SKY GOLD

King Of Obsession

Contents

Author's Note

This is the second book in the 'Kings of Omertà series, which follows the four Calibrese brothers, Mafia fixers, and secret keepers- the so-called Kings of Honor, who enforce the sacrosanct code for several powerful Mafia clans.

This book promises:
- 💍 An Alpha Mafia Grumpy Obsessive Dark Romance
- 💍 Brooding/Borderline Asshole MMC / Strong FMC
- 💍 Isolation and
- 💍 Major groveling
- 💍 Found family
- 💍 Morally gray themes
- 💍 Forced proximity
- 💍 Antihero
- 💍A Perfect Blend of Light and Dark
- 💍 Piercings & heated play
- 🌶️🌶️🌶️ Steam, sass and spice

This book contains all the aspects of a Mafia romance, with dark content not recommended for sensitive readers. It includes graphic scenes, violence, consensual steamy sex scenes, and mature language.

'King of Obsession' is perfect if you love mafia, dark + light, contemporary bad-boy romance packed with spice, steam, sass, and plenty of heat.

The characters are badass, unapologetic, and strong. They love and play hard, defend their loved ones, and uphold their code. They're loyal to a fault, true to the core, and will never cheat on their partners.

I've included a small glossary of Italian word translations at the end of the book for those who want it.

I hope you sincerely enjoy the series!

x, Sky

'Lose Control'

I lose control
When you're not next to me (when you're not here with me)
I'm fallin' apart right in front of you, can't you see?
I lose control
When you're not next to me, mm-hm
Yeah, you're breakin' my heart, baby
You make a mess of me

Problematic
Problem is I want your body like a fiend, like a bad habit
Bad habits hard to break when I'm with you
Yeah, I know, I could do it on my own
But I want that real full-moon black magic, and it takes two
Problematic
Problem is when I'm with you, I'm an addict
And I need some relief, my skin in your teeth
Can't see the forest through the trees
Got me down on my knees

Lose Control - Teddy Swims

Chapter 1

Ten years earlier

ALESSIO

F ive tulip glasses stood in a perfect row on the bar.

Beyond the marble buffet, the wedding churned.

Its setting was a grand castle whose ruins were lit with whimsical summer Neapolitan colors, each corner laden with vibrant flowers.

I crossed my hands over my chest with a smirk. Eyes on my eldest brother, Lorenzo, as he measured grappa out with precision into every glass, his tongue caught between his teeth in concentration.

Laughter rang out.

I turned my head to tag my cousin Daniela as she danced in the arms of her new groom, Davido.

I served her a chin jerk of approval as she whirled past, face flushed, hair escaping her crown, happiness radiating from her in waves.

'Fratelli.'

Coming toward us was Valerio, his ever-acerbic eye canted.

Behind him strode our youngest Vitto, and in his wake was our patriarch, Stephano, the man we all adored.

'A bene, we're all here,' our Don murmured, clasping us in his embrace. ' So proud of you, i miei figli, my strong Calibrese warriors.'

Bracing, athletic, handsome, clad in our wedding suits, we savored this rare moment together.

Lorenzo handed each of us a tot of chilled, light golden digestiv.

We stood in a semicircle, locked eyes, and muttered as one. 'Salute!'

We downed the grappa in a single slug, a ritual we always celebrated whenever we had the chance.

Slamming back our glasses on the bar for more, we leaned in, chatting and catching up.

Until Stephano eased towards me.

'Papà,' I rasped as he slid a hand around me.

My hero was a craggy-faced, salt-and-pepper-haired man with aqua-blue eyes that'd ice you one second and flame you the next.

His ever-lovin' patience with me and gentle guidance over the years had cast him as a god in my eyes.

'Mio figlio,' he growled, ducking closer to whisper in my ear. 'You're my favorite, sai?'

'Oh, I know it,' I huffed in mock disbelief, loving his attention. 'You tell that to each of us,' I grated.

He smirked, and then his face fell, turning somber. 'An old

2

friend just called.'

His eyes were shadowed, clouded with worry.

'Dimmi,' I grunted.

Leaning in, he murmured for a moment, extracted a faxed image from his breast pocket, and handed it to me.

I studied the features of the two photo IDs depicted.

Both were blurred and unclear, but it'd be enough for me to recognize them at first glance.

'You're the only one for it,' he ended.

I was.

I also was not one for parties, and any excuse to leave was enticing.

'You can count on me,' I growled.

'Bene,' my father rasped.

He tucked the paper back in his pocket and pulled me close into a hug imbued with his cologne and the scent of his cheroot.

After a buss of both cheeks, he left.

Heat seeking toward my radiant and beautiful mother, who stood with her sisters gossiping on the edges of the dance floor.

I found Lorenzo by the cocktail tables, where the stacks of towering antipasti and platters of endless deliciousness were lit up.

A golden light pierced through the trees on the castle ruins, leaves fluttering in the warm breeze.

'Arrivederci,' I drawled, tugging him into a farewell hug.

'Another not-so-delicate mission?'

'Si.'

With his brains, *sprezzatura*, and debonair panache, Lorenzo was destined to be the future head of the famiglia.

As such, the dirty work was left to me, head capo of the Calibrese clan, for I never ran from a good fight. I lived for it.

Lorenzo nodded, raising his glass. 'Va bene. We'll probably be here all night, so swing by after,' he said. His gaze flicked to our other two brothers, Valerio and Vitto, who were chasing girls in the garden arbors.

'Fuck, you won't be here. You'll be off rutting in between the legs of one of those women eyeing you from the singles table.'

'Cazzo,' he cursed after me, but already his eye was wandering.

Lorenzo adjusted his silk tie and flashed his signature debonair grin. 'Another conquest awaits,' he announced, winking at me.

I rolled my eyes and cracked my knuckles. 'Don't you get tired of running after skirts?'

The fading bruises on my jaw twinged as I spoke - souvenirs from my latest bare-knuckle bout in a seedy Neapolitan warehouse.

'Don't you ever get exhausted trading blows with ruffians and lowlifes?' Lorenzo turned to me, eyebrow arched.

His tailored attire and cravat were crisp perfection, not a hair out of place—a contrast to my wild leonine tresses and open-necked white shirt under my fitted suit.

'To each his own, I suppose,' I shrugged. 'Careful you don't break a nail out there, Casanova.'

'I can butter up a willing lay for you, mofo,' Lorenzo chuckled and clapped me on the shoulder.

I snorted. 'You can have the ladies. I prefer to let my fists do the talking.'

'Si, and what poetry they fuckin' weave,' Lorenzo murmured. 'Fratello, when will you let go and have some fun?'

I canted a brow and grumbled, 'Renzo, you know if there's one thing I avoid, it's letting go and having fun. Living it up is something I leave to you.'

'While you brood from the sidelines and look on.'

'Cazzo, it's so I keep an eye on y'all,' I growled. 'I see the details others miss. I also pick up the pieces so you can party. Like I'll be doing tonight, on famiglia business as you shake your ass.'

He lifted his hands to his lips, our family's double-fingered salute, wishing me well.

I checked my watch. 'I'm off. Don't wait up.'

Lorenzo smirked. 'I won't because you're a buzz kill.'

With a blasé wave, my brother sailed off, leaving a waft of expensive cologne in his wake.

I shook my head, a reluctant smirk tugging at my mouth. Lorenzo and I may have been born of the same mother, but we'd been stitched into different men.

Where he adapted the smooth charm and urbane airs, I retreated to shadowed alleys and underground rings.

While he glided across glittering ballrooms, I prowled the streets looking for a fight.

Massaging my bruised knuckles, I huffed a laugh. No, my brother and I were nothing alike. To be honest, I preferred it that way.

Lorenzo was the Lothario of our family, but I sensed that, like me, he was a one-woman-for-life kind of man who hadn't found his soulmate yet.

I was still holding out on finding a wife. Unconvinced anyone would ever handle all of me.

A loudspeaker screeched, and an uncle, once removed,

stumbled onto the stage to announce speech time.

I prowled away, thanking the gods I was evading the long-winded verbose from the wedding party.

Sliding into my Pagani Zonda sports car in the castle's parking lot, I headed to the center of Naples, away from its thriving neighborhoods with old-world homes, plunging into its gnarly underbelly.

The Europa Guesthouse loomed ahead, its neon sign flickering in the night. Caught between a hotel and a hostel, it was about as genteel as a motel got in this part of town.

I pulled into an adjacent side street.

The place was infamous for its small elevators, a slight chance of bedbugs, teens hollering from the bodega next door, broken glass, and half-drank bottles in the hallways.

It wasn't the Palazzo Caracciolo or the Ritz, but what did I fuckin' care?

I had a job to do.

No one was at reception, so I powered on, my nose wrinkling at the odor of stale cigarettes and cheap freshener rank in the air.

Music thumped from one of the rooms, and the sound of laughter and shouting from another.

I inched past a room where I caught the vigorous noises of banging against a wall and a woman's wails as she was plumbed to oblivion.

With a nod, I slipped by two wrinkled, sleazy men exchanging packages, light spilling from inside the drab room they stood in front of.

Moments later, I eased toward the darkened doorjamb of Number Fifteen.

My instincts churned like a beacon in superstition's night,

a loaded foretelling packed with omens of foreboding.

Weapon ready, I was about to tap on the door when my inner alarms went off.

The sliding casement next to the door glided open.

I stared at it as a slender arm reached out and dropped a bag and a pair of worn sneakers to the ground under the window.

An interesting turn of affairs.

Still, I prided myself on my fuckin' patience.

So, I waited to see how matters would unfold.

A body eased from the exposed chasm. One lithe leg extended first.

Then came a dark head, shaven in jagged streaks across her slight skull.

Yet the curve of her thighs and swell of tits beneath her torn tee made her out to be a full-grown-ass woman.

I recalled my father's words. 'Our package is eighteen, missing for a few weeks. Her grandfather is desperate to get her back.'

She turned her head, searching the darkness, her expression furtive, and I glimpsed her face in the dim light.

Fotto!

My entire being locked, eyes fixed on features so exquisite they'd make angels weep.

The photo ID printout had done her no justice.

Honey skin, plump, budding lips, and a slim nose.

Above that, eyes that sliced straight to my spirit.

Jade green, bottomless like an amethyst ocean.

Sad. Haunted.

Just as a second leg hitched over the egress, a growl erupted inside the room.

The slight figure jolted, their startled breath followed by a muted scream.

I moved, sidling toward the young woman, sliding a hand over her mouth, jerking her back to me.

'Stay fuckin' still, cara. Don't say a word,' I growled into her ear.

She disobeyed, scratching and flailing like a wild feline until I used my gun hand, banding it tight around her waist.

Even as she fought for her life, I was hit with a perfect fusion of scents. Pistachio, almond, vanilla, and salted caramel in a sweet and indulgent aroma.

Instantly lifting the darkness from my soul and transporting me close to unadulterated bliss.

It also thickened my cock, in a lightning jolt that had me biting back a growl.

She froze, feeling my throbbing hardness long enough for me to hiss into her ear. 'I'm here to help.'

The motel room door opened, and a body rushed at us, growling in outrage.

On pure instinct, I raised my weapon and fired.

He fell, writhing, his upper chest torn apart, shredded, blood spurting.

Another man emerged, handgun blasting.

I whirled, took cover, the girl still in my grasp, and squeezed off a shot.

A thump sounded, followed by a grunt, a loud thud, and silence.

I moved, still clutching my prize, to the room where two bodies lay prone on the ground.

Ignoring the struggling woman in my arms, I toed each man's body, flipping them over.

Both were quite dead, but none were my second mark.

I cursed.

Just then, a third man exited the washroom, eyes bleary, mouth slack.

Recognition was instant as I raked my narrowed gaze over him.

Fuck finally.

'Chi sei? Who are you?' he slurred.

His dilated eyes tagged the distressed woman still melded to me.

He lunged.

I lifted the butt of my gun and brought it down.

Blood spurted on his temple, and he fell to the ground, senseless.

The hellcat in my grasp bit my hand around her jaw so hard I growled.

At the same time, a hot heat seared through my left side.

Hell, not now.

My body ignored me and went numb, jerking, loosening my grip.

With a gasp, she twisted away.

But not before she stared at me, at my visible trembling, and realized her escape was involuntary on my part.

I saw her eyes understand and fill with an unexpected compassion.

I grunted, sucked my teeth, and clenched my muscles to try and control them, my gun hand quivering.

Taking the chance my incapacity gave her, she reached for her bag. Next, she slid her bare feet into the battered pair of shoes, her body shivering in the cold night air.

My shakes subsided, and I moved.

She froze.

Shaking my head to reassure her I meant no harm, I eased out of my Armani suit jacket and handed it to her.

She stared at me for a beat until I jerked my chin, and she took it.

While it'd been fitted and tailored to my contours, it hung over her like a drape. Yet it covered her up and provided her warmth, which I desired.

We locked eyes for another long moment, and I sliced my eyes to the world beyond, then gave her a slight nod.

'Grazie,' was all she whispered before turning to flee.

In seconds, she was gone, lost to the shadows.

My eye caught something shimmering in the faint illumination as it fell from her bag in a hurried escape.

I stalked toward it and picked it up.

The bracelet, a delicate cascade of luminous jade spheres intertwined with a silver feather, had slipped from her tote as she rushed away.

The gemstones were cool and smooth, gliding against my skin as I rolled them between my fingers.

I twirled the orbs like prayer beads, my eyes canting in the direction she'd disappeared, praying for safe mercies.

She'd long vanished into the night.

I let her.

Hell, I had no choice.

For she deserved her freedom. From what my father had shared, she'd suffered so much, so young.

I also knew our men would soon catch up to her and whisk her back home where she belonged.

I turned to the man flailing on the ground and committed his features to memory, just as I had hers.

For now and for all eternity.

Chapter 2

Present day

ALESSIO

The text came in at midnight.

My eyes flew open, and I knifed up in bed, reaching for my phone on the bedside table in my glass-walled, double-level penthouse.

Outside, New York was a living, breathing entity, pulsing with life even in the late hours, its neon glow and flashing strobes painting the sky in the distance.

I squinted at the words that radiated at me.

A development on CM & FC.

My eyes narrowed at the initials, the code for *her* – and *him*.

Two individuals whose fates had inextricably entwined with

mine.

I pushed a hand through my hair as I typed a quick response.

Call me. Now.

The device went off, and I stared at the screen for a beat before sliding a finger across it.

'Dimmi,' I announced in a raw growl.

'He's walking out of prison in three weeks,' the no-nonsense voice intoned in my ear.

'Cazzo. You've eyes on her?'

'No, we're stretched thin, but we know where she is.'

'Where?'

'On her farm in the outback. She uses it as a base and returns to it every few months. Only this time, she's stayed put for some time now. There's more, padrone. According to the local fuzz, she's alone on the property and had some trouble.

'From whom?'

'The neighboring estate. Which is where the fuckwit will return to after his jail term.'

I clenched my jaw. 'Fotto. I wonder if she's privy to his release?'

'Non penso.'

'Can you get eyes on her?'

'Like I said, we're thin on the ground, but we could stake her out for a few nights.'

I cursed, then sighed. 'I'm coming in.'

'You sure, padrone?'

'It's the right thing to do.'

'Also, along with the Contis and their shit, a local Mafia clan holds sway in the region. The Caputos.'

'Then they'll fuckin' pay me respect.'

I made my plans fast.

The following day, I was in my office, working with my PA, Sandra, to book tickets, move meetings around, and leave New York.

By the end of the day, reservations had been scheduled, and clients were informed. I had a global moving company locked in and a first-class fare to Sydney the following week.

I leaned back in my chair, feeling the familiar itch beneath my skin.

The restless energy that could only be sated one way.

I glanced at the clock—7:30 PM.

Plenty of time.

After checking that the door was secured, I shrugged off my suit jacket and loosened my tie, a transformation already underway.

I slipped into gym sweats and allowed myself a moment to roll my shoulders, to feel the coiled power waiting to be unleashed.

Then, I was out, navigating the city streets with a singular purpose.

I was apprised of the spots, the secret places where men like me gathered to test their mettle, where the only currency that mattered was the ability to take a punch and keep standing.

I snuck into a nondescript warehouse in the heart of the Bronx, the ambiance thick with the tang of sweat and blood. The crowd parted as I made my way to the makeshift ring, whispers of recognition trailing in my wake.

'*Diavolo d'oro*,' they called me. The Golden Devil.

A name earned through a wealth of gore and bruises, the ruthless efficiency of my punches, and the incongruousness of my features.

I stripped down to my waist, the chill air prickling my skin. My opponent, a tattooed brute with a broken nose, sneered at me from across the arena.

'Ready to dance, pretty boy?'

I smirked, settling into a fighting stance. 'Let's see if you can keep up.'

My world narrowed, coalescing on this perfect moment: winning the clash—the raw, visceral thrill of it—fists and feet, sweat, and snarls.

I lost myself in the rhythm of the blows, in the brutal joy of it all, relishing how wild, savage, and alive it made me.

In the fight circle, there was no pretense, no masks to wear. Just the pure, unadulterated truth of who I was. A fighter down to my bones.

As my fist connected with my opponent's jaw, I felt a sense of rightness settle over me as he crumpled to the mat.

I stepped out of the enclosure, my chest heaving, my knuckles raw and bruised. The adrenaline still surged through my veins, infusing me with invincible, untouchable strength.

Heading into the packed change rooms where influencers, brawlers, and fight organizers milled, I swiped a towel from a nearby bench, wiping the sweat and blood from my face.

I slipped into an empty cubicle, showered quickly, and

changed into clean gear: sweats, a tee, and slides.

Easing outside, I jerked a chin to familiar faces.

I grunted at the clapped hands on my back, congratulating me, their voices a dull roar in my ears.

Not one for small talk, I couldn't wait to leave and had just nabbed my gym bag when a pair of long arms reached from behind.

Mouth pressed to my shoulder, tits sliding over my spine.

'Alessio.'

I turned, arching a brow as I gazed down at a woman's face, the same emblazoned on ad campaigns and billboards all over the city.

She gave me coquettish pout.

I tried to recall her name as the high of my bout win faded.

Kristi.

We'd gone on some disastrous date on her insistence a few months ago.

'You were magnificent tonight. Want to celebrate?'

'Not now,' I rasped, easing away.

The last thing I needed was her brand of complicated. She was something crazy, borderline stalkerish, and I'd placed her pussy on serious probation.

She pouted and attempted a saucy eye-roll.

Despite her supermodel career, Kristi was another fan girl who hung around the fight clubs, chasing brawlers because they thought we were sexy.

Between my natural attributes, winning fists, and brooding over life's callous capriciousness, I drew the endless attention of women like bees to honey.

However, I had little to tell them when they came my way, for I'd never been as glib as Lorenzo or Vitto.

Talking taxed me, and I became impatient with chatty and flirty types. It pained me to open up.

Still, ladies chased me, enamored by my melancholic countenance.

When I declined them, they pursued me harder, doing backflips for my black heart and dark vibe.

Like Kristi was now, licking her lips in what she thought was an enticing, sexy affectation, the same she most likely fronted on her Instagram.

Fotto! It pissed me off.

My phone saved me, trilling in my hand.

My car was outside.

'I've places to be,' I growled at the stunning creature. 'You, I'm sure you've your beauty sleep to get to, magazines to pose for, that kind of thing. Rain check?'

I had no such plans.

She pushed her tits at me and tossed her hair. Hoping to entice me, to weaken me.

I was not moved.

Over the years, I'd built a shell around me. A thick one that belied my face.

Hell, I didn't care about my looks.

While I maintained my fitness and was partial to the occasional tailored suit, I'd found that focusing too much on my appearance drew the wrong attention.

Thank fuck for my father, Stephano, and his wisdom.

'Alessio,' he'd told me when I'd expressed frustration in my late teens with my physicality and the negative regard it attracted. 'No amount of handsomeness can make up for a rotten soul and slow mind. Like someone once said, beauty is only skin deep, but ugly goes clean to the bone.'

I'd taken the learning to heart and refused to let my ego or dick guide my actions. Leaning instead on my wits and fists.

My phone kept ringing.

'Got to go,' I grunted to the woman crowding me, rolling my jade bead talisman in one hand.

I headed for the exit. 'See you around.'

'Fuck you,' she spat, glared at me as I swept past. 'I can do better.'

I paused, tilted my head to her, and arched a brow. 'We all can. We just have to believe in ourselves.'

She cursed; I ignored her.

Stalking away, I savored the rush of being alive and in command.

Because control was fleeting in the real world, my condition saw to that: the shakes, the heated fevers, the perpetual battle to keep myself in check.

In the ring, though? I was the master of my fate—the king of my little kingdom.

Again and again, for as long as it took until my nightmares rested.

This was more than just a hobby; it was more than a way to blow off steam.

It was my lifeline. My anchor in a reality caught in constant flux.

A week later, I was on a plane headed to Sydney.

When I landed in the Harbor City, the bullish, tall, and scary mofo of our famiglia's guardsman was waiting in the airport arrivals lounge.

He whisked me to his SUV, and I settled in with a chin jerk.

'Good to see you, Mauri, but fuck, your ride reeks like a freakin' onion stand because of all your damn fried rings you never stop devouring.'

'It's the cat food, you fucker,' he growled. 'And show your consigliere some fucking respect if you're going to cruise with me.'

He gave me a fake glare, and we exchanged smirks, falling right back into our shit-eating grins and sketchy, crude banter on the drive to Sydney's North Shore.

We pulled into Lorenzo's home, and I fell into the arms of my brother and his woman, Mia.

Dinner that evening was a much-needed catch-up, filled with laughter and reminiscing about the old days.

Our youngest sibling, Vitto, showed up, and in no time, the warmth of family enveloped me.

Lorenzo's residence was a sanctuary where I could be myself and let down my guard.

We sat around the table, savoring Mia's delicious meal, sharing stories and jokes, and basking in each other's company.

But amid the merriment, the weight of my mission lingered in the back of my mind.

It was entwined with the memory of our parents' loss, which had hit me hard. I still did every fuckin' day.

Sensing my unshakable need for retaliation, Lorenzo attempted to talk me down from the precipice I was headed toward.

To jolt me out of my sheer rage of retribution.

But he was well aware, as were Valerio, Vitto, Mauri, and even Mia —that I was our only shot at exacting revenge. I was the only one with the balls to pull off what they would not.

The 'make it happen' man with a killer instinct, primed to yank out all the stops to get shit done. I had this sixth sense for sniffing out the enemy and gunning them down before they could react.

So, without saying it, my thirst for vengeance had my family's silent sanction.

After dinner, Lorenzo tapped out one of his herbal cigars.

I sat deep in a chaise lounge, one hand nursing a whiskey. The other rolled my jade beads in my hand, a habit I'd developed over a few years.

His eyes bore into mine, brimming with concern.

'Why don't you let Mauri and a few of our capos go check this out? I can spare them for a handful of days.'

On the flight to Sydney, I'd decided to go after Franco myself and keep a close eye on *her*, so I shook my head.

'This is my shit,' I growled. 'It will likely be a recon job, and I'll spend most of my days behind a pair of binoculars. Besides, it'll be a week tops.'

'You sure you're up for driving into the wild where you've never gone?' Lorenzo murmured.

'I've traversed the Alps, trekked on three-week survival camps in the Andes and Morocco, and trained with the best of the SAS; I'll be fine.'

In truth, I missed my days in the Italian Army's 3rd Alpini Regiment, whose soldiers were renowned for their expertise in alpine warfare.

Before active retirement and pivoting to the family business, I'd risen as high as a Maggiore, a major in the decorated, elite mountain corps comprising infantry and artillery.

I was well versed in traversing sierras, combat engagement in precipitous environments, and leading incursions.

'Are you sure, fratello? It's wild in the outback. Kangaroos, crocs, dingoes, peacock spiders, and drop bears who'll skin you alive in your sleep, the lot,' Lorenzo demurred.

When my brow furrowed, Mia, his partner, burst into laughter.

'Don't look so terrified, Alessio. Drop bears are a myth,' she teased.

'Or are they?' my elder brother hedged.

'Cazzo,' I shot back, my voice loaded with sarcasm. 'I'll go alone because it's a promise I made to myself, to all of us.'

I tipped back the whiskey, not even thinking twice.

Going into the wilds for *her* was my chronicle, my cursed purpose.

My moment to be a freakin' hero and villain all at the same time.

This shit would change my life.

I felt it in my core.

But fuck it.

There was no other way.

Chapter 3

ALESSIO

'**A**re you sure you don't want backup?' Mauri murmured to me, exchanging glances with my brother.

The three of us stood under the shadowed arch of Lorenzo's expansive front door, surrounded by an inky night and the silver fall of moonlight.

I caught the concern in our consigliere's eyes.

My seldom-seen weakness was always at the top of the pair's minds.

I'd stopped seeing it as pity but as a sign of their heartfelt care.

I shook my head. 'I need to do this alone. Less chance of drawing attention that way.'

Mauri nodded, yet a muscle ticked in his jaw. 'Be careful and call us if it all goes tits up.'

'Just get back in one piece,' Lorenzo rumbled raw and timbred.

I clapped them on their shoulders with a tight smile before climbing into the driver's seat.

'Si riguardi,' Lorenzo murmured through the window I was rolling down. 'Stay well and be safe.'

I raised a chin in acknowledgment.

'Bene,' I growled, unable to shake the shiver of foreboding that flew through me.

Tilting my head to the moonless shadowed sky, I inhaled the clean air, touched the Defender's ignition button, and the engine roared to life.

Mauri and I had packed all the off-roading gear I needed inside its generous storage cabin, from high-powered torches to an additional spare tire, petrol, camp swag, rations, weapons, and surveillance equipment.

I glanced at the pair backlit by the front porch light, ignoring the worry in their expressions, and rolled out of the driveway and into the dead of the night.

With a two-fingered Omertà salute aimed at both men, I lit out.

I navigated the empty streets of Sydney at 1 a.m., heading towards the Southern Tablelands.

The city's lights faded behind me, replaced by an eerie glow in the sky against the roaming clouds, casting shadows across the desolate landscape. I cruised for hours, serenaded by the engine's rumble.

The map directed me to turn off somewhere ahead of the sprawling regional city of Goulburn.

Deeper into the night and further from urban sprawl, I drove.

Soon, the bitumen thoroughfare gave way to dirt roads.

The outback terrain grew rougher, challenging my driving skills as I maneuvered through rugged trails and dense scrub.

As the first light of dawn began to creep over the horizon, I parked the SUV in a secluded spot and paused for a break.

Easing out of the car, I glanced up at a beaten trail that led deeper into the bush, twisting into darkness.

The air was crisp and fresh, with the scent of pine and earth. Birds chirped overhead, and a fresh breeze fluttered.

I chose a shrub close by for my release.

Midstream, I thought I detected a faint noise, but I wasn't too sure.

All of a sudden, the hairs on the back of my neck stood.

I zipped up my trousers and reached for the Sig Sauer revolver in its holster at my hip.

My senses were ratcheting, and instinct told me I was not alone.

I scanned the area, my hand clenched around the butt of the Sig at my waist.

A rustling sounded, and four men emerged from the brush.

Their faces masked behind printed kerchiefs, their matted hair under greasy caps, and their weapons glinted in the sunlight.

'Damn,' I muttered to myself.

'Hands where we can see them,' the lead man growled.

I made a quick threat assessment and sighed, annoyed at not being more cautious.

I was outnumbered.

Resigning myself to fate, I stepped forward, raising my arms, my left holding onto my Sig Sauer.

'Stay the fuck where you are,' another snarled.

'I don't want any trouble,' I stated, keeping calm, assessing the situation, and taking my time. The jokers exchanged glances, their body language tense and coiled for action.

The kerchiefs around their lower faces announced their affiliation—a bold logo of a cross with a skull over it.

Just my fuckin' luck. It appeared I'd stumbled across a trio of country mafioso fucks in the wild.

One of the masked men advanced, his eyes glinting with malice behind the mask's cover. 'You're in our territory, mate,' his local Aussie-fied Italian accent thick, his tone laced with menace. 'No one enters here without our say-so.'

I kept my gaze steady, attempting to diffuse the tension. 'Didn't see any boundary lines or fences.'

The group exchanged wary glances. The leader took a step closer, his firearm still trained on me. 'Really with that shit? Then why the weapon?' he declared.

I weighed my choices, aware that a misstep could edge to a dangerous confrontation. 'Purely precautionary.'

'Bullshit.'

Just then, a rock fell at the feet of the lead gangster.

My new acquaintances flinched and whipped around.

I did, too, brows flying at the unbelievable sight of a lithe figure with short dark hair on top of a nearby hilltop, a rifle in their hands.

Even from this far, I tagged their stance and multi-calibre long gun. Fuck, they weren't here to play.

Unlike the clowns with me who demonstrated piss-poor gunmanship and shitty weapons discipline, pawing over their triggers like this was some paintball game zone.

They'd lots to learn from the unexpected late entrant to our gathering. Whose index finger was placed along the frame of their firearm, still as a rock in the wind.

Silence fell as we all took stock of the unusual standoff.

'Back off, or we shoot him, and you,' one of the jokers shouted out.

The sniper aimed.

Seconds later, the ground spat at the foot of the lead gunman.

A warning, a freakin' well-targeted one.

The men flinched.

'Fuck! It's her,' one of them breathed.

I raised a brow and glanced at the rise.

My lips twisted.

It was *her*.

'You've got to be shittin' me,' I growled.

My nostrils flared, my eyes shuttered momentarily, unable to parse what I'd seen.

When I gazed out again, the hillock where the woman had stood only moments ago was empty.

She was gone.

One of the gunmen opened fire into the forest, pumping a rampant hail of bullets into the stand of trees she'd disappeared into.

My vision went fuckin' crimson.

I whirled, the gun in my hand, and with cold precision, sent firepower up their ass.

When they realized I'd turned on them, all four shooters switched their gunfire on me, and ammo began to fly in wild abandon.

'Cazzo,' I growled, aiming and obliterating the skull of one of the men firing on me.

Blood, brain matter, and gunk flew as I spun, heat-seeking.

A second assailant appeared from behind a tree and squeezed a shot at me.

I waited a split moment, eviscerating his chest with a trigger pull around a trunk.

One of the jackasses was too fast and barreled into my side.

The mofo pulled me off my feet, and I fell to the ground with a thud.

I struggled to fight back, but he was a hefty thug.

He punched, but I battered harder and kicked without mercy, even as the gun battle raged on.

He jammed his barrel into me, trying to fire it into my gut.

Twisting my torso, I succeeded in ramming him. Just as his weapon went off, a massive blast smacked into my shoulder.

Still, my survival instinct surged, and encircling his neck, I squeezed, and in seconds, he was out.

A flare of adrenaline hit, and I went numb, just managing to push him off me, and staggered to my knees, searching for my firearm.

I found it, spinning just in time as yet another of my attackers appeared, aiming a shotgun at me.

We paused, staring at each other.

His eyes flicked to his former companions, and he grimaced. 'Do you know what kinda hell that's about to rain down on you when the Caputos and Conti family find out you dared take their capos out?'

'Who's going to tell them?' I smirked.

'I am,' he snarled.

'Are you, though?'

I aimed and fired so fast; he'd zero reaction time.

The bullet got him dead center of mass, and he lurched, then flailed from the power-driven shot through his upper body.

Crimson bloomed on his trunk as he fell so close to me that his hand bounced off my leg.

I scrambled away, blood pounding in my ears.

Silence settled, my torso heaving.

I took quick stock of the fallen bodies on the roadside, thinking quick.

I needed to hide the evidence of the ambush.

Scouring the area, I undertook a few assessments.

In minutes, I was moving fast to roll the remains downhill.

The steep ravine made my work easy, and I used my boots to nudge the unexpected guests into the brushwood.

All in all, the four corpses disappeared, aided by gravity and my sheer doggedness.

Next, the reason for my mission.

It was imperative to find *her*.

Scanning the lay of the land, I deduced she was close by, regrouping.

Crouching to the ground, I crept through the underbrush in the direction I'd seen her disappear.

The scent of dirt and leaves filled my lungs with each breath.

I headed up the gradual slope toward the rocky outcropping.

Gritting my teeth, I drew down on my wilderness stalking skills from my time with the Italian army, running over the Alps, training in high altitude in ferocious weather, from sun to snow.

Dappled sunlight played across my taut shoulders as I moved in stealth, sensing she was close, lurking.

At one point, a sharp ache blossomed on my shoulder.

Glancing down, I pressed my lips as a gush of crimson stained my sleeve.

Merda, I was bleeding.

I had to find her, even more so now, aware I was in desperate need of medical aid.

With a suck of my teeth, I pushed forward, refusing to let the injury slow me down.

The pain worsened and was excruciating, radiating across my chest with every labored breath, but I couldn't stop now.

A sudden noise broke through my haze – the unmistakable scuff of a foot against a stone.

I froze, muscles coiled and ready to spring. Straining my ears, I waited for it to come again to pinpoint the source.

I gauged the wind direction and ascertained a location.

Without a sound, I rounded up on her, hiding behind a tree.

Impossible, and yet there was no mistaking her.

She was the shooter, evidenced by the long gun hanging off her shoulder.

I raked eyes over her as she stood to my left under a stand of trees.

Lowering my Sig a fraction, the pain of my wound faded as I thought through my next steps.

I inched closer as her stance moved from alert to relaxed, letting her rifle fall to her side.

If I approached her without the element of surprise, I feared she'd plant a bullet straight through my heart.

Scusa, woman. It's going to be fuckin' dirty.

I'd consider begging her forgiveness later.

Chapter 4

ALESSIO

I darted towards her in a burst of energy.

Seconds later, I'd divested her of her weapon, throwing it into a stand of bushes to her left.

I banded one arm across her waist, trapping her against me.

With a gasp, she reacted, thrashing, struggling, kicking hard, and bucking wild.

The back of her boot grazed my balls, my jewels almost sustaining a hit from her flailing.

I hissed, gripping her around the neck. 'Woman, relax!'

She'd no such plans.

Damn, she was a hellcat, kicking my knees, elbowing me, her swing sending shards of pure agony through me.

'Cleo, calm the fuck down,' I growled.

At the sound of her name, she froze.

Chest heaving, pulse jumping beneath my fingers.

I gentled my grip and let go with care, keeping a wary eye on her hands in case she decided to take a swing at me.

It wouldn't be the first time.

She whirled, and my gun snapped up in a reflexive motion.

A bolt of agony went through me, and I cursed at the throb of the wound in my shoulder.

For a suspended moment, we stared at each other.

I, down the barrels of my Sig, eyes piercing past the thick chasm of tension between us.

'It's you,' she whispered.

I tilted my chin up, letting her see all of me.

Hard eyes, clenched jaw, twisted lips.

'It's fuckin' you,' she repeated with something like wonder threading through her voice.

I exhaled, harsh and ragged. 'Si, bella. It's me.'

I gazed into her jade eyes and drank her in.

Still freakin' off the charts beautiful.

'After all these years,' she breathed.

I jerked my chin, too winded to say more.

'You let me go in Naples because, for some reason, you froze. So, have you now come to finish off what you started?'

I huffed at her husky intimation, a wild and inaccurate conjecture. 'You've quite the imagination, woman.'

She bristled.

'I've also got quite the fight in me. You're lucky I didn't aim higher with my boots,' she spat, her gaze flicking to my groin.

I winced, realizing just how close I had come to losing my jewels to her flailing limbs and deadly accuracy.

'Believe me, I'm counting my blessings,' I grated, trying to ignore the way my body responded to the sight of her, all coiled energy and barely leashed violence.

A wave of weakness came on the heel of my ratcheting desire.

I dropped to one knee.

'I'm flattered,' she growled, then gasped when I almost keeled face-first to the ground before her.

She rushed and caught me before I fell.

'You're hurt.'

She eased me down, and I slumped to the earth on my back, winded and unsure of my injuries.

Despite the waves of nausea assailing me, I kept my gun trained on her, and her eyes flicked to it, a flash of fear running through them.

I didn't give a fuck.

I wouldn't hurt her, but I was willing to do whatever it took to make sure she wasn't harmed.

Regardless if that meant hurting her feelings for a short while.

'You need to do as I say. I've got a first aid kit in my car. Take me to it,' I ground out.

Her eyes searched the knoll, finding my SUV tucked under the brush where I'd left it.

'Then what?'

I curled my lip at the defiance in her voice. 'Step by step, sweetheart. But first, bring your rifle to me. Attempt anything shady, and I'll shoot.'

She sucked her teeth but did as I asked.

'Disarm it,' I growled, waving my silencer-tipped weapon at her.

She did, sliding the unspent casings from the stock and handing them to me.

I hissed as I pocketed them, the movement sending shards

of agony across my torso.

'Lift me,' I rasped.

Somehow, she managed to help me to my feet, her arm encircling my waist.

'Don't try a fuckin' thing,' I warned.

My gun hand wrapped over her neck as we staggered down the slight incline to my vehicle, where she helped me into the back seat.

She didn't respond apart from a deep inhale.

'The fob is in my back pocket,' I growled when we got to the car, and she set me against its back wheel.

I lifted my ass so she'd rummage through my backside.

Her so close, so visceral, so sexy, her tits in my direct line of sight sent a bolt of need straight to my cock.

She inhaled as her fingers located the keys and pulled them out.

She turned, refusing to meet my eyes.

I kept my Sig in my clasp, resting on my chest, as she rummaged in my SUV. She found my first aid kit and went to work.

She was efficient and knew what she was doing.

She cleaned and dressed the wound with practiced efficiency.

While giving me furtive little glances, the pulse in her neck jumping, her breath hitching.

I was having a severe effect on her.

As she was on me.

'Cleo -.'

Her name fell from my lips like a prayer.

She glanced up, her eyes meeting mine.

In their depths, I tagged a flicker of fear.

33

But there was something else - a vulnerability, a rawness that twisted my guts.

'What?' she growled.

'I'll have you know that if I pass out, you can't leave me here to bleed out.'

'And why not?' she murmured, soft, not raising her voice. Yet it was edged with steel like she was considering the idea.

'One name,' I grated, hating myself as I rasped the words.

'Whose?'

'Guilia.'

Her whisper fell lower. 'Who?'

'Your Nonna. '

She jolted, her eyes flying up to meet mine, hands stilling.

'What the fuck?'

Still, she didn't raise her tone or volume.

She was a fuckin' mirror of calm.

'I have a man,' I told her, my face brutal, 'he's watching her; in fact, he's got a straight line to her door at Our Lady of Mercy Aged Care facility.'

My intonation was distinct, and she got the message loud and clear.

Her face blanched, and she glared at me for a lengthy time. 'You bastard.'

Her whisper coiled around my heart.

'You total fuckin' bastard.'

'Some have called me that,' I growled, a muscle in my jaw ticking.

She sucked her teeth at me, glowering all the while.

'Save your anger,' I rasped. 'You'll have plenty of time to unleash it on me after we're far from here.'

I tamped back the desire to reach out and stroke her face, to thumb the pulse at her nape.

'I'm not going anywhere with you,' she shot back. 'What do you want anyway?'

'Fuzzy alpaca slippers, a 'flippy' garden gnome, and a freak in the sheets tee. Pick any of the above.'

'Fuck you.'

I raised my Sig and made a play for the trigger. 'In due time, Cleo.'

She jolted at my intimation, and my lips curled.

'What do I want? For you to take me to your home, woman.'

Her jade eyes flashed. 'If I refuse?'

'You want to fuck around and find out?' I growled.

She studied me, eyes raking the stark planes of my face, brought to sharper relief by my pain. 'Fine,' she clipped. 'We'll do it your way, for now.'

Still a spitfire, I thought.

I jerked my chin. 'Get your ass and mine in the car, woman.'

The harsh brutishness was necessary to get my way with her; it was the best way to keep her moving and on her toes.

She helped me recline on the back seat, her touch scorching as she adjusted a safety belt over me. Regardless of my suffering, every brush of her fingers against my skin sent sparks dancing along my nerve endings.

Fuckin' keep it together, I chided myself.

But I couldn't deny the effect she had on me. Despite being battered and bruised, with my defenses stripped away, I was freakin' aware of her allure.

Cleo hovered for a beat, like she wanted to say something more, her eyes seething, jaw clenching and unclenching.

My breath hitched, waiting.

After a long moment, she jerked her chin to me, stepped

back, stored her weapon away, and closed the door before sliding into the driver's seat.

Her slender fingers touched the ignition, coaxing the engine to life.

My eyes locked on her as she pulled out onto the dirt track, gravel spraying. I leaned back and fixed my eyes on her, my Sig tight in my hand.

The road unspooled ahead of us, the dense forest giving way to rolling hills painted in the hues of a dying sun.

Exhaustion tugged at me, but I resisted its siren call.

I tried to focus on the landscape. But my eyes kept straying to her profile, flicking over the elegant lines of her nape.

To the stray wisps of hair curled against her neck and how the fading light caressed her skin.

Up close, she was the most fuckin' beautiful thing I'd ever seen, regardless of her being disheveled and splattered with my blood.

I tamped back the desire to reach out and pull her into the backseat with me and plumb her senselessness until we both forgot our names.

Damn, I was torn.

On the one hand, I wanted to tear off her clothes and bury my cock in her.

On the other, once Franco was taken care of, I'd need to walk away from her.

The fuckin' problem was what I was going to do with her afterward.

My mind whirled, but truth be told, I needed to close my eyes.

Fatigue was claiming me, the blood loss and shock taking their toll.

I slipped into unconsciousness, my Sig slipping from my bloodied hands as I slumped into my seat, and everything went black.

Chapter 5

CLEO

It *was him.*

It had always been him.

In the shadows and folds of my life.

Since his power-driven arms had wrapped around me that fateful night in Naples, I'd felt his presence with me, haunting me.

Those golden, unyielding, blazing eyes, that dark blonde mane, and his leonine gruff aura had remained on the periphery of my senses, just out of reach.

In some moments, I'd sensed him in the street or about a corner, those flaming eyes on me.

I'd thought it a figment of my imagination, but then again, he'd appeared so real.

But never had I come so close to his fullness and manhood.

For he was all man.

6'2, hard, muscled, lean, and angular, with thick thighs and tapered legs.

My eyes flickered over his shoulder-length, salon-styled dark gold, lustrous hair highlighted in amber and copper, groomed mustache and beard, and the bulk of muscle he carried.

Freakin' like the devil himself in a snug inky tee, black jeans, and feet in high-spec hiking boots.

But those eyes made my breath hitch, recalling them from so long ago.

They were the color of fire, flames, and incandescent cinders, burning through, scorching me.

When our gazes had met that fateful night in Naples all those years past, I'd been hit with a jolt throughout my body by the heated blaze radiating from his intense stare.

Damn him and his freakin' flaming eyes, which up close sent the fear of Dio through me.

They were now shut, but I still re-imagined their intensity and shivered.

I kept peeking at his supine form in the backseat of his high-spec 4X4.

Given the quality of the armament in his vehicle, his gear, his rugged fighting style, and his knowledge of weapons, he was a badass.

I wagered he gave zero fucks most days, a fuckin' monster when he wanted to be.

I recalled his threat to Nonna if I didn't do as he said, and a shiver of panic went through me.

It was clear he was ruthless and a freakin' inconvenience appearing now in the weeks leading up to my ultimate revenge.

For years, I waited, planned, and trained for the moment

when my monster would return to claim me.

I had vowed vengeance when he did. I had learned hate. I had sworn to destroy the evil soul who'd ruined my life and go down in flames with him.

After all this time, why had the man behind me shown up when I was on the verge of enacting my plans?

Why, when I'd sensed his far-off presence in my life, had he chosen to step out of the shadows now?

I'd had eyes on his ride early this morning when I spotted the dust from his fancy wheels roar up the gully.

I'd considered leaving him in the hands of fortune when I'd spotted the pitiful Caputo cunt capos hunting him down.

I hadn't heard the nature of their discussion being so far downwind, only that they were on my side of the fence line, and I'd needed them fuckin' gone.

Their Contis and, recently, the Caputos have terrorized me for years, trying to wear me down.

They were always pushing the boundary lines and bullying me along with the farmers that bordered mine to handing over our land to them for their hemp fields.

It was all taking its toll, and I was at the end of my rope. I had just enough in me to take out my monster, anything more, and I'd implode.

The man in the backseat was the icing on my nightmare cake.

For a moment, I contemplated stopping the car and rolling him down a steep gully, never to be seen again.

Except he'd unveiled Nonna Guilia's name and that his minions had her in their sight. If anything ever happened to her, I'd never live with myself.

So I shelved my murderous thoughts and drove on, hands

shaking with rage, until I pulled up to an armed gate.

It led to my daydream-perfect, 100-acre, off-grid, cozy, and self-sustaining acreage nestled at the crook of a mountain valley.

I unlocked the secure barrier, steered the car into my property, and turned back to lock up again.

I headed for the side lean to, unbolting that too to ease the vehicle inside, out of view.

After pulling the roller door down, summing up all my strength, I nudged the man awake.

His leonine eyes opened, dilated, and then refocused in seconds. They locked on me as he let me maneuver him out of the car.

Half-dragging his heavy frame through the connecting doorway into my primary shed, I brought him into my one-bedroom, corrugated iron home.

It featured a decent-sized singular kitchen, small bath, study nook, and a native-timber veranda overlooking a sandstone escarpment plus thousands of trees across the valley. Beyond the treelike were open fields where my windmills stood like silent guardians against the skyline.

I laid him on the only bed, mine, and rolled him into one end.

He blacked out once more, eyes rolling to the back of his head, lids shutting down.

I tucked a towel under his injured joint, which I'd treated with a clean compress from his car's emergency kit at the site of origin.

I shucked his boots and turned to my first aid supplies, using them to sanitize and sew up his wound. It was a pure through and through the upper shoulder, he'd live.

It also wasn't bleeding, so I wrapped, looped, and pinned a compression bandage on top of the wounded deltoid.

He remained knocked out right through it.

As a precaution, I ran my hands over him, checking for any other injuries. That's when I found the generous bump at the back of his head.

He must have hit something when he fell after being gunned down.

There was no broken skin, thank fuck, so I positioned a dressing on it to cushion it and jammed a painkiller injection into his thigh.

He didn't react, not even a grunt, still out cold.

Tugging off his boots, I adjusted and placed a duvet and blanket over him.

He settled, no, he fuckin' snuggled in, his free arm flung above his head, socked feet splayed on my hella clean sheets.

His tresses spread on my pillow, and I fought the urge to run my fingers through them.

His tee slid out of his jeans, showing off his designer underwear and, peeking from it, dark golden hair coiling toward his groin.

Damn, I had to admit he was freakin' hot—a dreamy thirst trap.

My clit pulsed in a stir that I'd not been detected in years.

Fuck me.

I cursed under my breath.

I could not afford any Stockholm Syndrome shit.

Besides, it'd be a fantasy to think he'd ever want me.

Life had taught me I was not important enough to be wanted by anyone.

I'd never been anything but a play-toy to men and to those

who wielded power over me.

Love, sex, and passion were not mine to have.

The only tendril of life I held onto was the revenge I intended on the man who'd stripped away any chance at everyday life.

This new conundrum in my bed was only a distraction I had to eliminate: body, soul, and mind.

ALESSIO

I jolted awake, my breath catching in my throat.

With a groan, I attempted to sit up but was cut down by a rush of agony emanating from my shoulder.

I fell back, heaving with pain, almost to the point of throwing up.

I closed my eyes and took deep breaths until the discomfort subsided.

Only then did I allow myself to open them once more.

Where was I?

My eyes adjusted to the dimness of the room.

A cabin.

The queen bed I lay in was covered in quilts and throws.

Side tables, lamps, and wardrobes against timber siding.

As the initial disorientation waned, I took in more details: the dresser standing sentinel by the door, the soft glow of embers in a fireplace in the living room in my line of sight.

A sheer white curtain fluttered in a night breeze that carried the scent of pine, eucalyptus and earth into the room.

The wooden beams overhead creaked, a lullaby sung by the cabin's sturdy frame.

I pushed myself to a propping position on the headboard, the rough-hewn logs of the wall to my back.

The room was nothing like my New York loft's sleek lines and glass surfaces.

I inhaled, the fragrance of cedar filling my lungs, grounding me in this reality far removed from the cacophony of yellow cabs and the perpetual twilight of skyscrapers.

At that moment, I sensed a soul hovering close by.

A silhouette sidled into the room, and there she was, her piercing jade eyes fixed on me from the shadows.

Cleo.

Dark brown, wispy hair in a pixie cut, small heart-shaped face, eyes so green they appeared to glow in the darkness.

Her gaze remained locked on me as myriad scents assaulted my senses - a perfect fusion of pistachio, almond, vanilla, and salted caramel, creating a sweet and indulgent aroma.

It was the same blend, so unique it had haunted me for years.

It had invaded my dreams and plagued my waking hours, an essence I could conjure at will.

Now, more potent than ever because it was real and right there in front of me.

Summoning all my strength, I forced myself to focus on her as she stared at me with unwavering intensity.

My cock jolted as desire surged through me.

She wore jeans and a tee that hugged her curves and accentuated her lithe frame.

The contours of her body beckoned to be touched and held;

her full, sensual lips, now pressed thin, only fueled my arousal further.

'How are you feeling?' she asked, her voice melodic yet edged with 'don't-fuck-with-me' steel.

I nodded, still trying to process the whirlwind of events. 'I've been better,' I rasped, cringing as I tried to sit up.

My hands hurt, and I glanced at them, wincing at the scabs and broken, seeping skin.

Looming over me, her eyes flickered over my injuries. 'Those Caputo jackasses are in with the Contis, and they all think they're hot shots. But in truth, they're nothing but dial-a-dealers and knuckle draggers,' she snarled. 'Do I have to worry about them knocking on my door for retribution?'

I arched a brow. 'Those particular fuckers? No.'

She slow-blinked, catching onto my meaning.

'We're good. I'm hoping they'll disappear in the escarpment for good.'

She took a sharp, hissed inhale.

I attempted to push myself up, but she touched my upper arm, preventing me from moving.

'Easy,' she murmured. 'You're patched up, but I'll need more supplies to heal that wound fast.'

Once more, my cock lurched.

Traitor.

I willed a scowl onto my face.

My jaw clenched tight to suppress the surge of desire threatening to overwhelm me.

The temptation to reach for her, slide deep into her, and blow my rocks off tugged at me.

Add to the fact she'd transformed from the waif I'd rescued into the badass woman now before me.

45

My chest rose and fell as our gazes locked.

I feigned indifference while turmoil churned within me.

'Your name?' she uttered.

The sensual vocalization sparked a rush of pure fuckin' need through me as I drew in a sharp breath to contain myself.

'Alessio.'

'The man on that night in Naples, the one who lent his jacket to me.'

I offered the truth without buffering it. 'Si.'

She pursed her lips. 'You've been watching me all these years.'

It appeared she'd noted the times I'd ghosted into her life, monitoring from afar, making sure she was OK.

To be honest, I'd done more than that.

I'd been her unseen guardian, her fuckin' fairy godfather.

Apprised of her grandfather's death, I'd arranged for her and her Nonna to receive an all-paid holiday to Europe, claiming it was from a friend of her father, which was true.

She'd taken it, and I'd flitted into Paris after the pair. Witnessing their pleasure as they wandered the quirky lanes, ate at cafes, explored its museums, and strolled along the Seine, healing from their loss.

As I'd admitted, her Nonna was in my purview, as was her property.

I'd ensured Cleo's farm won a private equity contract to install windmills on its land, which gave her a steady income.

Per my wishes, Mauri had maintained eyes on her, whether in person or via digital networks, a permanent, discreet watch as promised to her kin.

I'd kept away yet offered protection, which had been her grandfather's last ask of the Calibrese famiglia: that we extend our wings over her but that she remained unaware.

Until now, when Franco was about to be released from prison, which I suspected would upset the delicate balance of her life.

Or so I'd imagined, for she was nothing close to delicate.

Still, she needed me here till his brand of trouble was gone forever.

'You're Alessio Calibrese,' she stated, revealing she was apprised of my name.

I canted a brow.

'I went through your wallet,' she murmured. 'I'd have been a fool not to. Your ID is a New York State driver's license.

She crossed her hands over her chest, her tits rising in her tee. I dragged my eyes away from them, cock twitching.

'What brings you here, this far from home?' she continued.

'Woman, like I said, family business.'

'Like you had on the night we met?'

'Si.'

She considered my words, pursing her lips. 'Who sent you that night?'

'My father. He'd heard Franco Conti was in town.'

'Who told him?'

I shrugged, hesitant to say more. She caught onto the clench in my jaw and let her line of questioning go.

'Why are you really here? Why have a man on my grandmother and come after me? I'm of no value to you.'

Oh, but she was, she always had been.'

I glowered at her for a handful of moments before rasping. 'I know Franco Conti is about to be released from prison and that he's vowed to come for you after his release.'

She didn't look surprised, and I knew she'd visited the jail-

47

house a few times, attempting to uncover his exact discharge date.

Her lip curled in scorn. 'I'm well aware he's walking out in a several days or weeks. So you're here to what? Protect me from him?'

I huffed, then nodded. 'Something like that.'

'Why would you be concerned for little old me?' she shot out, her eyes flashing with bitterness of long-held ire at the man. 'My problems are not your own.'

But they are bellissima. They always were, I thought, infused with a violent urge to exterminate Franco Conti.

For both our fucking sakes.

'You're not here for me,' she surmised, her jade eyes narrowing on me as she came to an astute conclusion. 'You're here to use me as bait to reach him.'

She said it matter-of-fact and with a sadness that caught my attention.

Arching an eyebrow, I narrowed my gaze on her, noting the pulse hammering away at her nape, the one I wanted to run my tongue over.

'Regardless, Franco Conti will return and rip your life apart. You need me, cara. To prevent that.'

Her chest rose and fell in ratcheting agitation at my cold-as-fuck tone. 'Why are you so vested in Franco?'

'He owes my family a debt.'

'So you're going to use me to make sure he pays it?'

'Among other things. But if you hand me to the cops or try and run away, he will come after you. I'm your best insurance against him.'

With lightning speed, I leaned into her and jammed a hand in her hair, pulling her face near.

She winced.

I wasn't hurting her, but my sheer strength was enough to immobilize her.

Up close, her eyes glittered with pure ire, her mouth parting to curse me. 'You're a jerk, just like all of them.'

I ignored her characterization, growling, 'I'm giving you fair warning, woman, attempt any shit, and I'll make you regret it,' I whispered. 'You have been warned.'

She huffed. 'Not much I can do with you holding my Nonna hostage.'

'You'd better believe it,' I growled. 'If you run off, I'll find you wherever you go.'

'I've got that garbage from all the men in my life. Your threat means nothing to me,' she spat.

Despite her defiance, I tagged her fear of me in her eyes. Hating it, wondering if those jade beauties would ever pulse with wild craving and heat—anything but her twisted rage.

I released her, and she yanked away from me, standing over me, arms crossed, tits heaving.

She sucked her teeth. 'Regardless, you can't come after me. Not with that shoulder injury.'

I canted a brow.

'You also won't be able to fire any of your fancy weapons at him without my help,' she said.

Her husky voice sparked: more ratcheting desire mingled with intrigue.

'Scusa? Your help?'

'To put it plainly,' she continued, 'You saw my action out there. If Franco comes for us, we'll need to fight side by side, given the small army his sons have amassed at the farm.'

I was surprised by her intimation. 'Fight with me, cara?'

She shrugged. 'I want to end him, personally. You can fight him and his sons, but it has to be my bullet that goes through him.'

I shook my head nonplussed, impressed by her savage moxie on one hand and worried for her on the other.

'How' d'you know your fuckin' way around weapons?' I growled, hiding my concern with a scowl.

She gazed beyond me at the view out of the window. 'I've had to learn how to protect myself.'

I raised an eyebrow. 'That's ice, woman. Badass.'

'Living next to the Contis, I had to get training. But I'm low on ammo and guns, and your stash will supplement mine well. For when he dares come after me.'

I muttered a few choice words under my breath.

Her facing Franco in a gunfight made me want to break out in hives.

Still, I let my shoulders lift in a nonchalant shrug. 'I need time to think it over, woman. About me giving my shit to you and about you helping me.'

She shrugged. 'You're not quite in a position to negotiate, Calibrese.'

I sucked my teeth, helpless in her bed.

With a jerk of her head, she twisted away from me, hips swaying as another surge of lust shot through me.

At the dim doorway, she turned and caught my gaze again in her emerald allure before she vanished beyond the door.

Chapter 6

CLEO

I lived alone, and I liked it.

I adored the isolation of the mountains I sheltered in, the quiet, the freakin' peace.

Secluded, away from the world that wanted to tear me apart.

I wondered how Alessio would survive without the luxuries I assumed he was used to.

For all his pushy as fuck, gruff, and downright crude ways, he still had an air of sophistication and wealth.

He was probably accustomed to gilded bathrooms, king-size beds, and crystal chandeliers.

None of which was on offer here.

It was a simple life.

How would he react to the fact that all clothes were washed in a creek and that the toilet was of the composting variety?

There was no running water nor electricity, just a tiny

generator hooked up to my solar farm, a tank reservoir, and a fireplace.

His potential reaction rankled me as I imagined how he'd judge me and my eked-out existence.

For I'd never shared this roof with anyone other than my grandparents.

Alessio Calibrese was intimidating, no doubt.

His furrowed brow was daunting, eyes often narrowed and intense, scanning the room for probable threats.

His leonine hair and eyes afforded him the look of a sultry golden devil. Yet I sensed his soul and spirit were craggy as a granite cliff and rough as the sea carving its jagged edges.

The fact he was holding Nonna Guilia over me as a threat bestowed him with a layer of underlying danger and unpre- dictability that sent shivers down my spine.

My worry ratcheted for my grandmother and myself as the makings of a panic attack fluttered in my chest.

Taking a deep inhale as I eased out my front door away from him, I vowed not to let yet another man own me, my thoughts and soul.

I jumped on my ATV and rode the length of my farm's border on a perimeter check.

I headed east of the property, where the Conti farm lay. Also where, a local mafia militia, the Caputos, had commandeered the holding and turned it into hemp fields.

Desperate for real estate where they could conduct illicit operations like theirs, the ruthless gang had made properties in the area an easy target.

Unless one patrolled their land on a regular basis, they'd find the mafia group had taken over with their shitty illegal crop. The few farmers who'd protested had been subject to harassment, mysterious fires, and livestock killings.

For some reason, they'd kept away from my property, perhaps due to a mandate from Franco.

Still, the Conti sons harassed me, attacking my fences and trees, sabotaging my windmills, and making my daily life a constant worry as they tried to wear me down. So, I'd give in to their demands.

I'd repelled them so far with a tight security setup. However, it was difficult for me to monitor the entire acreage.

I could only be in one place at once, after all.

While cameras and alarms worked for urban properties, farms needed more.

My spread had one too many hard-to-reach corners that required a connection to power to work.

Electricity cabling was too damn expensive to install over vast land, and trespassers in the past had taken full advantage of these blind spots.

So, a few months ago, I'd stretched my budget and invested in solar.

Thank the gods that sunshine was abundant in Australia. I'd installed photovoltaic panels linked to an electrified fence and a network of cameras. I'd also rigged rechargeable batteries to a CCTV system to record and store footage.

A WiFi signal alerted me of suspicious activity, and I could view live video on a monitor in my shed.

Still, nothing was comparable to inspecting my fence lines in person, searching for signs of ingress or broken hedge posts.

An hour later, I returned to the cabin, where I inspected the alarms in all my outhouses and buildings in the storage barn, which also served as my office.

Nothing stood out, and I sighed in relief.

I eased into my cottage and checked on my unexpected guest.

He lay in bed, eyes half-mast, chest bare.

I paused at my bedroom door, and we stared at each other for a beat.

'I regret to inform you I'm still alive,' he drawled, eyes simmering with an indecipherable gleam.

In irritation, I pushed my tongue into my cheek and moved away, not trusting myself to speak.

I brought him a plate of sandwiches, fruit, and tea.

He jerked his chin in appreciation, picking at the offering, using his free hand to bring the infusion to those sensual lips.

My eyes flicked to his weapon, which sat on the bedside table closest to him, a reminder he was not just any guest but of the lethal variety.

Fleeing him, I tidied the kitchen and living area, and he sipped, eyes on me, following me with a flaming gaze that sliced through me with a crawling awareness.

He remained silent, as did I.

I tried ignoring him, but we exchanged fleeting glances, our gazes colliding across my cabin.

Like wild polarities clashing and repelling.

His overwhelming magnetism dominated my tiny home, and I was hit with a stab of panic. My anxiety was compounded by the fear of what he might be capable of with his sizable strength.

Despite my growing angst at his presence, I was also overcome with traitorous need. Wondering how it'd feel to have his sinewed arms around me, his sensual mouth on mine, his hips driving into me.

Fuck, was I that sex-starved? I had to escape him.

I needed bandages, more supplies to redress his wounds, and more food, milk, and meat for my freezer because, given his size, he'd require a good feed.

Just after 1 p.m., I decided I had enough time to run into Moss Vale, where I'd find the closest pharmacy.

I peeked into my room and found he'd slipped into sleep.

Relieved I didn't have to speak to him, I wrote a note and propped it on the pillow beside his golden mane.

I also left a fresh carafe of water, a thermos of tea, short-bread, fruit, and painkillers on the side table beside him.

Uneasiness gnawed at me, knowing I was leaving a stranger in my home. But I had no choice but to sneak into town for the supplies necessary to take care of him.

I hoped he wouldn't wake, miss my message, and assume I'd run from him.

Somehow, I sensed he'd move heaven and earth to find me, with a wrath I'd never recover from.

I hated crowds, cities, inquisitive eyes, and needless attention.

But needs must.

Even though I dreaded the drive and, even more, being spotted by curious onlookers, I tracked to my old beat-up Toyota Hilux parked in the shed.

For a moment, I stared at my unwanted guest's brand-new,

sparkling V8 luxury 4X4 with some longing, then shrugged.

It'd bring me too much scrutiny I didn't need.

My old, reliable truck, Sugar, was a rough and noisy ride, but it was also the least obtrusive option.

After a quick thought, I opened the trunk of Alessio's 4X4 and pulled out a shotgun and bullets from his extensive ammo collection. Placing them in my front seat, next to me, in case of any trouble.

I reversed out of the barn, locked up, and headed outside my property after checking and rechecking every lock and gate.

The roads were dusty, and the ute bounced along, the drive shitty from its lack of shock absorbers.

Still, the scenery made up for it.

As I navigated the winding route, the winter sun illuminated a lush, foliage-covered landscape that was only distinctive to Australia.

It was June, and the outback grasslands had just cast off their morning frost.

Houses and farms dotted the countryside, livestock grazed in paddocks, and wild kangaroos hopped across fields.

The trees were in the wane of autumn, but their pretty orange and red leaves still created bursts of color through the green panorama.

My rural life gave me the space to rebuild my life from scratch. For the most, I'd remained unobserved, finding the solitude I needed to keep the past at bay.

A privacy I guarded, avoiding cities and towns as much as possible.

Not by choice but necessity, I sighed as Moss Vale came into view within an hour.

I headed to a small village at the edge of the borough, on a quaint street with petite shops and eateries scattered along it.

In recent years, the country town has become fashionable, offering stunning lifestyle stores, fab cafes and restaurants, and a popular tap house. All of which had attracted a robust, creative community of former city dwellers.

I pulled into the pharmacy's parking lot, threw my hoodie over my hair, ducked as I sidled inside, and grabbed a shopping cart.

While I did, I avoided all contact with my fellow humans.

I'll always be a freak, a grumpy freak, I told myself as I hankered down and strode through the aisles.

I was way up on the scale. Somewhere between Angela Bassett's Queen Ramonda in Black Panther and Sigourney Weaver's Ripley from Aliens with a touch of Florence Pugh's Alice in 'Don't Worry Darling.'

I'd never been 'fun'.

That's because nothing in my life had been a laugh.

What irked me was that nearly all souls in the locale were apprised of my past and tribulations.

Which made every trip to Moss Vale a pain in the fuckin' ass; most all times, I spent them gritting my teeth, jaw clenched to stop myself from thwacking the curious locals over the head with their umbrellas.

Whenever they saw me and recognized me, they stared.

Then came the avalanche of questions and the pitying half-smiles.

So, to avoid them all, I power-walked like a booted missile, bobbing and weaving through crowds with heated intent.

I refused to meet other shoppers' eyes, guarding my privacy with a fierceness born out of necessity over the years.

However, my inconspicuous ingress soon ended in the

medical supplies aisle.

'Cleo, is that you?' a woman's voice called out.

I groaned on the inside.

I turned around, my heart pounding.

'Hey, Angie,' I answered, facing the bubbly, short blonde woman with sparkling blue eyes who stood at the makeup station with an eyeliner wand.

'I haven't seen you in ages! How have you been?' she asked, her curiosity evident.

I forced a smile. 'I've been good. Just busy with work and taking care of the property.'

She nodded, understanding the overwhelming nature of our lives. 'Oh my, I haven't visited the old place in months. We need to plan a catch-up so I can see how you're going.'

There was a light in her eyes, a strand of sympathy in her voice that I hated.

She meant well, but I couldn't shake the feeling I'd be trapped by her concern, pity, and the gossip in this town. 'Thank you. I appreciate it.'

'I haven't seen you since you got back from where was it again -'?'

'Sydney,' I proffered, trying to mask my annoyance.

'Why'd you go?'

Her utterance carried, and I sensed several eyes turn my way.

Angie wasn't a bad person.

She was one of a handful of women closest to my age who lived my way, which meant a homestead a few hundred klicks from me - in this part of the world.

Her father and other townspeople had convinced me to invest in a solar farm and wind turbine initiative.

I'd also qualified for a very generous grant to install the windmills.

Now, the spinning shadows of the 50-meter-long blades sweep across the north of my property at sunset.

The eco-farm had made good money, feeding power into the grid and bringing me a tidy income for which I was grateful.

However, the meetings of its shareholders always left me in tatters. People needled me about my life and my dating status and gave me those narrowed eyes, asking if I was doing OK after 'all of that.'

The reference was to a traumatic start to my life, fifteen years of my life I'd rather not have experienced.

My inadvertent background, which I'd preferred to have forgotten, added to my shame.

Everyone in this town appeared keen on my business, making me feel under a microscope. I'd avoided meetings for over a year now, unable to face the world.

I shrugged and chose silence.

'Like tell me, where were you?' she insisted.

I'd been in the city, nosing around the libraries and courts, trying to find out when Franco would be released from maximum jail.

He was my cause and also my utmost fear.

I knew he was returning anytime, but I'd hoped to get a date from my last excursion to his jailhouse.

I'd had to quit my waitress gig in Moss Vale and eat into my savings to fund the travel to Sydney's Silverwater Correctional Prison.

Where I'd been fobbed off at the office.

Worse still, I'd come back with no answers.

Bereft, I'd hunkered down on the farm.

'I took a much-needed trip,' I admitted, my tone clipped.

It had to be freakin' enough to shut her down.

It wasn't.

'Oh, that's lovely,' she replied, her smile widening. 'Any sightseeing?'

Damn, would this agony ever end?

'No.'

When I lapsed into silence, Angie gave an awkward, tremulous beam.

I widened my eyes and tilted my head, shutting down, not wishing to discuss it further.

She didn't get the memo.

Instead, she leaned in, eyes narrowed, lips pouting in conspiratorial curiosity. 'Go on, Cleo, what were you up to? Please, I won't share it with a soul.'

There was a rationale for why I'd ghosted Angie over the last few months.

She gossiped too much, and I'd become fodder for her stories.

At that moment, the store's aisles closed in, and the weariness from a restless night and my nagging worry about Alessio all hit at once. 'Let it fuckin' go, Ang.'

A gasp sounded to our right, and I glanced up, only to lock eyes with a woman who stood by clutching her pearls.

'How dare you, Cleo? Cursing? Is this how low you've sunk?'

I was beset with immediate regret as Angie's mother caught me red-handed in my tantrum. 'Mrs Davis, I'm sorry. I didn't mean to be rude. I'm just -.'

Her face softened at my obvious discomfort. 'How are you?'

Yet another person extending their pity toward me.

I pushed back my shoulders, met her gaze, and jerked my chin. 'I'm well.'

'I see I need to drop by with some cooking and maybe a cake or two -' she rambled on, her eyes flicking over my form. 'You're too thin.'

I'd had enough. 'Nice to see you both,' I mumbled. 'I've got to go.'

The pair waved at me, their faces incredulous, as I turned away, palms sweaty as I procured the supplies I needed from the shelf.

The daughter-mum duo sidled away as I let out a huff of relief.

Working fast, I filled my shopping basket.

Antibiotic ointment, sterile bandages, disinfectant, and pain relievers.

Next, I strode to the local butcher to purchase more meat.

Followed by the grocer for additional staples and sundries—enough to stock my pantry for two weeks—with extra provisions for my unexpected guest.

When I'd ticked all the items on my list, I pulled my jacket close and hopped into the truck's cabin.

It was getting to mid-winter, and the chill that fell from about 3 p.m. was setting in.

I drove fast, unwilling to have darkness fall while I was still on my way home.

I got to the cabin just as the last light sank behind the hills and slowed at the sight of the reflection off the turbines during sunset.

It was stunning.

Serenaded by the distant whoosh of the windmill blades, which sometimes sounded like the ocean, I eased the ute back into the shed, locked it up, and went inside.

A glance into the bedroom told me that Alessio was still asleep.

I sighed in relief, not quite ready to deal with all of him.

Making as little racket as possible, I set the supplies on my kitchen table.

All I wanted to do was finish my chores for the day, stoke the fire, and prep a light dinner.

If my guest slept through the night, I planned to enjoy my meal with a glass of wine, feet toasty under a blanket on my cherished chaise lounge, reading the next installment in my favorite thriller series.

I'd just placed the crusty loaf of bread I'd baked before on the cutting board when I caught a slight noise.

Without warning, I was lifted and thrown against a wall of hard, solid muscle to my rear.

A hand went over my airways, and another twisted one hand behind my back,

I struggled, kicked, and writhed; I tried to pry his hand away from my mouth and nose, to no avail.

The grip on me was too firm.

I recalled the size of this man and the sheer menace I'd tagged on him when I first spotted him.

He'd overpowered me, and I realized it'd be pointless to

fight him.

So I sagged against him in submission.

'Alessio, it's Cleo,' I croaked, my voice muted under the pressure of his hand.

He hesitated, withdrew his hand from my face, and released me.

I spun around, putting my hands up in mock surrender.

'Calibrese, why do we keep meeting this way?' I said with a biting edge.

That's when I noted his eyes were reddened, hot, and dilated.

He pulsed with heat.

Damn, he had a fever which was most likely scrambling his senses.

'Fotto,' he breathed, reaching to clutch the back of my sofa.

'Park yourself on the couch,' I urged. 'I've got your meds. Let's start with something to bring down that temperature.'

He nodded his head, and I tagged the tension in his body. 'I feel like shit.'

I assented, feeling a momentary compassion for him. 'All good. I'll get you some water to drink. Sit.'

He eyed me with wariness but jerked his head, settling into the lounge.

I handed him a glass and two pills, which he chugged down with greedy thirst.

'Scusa, cara, for manhandling you,' he growled after a beat. 'I was hallucinating for a moment. I thought you were some intruder.'

'You've had a hit to the back of your head,' I said with some reluctance, 'perhaps you need to see a doctor. It could be a concussion.'

'Fuck no,' he snarled. 'It'll bring us heat we don't need. It's you and me, woman.'

I conceded with a shrug. 'Your funeral. At least let me check on your injuries?'

'Bene,' he rasped.

I rose and approached him, bending over his seated form.

I plumped and set some soft pillows behind him so he'd be comfortable.

Then I got to work.

Silence fell between us, thick and unyielding, as I busied myself with unraveling my initial bandages and cleaning up any mess in his wound.

I observed that he was healing well, and I attributed the fast recovery to his freakish fitness, evidenced in his bunched muscles and sinewed bulk.

His eyes never left me as I wrapped him up.

They raked over my face, my shoulders, even my tits, unabashed.

The color shifted from gold to amber and yellow, and even a flaming coppery russet was unusual, but apart from tiny sneak peeks, I refused to meet his eyes.

With the last of the bandages secured, I patted his healthy shoulder. 'You're all done.'

Eyes still dilated, and out of focus, he lifted a hand to stroke my cheek.

I flinched and stepped back, creating a physical distance to match the emotional chasm that had formed.

His hand dropped, even as his lips curled at my reaction to him.

'So where are we sleeping tonight?'

'We?'

'Si,' he rasped. 'You and I,' he continued, unabashed, as if we were discussing the weather rather than an invasion of my private space.

Still, I tagged a gleam in his eyes.

Was the fucker flirting with me? Or was the fever scrambling his mind?

'What the actual hell?' I whispered.

My vocalization only served to heat him further.

His gruff mask fell away, and in place was a sensual, brooding vibe, complete with roaming, scorching eyes, all over me, undressing me.

Damn, he was brazen.

'Are the painkillers doing a number on you?' I snapped, letting my annoyance at him leak through.

'Temperare, woman,' he drawled, enunciating the 'r's' with a rolled inflection.

I bristled. 'I don't have a temper, but I do have a quick reaction when it comes to bullshit, Calibrese. So turn down whatever the fuck you're trying to dial up.'

He tilted his head with an arch of his brow.

'Calma,' he murmured, easing into his native Italian with a rasped tone. 'I'm just aiming to get acquainted with my bedmate for the evening.'

His voice was laced with an undertone that made my blood simmer.

'Just endeavoring to understand who I'll share dreams with tonight.'

His words hung in the air, a cloud of presumption that filled the tiny room.

My hands balled into fists at my sides.

With every guttural growl and sardonic lift of his eyebrow,

he trampled over social niceties as though they were nothing but dust beneath his feet.

My glare bore into the table's wood grain, wishing it were his smug face.

His audacity was astounding.

Here I was, offering sanctuary - albeit under duress - to a man with more secrets than sense, with the nerve to presume there was more on offer.

I gnashed my teeth so tight it hurt. 'You're unbelievable.'

He twisted his lips, his eyes glittering with an indiscernible gleam. 'It has been said more than one time.'

I huffed in annoyance. 'You'll take my bed. I'll couch it,' I muttered.

He knifed up, groaning at the fast movement. 'Fotto! Blood rush.'

Shaking his leonine head to clear the sensation, he clenched his jaw and leaned into me, propping himself up with a wince. 'No, I won't take your bed. In my world, women are goddesses. They never sleep on the floor or sofa.'

Despite the sultry deliverance of his words, his expression was loaded with cold menace.

This was a man not used to being defied.

I served him with equal fire. 'I'm not in your realm, so whatever you say is irrelevant. Besides, you have to rest and take care of your wounds. So you can be on your way sooner. Savvy?'

His eyes narrowed, and then that gold-tipped brow rose, and his lips curved, stabbing my chest again with need. 'Have it your way, cara, for now. But know this: I'm never wrong; you'll soon want your bed with me in it. You'll be fuckin' begging for it.'

Chapter 7

CLEO

I chose to ignore Alessio and his presumptuous yet oh-so-tight ass.

I made dinner, avoiding his eyes, face, and presence like the plague.

Irritated by how his essence flipped me from unease to arousal and back again in an ever-ratcheting cadence.

His fever appeared to have subsided, replaced by his rest-lessness.

While I worked, he prowled my sanctuary like a caged animal seeking an exit.

He also pulled a gold coin from his trousers and ran it over his knuckles, rolling it so fast it was a blur.

He jammed into his other pocket with his free hand, reaching for something inside it as if twirling an object to channel his energy.

It was curious; it was fascinating.

I had to admit he was intriguing.

Despite his golden looks, he had a soul of unruly wildness, the spirit of a brawler.

His hair was tousled like a lion's mane, framing a strong jawline and piercing eyes. His broad shoulders and muscular frame exuded strength, like a warrior from ancient times.

His presence was majestic and predatory, potent as he prowled through my surroundings with a sense of ownership and dominance.

Like a caged beast, his muscles rippled beneath his skin with each step. His essence was a mix of elegance, danger, and a primal, untamed energy.

It was clear Alessio was a mess of torment and sensuous ardor, his nature hinting at a tortured soul who'd broken the hearts of many.

I wondered what made his heart so black and his expression so ascetic in one moment and sultry in another.

I checked myself, unable to afford to fall prey to the temptations of rescuing a tragic, sensual hero with baggage who needed to be rescued from himself.

Ever so often, I sensed the scorching burn of his gaze, and under the cool, frightening menace was an indistinct emotion.

I tossed onion, garlic, and tiny diced carrots into the sizzling pan.

The aroma of cooking food began to fill the room, but it did little to soothe the tension that knotted between my shoulder blades.

It curled around me, invasive as smoke, as I stirred the stew with mechanical precision, helping to calm my frayed nerves.

He paused by my bookshelf, fingers dragging along the

spines of well-thumbed novels and limited-edition hardcovers.

My eyes flicked toward him, watching as he plucked out a paperback and a second and flipped through them, sliding both back into their place, out of order.

I bristled.

My rare editions were my world; anyone who touched my exclusive print editions might get a bullet in their heart.

His wanderlust continued, his shadow dancing across the walls as he paced, a caged animal in a too-tight space. Restless energy personified, he flipped through more spines of books on my shelf.

Next, he riffled through a stack of old postcards I'd collected in another lifetime.

Causing my focus to splinter, undoing my concentration as I chopped vegetables with more force than necessary.

'Would you just sit still for five minutes?'

The words left my lips sharper than I intended, echoing off the timber surfaces of the cabin.

He raised his eyebrows, adding an almost imperceptible shrug, lifting his wounded shoulder before he winced.

'Scusa, I'm not very good at being idle,' he rumbled.

He found my music corner and whistled under his breath.

The gentle strumming of my guitar came next.

One-handed and awkward yet somehow melodic, each note vibrated through the floorboards, up the legs of my chair, and straight into my core.

'You play?' I murmured, setting the wooden spoon down with a clatter.

He only glanced over, a slight curve playing on his lips— unruffled, unapologetic.

I raised my brows and turned to the stove, stirring the pot as if the simple action had the power to stir away the irritation inside me.

He knew his way around the strings, albeit in a mangled sense, given his injury.

His fingers danced over the cords, eliciting a discordant melody.

Most days, I loathed any stranger's intrusion into my peaceful, quiet, and sacred silence.

Yet Alessio's presence and his strumming gave me a certain peace.

I relaxed into it, let the chords soothe me, a sensation I'd not experienced in months.

'Dinner is ready,' I announced in time.

He joined me at my humble table with a gruff grunt of thanks.

Still unable to meet his gaze, I served him a rich vegetable and meatball stew and a fresh loaf I'd baked the day before.

The butter was sourced from a farm down the mountain, and the herbs, carrots, and broccoli came from my garden.

Our food was consumed in silence for the most part.

I kept my eyes on my plate.

He asked about the food, using spare words.

I noted how he listened to me when I used halting words to share my one passion: my recipes and the ingredients from my garden.

His appreciation of the fare came in murmurs in Italian, no less.

He was not a conversationalist. He didn't say much about himself, unaware—or perhaps well aware—of how his raw yet timbered, deep, rough, gravelly growls and concise responses turned me on.

Because, hell, was he intense.

His entire attention fixed on me on me through the meal, assessing me, raking me, breaking me down.

When he'd cleared his plate, he leaned back in the chair, spreading out his arms, wincing as his shoulder twisted.

'Promise me Guilia is safe?' I blurted, fighting the invisible shackles he had on me.

His gaze flicked over me, his tongue playing with his inner cheek. 'You've nothing to fuckin' worry about, bella.'

His delivery was crude, but when I glanced for a moment at his face, my instinct told me his word was bond.

While my eyes danced away, he kept his leonine stare on me. Rolling his gold coin over his knuckles and licking the corner of his lip in a freakin' sensual habit.

My face heated.

With a deep inhale, I gathered the used cutlery and plates.

He reached his free hand to me when I part rose from my seat.

'Grazie,' he growled, reaching for my cheek, cupping it, and stroking a finger on the edge of my mouth. 'For dinner.'

I tilted my head at him, eyes flashing with warning.

'You're impossible.'

'You don't know the half of it,' he rasped.

I left the table in a huff, retreating to the kitchen basin under the long, expansive window.

I fussed with clearing the plates, not quite seeing the darkening sky beyond the glass as my skin pulsated where he'd touched it.

Alessio lingered.

I sensed his eyes on me, probing and unrelenting, as if he

sought to unravel the layers I had wrapped around myself.

It was unnerving, this scrutiny, this intrusion into the fragile boundaries I had erected for my protection, his never-ending regard breaking through the room's peace.

I offered my silence as a shield against his persistence, but unable to resist, I sliced my eyes toward him.

Only to find the last rays of sunlight bathing his features in a warm glow, softening the hard angles of his face and casting long shadows behind him.

His profile was one of a god, and I hissed at the jolt it sent through me.

Fuck, I had to escape him.

'I'm going to wash the dishes outdoors,' I declared.

His head whipped toward me. 'Why? No running water?' he growled, his brow canted in disbelief.

'Nope,' I clipped, easing away with my burden of plates.

I made for the door, seeking refuge in the crisp night air.

The freedom of being away from him was a welcome relief.

Outside, the fiery hues of sunset painted streaks of orange and pink across the horizon, contrasting the shadows creeping over the landscape.

I marched towards the creek, just a few hundred meters from the cabin.

I knelt at its edge and scrubbed the remnants of our meal from the dishes.

My breath formed little puffs, and above, the stars blinked down through the skeletal branches, indifferent to my need for solitude.

But seclusion proved elusive.

Pebbles crunched underfoot, betraying his approach before his shadow fell over me. He crouched on a rock nearby, thick thighs bunching under his jeans in casual nonchalance as if he'd been invited to join.

He glanced up at the sky, eyes narrowing on the gleaming moonscape.

Silver light outlined his silhouette, and his features stood out. Carved in hardness and darkness, they evoked a timeless deity of vengeance.

I followed his gaze, blurting, shattering the quiet, needing to release the nervous energy building up in me. 'It's so full tonight it hangs like a coin tossed by some cosmic gambler.'

His timbered huff was laced with amusement. 'A poet, cara?' he drawled.

Embarrassment and irritation flared in me, and I shot my eyes to the ground, rinsing off a plate. It clattered as I flung it onto the pile with more force than necessary.

I exhaled, trying to rein in the frustration simmering beneath my skin. I sensed his gaze following me as I moved about, assessing me, breaking me down.

The nerve of this man.

I ignored him, pressing my lips together and focusing on my cleaning.

He turned his attention to the darkness, head tilted as if listening to the night.

I sneaked a glance as he nodded to himself, content there was no danger.

My pussy rippled as his thighs once again bunched when he executed a smooth ruse.

Without a word, he dusted off his trousers using his free-hand with a nonchalance that made me clench my jaw.

Without a word, he strode back toward the shack.

The screen door creaked and slammed shut behind him,

leaving me alone at last with the gurgle of the creek and the sigh of the wind.

I finished the dishes in silence, trying to shake *him* out of my freakin' mind.

When I slipped back inside, I found him in my bedroom, the door open, where the lamps cast a soft glow over the interior, throwing his figure into sharp relief.

He lay sprawled across my bed, under the sheets and a duvet to the side, his chest bare and gleaming.

My shake-off plan detonated.

Damn him and his sleek golden, muscled physique that had my clit pulsing in ways it had never done in years.

I averted my eyes from his beauty, nabbing my pajamas and socks from my wardrobe.

'Socks? How can you bear it? It's too hot in this one-room shack,' he declared from behind me, his timbre languid, lazy, so after midnight.

'Find a cooler shack then for yourself,' I shot back, my hands balling my nightclothes.

I swept past and caught sight of his lips curling, his heated gaze weighted like a physical touch.

Swiveling from the bedroom to the kitchen, where he had a line of sight, I stored the dishes and banked the fire.

Using the entryway to change, where I was hidden from his view, I slipped on my nightwear, shivering.

Unlike Adonis in my bed, I felt the cold, even more so when I was agitated.

The fireplace embers glowed a soft orange as I pushed them around, the poker clinking against the stone hearth. The flames subsided with a final flicker, resigning to a gentle smolder.

Shadows stretched and yawned across the room, reaching for the corners as I turned off the battery-powered lamps and plunged the cabin into near darkness.

A bold shaft of moonlight spilled through the window, casting a silver radiance into the room.

Settling on the couch, I wrapped myself in a thick blanket that did little to ward off the cold and restlessness gnawing at me.

All the while, I cursed him for imposing on my space, for being so undeservedly comfortable in my bed.

The room was shrouded in shadow, save for the faint glow of cinders dying in the fireplace.

Silence hung heavy, punctuated only by the occasional hoot of an owl from somewhere in the dark woods and my muted curses.

The sofa groaned beneath me as I shifted for the umpteenth time, trying to find a sliver of comfort on the cushions.

'Scusa,' his timbre cut through the stillness.

I half sat up, eyes slicing to his moonlit silhouette across the cabin.

His sheets rustled with his movement. 'Woman, take the fuckin' bed. I'll sleep on the couch.'

I squinted through the darkness towards the form brazenly sprawled over my mattress.

'I'm fine,' I said, my intonation more a growl than intended.

'Doesn't sound fine, with all that tossing and turning,' he observed, the amusement apparent even without seeing his face.

'I'm good,' I insisted, pressing my back into the sofa to prove its sudden transformation into a haven of comfort.

There was a pause, a moment where I sensed his mocking

75

disbelief.

I pictured the smirk likely tugging at the corner of his lips—smug and knowing. My fists clenched onto the blanket over me, imagining my hands around his corded neck, squeezing the air out of his freakin' muscled chest.

'Suit yourself,' he growled. 'But you'll be by my side soon enough, bella.'

What an ass, I thought to myself, but the ache in my lower back and the constant shifting to find some semblance of comfort wore me down.

In time, however, the couch transformed into a small boat in a sea of restlessness, each toss and turn a wave threatening to capsize me into wakefulness.

After many long minutes, pride lost out to exhaustion.

Exasperation became my north star, guiding me to rise in defeat. The floorboards were cool under my feet as I tiptoed toward the inevitable—my bed.

I saw him lever one of his leonine eyes open and use his free arm reach to rearrange the duvet for me.

'Don't you dare say it,' I warned with a growl.

'Wouldn't dare it,' he rasped, but I tagged the smug look on his face.

I climbed in with my pajamas and thick socks, his brow cocked, 'Quite the ensemble.'

'Thank fuck they're not for your benefit.'

'Still, they're -,' his lips curled, 'sensuale.'

His voice was a timbred rumble in the dimness, laced with that damnable cocksure attitude.

I grabbed the sheets at the foot of the mattress and pulled them over me. 'Just shut up. For a man who says little during the day, you're hella chatty at night,' I muttered.

'That's because we're in bed, and I'm always filthy when horizontal,' came the raw, graveled drawl.

I hissed, and he chuckled, his chest rumbling.

'Go to fuckin' sleep,' I shot back, tugging the blanket to my chin despite the heat.

'Damn, she's just as dirty as I am.'

This man was undaunted by my iciness, which only heated me more.

The sheets rustled as I adjusted myself, my back turned to him.

The room's silence was punctuated by the rhythmic pulse of cricket song outside and the occasional hoot of an owl.

I wriggled, trying to find my spot.

'Uncomfortable?' His voice was softer now, above a whisper.

I remained mute, bristling because he was in my usual spot.

Instead, he shifted, and the mattress dipped with his movement.

The bed realigned under his weight as he moved flat on his back.

I shivered.

In this small space, every inch counted, and our arrangement now required a closeness that set my nerves aflame.

'Slide over,' he murmured, his arm lifting, making room in the only way the cramped quarters allowed.

It was a gesture that called for compromise, a silent agreement that we were two beings trying to rest in a shared patch of night.

I edged closer with great reluctance, aware of the heat emanating from him even before our sides touched.

The air thinned, and I held my breath as I tucked into the

space beside him, our bodies aligned yet separate. It was a dance of distance within closeness, the careful choreography of sharing a bed without partaking in anything more.

'Better?' he asked, a note of genuine inquiry softening his gruff bravado.

'Fine,' I lied, the word bitter on my tongue.

'Fine' was a world away from the truth, but it was the only option to offer to avoid betraying the turmoil within.

His steady breathing was like a metronome, piercing the cabin's silence.

That and the scent of his cologne sent my senses spiraling from annoyance to unbidden lust.

Each rise and fall of his chest was an inexplicable pull—a gravitational force that both unnerved me and set my blood to simmer.

I wished it was a chasm to put all available distance between us.

So I'd escape all this shit sensation I was experiencing.

There was no contact, not the slightest brush of skin against skin.

Yet the atmosphere appeared charged with his presence, vibrating with an energy that crept along my nerves, teasing them into reluctant arousal.

I closed my eyes, willing away the sensations, focusing instead on the darkness behind my lids.

A sigh escaped me, misting in the air before dissipating like a wisp of unspoken dreams.

It'd been too long since I'd shared any bed.

Since I'd allowed someone close enough to break through the barriers of my solitary existence.

I cursed the heat, the sweat that clung to my brow, and

above all, him for being there, for breathing, for existing so with such ease in a space that was mine.

Yet, I was unable to ignore the pull of his body heat, fighting the pulse of desire between my legs.

I fought the gnawing in the pit of my stomach, a yearning I had long suppressed was powerless to disregard—a hunger for warmth, connection, and the basic comfort of another's touch.

It was more than just the bed—it was the principle, the invasion, the casual disruption of my solitude, and the realization that living alone fucking sucked.

It ate at me, this grudging acknowledgment that Alessio was making me feel, want, and yearn despite my resentment.

I hated that he'd been my rescuer those years ago and, as a result, held some perverse power over me.

I loathed that he had my Nonna under his control, effectively placing me in his.

I detested how sensual he was, how freakin' sexy when I had no time for his brand of problematic entanglement.

Damn, I despised everything about him, I thought with fierce annoyance.

The resentment swirled in a bitter cocktail of anger and longing.

I balled my fists, digging my nails into my palms, hating him for the ease with which he occupied my bed and my turbulent thoughts.

Turning to my side, I squeezed my eyes shut, willing sleep to claim me and quell the storm of emotions brewing within.

'Cleo,' came the quiet rumble from behind me. 'Calma. I'll watch over you.'

I froze, as, to my freakin surprise, my limbs relaxed, and

my breathing slowed.

I realized with a jolt that the relief in my body came from having someone else beside me.

It'd been so long since I'd shared my space and life with anyone.

Too long since I'd experienced the paradoxical mix of irritation and intrigue that another human being in my domain provoked.

Years since I'd allowed myself to feel anything but self-imposed isolation.

Too fuckin' long.

Despite my annoyance at his intrusion, Alessio's presence permitted me to surrender—to allow someone other than myself to provide me with a measure of security, to let some other soul share my unseen load.

I breathed in his musk, my heart settling, my mind resting, and my spirit falling into a deep, dreamless sleep.

Chapter 8

ALESSIO

I *woke.*

Gasping for breath, I jolted, my heart pounding with the remnants of a dream so potent it clung to me like a second skin.

The sheets twisted around my waist, knotted by the nocturnal tempest that had just torn through my consciousness.

With a start, I realized I was in a bed—not my own.

Blinking to dispel the fog clouding my vision, I darted my eyes around the room.

Sparse shadows played across the walls, thrown by the intermittent light of a waning moon peeking through the window.

A sudden realization pierced the hazy afterglow of sleep.

The weight of another presence pressed close, an undeniable warmth that was not my own. Swallowing hard against the dryness in my throat, I dared a glance to my side.

A body lay in quiet repose, cocooned by the same quilt draped over my waist.

Her breaths were even and deep, the rhythm a silent testament to her slumber. She was real—flesh, blood, and bone.

Cleo.

Fuck, I liked this woman in particular. At least my cock did.

From her jade eyes to her sensual mouth, her graceful hips, hell, all of it.

But she had no clue that her proximity was messing with my head.

Those haunted eyes that had seared themselves into my soul and psyche were now again ratcheting up an obsession in me.

Fotto, her essence was ensnaring me.

Just as it had all those years ago.

Then, she'd been off-limits to me, under my father's and our family's protection.

I'd tried to bury her memory below countless others, beneath the lure of beautiful bodies and meaningless sex, but failed.

Yet I hadn't managed to burn her essence out of me, to extricate the fuckin' cock jolt I'd felt for her when I'd first laid eyes on her.

Not a soul knew of my lingering obsession with her, not even my brothers – for we Calibreses excelled in the art of silence unto death.

I'd kept an eye on her from afar, confiding only in Mauri, our family's consigliere, about my clandestine quest.

With her now tantalizingly close yet still out of reach, I leaned against the bedhead, gaze focused on the rise and fall of her chest.

Her essence sent a shiver down my spine, and it had nothing to do with the chill of the mountain air seeping through the log walls.

It was sheer need hitting my cock and hardening it.

'Cazzo,' I groaned, the word a half-whisper of both frustration and raw need.

She moved, reached, and flung a hand over my chest.

Her breath was now a whisper on my skin.

Beneath the tangled sheets, her limbs were an intricate weave with mine, as though in sleep, we had found a way to converse without words.

Her tits pressed against my rib cage, her thighs over my own, her scent arousing me like crazy.

My cock jerked and went so fuckin' stiff and numb in seconds that I thrust my free, unharmed wrist on it, choking it to stop it from erupting, riding the wave of agonizing desire, tamping it down as my dick complained, seeping with the undeniable evidence of my longing for her.

I lifted a knee to hide my dick's jutting diamond-hard length and throbbing jewels, struggling to keep my chest from heaving and waking her.

I managed an exquisite level of self-control but would pay for it in bucket-loads of blue balls.

Fotto! Why me?

I lay still, not daring to disturb her, cranky for being so close to beauty and not having a touch of it.

My mind went wild, wondering how soft her breasts would be, how turgid her nipples under my tongue, how wet her slit would be for me.

Cazzo, I was losing it.

I fought to calm down by keeping my eyes on her face.

Her silhouette was serene in the delicate dance of dawn's darkness and light.

I studied the shape of her face, her brow's soft arch, and her nose's gentle slope—the restful curve of her lips—all bathed in the gossamer touch of lunar radiance.

Her short, pixie dark hair lay tousled around her head, like the shadow of a raven's wing against the pale pillowcase.

Her long lashes rested upon her peach cheeks, casting feathery shadows on her skin. Her allure was undeniable—a siren call to my weary soul—and in the dim light of morning, I acknowledged just how beguiling she was.

Even as my soul was drawn in, entranced by the dance of shadows playing across her features, accentuating the delicate frame of her pixie dark hair.

The sensation was intoxicating—strands brushed on me, cool and smooth.

As she cuddled into me, despite my throbbing cock, I found tranquility that I hadn't realized I was seeking.

I lay still, relishing how she nestled into me with a soft sigh, her body a natural fit fitted to my side, molding to mine in an instinctual search for comfort and warmth.

And I, even in the hazy edges of sleep, welcomed her without question.

There was no guilt, no second-guessing the rightness of it all.

Damn, this yearning was the last thing I needed.

Yet, for the first time in a long time, I wanted to play. To tease, to seduce a woman.

To entice her. Fuckin' have her horizontal under me. Keening for me.

That shit hadn't happened in almost a decade.

I threw my neck back, thinking of how to navigate her and my mission as morning seeped into the room.

A tendril of light grew bolder as it stretched across the floorboards and climbed to where we lay.

When dawn's chorus began its symphony outside, I disentangled myself from her, cool air rushing in to fill the space I vacated.

'Fotto,' I hissed at the pain from the back of my head.

Confirming Cleo's assessment that I must have hit it on something during the gunfight.

Her breath hitched at my vocalization, yet she remained in slumber.

I lingered beside the bed, staring down at her for a beat before I turned and left.

My muscles protested each movement, and the ache in my shoulder was a constant reminder of the previous night's chaos.

The cool wooden floor grounded me as I crossed the room.

I found a jug of water and drank straight from it with thirst, liquid splashing down my chin and chest, restoring a fragment of myself.

Only then did I look around. Seeing her cabin bathed in a new light.

The space was simple, practical, and ordered.

Books lined the shelves, their spines perfect in alignment.

A small dining table displayed a single, vibrant potted plant, and no stray paper or utensil was in sight.

Cleo valued order, perhaps as a counterbalance to the unpredictability of the outside world. Her environment was austere but warm, inviting an appreciation for simplicity.

I trailed my fingers over a plush throw on the sofa, then winced as a sharp twinge shot through my side. With a sigh, I tested the limits of my discomfort.

At least I could still manage the basics. Pouring water, reaching for something on a high shelf, and even driving if necessary. However, I had to stabilize my joint to prevent further pain.

Gritting my teeth, I found Cleo's first aid kit.

The contents were organized, just like everything else in her home. I fumbled for a moment before grasping the bandages, then fashioned a crude brace across my chest to immobilize my shoulder. My free hand did most of the work, tightening the fabric and securing it with a pin.

As I leaned against the cool sink, another discomfort demanded attention—I needed to piss.

A quick scan of the shack revealed no bathroom. I pushed aside a sheer window curtain, my gaze settling on a small outhouse adjacent to the cabin.

With a sigh of resignation and amusement, I shook my head at Cleo's rustic lifestyle.

Finding my boots beside hers at the door, I tugged them on and slipped outside, careful not to wake her.

The early dawn greeted me with a biting chill that stung my cheeks, oddly purifying. The trill of birds pierced the silence, a symphony of wild calls.

As the sun crested the horizon, painting the heavens pink and orange, I understood the primal allure of this isolation.

This stunning wilderness contrasted the urban chaos that had often ruled my life as a Son of Honor and one of the Kings of Omertà.

How easy it would be to lose oneself in the embrace of such

solitude, to become a mere echo among the trees and the endless sky.

The morning chill nipped at my skin as I made my way to the outhouse.

As I entered, the door creaked on its hinges.

The smaller shingled structure was unique. Its floor-to-ceiling window canted over the green valley, capturing spectacular views and plenty of natural light.

After lingering on the stunning dawn panorama for a beat, I attended to nature's call and, minutes later, trekked back, my boots crunching on the frost-kissed grass.

I powered into the modest kitchen, where a coffee maker squatted next to a canister of aromatic beans.

A longing for the rich, dark brew tugged at me.

But then I glanced back at Cleo's bedroom and cursed my craving.

The rattle and hum of the machine grinding would wake her, and she deserved this rare surrender to sleep.

Instead, I focused on the alternatives; a compromise presented itself as a tea caddy nestled among the pots and pans.

With care not to clink metal against metal, I selected a brew that promised robust flavor.

The kettle burbled, and I filled the billy tin mug with steaming water.

I dropped it in an infusion bag, and it began to steep, releasing its earthy scent into the air.

When the brew was ready, hot, black, and dark the way I preferred, I stepped out onto the veranda.

A long outdoor lounge stretched across one side of the space.

With socks muffling my footsteps, I made my way over and eased into a corner of the three-seater, crossing an ankle over a knee.

Leaning back, I sighed, luxuriating in the stillness of nature and the company of my thoughts.

The scenery was fuckin' out of this world. The wind was crisp, filled with the subtle fragrance of pine and the fresh earthiness that followed dawn's dew.

The tea in my hand radiated warmth, and I sipped, taking my time and letting the strong brew work its soothing magic.

The rhythmic hum of turbine blades in the distance swirled through the air, mimicking the ebb and flow of ocean waves.

In Cleo's domain, I found a moment of pure peace.

In this quiet awakening, there was no rush to move, no immediate pull towards action or thought.

This was the embodiment of 'la vie et bella.'

My cynical, dark heart demurred.

It wouldn't last.

Nothing this beautiful ever did.

Chapter 9

CLEO

Sunlight warmed my closed eyelids, teasing me from sleep.

My eyes snapped open, squinting against the intrusive brightness, adrenaline coursing through me.

Heart pounding, I scrambled upright, breath quickening, confusion clouding my thoughts.

What time was it?

I spun, searching the room until the clock's hands came into focus—9 a.m.

That couldn't be right.

'Shit,' I muttered, untangling myself from the sheets as I stood. Pressing a hand to my forehead, I tried to clear the fog.

Sleeping in wasn't like me; dawn was always my alarm.

So—why had I slept in?

My gaze landed on the pillow beside mine. Its center

was pressed inward, preserving the impression of another person's head.

A scent lingered in the air—cologne, musk, and maleness.

Alessio.

The man I'd shared my sacred space with—and because of it, I'd rested deeper than I had in months, perhaps even years.

I recalled his heat, scent, and solidness, which, while not touching me, had soothed me inexplicably.

A chill seeped through my pajamas, sending a shiver down my spine as realization hit—he'd seen me at my most vulnerable.

My cheeks flushed with embarrassment.

No man had woken in my bed with me still in it.

What had he glimpsed?

Had I drooled?

Talked in my sleep?

Stunk of morning breath?

Made a freaky fool of myself?

I took an inhale, needing to calm the fuck down.

But where the hell was he?

The faint scrape of furniture outside on the veranda triggered a stomach lurch.

I scooted from under the sheets and shuffled to the living space. My pulse quickened as I focused on the outer door, the wood mocking me with its silence.

My mind spun with self-doubt, imagining his judgment.

With a suck of my teeth, I silenced the unwarranted shame and crossed the floor, pushing the door open.

The veranda greeted me with a chill breeze, as did the sculpted mountain of a man sprawled on the outdoor lounge, sunlight casting a halo around him.

He was rolling his freakin' gold coin over his knuckles, eyes canted to the view.

Holy fuck.

It was unfair for any human to look this good in the morning.

His lips curled in awareness of my presence, and the penny paused for a beat, and then he continued.

His movements were smooth and deliberate, each flick of his lean fingers sending the golden coin spinning in a mesmerizing dance.

I'd learned from an early age that men could be dangerous.

I'd picked up on how to judge a man's level of menace so I'd escape it, fast.

Now, this man was beyond menacing.

Every move of his fingers was calculated, a display of control that intimidated and fascinated me.

Like he fuckin' held all the power and cards in the wicked game he was playing on me, toying with me with a sinister charm.

Yet, his essence had an allure, a wild appeal that drew me in despite my fear and uncertainty.

He turned his head, and flaming eyes hit mine, brimming with a dark emotion I couldn't place.

He jerked his chin at me in a silent invitation, and I responded with a slight wave, feeling absurd in my printed night gear.

His eyes raked over them with a gleam like he'd had the night before.

'What?' I groused.

'I'll repeat it: leaping cartoon kangaroos are so fuckin' sensual,' he rasped.

I rolled my eyes. 'You're out of your mind.'

91

'Your fault, bella,' came the amused drawl, obscuring half his face in his tea mug. 'You wear that sexy get up to bed tonight, and I may have to strip it off to maintain my sanity.'

I buzzed on the inside, hiding it with a glare. 'You're certifiably an asshole.'

He stuck his tongue in his cheek and met my defiant eyes until the heat sizzled so hot as to scorch, and I tore my eyes away.

A palpable silence settled, my heartbeat echoing in the stillness of the morning.

It was interrupted by the subtle scrape of his voice.

'Coffee?' he rasped, the word rough-edged.

I nodded, a mute puppet jerked to life by the simplicity of the offer.

My throat tightened, not from sleep but from the uncertainty that filled the space between us.

The nod was all I could muster, an agreement to something as mundane as a beverage, and yet, at that moment, it felt like so much more.

He pushed himself up from the couch, a grimace shadowing his features.

The makeshift brace cradled his left arm at an awkward angle, the white bandage stark against his skin's tan.

The jerry-rigged support was clumsy at best.

'That'll require a rework and some tightening and re-tying,' I whispered.

He turned his gaze to the injured limb, a single brow arched in response.

'So fix it.'

He finished the demand with a curl to his lip, revealing a dimple in his cheek under his beard.

Need streaked - to my freakin' clit.

The morning light played across his face, highlighting the stubble that framed his lips and the gleam in his eyes.

Damn, this man, I thought.

He stood waiting, expectant.

'Cleo?'

'Of course,' I replied.

He sat back on the sofa as I leaned in and re-tied the rudimentary brace, stretching the two reinforced elastic straps on the upper arm, across his chest, and under his other arm to provide extra support for the shoulder and give him more unrestricted movement.

'You're good now,' I soon announced.

'Bene,' he grunted, moving past me with the deliberate care of a man who respected his body's limits.

As he did so, the air around us shifted, carrying with it the essence of his skin—a blend of heady cologne and an indefinable spice that was so him. It came off him in waves, a musk that seemed to settle over my senses and leave me disarmed.

To avoid him, I canted away from him, albeit too fast, and he paused, a smirk on his face.

'Don't fret, woman,' he growled. 'When I touch you, it's because you'll be begging for it.'

I jolted at his crude estimation.

'You're so up yourself,' I whispered.

He raked his eyes over me, lips twitching.

I took a ragged breath.

'The only thing I want to be up in is you, carissima, drilling you deeper.'

He rasped the vulgar sentence, and I inhaled at his moxie,

my response tumbling out unbidden. 'You going to do what?'

He bent his head, drew his mouth parallel to my ear, and drawled into it. 'Up you, in you, balls deep.'

The undertone, raw, sultry, shredded me on the inside and sent ecstasy through every fiber of my being.

I struggled not to fumble my outrage. 'In your wildest dreams.'

He pulled back, the whisper of his breath playing on my skin. 'See? It's intriguing, no? Pensaci. Dream on it.'

He straightened with a lionizing gaze, his mouth curling, eyes predatory like a hunter's.

'Never.'

The unholy nerve.

I sliced my eyes away from his colossal frame, biting my lip to stop hissing at the jolt between us.

Italian men were bold as brass, but Alessio took the cake. His balls had to be coated in freakin' gold and diamonds.

He huffed, leonine eyes gleaming in triumph as he stalked off.

Leaving me sopping wet, nipples throbbing.

The sensation wasn't just physical; it was as if his presence was shattering my control, dismantling the walls I'd built over the years.

He was raw and aggressive, with a bullish sensuality that reached out and wrapped itself around the stony resolve I prided myself on.

His scent lingered where he'd passed, and I hissed, drawing it in.

Damn, he was a portrait of male beauty as he made his way to the kitchen, the fabric of his jeans hugging him in all the right places. He walked with stealthed grace, silent, raptorial, the kind of energy that slayed.

My eyes traced the muscles in his back shift beneath the cotton shirt that stretched across his broad shoulders.

Fuck, he annoyed me.

Yet somehow, he also calmed me. How else had I slept so well?

How was this man who, before yesterday, had only been a distant whisper of a memory, now become a bedrock in my uncertain existence?

Those questions and more danced in my mind, unbidden and unanswered.

Gingerly, I sat on the outdoor sofa, resting my head against the backrest. I exhaled an extended, measured breath, allowing the tension woven through my muscles to unravel.

To let go.

Of the apprehension, the need for control, and the fear of the unknown that had kept my world contained.

I closed my eyes, surrendering to the silence, my thoughts searching for peace in the wake of chaos.

The sun climbed higher, its rays filtering through the leaves, projecting a dappled pattern on the wooden floorboards.

Its warmth touched my skin, casting me adrift in a rare serenity when his quiet stride signaled his return.

A mug clinked onto the outdoor table before me.

The scent of fresh-brewed coffee wafted, waking my senses.

Still, with my eyes closed, I sensed his presence as a subtle shift in the air—a displacement caused by his solid frame moving through the space.

His arm brushed against the back of the sofa as he settled down, his steady breathing blending with the rustle of leaves outside.

I let a slow exhale escape, not ready to break the spell or open my eyes to acknowledge him.

But I nodded in a silent thank you for the coffee.

Settling into a fractious understanding that didn't demand words or action, just simple, shared existence despite the fact I wanted to slit his throat.

ALESSIO

I tagged the slight upturn to her lips as the sun warmed her.

Her eyes parted with an inhale, and she sliced her gaze to the mug I'd set in front of her.

Neat, elegant, unadorned fingers curled around its heat, bringing the lip to her mouth, sipping.

It was proving too hard not to resist needling her, pushing her buttons, talking dirty and crude-as-fuck.

Just to see her reaction, loving how her cheeks pinked up at my outrageous utterances, how her eyes lit up, and her lips tightened.

I was enjoying this shit a little too much.

However, I wasn't driven by pure lust alone. I wanted to pull her mind away from her present troubles, to see her light up with anything other than sadness. To witness an eye roll or curse that took her away from her loneliness.

Still, the sensuality of the game I was playing sent a jolt to my traitorous cock, and I found myself rasping out words to refocus my wayward body.

'The men who ambushed me, where do they operate from?' I growled.

'Why?'

'Like I said, I'm after Franco Conti. But I need to know of all possible threats in the area.'

She sat up, and I tagged the worry - the shit I didn't like to see - crowding her eyes.

'They're Caputo capos and work with his sons, who've been running the farm since Franco was put away.'

Her voice was a hushed whisper.

I nodded, taking my time before answering. 'Sons? How many?'

She shot me a narrowed glance, hesitating.

'Three.'

'Their names, cara?'

Her face clouded over for a second. 'Rocco, Fabio and Bruno Conti.'

I huffed at the cliche names. 'Stai scherzando. The sound like the members of a shit boy band. You're joking?'

Her lips twitched. 'I kid you not.'

'Tell me more,' I demanded.

Cleo gave me pressed lips, and I sensed turbulence under her calm waters. 'The Caputos are paying the Contis for their farmland to grow weed and manufacture meth. At least, that's what the rumors are. The Caputos have sent in a small army of capos to protect the drugs they're cooking on their farm. They're fuckin' nuts who walk around brandishing guns and their collective outrage, frustration, boredom, and weak-ass gangster fakery.'

I searched her face, aware of the reason for her ire. 'You hate them,' I noted.

Her lips twisted. 'I loath all of them. They have a wanton disregard for the lives and livelihoods of their fellow human beings. They've destroyed so many families, and the flow of narcotics has created a serious problem in the area.'

'Sounds like someone needs to take them out.'

Cleo's jaw clenched. 'Not me. My beef is with Franco.'

Her tone carried with it a measure of pain.

'You're waiting for him, aren't you? For revenge?' I growled.

Her eyes burned when she turned them toward me, confirming my suspicions she was planning to end Franco if she ever encountered him.

'You're well within your right, tesoro.'

She jolted. 'Why are you calling me that?'

Her voice was sharp, her face panicked.

I'd struck a nerve.

'It means treasure,' I offered. 'That's all.'

'I'm no one's treasure.'

Her bleak, stoic statement hit me so hard I sucked my teeth.

I pushed a hand into my trousers and found my jade talisman. Rolling the beads in my fingers, I growled at her. 'Woman, if you look like a fuckin' treasure; you talk and walk like one, and your body, tesoro, is out of this world, then you're a treasure.'

I smirked at the rush of color into her face as she canted away from me.

My eyes lingered on the curve of her spine. Wanting to take her in my arms and soothe away the strain on her face.

To kiss her shoulder and nape, lick her perfect ear shell,

make her come so hard she'd forget her momentary troubles.

Again, my cock jolted in my pants.

This woman was something else.

Vulnerable yet strong as hell.

Sharp nonetheless sweet under her orneriness.

Damn, I wanted to fuck her so bad.

With a long inhale, I reclined back on the couch and pulled a knee over the other thigh again to hide my tenting situation.

She seemed not to notice, her eyes fixed on the horizon.

I sensed her agony and twisted my lips.

Seeking to shift her attention, I leaned in. 'I have to find out how well armed the Contis are in case they attack. I'd also like to see this operation they're running,' I growled.

Her eyes flicked to my upper arm. 'With that injury, you're constrained with what you can do. Infiltrating the Conti farm means jumping their fences or digging under them to approach at night in stealth. You won't do it on a bum shoulder.'

'What makes you think I need to stealth it? Or attempt an infil at night?'

Her eyes widened at my audacity. 'A daytime raid? You're bodacious.'

'It is my middle name,' I drawled back. 'I've done it before.'

'How about I provide some support once you're healed,' she whispered. 'I'll point you in the right direction and maybe even help you over their fence line, but that'll be it. I don't want to be involved with the Contis unless it's on my terms.'

'Which are?' I pushed.

A wild light flared in her eyes. 'None of your fuckin' own business.'

With that, she rose and stalked off, empty mug in hand.

Just as she yanked open her cabin door, I drawled. 'So what does one do on a farm all day today?'

She paused for a second at the door. 'Breakfast, followed by repair work. We've got some freak storms, sometimes even the promise of tennis ball-sized hail. I must fix the roof and hammer a few loose nails in the shutters.'

I raised a brow.

'Feel free to watch me for your pure entertainment, or otherwise string some guitar song together, perhaps even read a book,' she shrugged.

I sighed and pulled out my phone from my pocket.

It had sustained a crack in my ambush with the Contis, but it was still working.

However, the internet symbol was grayed out.

I tipped my chin to her. 'You have WiFi?'

She'd just stepped into the house and reversed, with a twist to her lips, before disappearing into the cabin.

She emerged with a transistor radio and plopped it on the outdoor table. She punched in a button, and the strains of jazz and the muted sound of an announcer set up the next track.

I stared at it with narrowed eyes.

'Is this shit real?' I growled, disbelieving, arching my brow.

She smirked. 'We have ABC transmission. Enjoy. It's good enough for me, so it should be for you.'

I scoffed in shock. 'So no Internet? How do you survive?'

'I login at the library in town if I need it.'

She strode off with a small smile.

No WiFi? What the bumfuck was this place?

'I heard that.'

Chapter 10

CLEO

He was so damn restless.

Guitar strings twanged as his calloused fingers danced across them with caged energy.

One moment, he was strumming out a melancholic tune; the next, he set the instrument aside with a huff and paced the creaky wooden floorboards.

With a growl, he pushed the front door open and strode outside, prowling like a lost man around the property.

Moving like a caged panther, shoulders hunched, head down, wearing a trail in the green grass.

His gold coin bounced off his knuckles as he paced back and forth.

His leonine eyes darted, scanning the horizon, the trees, and the sky—searching.

His other hand was thrust into his trousers, clutching

something inside his pockets like he had a few times now.

I assumed a lucky charm.

Given his girth, strength, and brooding menace, I supposed he was the last man who needed one.

Still, we were all allowed a measure of weakness and a reprieve in how we sought to relieve our worries.

I wondered what it was, for he'd kept it away from my view.

I guessed a rosary, but as I'd never sighted whatever it was, fuck if I knew.

He strode along the edge of the creek, his gaze sweeping over the water, the rocky banks, the towering trees.

He moved with a predator's grace, all coiled strength and sharp edges.

Like he was casing the place, searching for what? Weaknesses? Escape routes?

I shivered despite the warm sun filtering through the leaves.

While I now had an idea about what had brought him to my doorstep, with his brooding energy, I still sensed murky waters and secrets.

Underneath the gloss of his golden eyes, I perceived a wolf lying in wait. But only time would tell who his ultimate prize and prey were.

I busied myself with other more minor chores inside, determined not to look outside.

A few minutes later, I heard his footsteps thumping up the porch steps. He paused in the doorway, his bulk filling the frame.

'Place looks secure,' he growled. 'You've got good sight lines, natural barriers with the creek and boulders.'

Then that cold as fuck predator light in his eyes went on. 'But your fence needs some work. And a dog wouldn't hurt.'

I bristled at the implication that I couldn't take care of myself. 'I do just fine on my own,' I murmured. 'The neighbors look out for me.'

His gaze sharpened. 'What neighbours?'

I sighed, leaning my hip against the counter. 'The Hendersons, about a mile down the road. And old Mr. Jameson across the way. They keep an eye out, but most times, they mind their own business.'

He grunted, unsatisfied.

He stalked the living area, hands stuck in his pocket, rolling whatever was in his pants.

His restless energy filled the small kitchen, making me twitch.

I needed to find something for him to do before he drove us both crazy.

'I've got some loose tiles on the roof that need nailing down,' I murmured. 'Think you can handle holding the toolbox for me?'

His eyes flashed at the challenge. 'Lead the way.'

I did, first, to the shed, where I wordlessly pointed to the ladder.

He understood the assignment and lifted it onto his shoulders, his solemn expression unchanged despite his injury.

I reached for my toolkit, then stopped short as he extended a hand for it, too.

We locked eyes in a battle of wills until I gave in to his icy glare.

I handed it to him and marched outside.

The sun beat down on our backs as we placed the ladder along the roofline where I needed it.

I clambered up the rungs, hammer in hand.

He followed more with care, his movements stiff and careful. I pretended not to notice his grimace of pain as he settled himself on the roof beside me.

We worked, not speaking, for a while; the only sounds were the hammer's steady thump and the birds' distant trilling. Sweat trickled down my neck, plastering my hair to my skin.

At one point, he descended to the ground and disappeared into the cabin before returning.

Damn, he was athletic and freakin' resilient.

Most men with the injury he had would be writhing in bed, yet here he was on a canopy, handing nails to me at the same time, keeping an eagle-eye view of our surroundings.

Granted, I was doing the hammering, and he was on light duty, but still, it gave me insight into his dogged spirit. This was a man who never yielded to anyone.

'Here.'

A bottle of water appeared in my peripheral vision.

I took it with a grunt of thanks, chugging half of it in one go.

His eyes studied me, something unreadable in his eyes.

'You know your way around a toolbox,' he muttered.

I shrugged. 'Had to learn. Repairmen charge an arm and a leg to come out here.'

'I'll help out while I'm here. Earn my keep.'

I squinted at him, trying to read his brooding energy. Was it a genuine offer or just a way to ease his boredom?

In the end, my practicality won out. 'I won't say no to an extra pair of hands,' I allowed.

He nodded, something like satisfaction flickering over his face. We returned to the task, the silence between us less strained.

The temperature became oppressive as the sun rose, baking the shingles beneath us. I wiped my brow with the back of my hand, smearing gritty granules of sand and tar across my skin.

'Time for a break,' he announced, easing himself upright with a slight wince. 'I'll rustle us up some lunch.'

I opened my mouth to protest that I wasn't hungry, but my stomach let out a mortifying growl at that moment.

Heat that had nothing to do with the weather rushed to my cheeks.

He smirked, a glimmer of amusement shining in his eyes. 'I'll take that as a yes.'

So he had a sense of humor under his fuckin' brooding facade.

It was refreshing to witness, for it meant he also had a heart beating beneath that tight, muscled chest.

He navigated back down the ladder, my gaze on his taut ass, admiring the fluid grace of his movements despite his obvious discomfort.

It set off a mini fantasy in my mind, the heat and hazy weather adding to my fervor.

Lost in lust, I almost missed the enticing aroma wafting up from below. The scent of fresh-brewed coffee mingled with something savory and rich. My mouth watered in anticipation.

He reappeared bearing a tray one-armed, laden with a platter of sandwiches and two steaming mugs.

'Cleo,' he growled, striding toward a log in my garden without waiting for my reply.

I descended, tracking to the outdoor sink to wash my hands.

I found him sitting on one of the alfresco benches. One thigh crossed over his knee, mug in one hand, fist cradling his chow.

The subs were simple but appetizing - thick slices of fried steak, cheese, and crisp lettuce stacked between hearty whole-grain bread.

The brew surprised me. It was a flawless macchiato, with espresso and crema layered in the glass vessel.

'How did you -?' I trailed off, gesturing to the heavenly creation.

He shrugged, lips curling. 'I noted you had a machine in the kitchen. Thought you might appreciate something a little fancier than plain black espresso.'

I took a sip, letting the velvety foam coat my tongue. It was delicious, the espresso's bitterness balanced by creamy sweetness.

'It's perfect,' I murmured. 'Thank you.'

His eyes met mine, heated and unfathomable. 'You're welcome, mia sola.'

The endearment slipped out, so natural, it took me a moment to register it. I glanced away, busying myself with grabbing a sandwich.

As we ate in companionable silence, I couldn't help sneaking glances at him from the corner of my eye. The dappled sunlight played across the planes of his face, highlighting the gold threading through his hair.

His tongue peeked out from his lips, and I bit back a groan.

'Like what you see, cara?'

The drawl threw me. As did his following words.

'You'd like it more if I was over you, inside you, loving you. Making you cum.'

I jolted. 'Are you hardwired to speak shit, or do you have some kind of verbal diarrhea ailment you'd like to share?'

I tagged the shameless smirk play at the end of his mouth

and inhaled, glowering at him.

Hating the stirring in my heart for him.

I dampened it seconds later, whispering my Nonna's name to remind me of what was at stake if I swooned over him.

Or let his unabashed sensuality lure me in.

After a few minutes of quiet chewing, he cleared his throat. I glanced over, catching his searching gaze.

'Tell me about this area,' Alessio rasped.

Eager to move our conversation away from his feral mind, I obliged him. 'It's rural, with a healthy Italian population. Migration from Italy to the Goulburn Valley began in the 1920s. Today, over 5,000 residents have Italian heritage, with many migrants coming from small towns with farming backgrounds attracted by work in the fruit industry. Over time, they bought farms and introduced traditional Mediterranean vegetables and horticulture. The Italian community, now in its third generation, is well integrated into various sectors, including medicine, law, and business.'

'And this farm?' he rasped, gesturing to the expansive property stretching before us. 'How long have you lived here?'

I swallowed the bite of my sandwich, considering my answer. 'A few years now. It was my grandparents' old place. When Grandpa Cesare passed, and Nonna Guilia went into aged care, I took it over.'

He nodded, taking another sip of his espresso. 'Bellissima.'

'Yeah, it is,' I agreed, looking out over the distant mountain ranges. The view never failed to take my breath away.

'Tell me more.'

'I have an organic veggie patch and fruit trees, indigenous bush tucker, and wild medicinal herbs growing in some of the most fertile black soil you've ever seen. I have an off-grid set-up due to a near-new solar array and batteries. I run a range, air conditioner, kettle, and a coffee machine. Just not all at once.'

He huffed.

'The fireplace and wood stove heat the whole house in winter, and with 50 acres of pristine and wooded forest, you'll never want for quality firewood. The land is half clear valley floor and bushland with wattles, grevilleas, red, both yellow and white box plus eucalypt trees.'

'Lonely?' he mused, his tone casual but his eyes sharp on my face.

I shrugged, brushing a few stray crumbs off my jeans. 'I like the solitude. And I've got good neighbors, even if we keep to ourselves.'

His brow furrowed. 'Still, a young woman living alone in the middle of nowhere. Aren't you worried about your safety?'

I bristled at his words, my spine stiffening. 'I can take care of myself,' I clipped. 'I'm not some helpless damsel in distress.'

He held up his hands in a placating gesture. 'Scusa. Just concerned.'

My anger deflated as fast as it had risen.

He sounded sincere, his worry genuine.

'I appreciate that,' I murmured. 'But I'm fine. I've got my wits about me and a shotgun under my bed. I can handle whatever comes my way.'

His mouth quirked. 'Somehow, that doesn't surprise me at all.'

I gave him a slight turn of my lips, the tension between easing off.

We lapsed back into silence, but it was a comfortable one

now.

I gathered our empty plates and mugs, ready to head back inside, when his voice stopped me.

'These neighbors of yours,' he said with casual nonchalance, his gaze fixed on the distant hills. 'They make sure you're okay?'

Damn, still on that?

I nodded, balancing the dishes in my hands. 'Yeah, the Hendersons next door. They're an older couple, sweet as can be. They've adopted me as an extra daughter.'

He glanced at me, his eyes unreadable. 'And how does that work? They check up on you from time to time?'

I shrugged, a smile tugging at my lips as I thought of the kind-hearted pair. 'We chat over the fence sometimes, swap recipes and gardening tips. But they make sure I'm still kicking. If they don't see me for a day or two, they'll come knocking, just to be certain.'

He hummed, his fingers drumming against his thigh. 'Bene. I like that they care. That you've got someone looking out for you.'

I tilted my head, studying him. 'I'm glad we meet with your approval, oh wise King,' I taunted.'

He huffed, but his intensity of narrowed eyes made me wonder what he was thinking.

'It is good,' I agreed. 'But like I said, I can handle myself. I'm not seeking for anyone to save me.'

His gaze met mine, a flash of something fierce and protective in their depths. 'I know you can. But everyone needs an ally in their corner. Even the strongest among us.'

I swallowed hard, my heart doing a funny flip in my chest. He held my glance for a long moment, something unspoken passing between us before he spoke again.

'Your face is sad, cara,' he murmured, his voice rasped and intimate.

I fought the urge to look away.

His words, spoken in a timbered burr, like a caress against my skin.

I couldn't remember when somebody had taken note of my sadness and cared enough to comment.

'I'm fine,' I lied after a beat, stammering, the monotone automatic, a reflex born of years of practice.

He studied me for a long moment, his eyes searching mine. I had the unsettling inkling that he perceived all of me and knew how not fine I was.

'You don't have to pretend with me,' he said with quiet emphasis, his gaze never leaving my face. 'I know what it's like to carry pain, to feel like you're all alone in the world.'

His words hit me like a gut punch, stealing my breath from my lungs.

How might he understand the depths of my loneliness, the aching void that ruled my existence for so long?

I opened my mouth to respond, but my self-doubt kicked in. All utterance escaped me, helpless as I gazed into his eyes.

Raw, exposed.

He'd somehow managed to strip away all my constructed defenses with just a few simple phrases.

And yet, even as I sat before him more vulnerable than I had in years, I couldn't help but feel a flicker of something else. Something that bordered dangerously close to hope.

I blinked, trying to keep the tears at bay. I wouldn't cry in front of him. I couldn't.

For so long I'd painted calm on my face, keeping my

composure, like everything was cool.

Crying was a weakness I couldn't afford to show, not even to this man who appeared to see straight into my soul.

'You don't know anything about me,' I said, my voice rough with emotion. 'You don't know what I've been through, what I've lost. You may have stalked me from afar but never saw me, not into my core. No one ever did!'

I spat the words with some venom, dialing down after a beat, realizing how petulant I sounded. 'I had no parenting to speak of, and my grandparents, though kind, were too told for me to bother with my problems.'

His eyes narrowed. 'You're right. I don't know your story. But I know what it's like to feel alone, like you're carrying the world's weight on your shoulders.'

Gazing into his eyes, I detected a depth of suffering that matched my own—anguish that spoke of loss, heartbreak, and loneliness that can break a person.

It blew me away when he continued. 'I lost my father years ago. He and my mother were killed in a car bomb.'

I inhaled, rocked to the core.

I reached a hand to touch his arm in instant commiseration.

His gaze tracked my gesture, eyes narrowing even further, teeth clenched, a tic in his jaw.

'I'm so sorry,' I breathed.

He shrugged and glanced away, his face dark and clouded. Ever the brooder, he was a tortured soul. Dangerous, too, he wielded power with ease, which drove me crazy but also enticed me.

He electrified me not only because he was ruthless but because he was aware enough of it and didn't try to apologize for it or cover it up.

'I lost my granddad,' I whispered, the words spilling out before I was able to stop them. 'He and Nonna were the only ones who never let me down and always had my back. And now he's gone. My grandmother is in hospice, and here on the farm, I'm alone again.'

My voice broke on the last word, and a tear slipped down my cheek. I brushed it away with anger, furious with myself for showing weakness.

Alessio didn't serve me with pity or condescension.

Instead, he gave me a searching look with such meaning that its intense power hit me. 'You're not alone,' he growled.

As I gazed into his eyes, a flicker of something I hadn't sensed in a long time went through. Something that bordered on hope.

I took a deep breath, trying to calm the sudden racing of my pulse. 'I should get these inside,' I muttered, lifting the dishes.

He nodded, pushing himself to his feet. 'Let me help.'

He followed me into the cozy kitchen, the worn floorboards creaking beneath our soles. I busied myself at the sink, rinsing off our plates as he leaned on the counter, his presence filling the small space.

'Cleo.'

I turned, the hotness of his raw, timbered whisper on my back.

He cupped my jaw.

His eyes searched mine as if trying to read something hidden below the surface.

My heart lurched.

His head lowered, and he brushed his lips to the corner of my mouth.

When he bent over, my breath hitched, all out of my element.

His hand brushed my cheek with a gentleness that undid me.

Then his lips touched my mouth, soft, testing the waters.

Heat spread through me, starting from where our lips met and radiating outwards, filling each cranny of my being.

The kiss deepened, every movement careful, deliberate.

Holy fuck, how he kissed me, a mix of tenderness and desire that made my knees feel weak.

I surged into him as our lips melded into a heated, searching exploration.

I reached up, threading through his golden locks, pulling him closer. His other hand found its way to the small of my back, the scorching heat of his touch imprinting through my clothes.

Time appeared to blur, and all that existed was the two of us wrapped in that perfect moment.

When we pulled away, our foreheads rested against each other, breaths mingling. My heart raced as the world around us faded back into focus.

Yet, I was different now, touched by something beautiful, something I never wanted to let go of.

A long, sinewed finger lifted my jaw, canting my eyes to his.

'Carissima, even the most capable people need relief. A companion to lean on, hope with, and fuckin' play and laugh with.'

I stilled, my hands gripping his shirt. 'Says the lone wolf,' I quipped.

'You've got me wrong, carissima. A Calibrese is never alone. We're a pack of wolves.'

I huffed at his apt description.

'I'm not sure I know how to do that anymore,' I admitted. 'Leaning. Trusting. I feel like I'd be weaker to rely on anyone else.'

'It's not about weakness, mia sola,' he growled. 'It's about knowing when to let someone help carry the load. Like I do for my family, and they for me.'

My eyes searched his. 'Is that what you're offering? To help carry my load?'

Something flickered in his gaze, a heat that made my breath catch.

We stood in each other's arms for a long moment, the ambiance thick with unspoken tension. My heart raced in my chest, my skin prickling with awareness of his closeness.

He opened his mouth, but I preempted him, raising a finger to stop his roll. 'Don't answer that. Not when you're holding me hostage so you can achieve whatever the fuck you're up to.'

He shuttered down. His soul retreating, the warmth leaking from his eyes, his withdrawal causing such a whiplash that I hissed.

'Cazzo, I need air,' he growled.

I'd insulted him, somehow.

The realization sent shame flying through me.

He stepped away, turning and heading out of the kitchen, leaving me alone with my thoughts.

I listened to his footsteps fade as he retreated outside.

With a sigh, I forced myself to move, busying my hands and tidying up the meal's remnants. But even as I went through the motions, my mind drifted back to him.

Damn, Alessio Calibrese unnerved and intrigued me.

He studied me as if he saw straight through to my soul. The way his presence filled a room, commanding attention without even trying.

And, hell, how he made me feel like I wasn't alone.

Maybe, just maybe, I didn't have to carry the world's weight by myself.

I finished cleaning up and headed outside, needing the fresh air to clear my head.

As I stepped onto the porch, movement caught my eye.

He stood by the fence line, his back to me as he surveyed the surrounding landscape.

For many long moments, I studied him.

Taking in the strong lines of his scapulae, the set of his stance, the golden mane lifting in the wind, and the menace of his prowl.

He was like a gilded warrior surveying the lay of the land before a battle.

Like a man who foresaw a darkness and dread so terrifying it foreshadowed Hades.

Chapter 11

CLEO

At some point, Alessio wandered back inside and disappeared into my bedroom.

I stood in the kitchen, back to him, as he stalked past me without saying a word.

The old floorboards creaked as he settled onto my bed.

For a moment, I imagined his beautiful, tight ass easing between my sheets.

I shook my head, trying to dislodge the heated thoughts.

Yearning for him was out of the question.

That said, the man was infiltrating every corner of my cabin.

The signs of him being here were scattered, subtle but unmistakable.

His leather boots sat by the door, carelessly kicking off as he entered.

His large gym bag sat in the bedroom, his gear folded inside.

More of his clothes draped over the back of a chair, and a crumpled shirt lay abandoned on the floor beside his jeans.

On the nightstand, a watch—his, not mine—rested beside a half-drunk glass of water, and one of the paperbacks from my shelf he'd been reading sat with the pages bent at the corner.

In the outhouse, his stark blue toothbrush against my white one leaned casually in the cup by the sink.

His razor had found its place beside my makeup bag, and his sharp, woodsy cologne lingered in the air as if marking his territory without effort.

In the living room, a hoodie he had left behind was tossed across the arm of the couch, and his heavy and unfamiliar keys rested on the entrance table as though they had always been there.

These little pieces of him, unspoken signs of his presence, quietly claimed corners of my space.

Still, I couldn't permit myself to get attached or used to his freakin' disarming presence and sensual, scowling essence.

I had a goal I was working toward. No matter how tempting, I couldn't allow Alessio's existence to jeopardize everything I'd labored for.

He also needed rest to heal, and then he would be on his way out of my life as fast as he had burst into it.

So I let him be.

The remainder of the day yawned before me, empty and quiet.

Restless energy thrummed through my limbs. I had to keep busy and occupy my mind and hands.

Nabbing my wide-brimmed hat, I headed out the back door into the brilliant afternoon sunlight. The garden beckoned - overgrown vines to untangle, weeds sprouting among the vegetable rows, leaves to pluck from the towering tomato plants.

I lost myself in the work, relishing the feel of rich soil between my fingers, the sweet scent of herbs crushed beneath my knees.

Out here, I could breathe. The simplicity and solitude restored a measure of peace to my rattled nerves.

But even as I labored, my awareness remained attuned to the man sleeping in my bed, just beyond the weathered walls of the cabin.

His essence lingered like wood smoke on a breeze.

I couldn't escape it, no matter how I tried to lose myself in the earth and toil of the plot.

Alessio had tilted my world on its axis, and I feared it would never right itself again.

The sun was starting to dip towards the horizon, painting the sky in shades of orange and pink, lengthening the shadows across the garden.

I sat back on my heels and surveyed my handiwork. It looked tidier, the plants standing tall and green, free from the choking embrace of weeds.

Satisfaction thrummed through me, the profound pleasure of hard work yielding tangible results.

I paused, wiping the sweat from my brow with the back of my hand.

I was aware I should return to the cabin, check on Alessio, and prepare dinner.

But a part of me hesitated, reluctant to face him again so soon after our earlier encounter. His words echoed in my mind.

The sincerity in his eyes and how he appeared to see straight through my soul's high walls terrified me.

He had a way of stirring up emotions I'd thought long buried, the way he made me want things I couldn't have.

With a sigh, I gathered my tools and headed back towards the cabin, steeling myself for whatever lay ahead.

I had to remember who I was and what I'd been through. I had to stay strong, no matter how much my heart might yearn for something more.

He was awake when I got inside.

This time, his shoulder was free of its brace, wrapped in a bandage.

He was seated on my couch, devastating and handsome, as he strummed the guitar once more.

Wordlessly, his eyes raked over me and my dirt-streaked face and overalls.

I tilted my head. 'Hey.'

He jerked his chin, eyes dark, distant.

I set down my basket of fresh-picked vegetables on the kitchen counter.

Keep it together, I reminded myself, taking a steadying breath. *Don't let him get under your fuckin' skin.*

I headed to the sink and washed my hands, gathering my ingredients for dinner.

Yet I kept stealing glances at him.

He sensed my sneaky peeks and glanced up, lips curled.

'You know, if you took a picture, it would last longer,' he growled.

Under the flaming golden gaze was an unnerving heat. He appeared to see right through me.

I rolled my eyes but couldn't quite suppress the twitch of my mouth. 'Don't flatter yourself, rockstar. Just checking you weren't about to keel over from all the hard work.'

He scoffed and set the guitar aside, standing up with a wince. 'Your concern is touching, cara. But I assure you, I'm made of tougher stuff than that.'

I huffed and sliced my eyes from him as he sauntered to the kitchen, peering over my shoulder at the ingredients I was assembling.

He jerked his chin in question.

I was beginning to understand his language, his silent, gruff style of communicating.

I shrugged. 'It's a Moroccan chicken pie.'

'From scratch dough?'

I hmmed in confirmation.

He curved his mouth and jerked his chin as if approving my choice.

I hunched my shoulders, self-conscious. 'It's something I picked up along the way. Helps me relax.'

Alessio assented, his eyes canting to the view. 'I get that. My brothers and I love cooking too to release the strain of life.'

My lips quirked at his words, and for an instant, we stood there, looking at each other. It was strange, but at that moment, I felt a connection with him that went beyond mere physical attraction.

But the mood passed, and I shifted. 'Well, don't get too used to it. You'll be on your way as soon as you're healed, and I can return to my bliss-filled solitary existence.'

Alessio was quiet for a beat, and his voice was soft when he spoke. 'Is that what you want, cara? To be alone forever?'

I stiffened, my hands clenching the dough under my fingers. 'It's what I need,' I whispered. 'It's the only way I know how to survive.'

I turned back, ignoring him, as his presence left me.

As the last rays of the sun dipped below the horizon, Alessio settled back onto the couch, picking up the guitar once more. His lean digits moved with deftness over the strings, coaxing a gentle tune that floated about me like a melodic caress.

He was improving, and the melody of his play was soothing as evening fell.

For a moment, I marveled at the strangeness of the situation. Here I was, a loner by nature and necessity, sharing my space with a near stranger—an irritatingly charming one, at that.

Despite my best efforts, I glanced at Alessio as he played. The way he danced over the cords and the concentration on his face as he lost himself in the tune were mesmerizing.

And infuriating.

Because as much as I wanted to hate him, to resent his intrusion into my solitude, I couldn't. Not in entirety.

Underneath his gruffness was a warmth that scared me more than anything.

I'd spent so long building partitions, protecting my heart from betrayal lurking around every corner. The thought of letting someone in, of making me vulnerable again, was terrifying.

But as the sweet strains of Alessio's guitar filled the cabin, the music washed over me, soothing the jagged edges of my soul.

My walls cracked a little. And for the first time in a sustained time, I wondered if maybe, just maybe, I didn't have to be alone forever.

I willed myself to forget about my past, about the pain and the anger that had been my constant companions for so long.

Setting the dough aside to rise, I began chopping vegetables for my one-all-in-one savory pastry.

The rhythmic thunk of the knife against the cutting board helped to settle my nerves. The repetitive motions were soothing, and soon, the dish was ready.

After placing the pie in the oven, I cleared up and glanced over my shoulder at Alessio. His eyes were closed, his face relaxed as he lost himself in the music.

Sensing my gaze, he opened those leonine stunners, his lips curving. 'Sit with me,' he rasped, patting the space beside him on the couch.

I can't let him in, I thought to myself.

He was dangerous. He'd destroy me and what was left of my living soul.

Besides, he appeared like a man who used and discarded women, and I was done with men who paid no heed to my heart.

No matter how sexy they were.

I hesitated, torn between the desire to keep my distance and the longing for human connection.

The latter won out, and I moved towards him, sinking onto the couch cushions.

Alessio continued to play, the melody shifting into something slower, more intimate. I relaxed, the tension draining away as I surrendered to the evocative sound.

This is dangerous, a voice in the back of my mind warned. *You can't let yourself get attached. You know how this ends.*

But as Alessio's shoulder brushed against mine, his warmth seeping into my skin, I couldn't care less.

I sighed, giving in to the present without the weight of my shitty past dragging me down.

And as the night deepened around us, the music weaving a spell of its own, my fantasies roamed wild.

Perhaps one day, I'd find happiness after all.

The savory aroma of the chicken and vegetable pie filled the cabin as I removed it from the oven.

Steam billowed from the golden-brown crust, and the fragrant blend of spices made my mouth water. I carried the dish to the table, where Alessio was already seated.

I cut into the pastry, serving a generous slice onto Alessio's plate.

A groan of appreciation escaped his lips as he took his first mouthful.

'Delizioso, cara,' he growled.

I shrugged, ignoring how my heart fluttered at his praise.

'It's a pie,' I said, taking a bite of my slice.

The flavors burst on my tongue, and the tender chicken and the complex blend of spices created a symphony of flavor.

He leaned forward, his eyes locked on mine. 'It's not any pie,' he said, his voice timbered and intimate. 'It's a work of art like you.'

My cheeks heated, and I glanced away, focusing on my plate. 'You don't know anything about me,' I said, my tone harsher than intended.

'What if I want to?' Alessio rasped.

Silence fell as I stared at him and he at me.

'What if I want to know about your hopes, dreams, fears, and joy? Whatever it takes to chase away the shadows in your eyes?'

You can't, I wanted to say. *You can't fix me, can't erase the scars that mar my soul.*

I found myself wanting to believe him.

'Then you're a fool, for I've nothing to offer you.'

An emotion I couldn't decipher flared in his eyes, and he pursed his lips. 'Bene, do you, Cleo.'

I forced a smile, but it was brittle and false on my face. 'I will,' I lied.

Alessio fixed his eyes on the horizon, and for that, I was grateful. I wasn't prepared to share my past with him and not primed to let him see the broken, damaged parts of my soul that I'd hidden away.

I wasn't ready to be teased and rejected, used and misused.

I loved me, and that was sufficient, recalling how Nonna had often told me, 'Baby, love yourself like you're not waiting for someone else to do it.'

So why did I ache with need?

Why the fuck had Alessio Calibrese torn through me and given me a deep yearning for that which was not mine?

I was not ready, not for him, not for love.

Maybe someday, I thought, as I began to clear the dishes from the table. Perhaps one day, I'd be strong enough to permit a man to adore me, to let them into my hidden corners.

Not today.

Not him, especially.

Because I sensed he was the one man who'd detonate my

world from within and eviscerate my heart and soul if I submitted to him.

Chapter 12

ALESSIO

I was a fixer, a brawler, a man used to force to get his way.
A freak of nature, a tempest of fists and words, a man who made proverbial mountains move and kingpins tremble with my sheer will alone.

A warrior in the game of life, wielding my strength like a weapon to carve out a path in the chaos.

But fuck I was tired.

Exhausted from deciding other's futures while my own hung in the balance.

Lorenzo's call a few months ago, letting me know that the Abrazzio problem had been resolved, brought me relief.

Staring then out of the windows of my penthouse into the skies over New York, I'd mulled the signs life was throwing me.

Our enemies had been cut off at the knee in utter and chilling finality.

Fuck, finally.

It paved the way for a new era for the Calibrese family and, perhaps, for me.

Soon after, the call came about Cleo and Franco's imminent release.

It hadn't taken much to persuade myself to relocate to Australia from New York.

After being obsessed with my role as the family's head capo for so long, my priorities and values became distorted, and I was burnt out from the constant hustle.

I'd departed the Big Apple without regret, escaping its dark mafia underbelly in the relentless pursuit of something better.

I was done with the grind, with the ambiguity of crime, corruption, and competition, which made it easy to forget what mattered.

What I wanted out of life now was a family, perhaps a woman of my own, even a baby.

That's what my soul yearned for; for some reason, my spirit, my inner oracle, told me I'd find it in the land down under.

I'd also be closer to Lorenzo, Mia, Vitto, and Mauri.

Valerio was still holding out in Napoli, but I was convinced he'd soon change his tune and move near us.

The fence line disappeared into the horizon, acres of rolling green pastures and grazing cattle stretching as far as I could see.

A light breeze ruffled the grass and cooled the back of my neck as I strode the perimeter of Cleo's farm.

Sunlight bathed the landscape in a golden glow.

I paused, hands on my hips, taking it in. No gunshots echoing in the distance. No smog and grime coating on every surface. Just open space, fresh breeze, and the tranquil sounds of nature.

I let out a long breath.

This.

I wanted this.

I craved what her world represented: an uncomplicated, uncluttered life in a place untouched by the darkness and death that had once defined me.

One where the sins of my past were washed away.

A life characterized by simple rhythms, pure food, sweet-scented air, and the gentle march of time.

A life shared with a woman, with her heart belonging to me, only me, one who'd remain in my arms forever.

My lips twisted, even as my hand bunched around a stalk of wildflowers and pulled the stems out of the ground.

Fotto.

Was my hardened mafia warrior spirit considering hanging up my guns and settling in a place like this?

There was always a first fuckin' time for everything, I huffed to myself.

I shook my head and continued patrolling the fence line, forcing my mind back to the mission: to protect Cleo from Franco Conti and give him his due justice by lying in wait for him and putting him in the ground once and for all.

Then, and only then, might I entertain foolish notions of a fresh start.

A flash of movement in my periphery made me tense as I returned to the farmhouse.

My free hand tightened on my gun as I spun around, ready for trouble.

But it was just Cleo, striding across the yard from the barn, a flashlight in hand.

I jolted, soul-lurching, as I followed her progress with a confident grace, her lean, lithe frame evident even from a distance.

The evening breeze tousled her dark hair, and the dying sun illuminated her striking features - high cheekbones, full lips, and eyes that missed nothing.

I exhaled, relaxing my stance but not my guard. Even in this peaceful place, I couldn't afford to let it down. Not with an enemy still lurking.

Cleo spotted me and altered course to intercept my path. As she drew near, she arched an eyebrow. 'Expecting company?'

She nodded towards my gun.

My fingers slipped from the weapon's hilt, and I shrugged. 'Old habits.'

I extended the hand I'd hidden behind me to her, thrusting the wildflowers in her face.

I tagged her instant joy and pushed my tongue into my cheek in triumph, watching as she took them and sunk her nose into them.

'You like?' I growled.

She tilted her head at me and rolled her eyes, but I detected the pleasure in her expression. 'Grazie.'

My gesture appeared to have unlocked something in her as her gaze tracked over me, astute and assessing. 'Walk with me. I want to show you something.'

I fell in beside her, trying not to lick my lips at how the faded denim of her jeans clung to her thighs. Or the graceful line of her neck disappearing beneath her worn flannel shirt collar. I tried and failed.

No doubt, she got me high, so high, on desire.

Dio mio, she was incredible.

A beautiful, cold-as-fuck badass.

And here I was, traipsing around her goddamn farm, having domestic and gentleman farmer fantasies.

I needed to get my head straight and remember my freakin' purpose.

But as we walked, our shoulders almost brushing, I couldn't shake the sensation that Cleo would be a distraction I was ill-equipped to resist.

She led me to a slight rise at the edge of her property. From the top, the view stretched for miles, nothing but wild, untamed bush as far as the eye cast out. It was breathtaking and humbling.

'This is what I wanted to show you,' she murmured.

Her eyes were on the horizon, and I followed her gaze with curiosity.

'Wait for it.'

I did, breathing slow and deep beside her.

Without warning, an unpredictable and astounding burst of color flared across the sky.

A celestial display of intense red and green collided into purple and blue lights that played over the firmament.

I raised a brow. 'What the fuck?'

'I caught it on the radio. A major geomagnetic storm is hitting the north and south poles. The result is this spectacular aurora over southern Australia and New Zealand,' she breathed.

I had to admit, the magenta, amethyst, and ruby skies were breathtaking.

'Feast or famine, or hope or fear, and in all things, land of chance, where nature pampers, or nature slays, in her ruthless,

red, romance.'

I lifted a brow at her exhortation and nailed her with a curious gaze.

'It's a line from a poem by Patterson that I've cherished for all my life.'

As she whispered, she turned to face me as the sky's unusual hues washed over us.

I was lost in all of her, at the soft smile on her lips, the fire of heaven reflected in her eyes.

At that moment, I understood how she loved this land, heart, mind, and soul.

Also, how much this slight, strong, savage woman was fast undoing me.

The realization hit me like a sucker punch.

The very thought made it challenging to breathe.

As if her spirit sensed my yearning, her hand reached for mine. Squeezing hard as the aurora above us flared with such magnificence that only reflected how stunning she was.

A stab of caution, doubt, and fear hit on the back of a wave of sorrow.

Memories of my parents and their love flooded my psyche.

Fotto. I hated thinking of how they'd been torn from us, my soul still ragged and worn with grief.

I'd witnessed so much death and destruction in my world.

Beauty never lasted, love never stayed the course, and if it did, it'd be blown apart by your enemies in a heartbeat.

What if I lost her too?

I was about to blow with emotion when she must have perceived something in my expression because her brow furrowed. 'Alessio? 'What is it?'

I shook my head, not trusting myself to speak.

131

I couldn't do this. I couldn't feel this way. Not now.

Maybe after I'd dealt with Franco's mess, I'd explore Cleo. Just not fucking now.

I stepped back, tearing my hand from hers, separating us. 'Enough of this shit,' I ground out.

Her eyes snapped to my face, confusion flitting on her face.

'We need to get back,' I said, hating how my voice sounded rough and strained. 'I'm done.'

Hurt flashed in Cleo's eyes, which she masked in a second, snatching back her hand. 'OK.'

I realized then that this was possibly the first time she'd touched anyone of her own volition in years.

Cazzo, what a dick move.

I tried to open my mouth to stay her, to say something, but she'd already turned on her heel and started back down the hill.

I let her go, chest tight, biting my lower lip in frustration.

As her figure grew smaller in the distance, I cursed.

Beating myself up for what was undoubtedly a major fuck up.

Chapter 13

Before going to bed, Cleo clipped that she needed to check my bandages.

She came to my side and, without a word, cleaned it and re-wrapped it.

'Who taught you triage?' I asked, wincing as I tested the mobility of my arm.

'Does it matter?' she replied with a terse edge, avoiding eye contact.

She was still shitty at me.

'Guess not,' I said, trying to catch her gaze. 'But you're good at it.'

'Nonna was a nurse, she trained me.'

Her voice was tight, hard.

I sighed, sensing her concern. 'Your Nonna is well. Don't worry.'

'Of course, I'm fuckin' worried about her. I also don't trust you.'

I winced, perceiving she was losing patience with me.

I'd need to come clean, and soon.

'Scusa, mia sola, if I'm being, how do they say it, too much. You're not obligated to count on me, even if I occupy your bed.'

'Damn right,' she muttered, gathering the soiled dressings and disposing of them in the waste bin.

I fell silent, eyes on her, back against the headboard, having run out of shit to say to ease the ratcheting tension.

She left the room, and I heard her change in her living area before she sidled back in, cute as fuck in her kangaroo-print pajamas.

Forget lace and silk lingerie; this number had my cock's attention, making it harder than diamond and steel.

She kept her face averted, her gaze and eyes away from me.

The punch of her disquiet hit, and I sucked my teeth.

The bed sagged as Cleo lowered herself onto the mattress, her back rigid and unmoving.

'Lights off?' I double-checked.

She nodded.

I turned the lamp down.

I shifted beside her, the thick duvet and sheets pooled around my naked waist and thin shorts, which I longed to shuck because, most times, I preferred to sleep nude.

The silence between us was impenetrable and heavy, broken only by the occasional pop and crackle of the banked fireplace in the living area.

I shifted to where her dark hair was splayed across the pillow, cheekbones casting shadows in the dim light.

Her stormy jade eyes stared unblinking at the rough-hewn

134

ceiling beams above.

'Cleo,' I rasped, addressing the stompin' massive elephant in the room. 'About earlier with the aurora outside. I didn't mean to -'

'Don't.' Her voice was flat, emotionless. 'Just don't.'

I ran my tongue over my teeth.

Cleo was not the warmest person, but this coldness was new.

It cut.

It was icy and impenetrable.

Like an invisible wall had sprung between us, leaving me stranded on the other side.

I wanted to reach for her, to break through that frozen exterior and find the real Cleo underneath.

But I didn't dare. Not when she was like this.

Not when one wrong move could shatter the fragile truce, if one remained at all.

So I lay motionless, my breathing faint, my body humming with tension. The frigid quiet stretched out unending.

In time, she shifted, rolling over so her back was to me. Her spine was a steel rod, muscles corded tight beneath her thin tank top.

I squeezed my eyes shut against the sting of rejection. Sleep would be a long time coming tonight.

If it came at all.

I cursed myself. My mind whirled with self-recrimination.

I'd spent hours chipping away at Cleo's defenses, coaxing her to lower her guard. And in one careless moment, I'd undone it all.

The memory of her face flashed behind my eyelids - the raw joy in her eyes as she touched my hand.

The softness in her voice had been so at odds with her usual steely control.

She'd trusted me with a piece of her heart. And I'd thrown it back in her face.

Stupid. So goddamned dumb.

I wanted to explain, to make her understand.

My words had come from a place of pain, not cruelty. Old scars that had never quite healed. But explanations meant nothing in the face of Cleo's hurt.

I glanced at her rigid back, the angry jut of her shoulder blades.

Every inch of her radiated 'stay away.' But underneath the sharp edge was a scared, scarred soul.

One which had been betrayed and abandoned too many times. She'd learned that vulnerability was a weakness to be stamped out early on.

I forced myself to be still. Giving her the space she needed, no matter how much it gutted me.

The minutes ticked by, each one an eternity. Inside me, guilt churned like a living thing, gnawing at my guts with merciless teeth.

Fuck, I felt like shit.

And hell, I wanted her so bad.

I frutti proibiti sono i più dolci.

Forbidden fruit was always the sweetest.

She'd been taboo to me for almost a decade, beyond a dream.

I had to fix this and find a way to earn back her trust.

As the night dragged on, exhaustion overcame self-recrimination. I drifted into a restless doze, my mind still whirling with thoughts of Cleo.

In my dreams, specters rose from the shadows. Twisted,

leering monsters with grasping hands and hungry eyes. They clawed at me, but they were too strong, too many.

I woke gasping for air.

That's when I realized, with a stab of shock, that Cleo was gone.

I knifed up, moving fast, slipping from bed in my socks and sweat bottoms, chest uncovered.

I burst into the living area.

Lit by dawn's weak rays, it was empty.

I caught the sound of an engine starting up and whipped myself around.

Nabbing my gun on the bureau beside the door, I ran to the front door and thundered into the early morning.

Just as Cleo's rugged ride sped out of the parking shed and raced past me.

She was alone in the driver's seat, her face hard and resolute in daybreak's light.

Her truck careened down the driveway, and I cursed, soft under my breath.

Lifting the barrel of my Sig, I fired.

Two shots to the rear wheels.

Exploding air and mini dust blooms erupted in the truck's wake.

It carried on for a few meters before its tires gave out.

It veered to one side of the roadway, then the other, rubber peeling and one tire coming clean off.

The vehicle came to a screeching halt, smoke rising from its engine.

I curled my lip and lowered my weapon, waiting.

She exploded from the car, clad in jeans, a zipped-up jacket, leather boots, and pure flaming rage.

Hair flying, eyes wild, arms pumping as she ran toward me.

She'd never appeared more fuckin' beguiling to me.

I braced as she came to a stop before me, chest heaving, hands clenched in fists at her side.

We locked eyes, caught in an intense standoff between us.

'What in the actual?' she whispered. 'You shot at me.'

I sucked my teeth. 'Let's be precise, mia sola. I blew out your wheels.'

'Bastard! What in devil's inferno were you thinking?'

'What the fuck were you?' I growled back. 'Of more importance, where the hell were you going?'

I reached my gun hand for her and wrapped it around her waist, pulling her flush to my front.

It gave me the advantage of height, intimidation, and commanding control.

Her hands fell on my chest, trying to pull away.

I scoffed, tightening my grip.

She'd no bloody chance of getting away.

Not now. Not ever.

'I won't ask again, carissima,' I rasped with menace, unleashing the full brutal extent of my ruthlessness.

Giving her flavors of my brutality.

She tossed her head back to stare up at me, fuckin' undaunted.

'To the Hendersons,' she hissed. 'To use their phone.'

'Who were you going to call? The cops?'

Her nostrils flared with rage. 'No, you paranoid freak. My Nonna. It's her birthday. I always call her on her flaming birthday.'

Her voice broke, and I jolted.

'I don't know if she's alive or dead, well or unwell,' Cleo went on, railing into me. 'I have no idea how she is. I need to know, especially today.'

Guilt, heated and lashed with condemnation, hit in a crushing wave.

I sucked her teeth and loosened my hold.

She whirled away as I turned from the pain flaring in her eyes, from the acid building inside her.

'How would you feel, Alessio Calibrese,' she snarled on, 'if you couldn't say happy birthday to the one blood relative you have left on this goddamn earth. The one person who means the world to you and the only soul who cares for you?'

Fotto, I was a monster, I thought as her words beat me up on the interior.

I sliced my eyes back to her, maintaining my mask of ice while howling at myself.

I should have been more clued-in, I raged in my mind.

I growled instead, 'You could have told me; I'd have driven you.'

'Fuck off, I don't believe you.'

She'd no reason to.

The immorality of my subterfuge hit, and I cursed.

She deserved the truth.

Not tomorrow, not next week.

Right fucking now.

139

I braced, aware her hatred of me was about to ratchet even higher.

'Cleo, there's something you have to know.'

She huffed, a little puff of irritation that cut deeper than her ire at me.

'What?'

Damn.

This tension was not knife-worthy; it'd necessitate a hatchet to get through it.

I sighed, inhaled in readiness for her inevitable attack, and growled. 'Your grandmother is not being held hostage. She's in care, with my men keeping an eye on her.'

She made a strangled noise in the back of her throat.

I threw my hand up. 'Not to harm her but to protect her if Franco attempts to reach her. I might have used the fact to try and compel you to keep me close. Which was a shitty thing to do.'

Cleo's head tilted as if scouring the heavens for patience.

Then she swiveled to face me, letting loose the full intensity of her disbelief. 'Repeat that?' she spat.

I did.

I also told her how three years ago, on discovering through Mauri that Guilia needed hospice support, I'd located the best aged care nursing home in the State.

Our Lady of Mercy was a well-regarded, clean, professional service.

I'd then arranged for a middle-aged couple, Joseph and Sofia, two respectable capos within the Omertà Alliance, to dine at Cleo's cafe in Moss Vale, where she'd held a job then.

Between coffee and generous tips, they'd initiated a conversation about the cost of aged care for their fictional dependents. Extolling the praises of said facility to her and its very affordable fees.

'You manipulated me?'

'No. I worked out you were living paycheck to paycheck and desperate for some bill relief. I made it hard for you to refuse the appeal of Our Lady of Mercy. In weeks, you had a bed for Nonna at a discounted price.'

'So when the administrators often returned my checks, citing overpayment, or sometimes waived the costs due to a generous donation from a wealthy sponsor, it was you?'

I shrugged. 'Si.'

What I didn't mention was that I'd bought the whole fuckin' facility, every brick, nail, and door.

She stared at me, astounded.

'You fucking piece of shit,' she snarled when I was done.

I twisted my lips and arched a brow. 'No thanks then?'

Her eyes blazed with fury as she unleashed a torrent of accusations. 'You know I'm not reaming you for the latter revelation, which I'll return to later. I'm freakin' outraged by you holding Nonna over me as a threat. Of making me think she was in danger.'

'Needs must,' I drawled.

'You selfish bastard! How dare you use my grandmother like that?'

I clenched my jaw, the muscles ticking beneath my skin.

Her words cut deep, each one a precise incision exposing the ugly truth.

'She is old and vulnerable, and still, you exploited that to keep me in line. What kind of monster does that?' Her voice rose, echoing in the early morning air.

I stood motionless, letting her verbal daggers pierce my

141

armor.

She paced, her hands gesturing as she laid bare my transgressions. 'Manipulating an aging woman, using her as a pawn in your twisted game. You're nothing but trash, Calibrese.'

She stalked closer, her eyes blazing with a fire threatening to consume me. 'I should have guessed you'd have no scruples taking advantage of the one person I adore most as a bargaining chip?'

The venom in her tone seeped into my veins, burning through my defenses.

I wanted to argue and justify my choices, but the words became ash on my tongue.

I raised a hand, a feeble attempt to stem the freakish tide of her fury.

But she was relentless, her voice rising to a crescendo as she laid bare the extent of my betrayal, her eyes glistening with unshed tears. 'You took advantage of my devotion, employing it as a weapon to keep me hostage. How low can you sink?'

Each accusation hit its mark, exposing the cracks in my façade. The truth was bitter, but I endured her righteous anger.

I chose silence, allowing her to vent the pain and treachery I had inflicted upon her.

The weight of my sins pressed down on me, a suffocating reminder of the depths I had plumbed in pursuing my goals.

She shook her head, a mirthless laugh escaping her lips. 'You're a boss manipulator, aren't you, Alessio Calibrese? Weaving your web of deceit, pulling the strings like a puppet master. Well, I won't be your marionette one second more.'

Her truth cut deep, exposing the ugly truth I had tried to

hide from myself.

The façade I had constructed crumbled under the force of her righteous anger, leaving me bare and exposed.

The words scorched like hot embers, but I forced them out regardless.

'I get it; I'm a piece of vile pig shit,' I drawled. 'Here's the deal, cara; you can continue spewing at me, or we can take my car to your neighbors as you want. So you can call and wish your Nonna a happy birthday. What's it going to be?'

Seconds ticked by, each one an eternity of its own.

The tautness between us was palpable, a living, breathing entity that threatened to suffocate us both.

I tagged the war behind her eyes, spiraling from anger at me to concern for her grandmother.

After an age, she spoke. 'Fine.'

The single word was clipped, choppy, and laced with a venom that made me flinch. But it was a concession, however grudging, even as guilt continued to gnaw at my insides.

I had a long way to go to make amends and earn back the trust I had shattered, but for now, I had to focus on the task at hand.

I jerked my chin towards her, a silent command, before stalking over to her still-smoking truck.

As I approached, the acrid stench of burnt rubber assaulted my nostrils, a stark reminder of the chaos that had unfolded mere moments ago.

With a grunt, I reached through the open window, grasping the steering wheel with one hand while the other found the clutch.

The muscles in my arm strained as I maneuvered the vehicle, my shoulder aching, and I hissed as the torture of it went through me.

I took it as my penance. Sweat beaded on my brow, a combination of the physical exertion and the simmering tension that hung in the air.

As I worked, I could feel her eyes boring into my back, watching my every move. I didn't need to turn around to know that her arms were crossed over her chest, a defensive posture that screamed her lingering anger and distrust.

With a final heave, I pushed the ute out of the way, clearing a path for my vehicle. I stepped back, wiping my hands on my jeans, and turned to face her.

She stood silhouetted against the stunning backdrop of the rising sun. The golden rays painted the distant ranges in breathtaking colors, but I took no notice.

My attention was focused on her, on the way the light caught the fiery glint in her eyes and her jaw clenched with suppressed fury.

Damn, even in wrath, she was a goddess.

The fog rose from the ground, tendrils of mist curling around my ankles as I marched past her.

Mocking me, the birds began their morning song, their melodic trills starkly contrasting our tense silence.

I entered the shed, the musty scent of old wood and rusting metal assaulting my nostrils, and slid into my SUV.

The engine roared to life.

I reversed the car out, the tires crunching over the gravel.

Turning in a tight circle, I pulled up beside her.

She stood, arms still crossed, her gaze fixed on some distant point, refusing to meet my eyes. I lowered the window, the cool morning air rushing in, carrying the smell of dew-soaked grass and the faint promise of redemption.

'Get in,' I said, my voice rough, the words scraping past the lump in my throat. 'Per favore.'

She hesitated, her jaw clenching, before she yanked open the passenger door and slid inside, slamming it shut with a force that made me wince.

I shifted into drive, and we rolled down the dirt road, the silence between us thick and oppressive.

My shoulder ached in a dull throb that pulsed in time with the migraine building behind my eyes.

Still, I drove on, jaw clenched, needing to get this shit over and done with.

The neighboring farm soon appeared, a picturesque scene of rolling hills and a red-roofed farmhouse nestled amid the lush greenery.

I pulled up to the front, the gravel crunching beneath the tires, and cut the engine.

Slicing my eyes to her, I found her gazing at me with pure disdain.

She unlocked the door, the sudden movement startling me from my self-flagellation. 'Stay here,' she said, her voice colder than the morning air. 'I won't be long.'

She marched towards the farmhouse, her shoulders squared, her head held high.

The door opened, and she disappeared inside, leaving me alone with my thoughts and the weight of my missteps.

I leaned back in my seat, pushed a rough hand through my hair, and closed my eyes as the sun climbed higher in the sky. The world around me came to life, oblivious to the battle within me.

Half an hour later, she emerged, her face an unreadable mask as she approached the car. The silence between us was deafening, a chasm growing with each passing second.

I started the engine, the roar of the SUV filling the void.

I risked a glance at her, hoping to catch a glimpse of some lightness in her spirit after her chat with her Nonna.

'How is she?' I ventured.

All I got was a baleful stare. Regret hit with a gut punch.

I'd shattered the little trust we'd had.

I fought the instinct to reach for her, sucking in air to keep calm.

Fuck. My. Life.

I spent the rest of the drive back to her cabin in a blur, the winding roads and lush greenery a mere backdrop to the turmoil.

When we arrived, the familiar ritual of securing the gate and locking my ride away was a welcome distraction from our taut agitation.

But as we approached the front door, I couldn't hold back.

I stopped her, my hand on her arm, my eyes pleading to understand.

'Cleo,' I growled, raw with emotion. 'I fucked up.

Her emerald eyes canted to me in a storm of conflicting emotions.

Anger, hurt, and betrayal all swirled in a vortex that threatened to consume us.

'Forgive me, carissima?' I murmured, reaching for her.

She yanked her arm away, her eyes flashing with a fury that ran my blood cold.

Her laugh was harsh, bitter. 'Who the hell do you think I am? Your get-out-of-jail-free card?'

Damn, her voice was sharp enough to slice through to the heart.

She stepped closer, her face inches from mine, the heat of her anger radiating off her in waves.

'Fuck off, Calibrese. And get the hella out of my cabin. I think I spotted tent swag in your fancy car. Use it!'

'Are you kicking me out?' I growled, incredulous.

She nodded. 'Believe it, soldier.'

I tossed the idea of arguing and pleading with her.

But that wasn't how I rolled.

I was no begging man.

Not now.

Not fuckin' ever.

So I did the only thing I could.

I twisted my lip, swiveled, and strode away.

Chapter 14

ALESSIO

Groveling fuckin' sucked.

My version involved physical servitude: trudging across Cleo's property with a spool of wire and a hammer hanging from my belt loop.

The sun beat down on my neck as I surveyed the crooked, splintered fence posts jutting from the soil.

I started at one corner, where the perimeter line disappeared into overgrown blackberry bushes. Cursing under my breath, I fought through the thorns, ripping my shirt sleeve.

There – a broken slat dangled limply, the rusted nails just about holding it in place. I yanked it free and tossed it aside.

Wiping the sweat from my brow, I selected a fresh board from the stack I'd hauled over in my SUV.

With precise whacks, I nailed it into position, the ringing of metal on metal echoing across the fields.

This shit was so far removed from the boardrooms and backstreet brawl clubs I'd become so used to.

It called on my military experience and brought back old memories.

It also purified the soul and helped to beat back my demons.

I took my time along the boundary, walking the fence lines and stopping every few feet to mend a weak spot.

I plugged knotholes with wood putty, twisted errant wires back into alignment, and replaced rotted posts knocked askew by fallen tree limbs.

I went as far as the Conti compound.

Studying the farmstead for a long time from beneath a stand of trees, as I'd done several mornings now, gathering intel and planning an infil while I paid penance for my sins.

Hours slipped by under the relentless Australian sun. My hands were nicked and raw, and dirt caked the sweat on my arms, but still, I continued, fueled by a grim resolve to do right by her.

The systematic work helped calm my restless thoughts.

I got back to the cabin by mid-afternoon.

Her door was still shut, and silence reigned.

I searched around for what more I could do and spotted the loose slates on her outhouse.

Clambering up the rickety ladder propped against the small building, I balanced precariously on the top rung, a stack of shingles tucked under one arm.

The old roof was a patchwork of rot and broken tiles, the exposed plywood beneath buckling from many rain seasons.

I pried off the damaged panels one by one, tossing them into the overgrown grass below with a satisfying thump. Sweat trickled down my back as I worked, the air heavy with the scent of pine sap and distant wood smoke.

With care, I aligned the new roofing, hammering each into place with precise strikes.

The shadows grew long, and the cicadas began their evening song when I hammered the last staple.

I stood back, surveying my work with weary satisfaction.

It wasn't enough to atone for what I'd done. But it was a start.

When I climbed down, the outhouse roof gleamed with tidy rows of fresh tiles, a small bastion of order amid the chaos.

I allowed myself a brief surge of pride before actuality crashed back in. Cleo was still fuming inside her cabin, nursing her grudge like a dog worrying about a bone.

Sighing, I stowed the leftover supplies and trudged towards my SUV.

Resigned to a different reality, pulling out the sizable swag bag from my car.

I found a secluded spot in her backyard.

Setting up the tent was a mechanical process. My body moved on autopilot while my mind replayed her last words to me over and over.

I rehearsed awkward attempts at an apology in my head. In my past, making amends was simple – I'd never offered any.
Fuck.

I mulled the matter, eating tinned minestrone, before falling back into the sleeping bag.

Closing my eyes, I let the day's events wash over me. It had been a roller coaster of emotions.

I couldn't help but feel a twinge of admiration for her stubborn resolve, even as I grappled with the sting of rejection.

Cleo was a force to be reckoned with, and winning her over

wouldn't be easy.

I considered knocking again, demanding that she hear me out. But something told me that pushing too hard would only make things worse. No, I would have to play the long game to earn Cleo's forgiveness.

Patience, I reminded myself. *Rome wasn't built in a day, and neither were second chances.*

I'd always taken pride in being in control and holding all the cards, but now I realized how fragile that illusion was.

The silence of the night was broken only by the distant howling of a solitary wild dog.

The irony wasn't lost on me. I was a lone dingo now, cast out from the warmth of her cabin, left to fend for solo in the wilderness of my own making.

'Cazzo,' I groaned.

I missed her, longing for her scent, skin, eyes, and laugh.

This was torture, to be lying a stone's throw from her, knowing I couldn't see her. So close, yet so far.

Sleep eluded me all night, my thoughts consumed by the weight of my mistakes.

When the sun rose, painting the sky in hues of orange and red, I felt none of its warmth.

Just an icy chill and hollow emptiness that threatened to swallow me whole.

Jumpy as a skittish savage cat, I sat up in my cot.

Fuck the long game.

I needed a resolution for us now.

I had one play.

With a twist of my lips, I decided to use it.

I marched to her door and banged on it.

I was about to hit it once more when the door was wrenched

open by a sleepy, angry woman.

'Alessio, for the love of -.'

I lifted a hand to pause her tirade before she went wild on me and wordlessly pushed an offering into her hand.

She unfurled her palm, revealing a jade bead bracelet.

The same one she'd lost on the night I'd rescued her in Naples.

She stared at me, at the weary, shitty lines on my face, and then down at the cluster of aquamarine beads in her hand.

I had no words left to say.

So I didn't.

Her eyes narrowed as she brought them closer, studying the beads.

Seconds later, her face transformed into a soft smile.

'No freakin way,' she whispered in that gentle way she had that threatened to send me to my knees in supplication. 'My grandparents gave me this to me on my sixteenth birthday. I thought I lost it.'

I shook my head, not trusting myself to speak. Still, I had to, and my vocalization was raw, hoarse. 'You dropped it when you ran. I kept it.'

I'd done more than keep the jade gems; I'd turned them into prayer beads, my aquamarine-stringed rosary.

They'd been my peace, my ritual in meditation, especially after my father's death.

I panicked if I ever misplaced them, even for one moment.

I'd never traveled, moved, or spent an hour away from them.

Many times, I'd thought about returning them to her.

I hadn't, needing to remain connected to her somehow.

She stared back at me, eyes wide in disbelief. 'You've held onto them all this time?'

I nodded, twisting my lips.

She took in my words, shaking her head in incredulity. 'What am I freakin' going to do with you?'

Her voice was edged with exasperation, and I sighed, almost stepping away until I caught the tenderness in her eye.

It shored me and gave strength to my weakened limbs.

'Is this your apology?'

I shrugged. 'It's what you want it to be.'

We locked eyes for a long moment before I bit my lip and made to leave.

She reached a hand to stay me. 'Wait.'

I turned back to her, hope rising.

'One thing, Alessio, you said you subsidized my grandmother's hospice care?'

I had to tell her the whole truth. 'I bought the fuckin' facility.'

'For her?'

I inhaled with sharp emotion. 'For you.'

She stared at me for an extended beat. 'Just double checking what you told me last night. You were the sponsor who reduced my fees and gifted me months of free accommodation for Nonna?'

I sucked my teeth and looked away, letting my silence be my answer.

'Why?'

'Because I wanted to.'

Now, she was apprised of how much of a hold she had on me.

Leaving me weak, exposed, vulnerable as fuck.

Still, I met her eyes.

I'd aggravated her and was now motivated to get us past it.

She tilted her head and searched my face for a long time. 'Calibrese, I see your heart,' she finally whispered. 'It's not as black as you'd have me believe.'

I sliced my eyes at her, letting my need for her bleed through.

To her credit, she didn't push me further. Instead, she took my hand and pressed an object into it.

I glanced down to see her jade bracelet in my palm.

'Take it, it's yours. If it has brought you peace all these years, hold onto it, Alessio. I won't take it from you.'

She could, but only if she surrendered her heart in its place.

Turning on her heel, she eased inside her cabin.

I lingered at its threshold, uncertain of whether I was welcome.

She swiveled her head and nailed me with those stunning emerald eyes. 'You coming soldier?'

I gave her a slight turn of my lips and followed, not unlike a battle-weary warrior returning from the cold.

'Hungry?' she murmured in her soft, sweet cadence.

I growled, as did my tummy. 'Si.'

'Minestrone?'

I cursed, wondering how she knew. She must have smelt it wafting from the tent out back.

'Too early in the fuckin' morning,' I grated, following her lush ass into her home.

'It's never too early for anything, Calibrese.'

I tagged the tease in her voice and clenched my fists. Fighting a craving to pull her into my chest, thrust a hand down her panties, and flick her clit until she came so hard she blacked out.

Fotto.

Chapter 15

CLEO

The strain of our night apart lifted as we spent the day slowly mending the unseen, broken fences between us.

I made us breakfast: scrambled eggs on toast.

Alessio brewed me coffee and finished the foam with a phallic shape, which I chuckled at for many long minutes.

His eyes remained shadowed, but his lips curled at my amusement as the coldness in my heart thawed.

'Scusa, mia sola, forgive me for being a dick to you.'

This morning, the man's golden hair hung in unruly waves around his face, giving him a wild and untamed appearance.

His sharp and intense leonine eyes gazed into mine, and I fought the urge to plunge both hands into his gilded tresses and kiss him.

Instead, I gave him a slight smile. 'Water under the bridge,'

I murmured. 'We're good now.'

I might have prolonged my sulking so he'd grovel harder, but the fact he'd revealed how he'd gone over and above to secure Nonna's care over the years had melted my last reserve.

His freakishly delicious coffee helped.

After breakfast, I nailed him with a keen look. 'So what now?'

He canted a brow, well aware of what was asking.

His leverage over me had evaporated.

He was healing well and had no reason to hang around.

'If it's OK with you, I'd like to stay a few days more until Franco is back and we have a handle on him. Does that work for you, carissima?'

His deep, timbered ask was hard to refuse.

As was the soft heat radiating from his eyes.

I nodded, conscious we'd turned a corner.

Fuck, I'd swept past it and fallen over the cliff.

He jerked his chin at me, and it was decided.

He was staying.

The relief that went through me was palpable, and I rose from the table in a rush.

The scorching heat of his gaze followed me, giving me shivers.

He dedicated a good part of the morning to fixing my piece-of-shit 4X4. He replaced the two wheels he'd shot at with two from my spares in one of my vast container sheds.

I spent most of that time drooling from afar as he worked in the sunlight, tee off, muscles rippling with primal strength.

'Woman, you're a hoarder,' he groused, rolling one of the tires from my storage space when I strolled toward him, holding out a mug of fresh coffee I'd brewed. 'Albeit a neat one.'

'You never know when the apocalypse will come,' I chuckled.

We locked eyes, and that sharp lurch I got when I glanced at him hit again.

I was warming to Alessio Calibrese very fast.

Ever since he'd shared about Nonna and then about the bracelet, I hadn't been able to keep my thoughts from him.

On my birthday call to her, Nonna had confirmed over the phone that she was safe and having a whale of a time with her new capo minders.

'They're young, tight, and sexy,' she'd whispered with a wicked chuckle. 'All the other women in the facility are jealous as fuck.'

I'd laughed so hard that Mrs. Henderson had come to check on me, offering a glass of water as I chuckled with my grandmother at her naughty, freaky mind.

I'd had to mask my amusement from Alessio when I'd emerged from the Henderson's farmhouse while hiding my intrigue and curiosity at his mindfulness to me over the years.

What he'd shared and laid down was a confession of sorts that he had some form of feelings for me.

I was unsure how to respond at first because *what-the-actual-fuck?*

All along, I'd thought the man was out to get me, that he was heartless and ruthless, without an iota of care for me.

I was so wrong.

While he'd never come close nor engaged me, he'd waved his proverbial mafia wand over me for years.

The concept was complex to wrap my head around.

More and more, I saw evidence of his care.

In the way his eyes leaked heat, smoldering each time they aimed at me, how his lips curved and softened when he now gazed at me.

He'd let his mask fall, letting me see his need for me.

It scared the hell out of me.

Not because he was petrifying. Well, he was.

But because of how much it moved me as well.

For some strange reason, it didn't feel creepy; it was righteous.

Perhaps it's because he'd been consistent for over ten years, giving me space yet looking out for me and mine.

Part of me was so unsure what to do with the revelation.

Another freakin' welcomed it like water finding its way over a desert that had been dry for decades.

I soaked it, cherished it in my heart, and pondered it.

Then I shelved it, my mind exhausted from thinking so hard.

I focused on keeping calm and creating a rich, chunky Spezzatino di Manzo, an Italian casserole Nonna had often made.

It was packed with chuck beef and braised until tender in a hearty stew of carrots, celery, mushrooms, and red wine.

I added rosemary and bay leaves for additional flavor and planned to serve it with chunks of crusty bread.

When he wandered back to the cabin searching for things to do, I put Alessio on baking duty.

It meant we stood close together in my kitchen's tight space.

I began to sense his flirtation ratchet up, heating me as he made slow, deep, timbered statements that left me weak in the knees.

At one point, as he kneaded the dough, thick arms bulging, his tee sticking on him in all the right places, he declared, nailing me with those leonine eyes.

'Bella to me you're buono come il pane. It means you're full of goodness like bread, with a heart of gold.'

Who knew I had a thing for men covered in flour rasping husky, sweet nothings?

I flicked a towel at him even as my soul lurched at his utterance.

Then, my logical mind kicked in.

All he was doing was tossing out words.

He was probably so used to mesmerizing women that this was one of his ploys.

'You think you're charming, don't you?' I said, crossing my arms over my chest. 'With your brooding personality and your sexy Italian prose.'

Alessio's scoffed, a gleam in his eye. 'I don't think, cara. I know.'

'Please,' I countered with a snort.

He threw the dough over, folded it, and pounded it. His posture relaxed like he'd been baking for years. 'You like it, no matter how much you resist.'

I rolled my eyes. 'Please. I've met plenty of men like you before. All talk and no substance.'

'Ah, but you've never come across a man quite like me,' he countered, his voice low and seductive. 'I'm one of a kind, bella. And I intend to prove it to you.'

God, he was insufferable, I thought, even as a shiver ran down my spine.

Why did he have to be so damn fuckin' sensual?

Why did his muscles bulge as he kneaded, and why was his body too tight and lean?

I almost moaned.

I turned away from him, busying myself with stirring the stew in the pan.

'You're all talk,' I said, my back to him. 'I bet you say that to all the girls.'

Without warning, his presence ghosted behind me, his breath warm on my neck. 'Not all the women,' he murmured, his rasp sending shivers through me. 'Only the special ones. Those who make me feel alive.'

I whirled around, finding myself face to face with him, our bodies only inches apart. 'I'm not special,' I said, just above a whisper. 'I'm just a girl with a messed up past and a lot of baggage.'

'You're also a woman who desires love, who craves me.'

Again, this man's balls had to be gilded, given how much golden bullshit he was spewing.

'Alessio, my mind knows the difference between wanting what I can't have and craving what I shouldn't. And I shouldn't want you. I don't deserve passion or you.'

Alessio reached out, tucking a strand of hair behind my ear. Flour from his sinewed hand sprinkled all over my nose.

I didn't fuckin' care.

He slid a powder-dusted hand to my nape and pulled me close, and my body pressed to his freakishly raw powered length.

'You're wrong, mia sola,' he rasped, his eyes holding mine. 'You're one badass woman who's fucking adorable at the same time. You're worthy of the world laid at your feet. And I'm going to make you see that, in the short time we might have together, perhaps even forever.'

Damn, he was fast-forwarding this show, and I was not ready for it.

Still, the words he used wormed their way into my keening soul.

Forever, I thought, my heart skipping a beat. A dangerous word.

Gazing into Alessio's eyes, I couldn't help but wonder if an endless love was my portion after all.

He remained tight to me, leaning his lean hips on the counter, eyes on me.

His tongue eased from between those luscious lips, and his eyes laser-focused on my mouth.

My nipples pebbled, and my pussy pulsed, wetness seeping into my panties.

'Alessio –,' I breathed.

'Che cosa?'

'We need to get that bread into the oven.'

His eyes smoldered. 'I know what I'd like to get into.'

I hissed at his brazenness as the hand around my waist slipped away.

'What more can I do ?' he asked when he'd slid the loaf into the stove to bake.

I swallowed hard, my heart pounding in my chest. 'I've got it under control,' I managed to say, my voice sounding strained even to my ears.

But Alessio was not one to be deterred. He reached for the wooden ladle in my hand, his fingers brushing against mine as he did so.

I jerked my hand back as if I'd been burned, my cheeks flushing with heat.

'Relax, cara, I don't bite.'

I raised my hand and pointed to the couch. 'I do, so get the hell out of my kitchen unless you want to know how hard I bite down.'

'Ah, mia sola, do you also swallow?'

I gasped, raising the utensil as if to whack him.

He tipped his head back and roared, strolling off, shoulders shaking.

He had an incredible laugh, rasped, hoarse, low.

A rumble came from his chest and through his neck as he threw that leonine head off his back, revealing his corded nape.

Fuck me.

I told him as much.

'Fuck you in particular,' I called, fighting the red color flying up my cheeks.

'Name the date and place, and I'll be there.'

I rolled my eyes, sliced them away from him, and returned my focus to the countertop.

He smirked and prowled back to the living area, picking a book from the shelf, which he settled down with.

Still, a small smile played on my lips as I continued to stir the pot.

Damn, the transformation in how we were relating to each other was blowing my mind.

That he cared so much under that gruff, brooding mask helped lower my barriers. For so long, I'd been used, manipulated, and discarded, which had destroyed most of my confidence, leaving it torn and ragged for years.

That he desired me heightened my self-esteem to stratospheric levels.

It also had my clit pulsing every single freakin' moment I was near him.

It'd been years since I'd slept with anyone.

Not that I hadn't wanted to; I'd just suppressed my needs, given my solitary life.

Until Alessio.

I sensed he'd be a fantastic lover.

It was in how he moved, with predatory power, powered by his thick thighs, six-pack chest, and corded neck.

I found myself obsessing over those erotic lips, his sinewed hands, and his lithe body.

He made me want to experiment, to explore, to go buck wild, unfettered by all the cares in my freakin' world.

He kept giving me glimpses of a sensual, seductive man with an unrestrained generosity I'd never be able to repay, enticing me to kiss him, stroke him, ride him.

Oh, Dio!

Seeking sanity, I focused on dinner.

The food was triumphant, and when I served it, Alessio cherished it, making appreciative moans while he ate.

I smiled, warmed by his appreciation, trying my damnedest to ignore the spikes of desire it sent through me.

I squeezed my thighs and hoped to goodness my hardened nipples weren't pebbling through my shirt.

At one point, I caught him flick his eyes to my chest, but his face remained inscrutable.

A small smile played on it as we shared a light-hearted conversation at dinner.

I asked him about his childhood, and he indulged me.

Relaxing with a glass of Pinot Noir, he launched into anecdotes about his early life in Italy. 'Growing up with three brothers was never boring,' he rasped with a chuckle. 'We were always getting into trouble, playing pranks on each other, driving our poor mother to the brink of insanity.'

Despite myself, the corners of my mouth twitched, a smile threatening to break through my stoic facade.

Alessio's eyes sparkled as he recounted a particularly memorable incident involving a goat, a paint bucket, and his eldest brother's prized motorcycle.

'Lorenzo's Ducati was covered in white pigment for months until my father agreed to restore it to its chrome beauty. All because a pair of fucking goats couldn't help themselves head-butting each other in the garden.'

'I love goats!' I exclaimed. 'They're so endearing and always look like they are smiling. They're so unbearably adorable. In my opinion, second only to kittens on the cuteness scale.'

'They're also little shits. Fuckin' butt heads. Can't tell you how many of them took me down for no reason.'

As he spoke, I was drawn into his world, one so different from mine.

It was filled with laughter, love, and carefree joy I had never experienced.

For an instant, I imagined what it would have been like to grow up in a family like Alessio's.

To have siblings to play with and parents who loved and protected me.

But the moment was fleeting, and reality came crashing back down around me.

My childhood had been nothing like his.

There'd been no joy nor affection, only fear, pain, and the constant struggle to survive. I'd been robbed of the innocence that Alessio had enjoyed, and the realization left a bitter aftertaste in my mouth.

I pushed my plate away, suddenly not hungry.

He fell silent, his brow furrowing in concern as his eyes raked over me.

'Cleo?' he growled. 'Che cosa?'

'I'm fine,' I said, forcing a bright note into my voice.

He didn't believe me, and his eyes searched my face for the next few moments as we cleared the table.

At one point, I had to slick away the tears in my eyes, and he tagged it.

With a suck of his teeth, he prowled to the bookshelf.

His fingers danced over the spines of the books until he found what he was looking for.

'Cleo, here.'

It was an order from a man unused to being disobeyed.

I went to him, eyes wide, as he patted the space on the couch beside him.

'Sit.'

Heart raw, I did as ordered while he opened the tome in his hand.

'You read books like these?' I asked, shock tinging my voice.

'I'm European and Italian. We were born with them in our hands.'

'That's my grandfather's,' I said, recognizing the title— Dante Alighieri's The Divine Comedy. 'He highlighted his favorite excerpts and read them to me at night.'

'So I shall do the same,' Alessio drawled.

I raised a brow.

'Hey?' he growled, meeting my bemused gaze. 'Can't reconcile a rough as fuck rogue like me with classic literature?'

I shrugged with a slight smile.

'The thing is, cara,' he rumbled, 'the modern mafioso doesn't fight with only fists these days. He needs his wits

165

and intelligence to stay alive and navigate a high-tech and fast-moving world. Books are like a whetstone, sharpening and keeping the intellect on guard. Now can I begin?'

I gave him a slight nod.

'We climbed, he first and I behind, until though a small round opening ahead of us, I saw the lovely things the heavens hold, and we came out to see once more the stars.'

I curled my feet under me and leaned closer, enamored by the deep timbre of his accented intonation.

At first, his gesture threw me.

I couldn't quite believe this burly, gruff, beautiful man was reading to me in the most poetic way possible.

His voice lulled me, comforted me, healed me.

Each word, like oil, was a balm to my troubled soul.

At one point, I found my head on his muscled shoulder, my hand creeping around his waist as he read on.

Eyes fluttering shut, I rested my weary spirit against the rock of Alessio's bulk.

On fuckin' hope itself.

Chapter 16

ALESSIO

I carried her to bed, tucking her in, lingering as she settled into sleep.

Fotto! She was a freakin' beauty.

I was utterly obsessed.

I crouched by her side for a long time, lost in thought.

She was incredible and beautiful, and with each day spent in her presence, she was fast becoming the kind of woman I'd never realized I wanted but now knew I couldn't breathe without.

I thought of the Italian phrase, 'colpo di fulmine' - a 'strike of lightning.'

Cleo was my lightning bolt.

Her fire and fierce attitude were a red flag to my bullish soul.

I was drawn to her savage courage, wanting to scale her walls, to fuckin' tear them down.

The thought that someone else breaking through and get-ting to her was enough to set off a tic in my jaw.

To even have her consider me, I'd need to jump the fucking hurdles of her distrust even as I flamed out the hell in her world.

My eyes stayed on her until my knees protested.

Only then did I rise and conduct a quick perimeter check outside.

I returned to the cabin and secured it.

It was close to midnight when I eased in next to her, vowing never to go another night without her in my arms.

I fell into dense slumber till a disturbance ripped through the night, yanking me back to consciousness.

I jolted upright, skin slick with sweat. Beside me, Cleo slept on, undisturbed.

I strained my ears, trying to pinpoint the noise source that had woken me.

A faint metallic clang sounded outside, like something striking against the fence. Every muscle in me went taut.

I checked the clock on the bedside table.

3 a.m.

I eased out of bed with care, wincing as my injured shoulder twinged in protest. I grabbed my boots and slipped them on, not bothering with the laces.

Then I reached for the gun I kept in the nightstand drawer. The weight of it was reassuring in my palm.

I glanced at Cleo, still lost to slumber, but chose not to wake her. Not until I was across what we were dealing with.

Silent as a ghost, I crept from the cabin and out into the night.

The air was crisp and cold, and the sky was a vast expanse

of stars. I scanned the darkness, my every sense on high alert.

There - movement at the edge of the property.

A shadow where none should have been.

Gritting my teeth against the pain in my shoulder, I palmed my gun and strode ahead. Whatever or whoever was lurking, they'd picked the wrong farm to mess with tonight.

Adrenaline surging through my veins, I advanced on the shadowy figure.

The rational part of my brain told me to stay back and assess the situation. But the primal, protective instinct that Cleo awakened in me propelled me forward.

As I drew closer, details emerged from the darkness.

It was a man hunched over something at the base of the fence—the dull gleam of metal in his hands.

Rage ignited in my gut.

I was only a few feet away now. The man was so intent on his subterfuge that he hadn't discerned my approach.

I tagged the curve of his spine, the vulnerable nape of his neck. It would be so easy to end him here and now.

But first, I needed answers.

Stuffing my gun in my sweats, I closed the distance between us with a burst of speed and lunged, wrapping my good arm around his throat.

The man gave a startled yelp as I dragged him away from the barrier.

'Who are you?' I snarled, tightening my grip.

He thrashed against my hold, but I only squeezed harder, cutting off his air. 'I suggest you start talking, fucker. Before I crush your windpipe.'

The man made a choked, gurgling sound, scrabbling at my hands with blunt nails. I eased up just enough for him to suck in a ragged breath.

'Fabio.'

I curled my lip at the name. 'Conti scum. What are you after?'

'Fuck off,' he wheezed.

I glanced at the fence and spotted for the first time a device wired to the generator housing that powered the surveillance network.

A crude bomb, my eye assessed.

Cold fury washed through me.

'You were going to blow it up,' I growled. 'Disable the security system. Why?'

'I had no choice!' His voice was high and thin with panic. 'He made me do it!'

'Who did?'

'My father. He sent the order from jail. We have to get the electric fence and network down so my brothers and I can retrieve his woman.'

I jolted. 'What the fuck?'

Turning the man, I twisted his hands behind his back so I'd see his face in the weak moonlight.

I found him smirking at me, hatred shining in his eyes.

'Don't you know? Cleo is my father's intended and soon-to-be wife.'

I lurched.

I wanted to roar, put my fist through something, and feel flesh and bone splinter beneath my knuckles. But I reined in the impulse, knowing I couldn't afford to be ruled by anger.

But first, I had an intruder to break.

The man whimpered as I wrenched his arm higher behind his back, sending fresh shockwaves of agony through my injured shoulder. I gritted my teeth against the pain. I'd endure far worse to keep Cleo safe.

'What the hell are you talking about? All he did was kidnap her over ten years ago. She was not then and has never been his fiancée.'

His lips curled. 'Oh, but she is. Did she deny it?'

Another jolt went through me. 'Context?' I demanded.

'If I tell you, will you leave me alone?'

'I might.'

'Are you a man of your word?'

'No. Still, you need to speak lest you lose your tongue. I mean, in a literal sense. I'll fuckin' chop it off.'

Fabio swallowed hard. 'He wants her back. Cleo. She's his property. He says she's his to marry.'

The words spilling from the man's mouth sent chills racing down my spine.

'Cleo was born into our Conti clan,' he mumbled. 'Her mother is a distant cousin. Everyone always said she was destined for amazing things. My father, Franco, also our leader, took a shine to her early on and started grooming her to be his perfect little wife from ten.'

Nausea hit, making me want to throw up.

The thought of a grown man preying on a child was enough to make my blood rage and boil. But I could ill afford to lose my damn head, not now.

'So what happened?' I demanded.

Fabio cursed. 'They were engaged within the cult. Father planned to have a fuckin' wedding ceremony, but she reported him to the cops, and Dad was arrested. He went to court, and they jailed him for minor endangerment. It was short-lived, and he returned when she was eighteen. Next, she ran off in the middle of the night and to Italy. Father was furious. He went after her after finding out she'd tried to return to Naples to her grandfather's people, who were meant to shelter her. He tracked her down, but somehow, she escaped him, and he went to jail. This time for a longer sentence, he served first in the old country, then Australia.'

I could only imagine the kind of fearlessness it had taken for Cleo when, little more than a kid, she'd dug deep to save herself despite being hunted down.

More so, she'd found the courage to break free of her captor twice.

The irony of my obsession with her didn't escape me, and I sucked my teeth, hoping I was nothing like the monster she'd escaped.

'She belongs to no one,' I snarled, seeing crimson.

My grip tightened on Fabio's arm, drawing a moan of pain from him. 'Cleo is her person, not some object to be owned.'

Revulsion churned through me as Franco's weak-assed son spilled out the details of his father's scheme.

'Cazzo! He hopes to claim his bride once and for all. His queen to rule at his side. He's been planning it for years, preparing everything for when he gets out of jail in a few months.'

I'd last seen Franco in Napoli years ago. Then and now, the idea of that sick fuck laying a single finger on Cleo made me want to tear him apart with my bare hands.

I tightened my grip on Fabio's shirt, hauling him in close. 'You listen to me,' I growled. 'Cleo will never be his, you understand? I don't care what kind of twisted plans Conti has. I'll shed blood before I let him lay a hand on her.'

Fabio's eyes were limpid and frightened in the moonlight.

'You don't know what he's capable of,' he stammered. 'The things he'll do to get what he wants.'

'I don't give a fuck,' I snarled. 'He's never getting close to her again. And if you've got any sense in that thick skull, you'll pray I never spot your fuckin' face near her residence ever again.'

I had to get back to Cleo, but first, I needed to send Fabio home with a stern message.

I dragged the man to the storehouse on the edge of Cleo's front yard.

I located a rope hanging on the external wall.

Shoving the younger man to the ground, I ignored his yelp of pain as I pulled a length of cord down. In seconds, I had his hands and feet trussed up tight, the knots digging into his skin. He squirmed against the dirt but found zero give in his bonds.

'You can't do this to me,' he whined, his utterance high and thin.

I crouched down beside him, my voice deadly calm. 'I can, and I am. This was a foregone conclusion the second you decided to attack Cleo. You didn't count on me being here.'

'You don't know what you're dealing with,' he spat, trembling. 'My father, the family, they'll never let her go. She belongs to us.'

Rage surged through my veins, white-hot and all-consuming.

I lunged forward and threw a lightning-fast fist into his face.

He screamed, but it was a dry, high-pitched wail, which I muted by wadding a cleaning cloth from a nearby bucket into his mouth.

He tried to fight back but was no match for my infuriated strength.

I laid into him, and he slumped, in shock from the beat down I meted.

When convinced he was suitably chastened, I nabbed a flashlight from the barn and pushed him outside.

I made the man stumble before me and herded him across the valley toward his family's homestead.

While he staggered on, groaning, my mind raced with the implications of what he'd revealed.

The thought of what Cleo had endured elicited a stomach churn.

I reached the base of the hill, where the Conti farm lay sprawled ahead.

With grim satisfaction, I stripped Fabio naked and bound him to a fence post on the Conti side, leaving him exposed for all to witness.

'Tell your fuckin' brothers and your jackass father that if they ever attempt what you tried tonight or worse, this hound of Hades will rip apart all your throats if your try to hurt Cleo. Let them know that I will stop at nothing to protect her.'

I left him mewling against the makeshift stake and strode back towards the cabin, my heart aching for my woman.

She had been through so much and had endured horrors I could scarcely imagine.

The nightmare in my head powered my energy, and in no time, I was taking the steps into the dim-lit interior, the floorboards creaking beneath my boots.

Chapter 17

CLEO

I woke to find the other side of my bed empty.

Instant panic and a flood of fear filled me and shook me so hard that I trembled for minutes.

Where had he gone?

I rose with shaking limbs, going to the living room.

It lay empty.

More dread ensued.

I peered through the windows to the outhouse.

There was no light visible.

Searching the room, I found his boots missing, as was his gun, which I'd placed on the sideboard for him the night he'd arrived.

It's like he'd vanished.

I had a sudden thought and rushed in my socks to the parking shed.

With relief, I tagged his ride, which was still parked by my 4X4.

Wherever he'd disappeared to, it must have been close by.

The two sides of me battled with opposing facts.

That he was a man who radiated menace and ruthlessness beyond my understanding.

Yet also the one person I'd come to depend on for my peace of mind.

After years of isolation and not letting anyone in, his dark, broody sensuality had slipped under my skin, pushed away my barriers, and turned into my safe anchor.

I shivered, hoping he'd not gone far and would return. Soon.

The alternative was nothing I wanted to consider.

Minutes passed.

I restarted the fire and thought about putting on coffee when the scrape of boots sounded on the front steps, followed by the silent easing in my door.

I spun as he pushed in, mane wild, eyes hard, gun in hand.

'What in the hell?' I whispered to myself.

We locked eyes across the room, and then, on impulse, I moved to him, and he to me.

His arms encircled me in seconds, holding me tight and close, murmuring Italian words into my hair.

His hands slid up and down my back and gave in to the stroke, welcoming the heat, warmth, and relief he offered.

In time, I stepped away, eyes flicking to his shirt, my hand reaching for him.

'You're bleeding.'

'It's not mine,' he growled.

That's when I tagged the fire in his eyes.

This was a whole new, different Alessio.

He was a vengeful god, a fearsome force of divine execution, the fuckin' punisher and lethal enforcer.

I did not doubt that whatever he'd witnessed outside, he was willing and ready to mete out swift justice and relentless vengeance without mercy.

'What the hell happened?' I searched his face, my gaze wary. 'Where were you?' I asked, voice hoarse with worry.

I caught his hesitation.

Finally, he took my hand and drew me to the couch, where the fire crackled. He jerked his chin at the sofa and urged me to sit.

He pulled the armchair close so he'd be eye-to-eye with me.

'I heard a noise and went outside to check on it,' he began, his deep timbre rolling over me.

'I found a man on your property, trying to cut through the fence,' he went on, eyes narrowed on me with close intent. 'I nabbed him before he could do any damage. Did a little questioning, then dragged him down the valley and left him trussed naked on your neighbor's land.'

My breath hitched, fingers tightening around the pillow I was clutching. 'Let me guess. One of the Conti brothers?'

'Si. Fabio.'

'Fucker,' I breathed.

'You're not surprised?'

I shook my head, plucking at the surface of the seat. 'It's not the first attempt. What was it this time? A fire, cutting down my trees, or a fence pulled down?'

His eyes flashed with anger, not at me, thank fuck.

'A rudimentary bomb, but enough to down your security system and fences. He was about to rig it up when I swung by.

Before he had a chance at –.'

'At kidnapping me.'

My voice was forlorn and weary.

Damn, I was so tired of this shit.

I closed my eyes to the pain of it all, only to fling them open at the warmth of a hand tracing my jaw, tilting my head up.

'He said his father ordered him to, so you'd become his queen when he exited prison. Is this true, Cleo?'

I swallowed as my throat dried.

That's when I took note of his tone.

Not hard-edged nor judgmental.

It was soft, kind, and burred, and I cherished its consideration despite the menacing light in his eyes.

Not aimed at me but at the man who'd tormented me.

Unable to handle Alessio's righteous wrath, I canted my face from his.

He waited, the heat from his brawling muscle enveloping me, his jaw clenching and unclenching.

In time, my fight-or-flight response calmed, and I found the courage to speak, keeping my voice to a murmur.

'I was brought up in a cult called the Outback Order, a bizarre quasi-religious sect active across Goulburn and Sydney. Franco was the local mayor once but was also its founder. A shitty, manipulative, opportunistic, cynical self-professed leader who groomed young girls in their early teens to become his wives and queens in his twisted harem. He'd pick one each year from the clan members' children and send them letters, court them, before marrying them. In a secret wedding on his farm and making her his concubine queen.'

'Fuck. A harem?'

'In essence. When I was twelve, I was selected to be one

of them. I was told what I was supposed to do, what I was expected to be, the 'shoulds and the should nots'. Life's little instructions were scaffolded around me until all that advice and good intentions became oppressive, like a cage. I was thirteen when Franco chose me to be his queen.'

The pain and anger in my depths spilled out. 'He wanted to own me, body and soul. To control every aspect of my life. And he would have if I hadn't escaped.'

'When?'

'At fifteen, I was commanded to prepare for a wedding ceremony. Knowing I'd never be free, I ran away one night. I went to the cops, got him charged, and was arrested with child endangerment. A few months later, I testified against him in court. He was imprisoned, and the entire cult turned on me. I was hated, still am, more so by his sons who've taken every chance to come after me.'

'How did you survive them?' Alessio growled.

'I lived on the farm with only my grandparents for company. My granddad would hide me away when the Contis came raging, angry at the fact I'd gotten their family head jailed. When I was 18, Franco was freed. Seeing no other option, my grandfather sent me to Italy to stay with his sister in Naples. But Franco found me, and you know the rest of the story. After you rescued me, I used the money I'd stolen from Franco that night and booked a ticket back to Sydney. I returned to find my grandfather was ill and my Nonna too weak to help much. So I nursed him until he died, put Guilia in care when it became impossible for her to live here, and took over the farm myself.'

Alessio reached out, taking my hand in his, stroking my cold skin and fingers. 'Scusa, mia sola. I can't even imagine what you went through.'

I shook my head, a bitter smile twisting my lips. 'No one can unless they've lived it. The fear, the shame, the constant feeling of being judged and controlled. It was a nightmare that kept going for years.'

'How about your parents?' he growled.

I huffed. 'They were lost to the cult too. My mother is a distant cousin of Franco's and married one of his capos after my dad died. She and her husband lit out for Victoria and haven't been seen or heard from her in years. Not that I care.'

Alessio's eyes darkened with rage. 'Did they do anything about how you were treated?'

I scoffed. 'Nope, they fucking encouraged it. They were caught up in the madness, raving lunatics for it.'

'How did you deal?'

I took a shaky breath. 'What d'you think? I was so bitter at a world that was cruel and mercilessly unfair. What had happened to me and women like me wasn't moral, fair, or something to be glossed over. I wasn't supposed to be angry or reject the control and manipulation. I was meant to play along. Until I didn't. Instead, I became furious. I still am.'

'You've every right to be,' Alessio agreed with a chin jerk. 'How have you stayed here, so close to all that pain, mia sola? Why haven't you left this place?'

I met his gaze and flicked an eye over his concerned brow, furrowed in genuine indignation and wonder. 'It's all I had. It was the only thing I owned because my grandfather entrusted it to me. Don't get me wrong, I tried living in Sydney but couldn't handle the noise, stress, and loneliness. When I almost became homeless one year, I returned to the farm. When Granddad died and Nonna went into care, I stayed on.

At least here, I could practice my gun skills to protect myself. Still, self-preservation is a full-time job,' I whispered.

Alessio held both my hands together as silence fell between us.

I met his leonine eyes after a beat. 'Does my story surprise or shock you?'

'No. It's made me fuckin' angry, cara, wanting to tear the whole valley down, find those Conti brothers and Franco, and slit their throats for you.'

I jolted at his impassioned growl. 'They've got a small army at the farm, one funded by the Caputos.'

He shrugged one shoulder, a curl to his mouth. 'They don't know who I am and what I can do.'

I eyed him, taking in the sheer menace on his face.

'I'm going to end it all for you, mia tesoro.'

I huffed. 'I'm no one's treasure; stop calling me that.'

'You're my treasure now,' he rasped, a new possessiveness creeping into his tone. 'And going through what you've endured would anger any human being.

'Anger's just the start of it. My experiences have often made me loathe people and even hate every waking moment of my life for how punishing it is.'

His arms reach for me, work around me, and pull me to his hard chest, murmuring words in Italian that I didn't understand.

I tried pulling back, rejecting the comfort he was offering, hating how it penetrated, incising the pain. I didn't get anywhere.

He held on.

I gave up fighting him.

I didn't cry, for my tears had long dried out. Instead, I sunk my nose in his nape, under his golden beard, and breathed him in.

We stayed that way for a long time.

He knelt on the floor, arms around me; I fell into his chest, head on his tee.

The fire kept crackling as my breath slowed from short, jagged inhales to a steady quietening.

The heat from his torso radiated through me, my limbs soft against his hard, muscled length.

For some strange reason, I chuckled.

He shifted and tipped my head up to him. 'I'd have liked to see Fabio trussed up like a hog.'

'He was a sight to see. Mewling like a cat.'

I laughed, shoulders shaking with mirth and the release of the strain I'd carried for so many years.

Alessio gifted me with a rare, dimpled, crooked smile. 'If you've had this much shit in life, carissima, anger is normal. It's happiness that's the real surprise. I look forward to seeing it on your face always.'

Chapter 18

ALESSIO

We went to bed and held each other.

I rocked her in my arms, heated by her limbs sprawled over mine.

Warmed by the thought that she'd shed her ice and shown me her true heart.

Which only stirred an unholy ire and a fierce, protective urge within me, a primal instinct to shield her from harm.

This, in addition to the fact that I was so drawn to her, so charged every time I saw her, it bordered on exploding for her.

I had to tread with care.

Cleo was an independent woman with layers and trauma.

Protecting her from danger didn't warrant me caging her like her cult had tried to do.

My work was to give her the security she deserved without

suffocating her.

I sensed she was done with aggressive assholes.

She needed tenderness, respect, and attention from some-one who could offer love and intimacy with no restraints.

Whether I was that man remained to be seen.

At the thought, my cock twitched, thinking of all the things I wanted to do to her.

I blazed with a primal urge, my skin tingling with electricity as my thoughts raced with the possibilities of passion and pleasure with her.

Every inch of me was hit with a visceral wave of yearning, longing to explore and claim her in all ways imaginable, to make her moan.

My breath caught in my throat, a growl escaping my lips.

She shifted, still awake, and tilted her head up.

I tagged her dark-haired pixie tresses, framing those jade eyes brimming with desire.

Shit, she was feeling this too.

The scent of arousal and passion wafted through the air, heavy and intoxicating.

I canted a brow, and she followed its arch.

'Mia sola,' I rasped. 'Sono pazzo di te. I'm wild for you.'

'Even after what I shared?' Her ask was tentative, vulnera-ble.

I growled. 'I want you even more after it. Not to save you or get off on your pain, but because I admire you, carissima. Now, you're a goddess to me.'

To my surprise, she reached a hand and touched the back of my head, tugging me closer.

'Kiss me, Alessio, make me forget.'

I huffed in a timbered growl against her lips, then let my

mouth skate over hers.

My hands found her waist, pulling her close as I deepened the kiss, losing myself in savoring her.

Cleo responded with a soft moan that sent a shock of electricity straight to my cock, her fingers tangling in my hair as she pressed herself to me.

The world around us faded away, leaving only the heat of our bodies and the intensity of our desire. Every nerve ending was alive and buzzing with need, aching for more of her touch.

When we finally broke apart, breathless and flushed, I rested my forehead against hers, trying to catch my breath. Cleo glanced up at me with eyes darkened with longing, a small smile on her lips.

'I want you,' she whispered, her voice husky with longing. 'Like really freakin' want you.'

I raised an eyebrow and quirked my mouth. 'Woman, two days ago, you couldn't stand the sight of me.'

She stuck her tongue in her cheek. 'Do you always have to ruin the moment?'

When I blanched, she laughed.

'I sometimes don't do myself a service, do I?' I growled.

She arched her brow this time.

'Don't get me fucking wrong. I've never wanted anything, anyone more. You're fast becoming my life obsession.'

'Then show me,' she whispered, her eyes dilating with need. 'Fuck me, baby. It's been so long.'

I bit my lip, caught up in all of her, welcoming how she spoke out her need.

I stroked her cheek. 'Woman, I want this too -.'

'But -?'

I huffed. 'Do you know of the phrase *l'uomo e cacciatore*?'

She shook her pretty head. 'No, I do not.'

'It means the man is the hunter. Italian men are expected to pursue a woman over an extended period, months, even during which time women are obliged to rebuff their advances.'

Her brows canted in disbelief. 'Is this why you're taking us slow?'

My mouth curled.

'What a fuckin' sexist, self-defeating practice.'

'But mia sola, it's molto romantico,' I growled, leaning in. 'I happen to like delayed gratification because the payoff is always mind-blowing.'

'Then you're a sucker for punishment,' she teased, her lips wandering in the soft light of dawn, seeking my neck and nape in a leisurely and sensual dance.

I growled at her wanton seduction. 'I want you too, mia sola, so bad. Mi ecciti, you're turning me on. Like you always have since I first met you. But I want to take it slow with you. To ease into it till your sadness disappears, to rock you to sleep in my arms until you forget. Because I need you to be ready for my brand of loving, it's wild, raw, untamed, and hot, and you must be freakin' primed for it, carissima.'

I struggled to maintain control as the primal urge to claim her consumed me.

I bent and pressed my lips to the corner of hers. 'Then I'll take you high, I'll kiss you senseless, I'll lick you, fill you, fuckin' plug you.'

Her eyes were limpid in wonder as she caught on to my meaning.

'Anytime, anyplace, I'll be ready,' she breathed.

My heart warmed at her lack of shame.

She lifted her mouth to me, and we fused into a fierce,

desperate collision of two souls yearning for connection. Her hands roamed my body with a hunger mirroring my own, igniting a fire within me.

I ground into her, lost in the overwhelming need for her touch, her presence.

Eventually, we slowed into a lazy sequence of kisses and caresses until sleep engulfed us both.

We woke to dawn leaking in through the windows.

To lips searching and finding each other, mouths melding in a slow and sensual dance.

Morning's soft illumination highlighted our faces, high-lighting the tangle of our limbs and the craving in our eyes.

Every kiss deepened, igniting a fire within us.

Our gentle moans and faint whispers filled the room, accompanied by our quiet keens and gasps as our mouths glided, exploring and tasting, fingers tracing patterns on our skin.

'Sei cosi seducente,' I growled into her ear, probing the shell of it with my tongue. 'So fuckin' seductive.'

She moaned back, thrusting her hips against mine, driving me wild.

I pull back, almost cumming in my pants.

'Woman, we're breaking the rules,' I grunted, waving at the air between us, 'of l'uomo e cacciatore.'

'I freakin' want to break them all.'

I hitched a thigh over her, claiming her, our bodies melting together in a symphony of desire, entwined and connected in a moment of pure intimacy.

'I should get up,' I rasped at one point, cock aching, wanting to blow but keen to keep my promise to her.

Cleo sighed, running her fingers through my locks, nails scratching my scalp in a sensual release of pleasure strobes.

She nodded, a small smile playing around her lips. 'Alright then, but you can't blame a girl for trying.'

I chuckled, slipping out of her grasp and sliding off the bed. 'A nympho, who knew.'

She shrugged. 'I look the part, don't I?'

With her swollen pink mouth, tousled pixie hair, and hot bedroom eyes, she did.

I took a moment to admire her.

Her beauty was nothing short of breathtaking. It took all my willpower not to look back at her as I left the room.

I headed for a brisk cold shower in the outhouse, my mind already set on the task ahead.

The water was fuckin' freezing, and I cursed like a trucker as it splashed over me.

Still, it was invigorating and helped me clarify my plan for the day.

'I'll stake the Conti farm for the day,' I told Cleo over breakfast.

'Hell no. We're doing this together.'

Her voice was firm, her eyes locked on mine across the kitchen table. Weak morning light seeped through the curtains. 'What if something happens to you out there alone? I'm with you, and that's final.'

I sighed and ran a hand through my locks. Part of me wanted

to argue, to insist on going solo. But I was beginning to recognize that stubborn set to Cleo's jaw. There would be no convincing her otherwise.

'Alright, we'll go together.'

I met her fierce gaze. 'But we have to be careful. Stay hidden; gather intel only. No engaging unless necessary.'

She nodded. 'Understood. I'm not looking to play hero, Alessio. I just can't let you walk into danger alone. Not after everything and your injury.'

Her words sent a pang through my chest.

After all, she'd been through, all the shit and heartache she carried, Cleo still had my back without hesitation.

I jolted, reaching across the table, capturing her hand, and bringing it to my lips.

'Sei fantastico. I'm honored to have you with me.' I quirked with a half-smile. 'There's no one else I'd rather have watching my six. Now let's get geared up and head out before the day escapes us.'

Cleo returned my smirk, her moxie shining through. 'Time to see what secrets the Conti's property is hiding.'

She stood, the scrape of her chair decisive.

We took off just after 7 a.m. as mist rose over the grass.

Again, I was reminded of my time with the Italian military, how we'd tramped across the Alps at a high elevation not so different from this one.

We navigated the winding paths from Cleo's acreage to the Conti homestead.

I took her hand, and she smiled as we navigated the brush around us. Which was alive with the sounds of hidden animals, the patter of invisible feet, and the trill of birds.

A comfortable silence settled, evidence of our growing

comfort and connection.

Also expanding in me was a ratcheting desire to love all of her.

At one point, I pulled her into my arms from behind.

'What was that for?' she murmured, facing me.

'Call it innamorato cotto.'

'Please explain,' she invited in a whisper, dragging a finger across my lips. 'What does it mean?'

'What you think it does. Fotto, I want to make you come so hard when I get a chance.'

She ducked her head, a touch of shyness in her eyes.

'Cleo.'

She twisted away from my rumbled growl with a roll of her eyes.

I caught the slight smile on her face and dragged her to me. 'Where the hell do you think you're going? I'm not done.'

She moved, eyes searching mine.

'Mouth, now.'

She jolted against me.

'Now?'

'Right here. I want more.'

I raked her face, loving how her jade eyes deepened with lust, how her lips parted for me, how her cheeks dusted with a pink blush.

I reached a hand for her nape and tugged her to me.

She slid her hands around my collar, and I lowered my head, capturing her lips, sliding my tongue in an unholy caress.

Before easing it into her, tongue fucking her until she squeezed my neck so hard, its imprint left a mark.

I kissed her with intensity, demanding, suckling on her lower lip till she whimpered against my mouth.

My cock pulsed, and I almost entertained stripping her clothes off right there and then and making her scream out here in the wilderness.

We'd work to do, my logical brain told me.

I pulled away from her swollen, wet mouth and brushed her cheek with a finger, chest heaving.

'You are pure, fuckin' beauty,' I rasped into her ear before tapping her ass and pushing her out in front of me on the path.

Tugging me forward, she stalked ahead, and I let her, drinking her in, her lush, tight behind, her hips, that waist, the small of her back and nape.

I couldn't wait to fuck her senseless.

The sun beat down on our backs, the air heavy with the scent of earth and a rich biosphere.

Cleo took the binoculars from me at the fence line and studied the compound below.

'I can't see any of the Contis, just worker bees, majority of them on the hemp fields.'

'See that?' I whispered, pointing somewhere above one of the barn structures. 'The last of the night's frost is rapidly turning to steam, which means they have massive amounts of heat inside.'

'Machinery?'

'Some large operation that gives out massive energy. I plan to check it out. Tomorrow morning.'

Cleo's lips pursed, and her hand tightened on my arm, her tone urgent. 'Alessio, we need to be careful. What if one of the Contis catches us snooping around?'

My mind was made up. 'I have to go in, Cleo. Maybe how we bring down Franco and his sons is by exposing the shit they're up to.'

Her eyes searched mine, and I tagged the fear and uncertainty warring with her fierce drive to end her nightmare. 'Alessio –'

'Woman, I know the risks,' I growled. 'But I also know that I can't walk away.'

'I –'

'You need me to do what no one else wants to,' I grunted, this time with a hard, unyielding edge.

Sei la mia vita.

She was rapidly becoming my hope of a fuckin' incandescent life, and I would never let her stop at any chance of bringing her happiness.

Cleo closed her eyes for a moment, taking a deep breath.

When she opened them again, she nodded.

'Okay,' she murmured. 'But we do this together. No rash decisions, no unnecessary risks. We go in smart, and we get out fast.'

I jerked my chin at the incredible woman beside me.

'Tomorrow morning. I've a plan for how all this shit will play out.'

CLEO

It was early evening, and I took a much-needed shower in the outhouse.

We'd spent most of the day gardening and knocking items off my never-ending chores list around the farm.

I'd got so much done with Alessio by my side. What it had meant, however, was heightened contact with his sensual, sexy self.

Which involved brushing close to his skin, his hands on the small of my back, a stroke, and frequent pulse checks.

By sunset, my lust for him was out of freakin' control.

Now, with a low-flow drizzle flowing over my skin, the jets in a stroking flow over my body, heat and desire pooled, making me sopping wet, sending fireworks through my pussy.

Not giving a second thought, I reached between my legs.

I slipped a finger past my lips and into my cunt, parted my thighs, and stroked, loving the fall of water off me as I flicked my clit.

I pulsed, thinking of him in those flippin' sweats, no tee, just pure muscle.

I moaned, reaching one hand to grab the wash rail as my fingers worked faster.

Without warning, the door to the outhouse opened, and cold air rushed in.

I turned, gasping at the sight of Alessio, brow arched, slicing away from my nudity.

'Scusa,' he growled, backing out. 'I didn't know -'

To his credit, I'd decreased the water flow.

He'd had no idea I was inside.

As he twisted away, I called out.

'Don't go.'

He froze, head tilting, eyes still canted away from me in respect.

Silence fell as I bowed my head, face flushing.

193

What the hell was I thinking?

'Did you fuckin say what I thought you did, carissima?' he snarled after a beat.

I took a shaky breath.

'Yes.'

I wanted this, no, I freakin' *needed this.*

To feel, be touched, and have a man's hands on me.

I hadn't ever experienced the skill of a masterful lover, just the fumbles of much younger, unschooled men.

I craved Alessio; sensing his masculinity and sensuality was what I sought to set me off. It was greedy, it was selfish, it was fucking white-hot.

I sneaked a peek at him.

Wind rifled his hair as he lifted a finger, his body still canted from me. 'Let me rerun this by you, carissima,' he growled. 'You want me inside. With you.'

My nipples pebbled at his growl, and not from the cool air from outside.

I glanced again at him over my shoulder, my hand holding tight onto the shower rail, the other still on my trembling upper leg. 'Yes.'

That's when he turned to me, eyes locking on mine.

Strangely enough, there was no shame.

Not with him.

How? I'd no idea, but Alessio Calibrese was the one man who made me feel so fuckin' beautiful in so long.

With him, I always felt so needed, so seen, not owned nor controlled, but adored.

His gaze flicked to where my hand lay on the apex of my thighs. He trailed his eyes over my back, ass, my tits, and back to my face.

'You yearning?' he growled, so raw, it sent shivers all over my skin and pebbled tits.

I nodded, mouth parted, not trusting my voice.

'You want me to make you cum?' he rasped.

I took a shaky breath and jerked my head once more.

He bit his lip, and for a moment, I thought he'd walk away to my everlasting mortification.

Instead, his eyes smoked out, and he stepped into the small space.

He still had no shirt on, and his chest gleamed with sweat and dirt from our day spent in the garden and working the land.

I couldn't tear my eyes away from his defined abs and how his muscles rippled with every movement. He was like an opus of masculine beauty, each sculpted line perfect and captivating.

The scent of his sweat mixed with the musky cologne he wore was intoxicating, filling my senses and heightening my desire.

My eyes drank him in like a thirsty traveler at an oasis, savoring the sight of his chiseled physique that spoke of strength and passion. Every hard edge and dip was a masterpiece, a work of art I longed to explore with my fingertips.

He strode to me, kicking off his boots and socks and throwing them outside.

In seconds, he loomed over me from the rear, his golden mane falling over his eyes, chest heaving.

Muscled and sinewed arms around me.

My breath hitched, my knees weakened, and my mouth went dry in anticipation.

First, he used the shower jets to wash his hands.

All the while, his torso hit my spine, his skin sliding over me, sending waves of need all over me.

With a grunt, he lowered his head to me from behind.

Pressing those sensual lips on my nape.

It galvanized me, and I turned, my grasp sinking into his mane.

His mouth met mine for a lush, scorching kiss.

Lips firm, sucking, biting, pulling.

When his veined, sinewed, heated hand cupped my tit, I lost purchase of his mouth as pure desire arced through me.

My head rested on his shoulder, panting, arms around his corded neck, holding on for dear life.

When he flicked my nipple and pinched it, making me moan.

His thick fingers moved lower, past my tummy mound, through the tiny nest on my pelvis, slipping in between my pussy lips.

I died and went to heaven.

Rotating into his nape, I lifted my thigh to give him all access.

'Oh Dio, I'm so wet,' I groaned.

He growled, thrusting a finger inside me, working me, exploring my folds with a tenderness that brought a sheen of mist to my eyes.

Gazing down at where his hands played in and over me, I held onto his neck and shoulders for dear life, hissing at the ecstasy, keening for more.

'Alessio, baby.'

I tried turning his face to mine for a kiss, but he pulled away. 'Only your pleasure today, carissima,' he rasped, his timbre rumbling through his chest from behind.

I was so caged, so protected in his grasp.

His focused attention flamed me more as water poured over us, slicking over my skin, soaking his gym pants, and pooling at our feet.

Still, he stroked, then slid two more fingers inside my slippery lips, deep into my cunt.

His other hand, banded around my back, twisted to cup my breast, tweaking, squeezing, rolling my nipple, driving me wild.

I arched my vertebrae as his lean, long digits fucked me, his thumb twisting my clit in rotations of unending, unceasing bliss.

I bucked my hips, pushing against his hand, wanting him deeper,

'Alessio,' I breathed, thighs shaking, waist swirling so lost in chasing the stratospheric high I sensed was coming with him.

His eyes smoldered, tongue between his lips as he gave me the most delight I'd ever experienced.

The tingle in the back of my spine spread out into a wave over my back and legs. Then, with a burst, concentrated at where his thumb and fingers slicked over me, I exploded.

Bucking with such wild abandon, his arm had to tighten to keep me from slipping.

I was taut, tight as a wire, as he worked me, my entire body convulsing for him, on him. His cock thudded through his pants, a scorching length against my inner thigh, driving me even more savage.

'Die on me, mia sola,' he growled.

I did, falling slack into his embrace, limbs aching from the tautness of arching so hard, panting even as I came down.

He pushed me up and on him, tits on his wet chest, eyes

closed, my face buried in his nape.

He rinsed me off, his hands stroking over me, until one hand slipped between us, a finger reached beneath my chin and tilted my face to his.

I blushed as unbidden words spilled from my lips. 'Was that pathetic? Was I a desperate slut?'

He rumbled, 'Cleo, cara, I won't have you talk about yourself like this. You were wild, you were fire, and you were the best non fuck I've ever had. I can't wait to undo you, make you scream with my cock in you.'

I let out a sigh, chest heaving, biting my lip.

Imagining.

'I want every drop of you.'

He huffed, eyes crinkling with pleasure at my greed for him.

Eyes flaming, he growled, 'Woman,' reaching for the shower gel.

He washed me with a tenderness that brought tears to my eyes before drying me off.

'Now get the hell out of here so I can cool down, bella.'

I nabbed my towel from his hands and kissed the corner of his lips.

And fled.

Chapter 19

ALESSIO

Shadowed in the dense treeline, binoculars pressed to my eyes. I scanned the perimeter of the sprawling Conti compound.

The early morning air bit at my cheeks, but I remained motionless, absorbing every detail.

I'd staked the property for a few mornings, gathering intel, piecing together their patterns, routines, and vulnerabilities—like a predator stalking its prey, biding its time.

Cleo's revelations about the Caputo clan's devout adherence to Sunday dawn mass in Moss Vale was a godsend, giving us a window of opportunity.

I lowered the binoculars as my woman stirred beside me in the SUV. Her short-cropped, sable hair caught the first rays of dawn light filtering through the forest canopy.

'They'll be on the move soon,' I murmured, my breath forming mist in the chilly breeze. 'The liturgy kicks off at 7:00 a.m. sharp.'

Cleo nodded, her green eyes alert despite the early hour.

I reached over, grasping her delicate hand in my calloused one, our unity a silent reassurance.

She stroked my arm, then handed me a thermos of piping hot coffee.

I drank it and gave it back.

Eyes on her, mulling her shower moment the night before.

When she'd left the outhouse, it'd taken minutes of sucking in air and sluicing cold, fucking water over my groin to calm down.

Still, like every instant I was with her, my cock throbbed, thickening and aching for her.

But I was also a man of extreme patience.

I'd kept away from her for ten years.

A few more hours was nothing in the grand scheme of things.

Loving her, bumping her, and making her scream would happen on my terms, and the forbearance only elevated the chances of heightened and titillating bliss even more.

So, I sat back, waiting.

For the right timing with her.

For the next fuckin' move from our marks.

The distant rumble of engines shattered the tranquil morning air.

I tensed and knifed forward. Cleo leaned, peering, squinting through the foliage.

She squeezed my hand in affirmation.

Her eyes flickered to the compound's gates. 'Showtime,

baby.'

I turned back to the binoculars, pulse-quickening. The game was on.

Two massive black Ram 1500 trucks emerged from the Conti property, moving with predatory intent.

'Damn, they're huge,' Cleo whispered, a mix of awe and apprehension in her voice. 'Like tanks on wheels.'

I grunted in agreement, my eyes never leaving the approaching convoy. The Caputos had spared no expense regarding their fleet - or their security.

But today, their arrogance would be their downfall.

The rigs rolled past our hidden position; close enough, the pulsations from their tires reverberated over my chest.

The acrid scent of diesel exhaust mingled with the earthy fragrance of the forest. I held my breath, willing our camouflage to hold.

Cleo's fingers dug into my thigh as the seconds ticked, an eternity compressed into a few heartbeats.

The growl of the engines receded as the vehicles continued down the winding road toward Moss Vale.

A third truck pulled up to the compound entrance, braking with a hiss of hydraulics.

My muscles tensed as a solitary figure emerged from the vehicle, his movements casual and unhurried. He strode, heading for the gates, and reached into his pocket for what I assumed were the keys.

I glanced at Cleo, a silent question in my eyes.

She nodded, her jaw set. 'Go. I'll cover you.'

Without hesitation, I eased open the SUV door and leaped out, my feet hitting the ground with a soft thud.

With a Sig in each hand, I darted across the road, my heart

pounding in my ears as I closed the distance between myself and the unsuspecting guard.

Halfway there, a flicker of movement caught my eye.

I'd been tagged.

Two other figures burst from the truck, weapons drawn, their faces contorted with rage. They'd spotted me, and they were out for blood.

I fired in rapid succession, my gun bucking in my hands as I squeezed off shot after shot. Gunfire shattered the morning stillness, echoing off the surrounding trees.

The first man went down, a bullet catching him square in the chest. He crumpled to the ground, his weapon clattering uselessly beside him.

The second man took a hit to the shoulder, spinning him around and sending him sprawling.

'You're a dead man!' the third man at the gate snarled, his eyes blazing with hatred as he fumbled with his firearm, his hands shaking as he attempted to draw a bead on me.

I didn't bother with a witty retort.

Instead, I let my Sig do the talking. I fired once, twice, and he stumbled back, a look of shock and pain etched on his face.

Blood blossomed on his chest, spreading rapidly as he fell to his knees. He tried to speak, his lips moving, but no words came out. Instead, a crimson spray erupted from his mouth, splattering his feet.

Two more quick shots, and he joined his buddies on the ground, either unconscious or lifeless. I didn't have time to check which.

I turned to tag Cleo behind me with her rifle, ensuring no one was at my rear. She jerked, her face dark and solemn.

'We must get rid of them,' I rasped, advancing toward the

fallen men. 'Roll them into that ditch over there. It won't hide them for long but'll buy us some time.'

Together, we worked fast, dragging the bodies to the deep trench on the side of the road and pushing them over the edge.

We found branches to cover the corpses.

It was grim work, but there was no time for sentiment or squeamishness.

'We have to keep moving, bella,' I cautioned.

With a nod, I loped to the idling Ram 1500, its robust engine growling like a caged beast. The sleek black exterior gleamed in the morning sun, starkly contrasting the chaos and violence outside.

I swung open the driver's door and climbed into the massive cabin, the leather seat creaking beneath my weight.

'Get in,' I murmured to Cleo, eyes scanning the surrounding area for movement.

She slid into the passenger side, slamming the door behind her. I reached over to make sure she was securely strapped in. The last thing I needed was for her to get hurt if things went sideways.

My gaze snapped to the metal barrier between us and the Conti compound. 'That Caputo bastard managed to shut it before I took him out.'

I gripped the steering wheel as I pressed down on the accelerator. The truck surged forward, eating up the distance between us and the gate in seconds.

'Ready?' I asked Cleo, my rasp tense with an edge.

Her eyes locked on the imposing barrier ahead. I slammed my foot down on the lead, the Ram 1500 roaring to life as we hurtled towards our target.

The impact was jarring, metal crashing against metal,

echoing through the air. But the entryway held firm, refusing to yield to our assault.

'Again,' Cleo urged, her voice tight with tension.

I threw the car into reverse, the tires shredding the dirt road, peppering the wheel arches with gravel as I backed up for another run.

'Come on, you bastard,' I gritted my teeth as I again floored the accelerator.

The truck slammed into the gate with even greater force this time.

The sound of splintering wood and twisting alloy was deafening as the logs gave way and crashed to the ground in a shower of debris.

We ran over the shattered remains and onto the Conti property.

The driveway wound around a curve, the barn emerging into view in the distance.

'Is that it?'

Cleo leaned forward, squinting at the rapidly approaching structure. 'It's the blue one,' she confirmed. 'With a big ass B emblazoned on the side. Can't miss it.'

I nodded, my jaw clenched tight as I pressed down on the accelerator.

'Mia sola, hold on,' I warned Cleo, my fingers tightening on the steering wheel. 'We're coming in hot.'

With the engine's final, defiant roar, I slammed my foot down on the throttle, sending the Ram 1500 hurtling towards the barn door like a battering ram.

The impact was bone-jarring, splintering wood and screeching metal filling the air as we smashed through the barrier and into the darkness beyond.

For a moment, the world was chaos, a whirlwind of debris and dust that threatened to engulf us. But then, as fast as it had begun, it was over, the truck skidding to a stop amid a pile of shattered wooden slats and twisted iron.

I blinked, my vision slowly adjusting to the gloom. Beside me, Cleo was already moving, her gun drawn and ready as she scanned the interior of the storehouse for any signs of movement.

I climbed out of the smoking vehicle, my boots crunching on the wreckage-strewn floor as I moved to join Cleo.

Inside, the barn was dark and musty, the air thick with the scent of hay and manure. Shafts of light filtered through the gaps in the wooden slats, casting eerie shadows on the dirt surface.

We moved fast, weapons primed, senses on high alert.

We froze as we came onto an enclosure of plastic sheeting.

Eyes clashed, brows arched.

I stepped forward, pulled aside one of the synthetic screens, and whistled under my breath.

Here was the reason for the Caputos' secrecy, what they'd gone to such lengths to protect, their dirty little fuckin' secret.

A freakin lab.

It stretched out in the vast space.

Workbenches lined the walls, each laden with beakers, test tubes, Bunsen burners, and microscopes.

In the center of the room, a series of massive, cylindrical tanks hummed and bubbled, their contents hidden behind a veil of frosted glass.

I reached to touch one of the reservoirs, my fingers hovering just above the transparent surface.

'Dio,' Cleo breathed, coming alongside me. 'They are

cooking meth.'

My eyes darted around the room. Bags of innocuous shit were stacked in the corner, waiting to be processed. The scale of the operation was staggering.

Sucking my teeth, I pulled out my phone and began snapping photos, documenting the evidence. We had to move fast before–

A voice cut through the silence like a knife.

'What the actual fuck?'

CLEO

Alessio's entire frame locked beside me.

His arm went to me, pulling me behind him as he sauntered out of the makeshift lab.

I followed, heart thudding.

Three men stepped through the mangled fissure we'd punched into the dim-lit barn.

The lead was thin and tall, with a jagged scar twisting down his cheek, distorting his fierce expression.

The second man's eyes were bloodshot, pupils dilated.

He was twitchy, fingers drumming restlessly against his thigh. Meth, probably.

The last appeared like he'd gone a few rounds with a brick wall and lost. One eye was almost swollen shut, mottled purple and black.

'If it's not the three Conti stooges,' I called out. 'Why'd y'all miss out on morning mass? Your black souls not good enough for church?'

'Well, well, look who it is,' Rocco sneered, his dark eyes glaring at Alessio and me. 'You the reason we were woken with a fuckin' bang?'

'Don't knock it. It's our one-off home delivered good morning,' Alessio drawled.

Rocco glowered, ignoring him, eyes fixed on me. 'Queen Cleo, scurrying around in our shithole barn like a rat. You could have knocked on the front door, darlin'? We'd have let you in. After all, this will be your forever home with our father.'

As much as I wanted to spit in his ugly, scarred face, we had to play this smart. We were outnumbered and outgunned at the moment.

I glanced at Alessio, who appeared at ease, leaning casually nonchalantly against a stack of hay bales. His calmness reassured me.

'Your freakish delusions are off the charts, Rocco,' I said. 'Downright weird.'

Rocco's eyes flashed with malice. 'Funny. I was about to say the same about you, Cleo. Isn't it weird to be slumming it in barns with some random jackass instead of prepping to be our father's long-awaited bride? Or did this shithead accompany you to hand yourself into us before our father arrives?'

'In his and your dreams,' I stated, voice dripping with sarcasm.

Rocco curled his lip at my derision and jerked his chin at Alessio. 'Who's this asshole?'

I felt Alessio tense beside me at the insult, but his face

207

remained impassive, that infuriating half-smile still on his lips.

Calm, not reacting one iota to Rocco's apparent provocation. 'Didn't Fabio share?'

Rocco didn't take well to Alessio's smirk. He cursed.

The hate in his one good eye was diabolical.

I sliced my eyes to Alessio and jolted at the pure, unadulterated wrath aimed at the Contis. I suppressed a shudder.

Despite his nonchalance, Alessio was after blood, and he didn't look like he'd have any problem spilling it on the dirt floor of this godforsaken barn.

Alessio shifted, angling his body so he stood in front of me. Shielding me.

'Fabio, how's the the shiner?' Alessio asked, his timbre rumbling through the open space.

'Fuck off,' Fabio snarled, taking a threatening step forward, but Alessio lifted a hand, stopping him.

'You need to slow your roll,' Alessio rasped. 'Before I give you a matching set.'

The Conti brothers exchanged glances, scowled, and kept coming.

Alessio raised a chin. 'I suggest you three clowns walk away now. While you still can.'

Rocco growled. 'Handover our father's bride-to-be, and we'll let you live.'

'Cleo's under my protection now. You want her, you go through me.'

Alessio's voice was timbred, dangerous. It sent a shiver down my spine.

Rocco's gaze flicked to Alessio, sizing him up with narrowed eyes. 'Who the fuck are you, pretty boy for real?' he sneered.

'Her guard dog?'

Alessio's lips curled into a cold smile. 'No one important, just the man who's about to jack your shit up and make sure your father, yourself, and your brothers pay for your freakin' arrogance.'

''Is that right?' Fabio stepped forward, fists clenched. 'You threatening us, asshole?'

Alessio didn't even spare him a glance. His eyes stayed locked on Rocco's. 'Not a threat. A promise.'

Rocco's hand twitched towards the gun at his waist. 'You've got balls, fuck boy, I'll give you that. But you're making a huge mistake, siding with this lying bitch.'

Alessio's smile widened, but there was no humor in it. 'The only error here was you thinking you could mess with Cleo and get away with it. Now, you've got two choices. Walk away now, or get ready for a world of pain.'

The trio exchanged glances, smirked, and rushed in.

Alessio moved so fast for a man his size.

He reached for a hoe idling on the barn wall as he did.

He swung.

So swift that none of the brothers had the chance to reach for their weapons.

Rocco went down with a roar and cry of agony.

Fabio followed, reeling into the dirt and hay strands on the ground.

Bruno tried to lunge at me and scratched at me, trying to slap me.

I launched into a roundhouse kick that threw him into the air and against a post, winding him.

It went down with such rapid fervor that it was all blurry until I realized Alessio and I had the upper hand.

Breathing hard, I moved in a hurry to secure them.

Using some loose ropes on the wall, I tied up Bruno and Fabio, then tracked to Alessio's side just as he placed the sharp edge of the hoe on the groin of a moaning Rocco.

'You're cutting off his balls?' I murmured.

'No, yet, cara. If I lean on them, I will.'

Alessio turned to the gasping man beneath him, who was struggling not to writhe in pain lest he lose his crown jewels. 'When's your father expected, shithole?'

'He's not here presently.'

'That's not the answer I was looking for, Captain Obvious. When does he arrive?'

Rocco spat at Alessio's feet. 'Any time this week. What do you want with him?'

'What do I want? Well, now that you asked, I want a getaway on the beach with my woman, it's the shit. Plus, the latest edition of the bestseller, 'How To Live With A Huge Penis.' Perhaps a free pass to rip you and all your clan apart if you decide to come after my woman again.'

Rocco groaned. 'Fuck you. You'll need to watch your back because we'll be drilling bullets into it.'

'Will you now?' Alessio growled.

With no warning, he crouched and threw a lightning punch at Rocco's visage.

'You broke my fucking nose!' the eldest Conti screamed, clutching his face.

'Only your nose? How about I get your whole fuckin' face for you?'

Alessio landed another blow, and Rocco's head whipped.

He lay keening, howling on the ground for a moment before blacking out.

I stared at my freakish superhero lover as he surged from his crouch. He canted away from me, and returned the hoe to its place on the wall, calm as fuck.

Maybe, just maybe, with him by my side, we had a shot at getting out of this mess after all.

Chapter 20

CLEO

We moved through the barn to catalog images and videos of the lab works inside.

It was a little after nine a.m. by the time we were done.

To my surprise, no one had disturbed our moment with the trio of siblings, so we left them cold and still snoring on the shed floor.

The Caputos were still at mass, so we returned to their Ram 1500.

Its bull bars meant it had sustained minor damage, and we roared out the Conti property the same way we'd arrived.

When we pulled next to Alessio's SUV on the road, he jerked his chin at me.

'Take my car and follow me.'

I arched a brow. 'You're keeping their truck?'

'Fuck yeah. They've jacked up enough of your shit that they owe you. Plus, you need a new ride.'

'After you messed mine up,' I noted with an acerbic wink.

His mouth twitched. 'Go, mia sola. We don't want to be caught out.'

I scrambled from the Ram 1500, shocked by his brazenness, still astounded by his brand of retribution.

I jumped into his Defender and followed him back home.

When we arrived, we went through the ritual of locking up before Alessio's strong arms captured me at the shed door, wrapping around my waist and pulling me close.

Alessio exuded sensuality, yet he held back as if he couldn't quite believe he was here with me.

'What a fuckin' day, hey?' he murmured, his breath warm against my ear. 'You OK carissima?'

I melted at his care, twisting in his embrace to face him, reaching up to caress his cheek. 'That was wild, but it was freakin' good.'

Alessio's hand covered my own, his green eyes searching my face as if memorizing every detail.

Then he dipped his head and captured my lips with his.

The kiss was tender yet passionate, conveying everything words could not. When we parted, breathless, Alessio rested his forehead on mine.

'Voglio rimanere con te per sempre,' he whispered, voice raw and hoarse. 'I want to stay with you, here, forever.'

I lost myself in his flaming gaze.

In that perfect moment, nothing existed except the two of us, our hearts beating as one, savoring the incredible gift of holding him in my arms.

Alessio tucked a finger under my chin.

I gazed at him questioningly, dazed by how the radiance danced across his golden features.

'Grazie bella,' he rasped, his eyes filled with tender emotion. 'For being my light in the darkness.'

'You talk like you've been thinking that way for some time.'

He tugged me into his embrace, nestling my head against his chest. 'Ah, carissima, but I have.'

'You saved me too, you know,' I whispered. 'In more ways than one.'

His mere presence in my world lifted my heart out of the shadows.

We held each other tight as we entered the cabin.

It was heaven.

ALESSIO

After dinner, we changed into sweats and sat in the living area, the fire blazing before us.

Cleo pulled a worn deck of cards from her mantelpiece, her eyes sparkling with mischief.

'Care for a game, amore?' I asked.

She grinned, settling across from him at the rough-hewn table. 'Prepare to lose, pretty boy,' she teased. 'I'm a card shark in disguise.'

I chuckled, dealing out the deck with practiced ease. 'We'll see about that, country girl.'

We played Five Crowns.

The radio hummed in the background, a soothing sound-track to our gentle banter and the occasional triumphant, gloating scoff as one of us took a hand.

Later, after our game, I sipped whiskey, and Cleo enjoyed a glass of Cabernet Merlot.

'Tell me your story, Alessio.'

I bit my lip at the husky rawness of her voice. 'I'm a simple man. Not much to say.'

'You talk sparingly, but you move a lot.'

If only she had a clue.

Fuck, she deserved to know.

I debated for a beat until I shared part of my truth. 'That's because I was born with a condition called MS that disrupts the flow of information within the brain and body. My experience keeps altering, and it manifests in fatigue, memory difficulties, mood changes, mobility issues, numbness, pain, and tingling.'

'I'm so sorry to hear, honey,' she whispered.

She set aside her glass and slipped onto my lap, cradling my head while she ran her fingers through my hair.

The sensation was incredible, and I let my head fall into her hands as I went on.

'Over the years, I have used exercise and movement to curb the symptoms and train my body to be healthier. Most of the shit has subsided as I'm now in great shape,' I murmured.

'Baby,' she breathed.

I shrugged. 'It's why when people compliment me on my looks, I hate it because they don't see the agony I sometimes go through.'

'When does it happen?'

215

'Sometimes, when tired or stressed, I get what I would describe as a numb feeling on one side. Also, if I've too much adrenaline in me.'

'Alessio, honey, all I can see is a man whose strength is forged through fire. You're as strong as steel, and I adore you for it.'

Her words melted any doubt or worry I'd ever had about how she saw me.

She leaned in, her lips brushing against mine in a kiss that was achingly sweet and full of promise.

As she pulled back from the tender embrace, I gazed into her eyes, tagging the swirling emotions within their depths.

Pain, grief, and anger still lingered, but there was also a glimmer of hope, a spark of something that had been missing for far too long.

We kissed, murmuring endearing words as our hands explored one another.

'I'm so obsessed with your mouth, eyes, and touch,' she murmured.

'I have only one obsession,' I growled against her lips. 'You. Only you, bellissima.'

Our kisses were sweet and hungry, each one imbued with pure euphoria, whiskey, and longing, fueling a more profound yearning for one another. The sweetness of her breath mingled with mine, creating a heady sensation.

Soft moans and whispers of adoration filled the air as we kissed, our exhalations coming in ragged rhythms.

My hands roamed her body, tracing every curve and eliciting shivers of pleasure. Her fingers danced along my skin, igniting sparks of electricity with every caress.

I slid under her thin tee and fondled her heavy tits, thumbing and flicking her nipples.

My cock went diamond stiff in my sweats, aching, throbbing for her, always for her.

Cleo's inhales grew heavier at my touch, and she began to explore me.

Her fingertips grazed the waistband of my sweatpants, mere inches from my pulsating erection.

She leaned in closer, her lips close to mine, and whispered, 'I want you, too, so bad - it's so hard for me to breathe, needing you so much.'

I pulled back, taking in her flushed face and heavy-lidded eyes.

'Then let me give you a flavor of the fuckin' bliss about to come your way, cara,' I murmured, my voice a timbered growl. 'I want to make you happy. I'm going down on you, and I won't permit you to think about returning the favor.'

Her eyes widened as I knelt before her and clutched the edge of her tee, pulling it off her.

Her bra followed, and I was transported to heaven.

Her body was a work of art, every curve and contour perfect. She was mine, and I wanted to show her just how much.

I glanced at her and said, 'You are a goddess, and I am here to serve you. I want you riding me right now, face between your legs.'

Cleo blushed at my words. 'Baby.'

I reached up and pulled her close, my lips finding hers in a passionate kiss.

She moaned as I stared at her tits.

They were a sight to behold, heavy globes crowned with caramel-tipped pebbled tips. I paused, not wanting to rush things, and let my eyes linger on their beauty.

217

My woman eyes locked on me from above, her lust-filled gaze making my cock twitch in anticipation. 'You can touch them, you know,' she whispered.

I gazed up into her eyes, lost in their depths. 'I fuckin plan to, but first, I want to show you how much I crave you.'

With that, I began to kiss her neck, nibbling and biting, leaving a trail of hickeys that would mark her as mine.

Her moans underscored the fact she belonged to me, body and soul.

My lips moved lower, teasing the tender skin of her collarbone. Cleo arched her back, her breaths growing shallow and quick.

'Oh Dio. More,' she begged, breathy and filled with desire.

I smiled against her flesh, my hands finding their way back to her breasts.

They were warm and soft, the perfect size for my palms. I began to knead them, rolling her nipples between my fingers until they hardened into small pebbles.

Cleo cried out, her hips bucking. 'I crave you, Alessio. I need you so much.'

'I'm here, my love,' I whispered, my timbre husky with arousal. 'Just let me adore you.'

And worship her I did, my lips trailing down her chest, over her stomach, and down to her waistband. She moaned, her hands tangling in my hair as I kissed and licked her skin.

I sank to the floor, pulling her legs apart.

'Alessio, please!' she begged, her utterance thick with yearning. 'I need you now.'

My eyes glinted wickedly as I grabbed her hips and slid her so that she was lying down, her thighs spread for me.

Without a moment's hesitation, I dragged her pants off and

pushed the lace of her panties aside, revealing the pink, wet folds of her desire.

I lowered my mouth to her, my tongue darting out to sample her sweetness.

Cleo's breath hitched as I traced gentle circles around her entrance, feeling her shiver at the feather-light touch.

'Dio, Alessio,' she whimpered, her groin bucking. 'Please, I can't wait any more.'

Her words were my undoing. My hunger for her was insatiable, and I'd lose my mind if I didn't feast on her now.

With a growl, I tore her panties and buried my face between her legs, my tongue diving deep inside her. She moaned out in pleasure, her hands gripping my hair as I licked and suckled at her most intimate places.

'Oh fuck!' she wailed out, her body convulsing underneath mine.

I was rocked by a sense of triumph at her surrender, and a kaleidoscope of emotions washed over me as she opened up to me.

I delved further, my mouth tracing every curve, flicking her clit with just the right amount of pressure.

'Alessio, yes!' she cried, her hips bucking into my face. 'Oh, please, more!'

My fingers joined my tongue, sliding inside her slick entrance, stroking her velvety walls.

She moaned my name, her muscles clenched around my hand, pulling me deeper into her.

Cleo moaned, her hands gripping the sofa as my tongue explored her. Her flavor was intoxicating, and I couldn't get enough.

My cock throbbed so hard as she mewled, thrusting into my

beard, soaking it, clutching my hair and shoulders as she rode me to her bliss.

My fingers moved in rhythm with my tongue, fucking her, driving her wild with every thrust. Her breaths became ragged and shallow, each moan and whimper music to my ears.

She trembled and shook, her orgasm building, her muscles tightening around my fingers. I increased my pace, my burred tongue tip dancing on her most sensitive spot as I pleasured her.

'Alessio, oh Dio!' she cried out, shaking as she convulsed in pleasure. 'So good!'

That was all the encouragement I needed.

I slipped two more digits inside her, thrusting her with a ferocity that matched her own. My thumb continued to flick her clit, sending her over the edge.

I bent over and suckled it as her back arched, her body convulsing as her orgasm washed over her. I moaned against her, savoring the feel of her wet coating my hand.

I flicked her nipples, pulling, plumping them for me before I descended on her left one. Licking and suckling her sensitive skin and turgid nerve endings.

'Oh, Alessio!' she cried, shuddering. 'Honey! I'm going to cum so hard!'

Her words were my undoing. I wanted her more than anything in this world, and seeing her so lost in pleasure only fueled my desire.

My cock had never been more rigid, more pulsing than it was now, my eyes scorching, raking over her as her ecstasy approached.

Fuck, it was the most I'd ever been turned on.

'Oh, Alessio,' she gasped, her voice barely a whisper. 'I'm

so close, please don't stop.'

Her utterances were like fuel for me, and I redoubled my efforts, descending to feast, so my tongue danced over her clit as my fingers thrust inside her.

'Yes, yes, yes!' she cried out, her body bucking underneath me. 'I'm cumming, baby!'

Her orgasm was a symphony of euphoria, waves of bliss crashing over her like a tidal wave. Her muscles clenched around me, her moans filling the air as she rode her high to its heart-shattering peak.

She came apart in my arms, wracked with pleasure. My desire threatened to break free as her climax washed over her.

Then I lost it.

With a roar, I surged back from her, rocked onto my heels, and arched my spine.

My hand instinctively went to my cock, over the tented material, kneading and massaging the pulsing, red-hot shaft.

While the other hand continued its ministration to Cleo's sensitive flesh, coaxing more and more from her.

I stiffened and shuddered as I reached my peak, sweat pouring down my chest in rivulets, muscles rippling with gratification.

I came so hard, with such a gush and torrent of cum, I spurted into my fuckin' pants.

The fabric straining, hips bucking and grinding as I rode out the waves of pleasure.

The tang of her lingered on my lips as I let out guttural moans, the scent only fueling my desire even more.

I convulsed, and my senses were overwhelmed by the rush and deluge of ecstasy.

It was damn pure and intense, as was Cleo's release, which

appeared to last forever. She still shook as I thrust into her with my hand.

My gaze worshiped her as she lay before me like a goddess, eyes still closed, limbs still twitching with the aftershocks of the overwhelming orgasm.

The perfume of our sex filled the room, spicy and musky, mixed with the slight tang of sweat and the lingering scent of her wetness.

I couldn't help but smirk, taking in the sight of her sprawled across the sofa, panting, legs thrown open, her hips glistening with her arousal and my saliva.

Canting forward, I slid my hand from her pussy and sought her lips as she came down.

'Brava, Cleo,' I whispered, hoarse with passion. 'You're a sensuous goddess; I am your obedient devotee.'

My fingers parted her mouth, tracing the delicate contours of her face and then delving into her mouth to savor the remnants of our shared intimacy.

Our breathing slowed, and our hearts decelerated in sync as we both shuddered in the afterglow of our intense encounter.

'Cleo,' I rasped, my voice still tinged with arousal. 'I adore you.'

I kissed her hot, sweaty skin, a trail from the top of her chest to the base of her throat. She gasped, her hands stroking my hair, tugging me.

'Alessio,' she panted, husky with the remnants of her ebbing desire. 'I can't believe how incredible that was.'

I chuckled. 'Cara, that's just the beginning,' I promised, my eyes never leaving her face as her breathing evened out, the ebb of her orgasm draining from her body. 'But for now, I need to clean up.'

That's when she noted the wet spot on my gray sweats.

'Did you just –'

'Si,' I growled with no shame.

She smirked. 'Early off the mark, soldier. In some places, that means instant disqualification.'

I growled. 'I've imagined you, this, us, often in the past ten years. Can't blame me that I blew when my dream came true.'

'You weren't celibate all this time, were you?' she teased.

I shook my head. 'They never meant anything. I never charged up with anyone like I have with you. How about yourself?'

She blushed. 'One or two, an old boyfriend and some fly-by-the-night hostel hookups when I was abroad and in Sydney. Nothing extraordinary.'

'Bene. That's because you were always destined to be mine, body, mind, and soul. Now, no one else will ever have you.'

'So obsessive.'

'You love it.'

I could tell she did by the soft light in her eyes and the part of her lips.

She yawned, and I tagged the post-orgasm lassitude hit her.

Shifting her in my arms, I cradled her against my chest as I stood.

She mumbled a sleepy protest, but I shushed her. 'It's alright, sweetheart. I've got you.'

I carried her to the bedroom, each step measured and careful as I accounted for my stiff shoulder, focusing on the precious cargo in my clasp.

I laid her on the bed. Finding a dry towel, I cleaned her and helped her wriggle into a fresh pair of cami shorts.

I tucked her in, pulling the covers to her chin.

She blinked up at me, her eyes hazy with fatigue. 'Stay with me?' she asked, her voice small and vulnerable.

'Where else would I sleep except for in your embrace, bella? But I need to freshen up first.'

She nodded, her eyes already drifting shut. 'OK,' she whispered, the words slurred with exhaustion.

I kissed her mouth and left her to go clean myself in the outhouse, where I shucked off my sweats with a curl of my lips.

Fotto, I'd come in my pants like a horny teen.

It'd been fuckin' incredible even as I thought of how much sliding in her would be even more enticing.

When I took her, our lovemaking would be off the charts.

Dressed, I returned to the cabin, finding her half drifted off.

I eased into bed and tugged her close, mouth descending on hers.

Her lips were soft and wet. My fingers pressed them as the will to continue was too overwhelming.

I growled, 'I think I've adored you for a long time, Cleo.'

She opened her eyes, blinking and smiling up at me. Her gaze was heavy-lidded and filled with emotion.

I moved my hand from her mouth to cup her cheek, my thumb stroking away a tear that escaped.

I leaned forward, my lips brushing hers. 'You don't have to say anything you're not ready to. But know this: I promise, always and forever, you will be mine, and I will be yours.'

'Alessio,' she murmured, cradling my face in her hands. 'You're fast becoming my sweetest obsession.'

Her words were music to my ears, and I nodded, my eyes never leaving her until she closed her jade beauties and fell asleep in my arms.

Chapter 21

ALESSIO

Early the following day, the sound of a gun firing and bullets flying had me knifing up from the bed.

I stumbled outside to the veranda, disoriented.

My eyes flew to the sight of Cleo standing in the extensive front yard of her farm, aiming a shotgun at a far-off target.

She fired once, twice, then in rapid repetition.

She was practicing her aim.

Next, she placed the rifle down and reached for a handgun. This, too, she discharged.

I lurched at the wild emotion in her shoot.

She was shooting with increasing anger and ire.

When she missed her target and let out a loud curse, I sucked my teeth.

I had to stop her moment in case she hurt herself.

Stepping off the terrace, I walked slow and easy to her.

I called out from a safe distance. 'Carissima, calma. Suffi-cientemente.'

She paused for a beat, silence falling, smoke curling from her weapon.

With an inhale and a low growl, she returned to her blasting at unseen enemies.

I'd had enough.

I prowled to her and, in seconds, hauled her to my torso, immobilizing her shooting arm.

She slumped against me, chest heaving.

'What the hell, cara?' I murmured into her ear, keeping my tone soft.

She whipped around to face me. 'Baby, I had a nightmare that they would come after us and burn all of this, all of us, down. That they'd take you, us, away from me. I have to keep practicing. I can't let them ever win.'

I took an inhale and a moment to assess. 'Bellissima, you're angry and frustrated, I know. But a firearm and emotion don't mix.'

'The fuck they don't,' she growled. 'When I've been made to feel like shit and treated like shit for so long, they do merge. They fuckin' have to. It's the only sanity I have left to hold on to. That one day I will find my revenge, that I'll empty my gun in that monster's face until it's obliterated.'

Shakes racked her entire body as she crumpled on me.

I caught her, steadying her trembling frame as her fingers clutched my shirt. Her anguish was palpable, radiating off her in waves that threatened to drown us both.

'Did you know on the night you found me in Naples that he and those two other fucktards he was with planned to rape me? Thank Dio, they drank and got high before they did much.

226

One even fell asleep as he was pawing me hard. That's when I escaped, and you arrived.'

'It's OK, mia sola,' I growled. 'Franco Conti will never hurt you again.'

With care, I pried the weapon from her grasp and placed it in the open case at our feet, snapping it shut.

In one fluid motion, I scooped her into my arms, cradling her against me as I carried her back towards the farmhouse.

Slight and fragile, she folded in my embrace.

All that mattered was getting her inside. To soothe the pain that had driven her out here, gun in hand, ready to pursue the vengeance that had consumed her for so long.

I wanted to love her until she learned to cherish herself, to give her everything she ever needed, and to adore her the way she was supposed to be.

When we reached the front door, she lifted her head, red-rimmed eyes meeting mine.

'I'm sorry,' she choked out between hiccuping breaths. 'You didn't need to see that. I woke with the devil riding my back, and I couldn't stop thinking of how much Franco and his Conti cunt family have done to ruin my life.'

Her voice broke.

'Shhh, it's alright,' I soothed, shifting her weight to push open the door. 'You have nothing to apologize for.'

I lifted her over the threshold, kicking the door closed behind us.

She was far from OK, the scars that bastard left her with cutting soul-deep. But I would help her through this in whatever way possible.

Easing her suffering was the only thing that mattered now, even if it meant ignoring the burning ache in my own heart.

I carried her over to the sofa, my shoulder aching in protest as I lowered us both down onto the cushions.

I gritted my teeth against the pain. It was nothing compared to the agony she was drowning in.

Settling back on the lounge, I pulled her into my arms, letting her curl up on my lap, seeking comfort. She clutched at my shirt with desperate hands, her whole body shaking with the force of her sobs.

'I hate him,' she whispered, muffled on my chest. 'I loathe him so much. Franco Conti's name, face, and voice are the poison and acid in my veins.'

'I know, sweetheart. I know.' I stroked her hair, loving the silky strands that slid between my fingers. She was so delicate, but a steel core also ran through her. The strength that had kept her going all these years was fueled by the hatred for the man who'd shattered her world.

He'd taken an abundance from her, from so many innocent people. And he'd keep on taking until someone stopped him.

Unless I shut his shit down.

She didn't know that, as well as protecting her, I'd come to these hills to un-alive the man.

I was a man with a mission behind the mask of the ruthless stranger, the tender almost-lover. A man who'd seen too much evil, and had vowed to put an end to it, one scumbag in particular.

Franco Conti was that scum.

He had to disappear for her sake and my own.

But that was for later. Right now, she needed me to be here, to hold her as she purged some of the poison he'd left inside her.

She wept in my arms until my shirt was damp with her tears,

till her breathing slowed, and her soft tremors eased.

I murmured soothing nonsense, words that meant nothing and everything, anchoring her with my voice and touch.

My fingers combed through her hair, silken strands sliding between my fingertips like silk. The repetitive motion seemed to calm her, and slowly, the sobs that wracked her body began to subside.

'You're strong,' I told her instead, meaning it with every fiber of my fuckin' being. 'Stronger than you know. And you're not alone anymore. I'm here now.'

She inhaled, clutching my chest. 'You're just one man, Alessio.'

I leaned back. 'Ah mia sola, on that, you are wrong. I come from a family that doesn't take shit, one that metes out justice in the highest order.'

She knifed up and canted her brow in disbelief. 'Is that the truth?'

I jerked my chin. 'Si. The Calibrese legacy is one in which we were the guardians of Omertà throughout most of Southern Italy. Meaning we were the honor protectors, the law among the unlawful. We trained assassins and trusted soldiers for various mob bosses. We upheld the families' paramilitary structures, influencing every level of our society. We oversaw the blood oaths of silence which restrained each initiated and made man.'

'You too?'

'I am the family's head capo, chief enforcer, and fixer, but we're less into crime now. We operate more as security experts, militia advisers, and vault guardians. While we focus now more on legitimate endeavors, our enemies are still bound. They think we're weak, but we are not. We still have the might, money, firepower, and balls to defend our own and avenge anyone who dares come for us and for whom we love. Including you, mia sola.'

The words were a vow, a solemn promise spoken in the hush of the fading day. As she lifted her head to look at me, her eyes were red-rimmed but achingly beautiful.

'Makes so much sense now,' she breathed. 'There was always an air of mystery with you. I've always wondered.'

'Now you know,' I rasped.

'I do.'

She wiped her eyes, a watery laugh escaping her lips. 'I must look a mess.'

I shook my head, brushing a strand of hair from her face with a gentle touch. 'You look stunning. You always do.'

A faint blush stained her cheeks, and she ducked her head. But I caught the glimmer of a smile, fleeting but real, and it warmed me from the inside out.

'I've spent so long focused on revenge,' she murmured, her fingers twisting in the fabric of my shirt. 'It's consumed me, driven me. I almost don't know how to exist without it.'

'You live,' I said. 'You heal. You let yourself be happy again.'

She scoffed, the sound bitter and broken. 'I don't know if I recall how.'

'Then I'll help you remember.' I tipped her chin up, forcing her to meet my gaze. 'I'm not going anywhere, sweetheart. I'm in this through hell and haul.'

Her breath hitched, her eyes searching mine for any hint of deception. But there was none to find. I meant every word.

'Why?' she breathed, her words cracking. 'Why do you care so much?'

I smiled, the answer as easy as breathing. 'Because you're

worth caring about.'

She stared at me for a long moment, her expression soft, pliant, freakin' sensual.

I wanted to fuck her so bad.

'Thank you,' she murmured, her countenance heavy with fatigue. 'For being here, for listening, for everything.'

I pressed a gentle kiss to the top of her head. 'Always,' I murmured the word as a solemn vow.

She sighed, her body relaxing further into my embrace. 'I don't deserve you.'

'You merit the world,' I countered, my tone leaving no room for argument. 'And I intend to give it to you.'

A soft laugh escaped her, the sound like music to my ears. 'You're stubborn, aren't you?' she said.

'When it comes to you? Assolutamente.'

We lapsed into a comfortable silence, the weight of unsaid words hanging between us. There was still much to discuss, many wounds to heal, and battles to fight.

But for now, this moment, the warmth of her body against mine and the knowledge that we'd face anything together took precedence over every other freakin' thing.

Cleo eased past a sack of potting mix into her barn.

It was mid-morning, and the sun was shining hard, and we

231

sweated under its heat.

Cleo was going through her supply shed, and I was enjoying watching her tight ass move in her work jeans.

'I don't get Australian winters,' I mused. 'One day, you're lighting a fire; the next, you're stripping off.'

'It's the outback, baby, comes with the territory,' Cleo shot at me. 'And if you think it is hot, wait for December and January when the temperatures go so high even the poor flies give up on life.'

Wiping beads of sweat from her brow, she surveyed the other supplies packed inside – cans of beans, bags of rice, cartons of vegetable seeds.

Slamming the doors shut, she turned to me. 'It's not enough, Calibrese. We need to go shopping. You and your brawny self are eating me out of home and hearth.'

I leaned against the side of the container, arms crossed. 'Don't blame me because your doomsday provisions are running low, woman. Why are you such a prepper? Planning to hunker down for the apocalypse?'

Cleo shot me a wry look as she brushed the dust off her faded jeans. 'You joke, Alessio, but it's pure survival in the sticks. The nearest supermarket's an hour away, and winter storms can cut us off for weeks.'

Her voice took on a serious edge. 'Girl's gotta be prepared to fend for herself.'

I nodded, conscious of how isolated and self-reliant Cleo was out here, a far cry from my cushy city life. What strength and resourcefulness it took to carve out an existence in this remote place.

I circled my arms around Cleo's waist, pulling her close. 'Well, lucky for you, cara, now you've got me as your survival partner. We might need to stock up on more coffee and wine to make it through.'

Cleo smirked, a mischievous glint in her eye. 'Oh? You think you're ready for the great apocalypse with me?' She placed her palm against my chest, the warmth of her touch seeping through my shirt.

I grinned down at her, relishing the playful challenge in her gaze. 'Bella, with you by my side, I'll survive anything. Bring on the zombies, the nuclear fallout, whatever doomsday scenario you've got.'

Quick as a flash, Cleo smacked my torso, the sting barely registering before I caught her hand in mine. 'Cocky bastard,' she muttered, but her lips twitched with a repressed smile.

I brought her captured palm to my mouth, pressing a slow, sensual kiss to the center. Her breath hitched as I murmured against her skin, 'Face it, carissima. You and me? We're unstoppable together.'

Cleo's eyes darkened with desire, her body swaying closer. The rest of the world fell away - the dusty hills, the cabin, the impending tasks. In that charged moment, nothing existed but the magnetism crackling between us, the unspoken promise of passion and partnership.

I caught the rapid thrum of Cleo's pulse beneath my fingertips. Betraying the effect of my touch and my words as this fierce, independent woman allowed herself to be vulnerable and trust in our connection.

It humbled and thrilled me in equal measure.

She laughed, the sound echoing through the air. 'You've sure got your priorities straight. Coming into town with me?'

'It'll be my pleasure.'

Chapter 22

ALESSIO

The drive into Moss Vale was picturesque.

The winding road was flanked by towering eucalyptus trees and sprawling fields of wildflowers.

The sun beat down from a clear, azure sky, the heat shimmering off the asphalt in hazy waves.

Cleo navigated the twists and turns with practiced ease, her hands steady on the wheel, her eyes hidden behind dark sunglasses.

I lounged in the passenger seat, one arm on the seat rest behind her, the other hanging out the open window, the hot breeze ruffling my hair. Despite my idyllic surroundings, I couldn't shake the unease that prickled my spine.

Cleo squeezed my knee as if sensing my thoughts, her touch grounding and reassuring. 'It'll be quick,' she said. 'In and out, no fuss.'

I covered her hand with my own, interlacing our fingers. 'I've got your back, bella. Always.'

She flashed me a grateful smile before turning her attention back to the road.

We lapsed into a comfortable silence; the only sounds were the engine's purr and the faint strains of a classic rock station crackling through the speakers.

Cleo killed the engine when we pulled into the parking lot of the general store.

I reached out and tucked a stray curl behind her ear, my fingertips lingering against the delicate skin of her cheek.

She leaned into my touch, her eyes fluttering closed for a brief instant when she opened them again, a newfound light burned in their depths. 'Let's do this.'

Together, we climbed out of the truck and entered the grocery store.

The bell above the door jingled, announcing our arrival to the handful of patrons milling about the aisles.

I sensed the weight of curious stares on my back as we grabbed a cart.

Ignoring the attention, we loaded it up with Cleo's supplies—huge bags of rice and flour, cans of vegetables and fruit, and jugs of water and oil.

Eyes on our surroundings, my senses on high alert for any signs of trouble. My woman moved with single-minded focus, ticking items off her mental checklist with quick, efficient movements. But even she couldn't ignore the whispers that followed us from aisle to aisle, the pointed glances and raised eyebrows.

'Is that Cleo Michele? Thought she'd left town forever.'

'Who's that she's with, a bodyguard or boyfriend?'

235

Both, I wanted to growl.

'Or a farmhand?'

The last comment had Cleo in stitches as she met my affronted gaze.

I guess I deserved the description given, as I'd let my beard grow out recently.

My dress sense, too, had dialed down from Italian *sprezzatura* to outback casual.

Boots, jeans, a white vest and shirt over it, sleeves rolled up, showing off my muscles and bulk.

I gritted my teeth against the surge of protective anger in my chest.

These small-minded gossips had no idea what my bella had been through, the strength it had taken for her to break free from their expectations and judgments. She deserved so much better than their petty speculation.

Cleo's hand found mine over the cart handle as if reading my mind.

She laced our fingers together, her grip fierce and unyielding. 'Ignore them,' she murmured, her voice low, only for me. 'They don't matter.'

I squeezed her hand in silent agreement, marveling at the sheer force of will that radiated from this incredible woman. She stood tall and unbowed in the face of adversity, a queen among peasants.

We finished our shopping without incident. The trolley piled high with adequate supplies to sustain us for months. I insisted on paying, waving away Cleo's protests with a firm, 'Let me do this for you, bella. Please.'

She relented with a small smile, her eyes soft and warm as they met mine. 'Grazie, Alessio. For it all.'

'Anything for you,' I murmured, meaning it with every fiber of my being.

I loaded the last of the sacks into the bed of the truck, flexing my arms and back with the effort.

I arranged the bags and boxes with meticulous care. I wanted everything to be perfect for her, to show her that she was cherished and protected.

Her hands trailed over my back as I locked up.

She waggled her sunglasses at me. 'Hungry?'

'Starving.'

'I know someplace. It's been a beat since I worked there, but if the chef is the same, the food is decent.'

We walked hand in hand through Moss Vale, the sun shining, the breeze blowing, and life golden.

The bell on the cafe door jangled as we stepped inside, the aroma of baking pies enveloping us like a warm hug.

Checkered tablecloths covered the tables, and framed photos of rolling pastures dotted the walls, giving the space a cozy, homespun feel.

'Cleo, so lovely to see you again!'

A plump, motherly woman with rosy cheeks emerged from behind the counter, arms outstretched. She pulled my companion into a tight embrace.

An older man with gray hair and a kind face followed close after. 'And who's this strapping young man?'

He raked eyes over me, glancing me up and down approvingly.

'This is Alessio,' Cleo said, taking my hand. 'My special someone.'

She smiled up at me, her eyes sparkling.

'Well, any friend of Cleo's is a friend of ours! Welcome!'

The man clapped me on the shoulder. 'I'm Bill, and this is my wife, Nancy. We're the Nichols and are so glad you're joining us today.'

'The pleasure's all mine,' I replied, shaking his hand.

Their warmth and easy smiles immediately put me at ease. I understood why Cleo had enjoyed working here.

Nancy ushered us to a corner table. 'You two make such a lovely couple! Now, what can I get you to drink? Some coffee, tea?'

'Two lemonades would be awesome, thank you.' Cleo slid into the booth across me, reaching for my hand again.

I laced my fingers through hers, loving how we fit together.

As Bill and Nancy bustled off to fetch our drinks, I surveyed the cafe, taking in its simple charm and noticing how the other diners—regulars and locals—chatted animatedly.

Cleo had described it well—the perfect cozy spot to steal a little time for ourselves, surrounded by kind, humble people who wouldn't pry or gossip.

My woman leaned in close, her voice warm. 'I liked it here because Bill and Nancy have always respected my privacy and never pried into my life. They let me just be.'

She glanced at where the couple bustled behind the counter, preparing our order. 'When everything else was spinning out of control, this place was my haven, even for a little while.'

I squeezed her hand, emotions welling up inside my chest. To know that she had struggled and had needed a refuge when I'd been blissfully unaware cut me deep.

But the fact that she was sharing this with me now, bringing me into her sanctuary, meant more than I'd ever be able to express.

'Grazie mille,' I murmured, brushing my thumb across her knuckles. 'For letting me in.'

Cleo's answering smile was radiant, her eyes misty. She was about to reply, but Nancy appeared with a laden tray just then.

'Here we are, dears! Two lemonades,' she said, setting tall glasses beaded with condensation before us. 'And an assortment of our finest - steak and kidney pie, bangers and mash, and fish and chips. You mustn't forget the sides, either. Coleslaw and garden salad, all fresh from the farmer's market this morning!'

My mouth watered as she transferred plates piled high with golden pastry and steaming heaps of fries, the savory aroma making my stomach rumble. It seemed like an endless bounty, each dish more tempting than the last.

'This looks incredible,' I raped, inhaling in appreciation. 'You've outdone yourself, Nancy.'

The woman pinked, waving a hand in modest denial. 'Oh, it's nothing special. You dig in and enjoy, hear? And mind, I'll be mighty offended if there's so much as a crumb left over!'

Cleo and I chuckled, promising to do the spread justice. Nancy topped off our lemonades with a wink before bustling off again, leaving us to the mouthwatering feast.

Cleo reached for a fry, but I caught her hand, bringing it to my lips. Her skin was soft and warm beneath my touch, pulse fluttering at her wrist. A heartbeat passed as we stared at each other, the air between us electric with longing.

'I treasure you,' I murmured, thick with emotion. 'So much.'

'I adore you too,' she whispered back, lashes dipping to hide the sudden sheen of tears. 'More than you know.'

Unable to resist any longer, I leaned in, capturing her mouth with mine. The kiss was slow and deep, a reaffirmation of the love we shared. When we finally parted, we were both breathless, cheeks flushed with desire.

Grinning, I released her hand and snagged a fry. 'Mmm, you're right. They're perfect.'

Cleo laughed, the sound bright and carefree. She picked up her fork and dug into the pie, humming with pleasure at the first bite. 'See? I told you so.'

We ate in companionable silence for a while, savoring each mouthful.

Now and then, our hands would brush as we reached for the same dish, sending sparks skittering across my skin. I couldn't stop myself from touching her in pulse checks - a graze of fingers along her arm, a palm resting on her thigh. I knew she sensed the overwhelming need for closeness from how she leaned into me.

All my worries faded at that moment, surrounded by excellent food and even better company.

For the first time in fuckin' forever, I was contented.

Without warning, the cafe's cheerful chatter died as a familiar Ram 1500 truck screeched into the parking lot.

I sliced my eyes to the unfolding view.

Four men swung out of the car, and I froze. I recognized

them as I locked on their swaggering progress toward the diner's front door.

Fuck.

All thugs were toting guns in open carry disdain.

I was not the only apprised of the impending danger.

I leaned into my woman as people scrambled to get out of the place from the second door to the eatery's rear.

'Trust me, stay put, I'll be back,' I growled to Cleo.

Her eyes widened, and her face lost color, but she nodded.

I melted into the departing crowd.

Chapter 23

CLEO

The cafe's entrance swung open with a chime.

The staff, bustling about moments ago, appeared to vanish into thin air, behind closed doors. An eerie silence descended upon the room, broken only by heavy footsteps against the linoleum floor.

Four men strutted into the cafe, their posture oozing arrogance and menace. Their eyes scanned the room like hunters searching for prey.

I froze, realizing, with a shard of frigid angst, why Alessio had slipped out.

The Contis were on the prowl, and not just the sons.

The father himself.

Franco swaggered into the space, a towering figure, his presence heavy and hard.

The years had carved deep lines into his weathered face,

each crease telling a story of violence, power, and survival.

His dark hair, cut close to the skull, had turned all silver. His skin, tanned and rough like worn leather, was marked with tattoos—inked symbols of his past that wound around his forearms and up his neck, disappearing beneath his top collar.

The faded designs, from the snapping shark on his bicep to the snake coiled around his wrist, hinted at the ominousness oozing from him. The tattoos were old, their edges blurred, but they still held a quiet warning, reminders of battles fought and won.

His cold and calculating eyes were the color of steel, hardened from years of seeing too much. They missed nothing, scanning the room with a sharpness that left no room for doubt—this man was vicious.

His thick and scarred hands rested loosely at his sides, but they held an underlying tension, like a tight spring ready to strike at the slightest provocation.

The sweats he wore, which I deduced were fresh from prison, couldn't mask the raw, nasty edge of him.

Seeing him sent splinters of panic over me, an anxiety attack threatening.

Here was a man who had built his largesse through blood and brutality, and the air around him crackled with terror.

Bill, jaw firm, body braced for trouble, emerged from around the counter, his smaller frame juxtaposed against the newcomer's formidable figure.

'Franco, you and your boys will either put those guns away, or you'll need to leave now,' he admonished.

The Conti Don pressed his mouth into a thin, bitter line.

'Fuck off, Nichols,' Franco snarled. 'I'm now back, and I

still run this freakin' town. You don't tell me what to do.'

Bill, however, was no coward.

He stepped forward, lifting his hands. 'Get the hell out.'

Without warning, Franco's firearm went off, the loud sound cracking through the room.

I jolted as Bill groaned in agony and dropped to one knee, clutching his thigh.

Franco advanced on the fallen man, gun smoking. 'You dare spew your shit?' he screamed. 'You attemptin' to order me around?'

The voice I remembered from all those years ago triggered ice-cold fear in me, my heart erupting and shaking, praying Alessio would make it back before this bomb went off.

'You damn fuck!' Bill cried, still prone, one hand to his wound, blood oozing between his fingers.

He tilted his head back and glared at Franco. 'What the fuck's the matter with you? You shot me! You aiming to return right back into the slammer?'

'I'm endeavoring to procure what's mine.'

I'd seen enough.

'Franco Conti,' I growled, rising from behind my booth, my voice dripping with disdain. 'Still a coward, going after the innocent.'

I clenched my fists as they trembled, willing myself to stay calm.

I laser-focused on the arrogant swine before me.

The cult leader had aged over the years.

Still, he was a commanding figure who'd managed to manipulate many with his cursed tongue and creepy, oily car salesman vibe.

He stepped forward with a cruel twist to his lips, his eyes

never leaving my face.

'There she is, my prize and lady,' his lecherous voice intoned. 'We got a call saying you'd be here. Why don't you come closer, wife, and give me the kiss I've been waiting for all these years?'

My breath caught as my darkest nightmare unfolded.

That's when I saw a silhouette ease through the open door and loom behind Franco.

I released a shaky exhalation in relief at the sight of not just any man; my man. He exuded a power taken, not given, commanding sheer fear.

My eyes locked onto his vortex of sheathed strength tower-ing behind the unwitting quartet.

Franco's hubris was about to get torn up.

ALESSIO

'Put your fuckin' weapons down.'

The men before me froze, limbs locking, breaths hitching.

'I've got a 12 freakin' gauge aimed at the back of Franco's head. So unless you want to be plastered by his brains and pulp, you'll do as I damn well say.'

I sliced my eyes at my woman and tagged her wooden expression, knowing she was tense and on the edge of panic.

I'd tagged how her eyes darted to Franco, jolting at his brazen ask for a kiss.

Like hell, I'd let him touch her, I thought, my jaw clenching with barely suppressed rage.

Over my dead body.

'Do it now!' I snarled.

The Contis exchanged glances and relented, raising their hands in surrender and bending to place their guns on the floor.

'Kick them to Cleo.'

They gave a collective groan.

'Fuckin' do it, or your old man's skull is egg salad.'

They did as I demanded, flicking their feet to slide the weapons towards my woman.

I jerked my chin, and she picked them up, turning one on the cursing men.

'Mr Nichols, are you OK?'

I addressed the injured man, who had fallen silent, clenching his jaw and still clutching his thigh.

'I'll live,' he murmured.

'Nancy, please help your husband.'

His wife rushed from the kitchen where she'd been hiding. She shot me a grateful look, then, with the aid of a server, helped her man to his feet, and they limped away.

Once they were clear, I prowled around the room until my body and weapon were between Cleo and the quartet.

I sized up my opponents, my muscles tensed, ready for action.

My eyes raked over Franco.

'Fuck, you've aged,' I growled. 'Prison sure sucked the life out of you.'

The jailbird's eyes narrowed, and he stepped forward, his fists clenching at his sides.

His sons flanked him, their stances aggressive and menacing.

'Who the hell are you?' he snarled, his gaze flicking from me to Cleo. 'This is a matter for me and my fiancee. Stay out of it, or you'll regret it.'

I barked out a harsh laugh, shaking my head in disbelief. 'Your fuckin' what? You delusional piece of shit. She was never yours, and she never will be.'

As I spoke, I felt Cleo's hand on my arm, her fingers digging into my skin.

I glanced down at her, tagging the wariness and defiance warring in her eyes. She shook her head, pleading with me not to escalate the situation.

I can't back down now, carissima, I thought, my resolve hardening.

I wouldn't let him hurt her again. Not when I was still breathing.

I turned back to Franco, my stance widening as I prepared for the inevitable confrontation. 'You want her? You'll have to go through me first,' I declared, my voice ringing with conviction. 'And trust me, that's a fight you don't want to pick.'

Conti's sons shifted behind him, their faces still bearing the marks of our last encounter.

Fabio's nose was crooked, a testament to the solid right hook I'd landed, while Bruno sported a nasty black eye.

The eldest Rocco appeared wary, his jaw still bandaged and his gaze darting from his father and me.

'You think you're some kind of tough guy?' Franco sneered, his lips curling into a mocking smile. 'You have no idea who you're dealing with. I own this town, and I always get what I

247

want.'

I took a step forward, closing the distance.

'Not this time,' I rumbled with a menacing smirk. 'You're nothing but a coward who preys on the weak. But you picked the wrong mofo to mess with.'

Franco's eyes flashed with rage, and he lunged at me, his fists swinging.

I lifted my gun hand, making a point of fighting them one-handed.

I dodged his clumsy attack with ease, my reflexes honed by years of training.

I countered with a swift jab to his solar plexus and a devastating uppercut that snapped his head back.

As Franco staggered backward, his sons moved to intervene, but I was ready for them.

I spun around, delivering a roundhouse kick to Fabio's chest that sent him crashing into a nearby table.

Bruno and Rocco hesitated, open-eyed with fear.

I turned back to Franco, who was struggling to catch his breath, his face contorted with pain and humiliation.

'Last chance,' I warned, my voice cold and unyielding. 'Walk away now, and don't ever come near Cleo again. Or I swear I'll make you regret the day you were born.'

Franco glared at me, his eyes burning with hatred and defiance. 'You think you can threaten me?' he snarled, spitting blood onto the floor. 'I've been dealing with punks like you my whole life. You're nothing exceptional.'

I let out a mirthless chuckle, shaking my head. 'You still don't grasp it, do you? I'm not some small-time thug you can intimidate with your cheap guns and sweet talk. I'm the man who brought you down the first time, and I'm here to bring you down once and for all.'

I took a step closer, my timbre dropping to a whisper. 'I know all about your dirty little secrets, Franco. The loose lips in prison that led to the deaths of my mother and father.'

Cleo's breath hitched from somewhere behind me, and I comprehended I'd have some explaining to do.

Not now, however.

All I wanted at this moment was to nail Franco's ass to the wall and tear his balls from his sack.

'Who the fuck are you?' Franco asked, this time with terror lacing his utterance.

'Who the fuck am I? Don't recognize me, mofo? I'm the man who gunned you down and handed you to the authorities all those years ago. I'm the reason you suffered in prison, but not enough, it appears. You can't stay away from Cleo. So now retribution won't keep away from you.'

Franco's face paled, and I tagged the fear in his eyes.

He sensed I wasn't bluffing.

'You're lying,' he stammered, but his intonation lacked conviction. 'Vaffanculo!'

I smiled a chilly, predatory grin. 'Damn, it seems you've no idea who you're insulting. Let me remind you. I'm your worst nightmare, the monster who destroys everything of yours that he touches and will never go away until you do.'

Franco's shoulders slumped, but he still blustered, snarling at me. 'What do you want?'

I leaned in close, my lips brushing against his ear. 'I want you to disappear,' I said, cold and unforgiving. 'Depart this town, leave Cleo, and never come back. If I ever tag your fuckin' face lurking again, I'll make sure mine is the last one you have eyes on. Capisce, you octogenarian?'

My ultimatum was more than he could handle, and Franco rotated to his sons and screamed. 'What the fuck are you waiting for? Get him!'

'Tsk, tsk tsk,' I drawled, aiming my shotgun at his three progeny. 'They can try and rush me and sacrifice two of your own in an instant. You may even lose Rocco because I'm that fast of a draw. Before you dismiss me, ask your boys what I did with a hoe. What I can do with a 12 gauge is way worse.'

Franco painted on a contemptuous smile, one mired in dark wrath. 'Cleo, so you've gone and got yourself a stand-in Rambo-type boyfriend. It's OK. I understand; you needed a body to keep you warm until I returned. Now I'm back, you can drop him, my queen. I'm back, and you can return to me.'

'I was never yours. I'm everything you want but can't have,' Cleo breathed.

Franco shook with rage as he shifted his gaze to me.

'Stronzo!' the older man said, spitting onto the cafe floor. 'This asshole has turned you against me, and he will pay. Watch your backs!'

His last words were an enraged shout.

'Get the fokk outta here,' I drawled, brandishing my weapon and hinting at their exit.

Franco hesitated, glowering at me in a long stare.

'Appears the gates are down, the lights are flashing, but the train isn't roaring through,' I rasped.

Finally, the message hit home.

With a snarl, the affronted cult leader and his offspring turned and lit out of the cafe, sending hot glares our way.

'Fuckin' good riddance,' I growled as they slid into their trucks and dusted off. 'Seems the kind of man who sets low personal standards and consistently fails to achieve them.'

I sliced my eyes to Cleo. 'You fine, cara?'

She tracked to my side and wrapped an arm around me. 'That was about to be the gunfight at the OK Corral. Why are you not acting more worried?' she scolded.

'You haven't seen me shoot, woman. They had nothing on me.'

'Are you saying you're fast?'

'As lightning. When you see my guns go off, you might come in your pants.'

She laughed soft and husky, which was my end goal.

Around us, the staff sidled back in, with Mrs Nichols striding to me.

She took my hands, tears in her eyes. 'Appreciate you clearing those shitheads away.'

'How's your husband?'

'It's a flesh wound. I've got the town nurse to come into the back. Thank you so much,' she whispered, her voice trailing off.

I jerked my chin to her. 'You're welcome.'

I turned to Cleo. 'I have to do something, bella.'

While my woman helped the cafe staff clean up, I strode back to our booth and sat, turning on my phone for the first time in days.

The network bars and Wi-Fi signal flickered as messages and missed calls, most from Mauri and Lorenzo, pinged in.

I chose not to call my brother.

Instead, I sent a text reassuring the mofo that I was okay and that I'd made an oath to help a friend and to be on standby.

I also flicked over photos Cleo and I had taken of the Conti farm to Mauri and Lorenzo.

In minutes, I received a response from Lorenzo saying he'd

send them to Sovereign and Saint Tahana, who'd ensure the AFP would look into it.

Fuck yeah.

Chapter 24

CLEO

The truck hugged the curves of the mountain road, tires crunching over gravel and dried leaves. Shafts of golden sunlight slanted through the pine branches, striping the rugged slopes in saffron and shadow.

I'd insisted on driving back. 'I know all the potholes and ditches from Moss Vale to home.'

Still, as I gripped the steering wheel, I inhaled quickly, needing reassurance from what was bothering me.

Alessio stared through the windshield, watching the ridge crests burn rose gold in the fading light, his handsome face in profile. The air between us was taut, heavy with unspoken words.

Soon, I couldn't wait any more.

I pulled the car to the side of the mountain track, the late afternoon radiance filtering through the trees and dappling the windowpane.

I turned in my seat to face him, my expression pensive, the weight of implicit thoughts pressing against my lips, a dam ready to burst.

He shifted in his chair, the leather creaking.

'Alessio,' trying to make sense of my spiraling thoughts. 'I need to ask you something -.'

My voice trailed off.

'Si,' he rasped, brushing a stray hair on my forehead. 'What's on your mind, cara?'

I caught his hand, lacing our fingers together. 'Alessio, I -' I paused, gaze dropping to our intertwined hands. 'You said something at the cafe. That you were the man who brought him down the first time. You also stated his loose lips in prison led to the deaths of your mother and father. What was that all about?'

He sucked his teeth and took a hissed inhale.

With a sigh, he rubbed a hand over his jaw, rugged with stubble.

'Cleo,' he began, voice rough with emotion. 'What I'm about to tell you is not easy to share. But you deserve to know the truth, cara. So here goes. Franco Conti has been on my kill list for many years. It all originated with your grandfather.'

My eyebrow arched. 'Poppa?'

Alessio nodded. 'Not sure if you knew, but he was an ex-mafia capo for the Omertà alliance.'

A jolt of shock hit me. 'What the hell?'

'It's true. Your grandfather went by the pseudonym Cesare Michele. His real name was Cosimo Matteo from Napoli. He was about to go to jail for murder when my Poppa, Constantino, helped him escape to Australia, where he changed

254

his identity and disappeared as best he was able. However, he and Constantino remained friends until my grandfather died. When you were kidnapped by Conti and brought to Naples to have your sham marriage blessed by the pope, that's when your Poppa called my dad, Stephano, to help. I was sent to rescue you.'

I stared at him, shaking my head. 'I'd no idea.'

'It's an old oath that we were determined to keep.'

I sat silent, eyes fixed on the road ahead, heart racing.

I faced him and touched his arm, still parsing what he'd told me. 'I thank you for keeping that promise, honey.'

He stuck a tongue in his cheek and growled, 'So you're not mad at me?'

'I might say fuck you, but that'd make me a bitch. You gave me my life back, Alessio, and I appreciate you for it. Please know that. Although using a gun on me this time and telling a white lie about my Nonna was scraping the barrel.'

'I'm so sorry, mia sola,' he groaned, raw and ragged, as moisture misted my eyes. 'Shit strategy, but I wasn't sure if you'd let me into your world unless –'

'Unless you bulldozed your way in! Typical man. Why didn't you just ask?'

I laughed in between my tears.

He reached a hand and stroked the corner of my temple. 'I froze. Just like I did when I first rescued you because I had an MS flare and went numb in the hand holding to you.'

'Is that right?'

'Si. You ran off, and I strung up Franco. When I'd tied him up, I searched his hotel room. I found weapons, drugs, and all the evidence that he'd kidnapped you and handed him and the proof over to the authorities. He got put away for a few good years. During that time, he somehow learned the Calibrese family was involved in his imprisonment, and he never forgave us for snatching his bride-to-be away and landing him in prison. So he started rumors in jail of how my father, Stephano, conspired against Carlo Abrazzio. The long and short of it, an already paranoid Carlo thought the hearsay was true and bombed my parents' and uncle's car, killing them. As head capo of my family, this was shit I couldn't let fly. Since then, I've kept tabs on Franco and you. Waiting for the right moment to strike.'

Alessio paused, the pain of that betrayal still fresh in his mind.

I tagged and squeezed his hand, urging him to continue.

'He couldn't get to me, so he went after the people I loved most.'

Alessio's voice cracked, and I swallowed hard against the lump in my throat, feeling his anguish. 'He had them killed, Cleo. And it was all because of me. I should have eliminated Franco on the night I found him with you in Naples. Instead, I let the fuzz take him. Not knowing how he'd knife us in the back in the worst way possible.'

The words hung heavy between us, the weight of his confession almost suffocating.

My eyes glistened with unshed tears, my hand tightening around his as I processed the revelation.

'Baby,' I whispered, voice trembling. 'I'm so sorry. I can't even imagine the pain you must have gone through.'

He shook his head, a bitter smile tugging at his sensual lips. 'It's grief I've carried with me every day since. A constant reminder of the consequences of my actions, of the price others paid for my mistakes.'

I reached up, palm cupping his cheek as I forced him to meet my gaze. 'You can't blame yourself, Alessio. You were doing your job, trying to bring a dangerous man to justice. What happened to your parents, that's on Franco, not you.'

He leaned into my touch, drawing strength from my unwavering support. 'I know that, logically. But it doesn't make the guilt any easier to bear.'

'Baby,' I breathed, stroking his jaw.

'What are you thinking?' he rasped. 'Does this change how you see me? Us?'

Silence stretched between us, and the only sounds were the distant chirping of birds and the gentle rustle of leaves in the breeze.

He turned to look at me, but I fixed my eyes on the road ahead.

When I spoke again, I kept my tone soft.

'It changes us for the better. You risked your life for me, honey, then and now. For that, I love you even more.'

His voice hitched, a hoarse timbre dragging out of me. 'You love me?'

I tapped my heart, giving him the fullness of my soul, smiling at him.

It'd been a short time together, but one so intense it felt like I'd known him for years. Which made my declaration that much more poignant given the shit we'd been through.

'Fuck woman, stop,' he grunted, those sensual lips curling, his leonine eyes flashing. 'If you don't, you'll need to give me your heartbeat because you're taking off with mine.'

He leaned in and took my jaw, gentle thumb caressing my cheek. 'Ti amo. Sei la mia anima gemella, you're my dream mate, Cleo.'

I slid across the truck's bench seat, burying my nose in his nape.

He inhaled, and his musk and scent filled my lungs as he held me close. The scorching heat of his body against me was all I needed to exist.

Taking my time, I pulled back, his hands stroking my face.

'I meant every word,' he murmured. 'Franco's carelessness cost my parents their lives. Bringing him to justice is the only way to honor their memory.'

I exhaled, my shoulders rising and falling with emotion under my thin sweater. 'Why didn't you tell me sooner? Did you not trust me?'

'No, cara, never that.' Alessio reached for my free hand, lacing their fingers together. My skin was cool, the slim bones delicate beneath his rough palm. 'I wanted to protect you from my past. From the man I was before.'

'The man you are is all that matters to me.' I shot him a glance, my eyes green and gold in the honeyed light. 'No more secrets, Alessio. Promise me.'

'No more,' he vowed, lifting my hand to brush his lips across my knuckles. 'From now on, you'll know everything. My heart is an open book.'

I sighed and glanced away from him, eyes canted to the view outside the car window.

'You're one of a kind man,' I whispered. 'Rare,' I added as if not quite believing it.

'Why do you say so?'

I turned to lock eyes with Alessio. 'Because most men I've encountered have been monsters. They've suffered no consequences for the horrible things they've perpetrated on women. Despite their behavior, I've had to retain hope and

258

keep fucking trucking, no matter what they'd done to me, or I'd have been too angry to live.'

My voice rose, the bitterness within me welling up. 'From my father to Franco and his sons, my lifetime has been spent witnessing others manipulating, lying, bullying, misleading, and freakin' forcing marriage on me — all consequence-free.'

'You've earned your anger,' Alessio rasped, his finger stroking my cheek.

'Damn right I have,' I growled. 'But I've worked hard not to let it poison me by isolating myself to heal.'

'And have you healed?' He murmured.

'I'm getting close,' I told him, facing him. 'You need to know, baby, that for me to love and trust you means you need to see me for everything I am. To recognize the façade of quiet calm I put on for the world is nothing more than a mask. The question is: Will you want to know and love it all? My flaws, my past, my shit?'

I raised my face in defiance, daring him, my heart pounding as his eyes narrowed in contemplation, never leaving my face.'

His hand moved to cradle my chin. 'Here's a question for you: Will you love me all with my kinks, my resting badass face, my morally gray sins, and my gruffness?'

He had a point.

'Cara, we're both broken to some degree,' he rumbled in his deep timbre. 'We both, unfortunately, or fortunately, carry the bullshit of our fucked up past. This means we understand each other more than anyone else would, making us each other's haven, our safe space. Will you trust that united and on the same team, we'll make sure Franco pays for everything he's done to you and countless others?'

I gave him a long look. 'Only if we do it by the book. No

more secrets, no more going it alone.'

'Fuck yeah, we're doing it together, and secret-free,' he grunted, pulling me into his arms and holding me close once more.

Chapter 25

CLEO

We drove back to the cabin with hands entwined.

Sunset serenaded us all the way home.

We arrived ready to call it a day, yet we still needed to unpack my truck and put away all the shopping and supplies.

Half an hour later, Alessio glanced at me as he closed the door of the supply shed.

'I don't know about you,' he rasped, 'but I need a shower.'

Sweat trickled between my boobs, and I nodded. 'I'm with you.'

'Is that right, bella, with me?

His eyes twinkled at his deliberate misunderstanding.

Gazing at him, the day's emotion overwhelmed me.

I reached a hand for his cheek, thumbing and stroking his beard and jawline, which I adored. 'Si, baby, with you.'

His eyes glittered as he got the memo.

'You're on protection?' he growled.

I assented. 'I'm on the pill. It's the best way to manage here on the farm as I can't have much downtime and I've got a history of bad cramps.'

'Scusa, bella, sorry to hear.'

'And honey, are you done with your *l'uomo e cacciatore* gameplay?'

He huffed, lips turning up. 'Forget that shit. If I don't cum inside you today, I'll blow. I crave you, woman, and I need you now.'

He drew me close, his mouth soft and warm against mine. Our bodies melded together, the previous hours of longing and anticipation unleashed.

Tongues danced and explored as his hands roamed all over me. He traced the curve of my back and the swell of my hips as we walked to the outhouse, our boots creaking on the wooden floors.

He pushed its door open, and for a moment, my knees weakened at the sight of his sinewed, capable fingers that would be soon on me, in me.

Oh my!

Inside, we kicked off our shoes and began to undress each other.

With slow deliberation, as if we had all the time in the world.

I traced the lines of his muscles, the scars telling stories of a life lived, the hardness of his physique speaking of the strength he possessed. He did the same to me, his touch feather-light and tender.

His hands roamed my curves, tracing the curve of my back and the swell of my hips.

I reached up under his shirt, the tension of our desire building between us. We broke the kiss long enough to remove our clothes, leaving only our hearts bare.

I stared at him, loving his muscled, beautiful body.

His build was a work of art, every muscle chiseled and toned as if carved by a master sculptor. He stood before me, uncovered and raw, with a confident stance, his dark blonde hair tousled and his deep hazel gold eyes filled with lust.

The whole of him was gorgeous, from the arch of his brows to the curve of his lips, his skin a canvas for his life story.

The dim light of the outhouse cast shadows across his sculpted chest and defined arms. Each tricep visible rippled with his movements. His toned abdomen led downward to a thick, distinct set of legs. He was like a masterpiece carved out of stone.

It was his cock, bobbing, long, throbbing, and its mush-roomed head that had me gasping.

'Is that a piercing?'

'Say hi to my Prince Albert,' he growled as I stared at the jewelry at the base of his head.

'Did it hurt?' I asked, reaching a hand and stroking it, squeezing his shaft head around it.

He hissed with pleasure, his golden head thrown back to the outhouse wall, the veins in his neck corded and rippling.

He bucked into my hand for a moment, speechless from the ecstasy.

'It wasn't too bad. I was fuckin' careful, though,' he snarled, moving his head and staring down as I palmed and stroked him in exploration. 'Because inexperienced piercers can cause irreversible damage to your jewels.'

He placed a sinewed hand over me when my strokes deepened. 'Fuck cara, give me time. I'll blow if you keep going like this.'

His cologne and musk mingled with the fresh air and cedar pouring from the half-open window. Creating an earthy and intoxicating aroma that made me crave him even more.

As my fingers trailed down his body, I ran them over the sometimes velvety skin, dotted with the roughness of brawling calluses and old wounds from a lifetime of Omertà work.

But underneath was hard, rippling muscle that I loved running my hands over.

He was a marble sculpture come to life, chiseled and perfect, with smooth contours and strong lines begging to be touched and adored.

My eyes roamed over his form, worshiping every inch and curve. Loving every fuckin' cut and sculpt of his abs.

Until my gaze settled on his face, the window to his soul and the truest reflection of his beauty.

Turning on the shower, he pulled me close.

I gasped as water cascaded over us, washing away the remnants of our day, each touch igniting a spark of electricity between us.

He found the body wash on the shelf and used it with liberal generosity, covering us both in frothy suds.

As he cleaned me, his sizable, rough hands traced my silhouette, his fingers leaving a trail of heat and desire in their wake. They explored my dips and curves, adoring the lines and contours of my form.

He had a way of stroking me that had me so wet.

I adored how his eyes flamed, his mouth pursed, oh so sexy, when he touched me.

The way he sized my body up and down with sensual lasciviousness, worshiping me with murmurs in Italian, slight hisses, and licks that made me hot.

When his fingers hit my sensitive nerve clusters, I keened, falling weak in his arms.

I wanted his touch in all my spaces, my folds, heating me, scorching me.

His hands were fire on my skin, igniting a spark of electricity between us. Calloused and scarred from a lifetime of work, they moved with a tenderness and gentleness that belied their rough exterior.

'You are so beautiful, mia sola.'

Every caress was a love song, each stroke a masterpiece painted with passion and devotion.

His mouth glided over my curves, my breasts, and my hips, his intensity pouring into me, a sweet and heady elixir that I couldn't get enough of.

When the water ran clear, he upped the ante, licking and suckling my tits, his fingers plumbing my pussy, thumb working my clit.

All I could do was hold on to his shoulders as he rippled over me, groaning against my skin.

'Alessio, I can't – I need you inside me,' I pleaded, my voice ragged with yearning.

I writhed my lower tummy and pelvis over his scorching, thick cock, seeking more.

He didn't have to be told twice. With a guttural grunt, he pulled away from my wet, sopping core, his hand glistening with my juice. He took a moment to admire me, my skin flushed and saturated, eyes dark with desire.

Stepping close, he banded a muscled arm around my ass

and lifted me, legs still spread wide for him.

He was hard and throbbing, the head slippery with pre-cum. I reached out, grasped it, and began to stroke him, my gaze never leaving his.

'Please, Alessio,' I whispered.

I needed to feel his rock-solid dick deep in me.

He took my cue, planting one hand on the shower wall behind me.

The other lined up his penis at the entrance to my wet, slick pussy. His eyes locked onto mine. My breath was snatched away by the desire burning within them.

'Are you sure?' he rasped, his voice heavy with lust.

I nodded as the urge to have him root me overwhelmed my entirety.

'Fill me, to take me in every way possible, honey,' I breathed, reaching up to pull him closer. 'Fuck me.'

He didn't need a second invitation.

With a groan, he thrust forward, burying his entire length in one fluid motion. I cried out in pleasure and arched my back, my nails digging into his shoulders as he began to push into me.

'Fotto!' he cursed, his eyes rolling back as I enveloped him, the nubbed edges of his piercing working all the way into my pussy until he was anchored deep within me.

I moaned as his cock stretched me open, filling me. His warm hardness was incredible inside me, and I bucked, unable to believe this was happening.

Once he was implanted all in me, he stilled for a moment, his eyes locked with mine.

'You OK, cara?'

My eyes misted at his concern, and I nodded I was okay.

Bene,' he growled.

With a melting kiss, he pistoned with abandon, thrusting so hard I nearly blacked out from the pleasure, giving in to the ride of my life.

His shaft, thick and stiff, hit all the right spots in me as he moved in and out. I wrapped my legs around his hips, pulling him deeper.

He began to move, his pelvis rocking against me, his member sliding in and out of my pussy with an intoxicating rhythm.

Each jab brought a different ecstasy crashing over me, my nerve endings lit. I responded to his with a fire that ratcheted with each passing moment.

He was a force of nature, and every movement was a testament to the raw, untamed passion that had been building between us.

His cock and that freakish piercing hit my clit, sinking into my G-spot with each forceful plunge.

The resulting exquisite sensation had me gasping for breath, shuddering with pleasure.

He was a master of lovemaking, every lunge calculated to bring me to the height of ecstasy.

As he continued to drill into me with a primal intensity, I reached up to pull his face down to mine.

Needing to feel his lips on me, to savor the passion that burned between us.

Our tongues danced and mingled, our bodies in perfect sync, as we lost ourselves in the raw, animalistic bliss of our union.

Alessio's hands gripped my ass, pulling me harder onto his cock, his groin moving in a frantic rhythm, his mouth devouring mine.

His shaft pounded inside me, ready to explode with his seed.

'Fuck,' he growled, eyes locking on my face.

I moaned, my climax building, wanting to reach it with him.

I neared the brink, Alessio's eyes fixed on mine, his expression intense, his face contorted with desire. 'Cum for me, mia sola,' he urged.

With that, I thrust my hips up to meet his.

'I'm so close,' I gasped, tensing, my pussy clenching around his dick.

He groaned, his cock twitching, throbbing, pulsing, and then he was roaring, cumming too, his thickness pulsating in me, releasing deluges and cascades of his hot, thick seed.

'Yes!' I cried, writhing, my orgasm bursting through me, my mind spinning with pleasure.

He kept fucking me, still buried in me, his lips still locked with mine, as we both rode out our climaxes together.

Shaking and trembling, we came down from our high, our bodies still joined, our breathing slowing.

The steam from the shower fogged up the floor-to-ceiling glass window as dusk's gold luminescence shone over us.

Chapter 26

CLEO

Alessio's fingertips traced light circles on the bare skin of my back.

We lay tangled together in my bed, the first rays of dawn peeking through the lace curtains.

I sighed, pressing closer to his warmth.

'Again, amore mio?' he murmured, voice husky with sleep and desire.

I smiled and shifted to straddle him.

'Always,' I breathed against his lips before losing myself again in his tender caresses and passionate kisses.

We'd made love for most of the night.

Each touch, kiss, rocking, and stroking of his fingers and cock elicited new waves of ecstasy, every one more intense than the last.

I quivered and shook, my pussy throbbing and pulsing as

he took me to the brink again and again, leaving me in a state of bliss.

I'd come so many times to count. My cunt wouldn't stop rippling for hours under his ministrations.

I was obsessed, addicted.

Now, still needing him, I swung a thigh over him and lowered my pelvis over his groin.

With a sigh, I pulled his thickness, headed with his cock ring, into me, sighing as his head tapped my damp curls and slid in, striking all my pleasure points.

He thumbed my nipples, and I flattened my hand on his chest and bent over him to give him purchase.

He sucked and plumped my tits, dragging a calloused finger, pinching and pulling as I writhed and rolled my midsection.

I gasped, 'I need you now, make me cum.'

'Your wish is my desire,' he growled, his thickness stimulating all the wild spots, his arm a warm anchor as I rode his hips.

He moved with me, his hands guiding my motion, his lips nuzzling my neck, his tongue a heated tease.

I cried out, 'I'm almost there. Deeper, harder, baby.'

'So greedy,' he rasped. 'Greedy for my cock.'

We locked eyes. Damn, those leonine eyes, they gave me fever.

I felt the heat through to my clit.

He thrust more forcefully, driving me over the edge, that fucking piercing hitting me just right, sending me into a frenzy.

'Oh fotto!' He grunted, his pelvis jerking, hips bucking, every drive bringing him closer to his release.

With a growl, he turned me over, his strength making the

interchange smooth as fuck, still powering in me as he shifted us.

My thighs went around his waist. I clawed at his back, my nails leaving crescents of pain, my climax coursing through me, my form on fire, my pussy throbbing, needing more.

'Love me harder, honey,' I begged, my voice husky with desire, my being trembling with need.

He pistoned into my G-spot, stretching me wide, driving into my sensitive flesh. My walls clenched and squeezed, yet another peak building, my thighs shuddering from the intensity of it.

'Cum for me, mia sola,' he growled, his eyes locked on me, his growl thick with lust.

When I sat up, staring at our joining to the hilt, shaking, he shoved a hand in my hair and snarled into my ear. 'Now.'

I cried out, shuddering, releasing oceans of pleasure that washed over me, my pussy clenching around his cock.

Alessio's hips bucked, thrusting deep in me, his jeweled head stroking at me, his eyes fixed on mine as he came.

He roared, jolting with the force of his release pulsating inside me, his cum filling me.

I milked his seed from him. It felt so wild, so heated, so fucking good.

Panting, I fell back, gasping, panting, unable to contain the waves of ecstasy washing over me.

'Lo e te tre metri sopra il cielo,' he growled into my nape, still jerking until his ecstasy passed.

Many moments later, I spoke into his corded neck, with him still buried in me. 'What did that mean?'

He pulled up, eyes gleaming. 'It's from some cheesy Italian film and means you and me, floating three meters above the heavens. Which is how this night was for me, bella.'

I appreciated the sanctity of the words, for this man had a way of making me fly higher than I'd ever done.

He knifed and kissed me long and slow before easing out of me to fetch a towel.

He cleaned me, then he fell back into my arms.

Sometime later, the insistent grumble of my stomach roused us from bed.

Alessio chuckled and swatted my behind. 'Up and at 'em, carissima. I'll tend the fire if you make us some breakfast.'

'Deal.'

I wrapped myself in the quilt and padded to the kitchenette while he crouched by the hearth, coaxing the embers back to crackling flames.

As I whisked eggs and warmed crusty bread, I couldn't help sneaking glances at my gorgeous, golden Italian stallion, all lean muscle and sun-bronzed skin in the firelight.

How did I get so lucky?

Alessio caught me staring and smirked. 'See something you like?'

'Always,' I quipped, echoing my earlier response.

Happiness bloomed warm in my chest.

In our cozy little love nest, the rest of the world seemed to melt away - no Contis, no threats of vengeance looming. Just us, basking in our newfound adoration and passion. I'd never felt so free, so utterly myself.

If only these perfect moments could last forever, I mused.

But I pushed those thoughts aside, determined to savor every second we did have.

'Breakfast is served, handsome.'

After devouring the simple but satisfying meal of scrambled

eggs and chives on toast, Alessio and I gathered up the dishes. Making our way down to the creek, shivering in the crisp morning air.

The water was bracing and ice cold, but we laughed and splashed each other while scrubbing the plates and utensils clean.

'You've got soap suds in your hair,' he murmured, reaching out to brush them away. His touch sent delicious tingles across my skin.

'Whose fault is that?' I retorted, flicking droplets at him. He grinned, unrepentant.

God, that smile.

It turned my insides to molten honey every time.

After the dishes were done, we stripped off our clothes and plunged into the creek, gasping at the shock of cold. Still, it felt glorious and refreshing, washing away the last cobwebs of sleep and sex funk.

We swam, stealing kisses and long, sensual strokes underwater.

When goosebumps prickled our skin, we clambered and dried off with the towels we'd brought.

'What's on the agenda today?' I asked as I tugged on my outfit. 'Gardening or perimeter check?'

Alessio's expression sobered. 'We'd better inspect the property lines first. Can't be too careful, with the Contis still out for blood.' A shadow crossed his handsome face, but he shook it off. 'Your prize tomatoes can wait a tad.'

I nodded, a frisson of unease creeping up my spine at the reminder of the danger lurking outside our refuge.

Sensing my inner tension, Alessio squeezed my hand in reassurance. 'Don't worry, mia sola. I won't let anything happen to you or this place. I promise.'

'I know,' I murmured, lacing my fingers through his.

Hand in hand, we set off to walk the perimeter, eyes peeled for any signs of trouble. Despite the looming threat, I couldn't help treasuring these moments. The solidness of his presence beside me, the whisper of the wind through the trees, the crystal-bright clarity of the morning light.

A thought struck me as we reached one corner of the property.

I turned to Alessio, searching his face. 'Why are we waiting for them to hit us?' I asked, puzzled. 'Why not take the fight to them, catch them off guard?'

Alessio's jaw tightened, a muscle ticking in his cheek. He was silent for a beat, staring out over the rolling hills. When he spoke, his voice was flat and hard.

'So I have the best excuse for un-aliving him,' he growled with a brutal edge. 'Going to him is murder and could land me in jail. He coming here is self-defense on my part.'

I sucked in a sharp breath, stunned by the icy logic of his words. Of course, I knew Alessio was more than capable of violence – I'd seen it firsthand.

To hear him speak so calm and collected of killing, even in defense of my home and our lives, however, sent a chill through me.

And yet, beneath the shock, I understood. Alessio's ruthlessness had been forged in the crucible of an unforgiving life.

He'd learned that sometimes, the only way to protect what you loved was to be harder, more ruthless than those who would destroy it.

I swallowed hard, my heart aching for the boy he had been,

for all the choices that had been ripped away from him.

Wordlessly, I stretched to cup his face, my thumb brushing the proud jut of his cheekbone.

'I hate that it has to be this way,' I murmured. 'I loathe that you have to carry this burden, Alessio.'

His eyes gleamed. 'I detest that you, too, had to endure so much because of him.'

He leaned into my touch, his eyes drifting closed for a brief moment.

Tears pricked at my eyes, and I reached for his hand, twining our fingers together. 'I know you will,' I whispered. 'I trust you, Alessio. With my life, with my love, with everything I am.'

He lifted our joined hands to his lips, pressing a fervent kiss to my knuckles. 'Ti amo, amore mio,' he murmured. 'Always and forever.'

When he opened them again, they were softer, warmer. He turned his head to press his lips once more on my palm.

He straightened, squaring his shoulders as if shrugging off a heavy weight. 'Come on, let's finish the rounds, and I'll do some work securing the place. Afterward, I'll make you dinner.'

I nodded, mustering a smile. 'Sounds perfect.'

Over the next few hours, Alessio threw himself into fortifying the farm.

After raising my barn and sheds for material, he loaded up his Defender and headed for the gate and perimeter fence leading off it.

I stood by him, handing him tools and nails as he strung tripwires along the perimeter and camouflaged snares in the underbrush.

He even rigged up some nasty surprises involving rusty spikes and well-placed boards.

'Who are you?' I asked him at one point.

'Being a Maggiore in the Italian Alpine units meant I learned much about stringing up traps,' he murmured.

I stared, awed and also unsettled by his single-minded focus. It was a stark reminder of the dangerous world he came from, the brutal life he'd left behind. But it was a testament to his fierce willpower to protect what was ours.

When night fell, we retired to the farmhouse, the crackling fire and soft lamplight casting a warm glow over the rustic room.

Alessio surprised me with a special dinner. The scent of garlic and butter wafted through the air, making my mouth water and my stomach growl.

'What's all this?' I asked, wandering into the kitchen.

My golden lion stood at the stove, stirring a pot of bubbling pasta with a look of intense concentration on his face.

He glanced up at me, a smile tugging at the corners of his lips. 'It's a surprise,' he said, his voice low and warm. 'An old famiglia recipe, straight from the heart of Naples.'

I leaned against the counter, watching him work. There was something almost hypnotic about how he moved, his hands sure and steady as he chopped mushrooms and grated cheese. I could have observed him forever, lost in the rhythm of his motions and the play of muscles beneath his skin.

'It's called 'miezi paccheri alla capa 'e' mbrello,' he said, the words rolling off his tongue like a song. 'Pasta with mushrooms and cream. Simple, but delicious.'

My stomach growled again, louder this time, and he chuckled. 'Patience, amore mio,' he murmured, brushing a kiss against my temple. 'Good things come to those who wait.'

And so I waited, the anticipation building.

When, at last, he set a steaming plate of pasta before me, the aroma was intoxicating, the flavors bursting on my tongue like fireworks.

'Alessio,' I breathed, my eyes fluttering closed in ecstasy. 'This is incredible.'

He smirked, looking pleased with himself. 'I told you,' he said, twirling his fork in his food. 'Simple, but delicious.'

We ate in silence for a few moments, savoring every bite. I couldn't remember when I'd savored something so perfect, so satisfying, imbued with Alessio's love and passion.

'Thank you,' I said at last, reaching across the table to take his hand in mine. 'For this, for everything. I don't know what I did to justify you, but I'm so grateful.'

He squeezed my fingers, his eyes soft and warm in the candlelight. 'You deserve the world, mia sola mio,' he murmured. 'And I intend to give it to you, one meal at a time.'

I laughed, my heart so full it overflowed with emotion. 'If this is what your pasta does to me, I can't imagine what other tricks you have up your sleeve.'

Alessio's grin turned wicked, his eyes smoldering. 'Oh, I have plenty of tricks,' he purred, his voice low and sultry. 'But those are best saved for dessert, don't you think?'

I shivered, heat pooling in my belly at the promise in his words. 'Dessert, huh?' I managed, my mouth dry. 'And what did you have in mind for that?'

He leaned forward, his breath warm on my ear. 'Let me surprise you,' he whispered, nipping at my earlobe. 'But first, we finish this masterpiece of a meal.'

I nodded, not trusting myself to speak. We ate the rest of

our pasta in charged silence, the air between us thick with anticipation. Every brush of Alessio's foot on my leg under the table sent sparks skittering across my skin, each heated glance stoking the flames of my desire.

By the time our plates were clean, I was vibrating with need. Alessio stood, holding his hand to me with a smoldering look that made my knees weak. I took it, allowing him to pull me to my feet and into his arms.

'Now,' he growled, his lips brushing against mine. 'Let me show you just how sweet dessert can be.'

That night, he took our loving to a new level, one so stratospheric I thought I'd never come down.

The pale moonlight streaming through the window highlighted the curves of our entwined bodies, slick with sweat and glowing in the dim light. My lover's face was a mask of concentration and desire as he pleasured me.

His tongue traced a path down my belly, his hand gripping my backside and pulling me down onto him, his hand moving in rhythmic motions between my thighs.

'I want to go so deep in you, mia sola, and make you feel like you've never done before.'

'How?' I whispered. 'How can you possibly take me higher?'

He bent over me, giving me a long look, and breathed into my ear. 'I want to take your ass.'

He pulled up to gauge my response.

I stared at him, slow-blinking, playing with the idea.

With a shaky breath, I nodded, granting him my most profound trust. My knees were weak and molten, and arcs of electricity soared through me. 'Whatever you want, have your way.'

'You'll never regret this,' he growled against my nape, doing away any last fragments of doubt with a soul-melting kiss.

Damn, he was going for it and freakin' going to balls to the wall.

His tongue traveled over my body, all the way to my pussy where he pushed my thighs as far as they could go, exposing all of me to him.

He dipped his head and took his time, edging me. Sucking my clit, then pulling away when I was about to peak over and over until I was soaking the towel he'd placed under my ass with my spurting need.

Priming me, oiling me, working my cunt and button with a gentle intensity that had me writhing.

I reached for his cock, grabbing it, stroking, squeezing as his head spurted with precum.

'Fotto, Cleo,' he snarled.

He returned the favor, fucking me with his fingers and hand, slipping and sliding over my folds, flooding his hand with my juices.

'Ready?' he grunted, neck corded, eyes so hot as he stared at me mewling, wanting so bad to come.

'Per favore, baby,' I begged.

'Il piacere e tutto mio, my utter pleasure,' he growled.

He sat up, legs tucked under him and tugging my hips so

my ass cheeks rested on his knees.

His golden tresses fell to his shoulders, veins standing out on his brow as he, with great care, guided his cock, so thick and throbbing, into my ass.

He went slow, allowing me to get used to his girth in my virgin cavity.

At first, I gasped at his thickness, and my gaze fluttered away, overwhelmed by the sensations crashing over me.

'Keep looking at me,' my man growled. 'Don't be shy on me, bella.'

I met his amber eyes, mine shimmering with tears, as ecstasy and feeling surged all around us.

He held my hand and squeezed, lending me his strength.

I flooded from my slit, and he stroked me, letting my wet coat our joining.

'Fuck yourself on me, carissima,' he invited, his growl thick with lust.

I hissed, arched my spine as I obeyed.

I placed one foot on his chest for leverage, canted my waist, and slicked myself over him as his fingers plundered my pussy.

It was beyond wild.

'Ride me,' he rasped, raw and coarse with need.

He held his hips still while I drove mine along his thick length. Rocking onto him, I took him into me one inch at a time as I got used to his girth, shaking from the growing euphoria of the wild sensation.

When he was finally buried to the hilt, he took over. His hands gripped my ass tighter, pulling me closer, his cock sliding deeper in and out of me with a rhythm that was equally maddening and exhilarating.

Each piston brought a different wave of bliss, my being

responding to his with an intensity that was both passionate and intense.

His fingers moved up and down my skin as I wailed, writhed, and screamed, pinching my nipples, moaning, the pleasure building within me, trembling with every touch.

He slowed his movements, his eyes locking onto mine, the desire in his eyes burning bright.

'I'm cumming,' I breathed, my muscles tensing, clenching tight onto his cock.

His shaft swelled even more inside me as if he was trying to reach deeper into my core, maximizing the ecstasy I was feeling.

He increased the intensity of his thrusts, his hips driving into me with incessant power. His piercing hit the most sensitive of spots, causing me to convulse in a combination of sweet agony and pleasure.

At the sound of my moans, he encircled my thighs, pulling me closer.

His lips found mine, melding our tongues and mouth me with an insistent hunger, his essence mingling with me as our bodies moved in perfect sync.

With a growl, he thrust into me one last time, his cock pulsing deep inside me.

Filling me with a burning heat, the sensation of his piercing sent undulations of delight coursing through me.

I sank my hands in his golden tresses as such a sweet bliss hit that I burst into tears.

'Let go, bella. Allow this moment to take you where you've never been.'

And so I did, surrendering to the intense ripples that washed over me. I shuddered and convulsed around him; my mind was lost in a blissful abyss.

It was unending, shattering, spectacular, and in my bliss, my thighs caged his torso, gripping so hard that my muscles flexed.

He powered into me, cumming hard, flinging his head back as he roared into his climax.

Falling on me, he groaned into my nape as I pushed my hands through his hair, stroking his golden mane as his hips kept undulating in his come-down.

And as the waves of pleasure receded, we lay tangled in each other's arms, our bodies slick with sweat and passion.

'You OK?' he growled at one point. 'You rode hard, bellissima.'

'I'm more than OK,' I reassured him. 'You blew my mind.'

He grunted into my neck, hands wrapped around me, his chest rising and falling, still buried deep inside me, his piercing pulsating in me.

Still joined, I couldn't help but feel a sense of peace and contentment wash over me.

He kept me tight and close, and I welcomed his weight, musk, and heat. Our hearts beat in sync, our souls entwined in a way that could never be broken.

I kissed him, my lips lingering on his, our tongues dancing together.

This wasn't just an act of love but a connection beyond the physical.

It was pure magnificence.

Chapter 27

ALESSIO

A sharp noise pierced the silence, jolting me awake.

My eyes snapped open, my heart thudding against my rib cage as I lay motionless, straining my hearing. The room was enveloped in an inky blackness, a darkness that only existed at night when even the moon declined to shine.

The cabin creaked and groaned, settling in the stillness of the night. Seconds ticked by, turning into minutes, but the eerie quiet remained unbroken.

Had it been a figment of my imagination?

With care, I reached for the nightstand, my fingers fumbling in the dark until they brushed against the cold metal of my phone.

The screen illuminated, casting a faint blue glow across my face—2:00 a.m.

A sense of unease crept up my spine, sending a shiver through my body despite the warmth of the bed covers.

I rose, untangling myself from Cleo's legs, and went to the veranda.

That's when I spotted lights and sirens wailing, their piercing cry carried on the wind, mingling with the distant thrum of helicopter blades.

Headed towards the Contis farm.

I smirked in the dark.

It appeared justice had finally caught up with the fuckers.

A soft rustling sound behind me snagged my attention.

I turned to see Cleo standing in the doorway to the terrace.

The faint moonlight illuminated her silhouette, her lashes casting feathered shadows on her cheeks in the molten light.

Even in the darkness, I tagged the concern on her face.

'What's going on?' she asked, her voice thick from sleep.

Taking a step, her hands slid around my waist. I pulled her tight, loving her scent, the gentle rise and fall of her breath as she nestled her face into the crook of my neck.

'It's going down,' I rasped. 'Looks like the feds decided to raid their little operation.'

I pulled my woman close, and we stood, eyes on the distant lights flickering and dancing.

Fotto! This was just the beginning.

The Contis were like cockroaches—they always found a way to survive and come back stronger and more vicious than ever.

They wouldn't let this transgression slide. They'd come after us, seeking blood for our betrayal. It was inevitable, and how so many desperate souls I'd dealt with in the past operated.

My mind raced with contingency plans forming and discarding themselves in rapid succession.

We had to be ready for whatever came next, whether it was the Contis or the Caputos chasing retribution for the fallout of their criminal hustle.

Those sons of bitches weren't going to go down without a fight.

No way in hell would I let my back down. I had to protect my woman and do it with ruthlessness while exacting my vengeance.

I turned to Cleo, pulling her close, burying my face in her hair, breathing in her scent. Franco and his progeny may have started this war, but I was damn well going to finish it.

After breakfast, we conducted our usual perimeter check of the fence lines.

We'd just arrived at the main gate when the rumble of an approaching engine caught our attention.

I tensed, turning to catch sight of a battered truck as I instinctively reached for the gun tucked in the waistband of my jeans, '

'Relax, baby,' my woman murmured. 'It's just my neighbor, Mr. Henderson.'

He pulled up in front of the entrance, his weathered face grim as he climbed out of the cab. 'Morning, Cleo,' he greeted us, his voice heavy with concern.

'Hey, Mr Henderson. This is a friend of mine, Alessio,' she said, introducing me to the silver-haired gentleman.

He nodded absentmindedly, his thoughts elsewhere. 'You caught the commotion last night?'

I jerked my chin, lips pursing. 'Hard to miss. What's the word?'

The old farmer sighed, taking off his hat and running a hand through his thinning hair. 'It's bad, real bad. The cops raided the Conti farm and found a goddamn meth lab and enough weed to supply half the state. Franco and his boys managed to slip away, disappearing into the mountains like the slimy bastards they are.'

Cleo's fingers tightened around mine, her voice tight with worry. 'They're still out there? Dio, they might be anywhere.'

Mr. Henderson's expression darkened. 'Oh, that's not the worst of it. Word is, the Caputos are pissed off, seeing as the Conti farm was one of their main sources of raw drugs. The labs got stripped, and the crop of hemp was poisoned in that raid. So if the Caputos decide to go after whoever called the cops on them, it may turn into a bloodbath.'

Cleo glanced at me and found me stoic, calm as fuck. I wasn't afraid of the local mafia. They were small fry compared to the Calibreses and the Omertà Alliance.

But they didn't know that, and I suspected they'd soon come sniffing around to initiate their brand of dick-twirling with me.

I squeezed Cleo's hand, my mind racing. We needed to act fast to shore up our defenses and gather our allies before the Contis and their new friends came knocking. It was going to be a long, bloody fight, but I'd be damned if I let them take what was ours.

'Thanks for the heads up, sir,' I said, my voice grim. 'We'll keep an eye out if they come knocking.'

He assessed me and the gun at my waist, the rifle in Cleo's grasp, and nodded. 'Be careful. Call me as soon as trouble shows up, and I'll do the same if they're spotted on my farm.'

With a tip of his hat, the gentlemanly farmer climbed back into his truck and drove off.

'That's a man with sizable balls,' I growled in respect.

My woman's gaze met mine, and she gave me a slight smile.

Her brow arched even higher. 'I much prefer yours, honey. Much bigger, too.'

I huffed into her mouth as our lips met in a melting kiss.

Dio, I was fucked.

Gone for her.

CLEO

That evening, Alessio found me in the kitchen, putting away the last dried dishes for the day.

I turned and tagged him, leaning against the counter, eyes molten on me.

'How do you want it? Tongue or cock between your legs?'

Still unused to his filthy tongue yet secretly loving it, I gasped, then laughed, throwing a dish towel at him.

His lips curled at the edges, and then he moved, prowling

toward me.

'Tits baby, fucking now.'

My man was a dirty talker; despite my blushes, I was here for it.

I reached for the edge of my tee and swept it off my head.

My bra sailed off next, and in seconds, his hot mouth descended over my left nipple.

Suckling, laving, flicking with the rough nob of his tongue.

I keened and curved into him. Hands clutching his back for purchase.

'She's so ravenous for it, so needy, so freakin' insatiable for it,' he growled, lifting away to kiss me. 'I had a hard-on all day from being so close to you.'

Our mouths met, so wild for him I lost all breath for a second.

The next thing I knew, my jeans were being tugged down, and my panties ripped away.

Throwing his sinewed arm around me, he hoisted me onto the kitchen bench.

'Legs spread, cara,' he growled. 'I'll take care of the rest.'

His heated lips lowered and fell on me.

Feasting, lavishing, pleasuring, making me with under him as I flooded his mouth, even as arcs of pure bliss flew through me, thrumming my core.

He lifted for a beat, his dark blonde locks wild about his face from how much I was tugging at them.

'I can't decide if your tits or your pussy is more delicious. Give me another taste.'

My right nipple got what it'd been waiting for, and I offered the plumpness of it to him.

The other hand buried in his hair as I moaned, arched back, toes canted off the kitchen counter.

I'd never been so open or vulnerable for any man before.

With a growl, he pushed back and divested himself of his clothes. 'Revealing his fuckin' beautiful body.

I heaved both hands, now levering me up, thighs apart and trembling as he came closer, one arm on the bench, the other on my tits.

His cock, thick, long, and crowned with jewelry, pulsated for me.

I reached for him, pumping him, while Alessio's eyes burned on the connection of my hand on his shaft, the veins in his neck jutting from trying to maintain control.

'Enough woman,' he growled, pulling my hand away.

He gave himself a quick squeeze at the root of his penis to hold off from cumming too soon.

'Ready?' he grunted, eyes half-mast with need as he stepped in and placed his head between my lips, running it over and over until our seeping desire mixed.

It was so sensual I began feeling my orgasm rising from the base of my ass.

'Now, baby, fuck me now,' I begged.

He obliged with a smirk, easing into me, his palms anchored on either side of my hips, our eyes on our joining.

'Fotto,' he grated, pushing in, widening me impossibly. 'You're so tight, I can't take it.'

I moaned, levering my pelvis up to take more of him. 'Honey, the way you feel beneath me is addicting. I can't get enough.'

His mouth lowered to mine, and we kissed as he began to move inside me.

One of his hands lifted to my tit, squeezing,

I reached for his ass and flicked his balls from behind.

It drove him wild, and his groin bucked.

'Cleo, you're not fuckin' in charge. Stop it, or you'll make me blow too soon,' he warned, eyes narrowed in warning.

I did it again, a cheeky smirk on my face.

'You'll pay for that,' he growled.

With a hiss, he pulled out of me.

I was still protesting as he flipped me to my tummy, captured my hands in his, and lowered them to the counter, caging me in.

His thick thigh pushed between my sopping ones, and I gave a half scream as he surged back into me.

This time, there were no slow, sweet, melting thrusts.

He pistoned, hard, fast, wild, into me as I gasped, over and over until, with a roar he muffled into my nape, I felt him cum.

Hot, scorching jets of his ecstasy pulsated into me, even as I convulsed, my entire pelvis in heated release.

Every nerve end flamed as I quaked through one of the best orgasms I'd ever experienced.

Chapter 28

FRANCO

My breath came in ragged gasps, each step a struggle.

Still, I made my way toward the towering iron gate of the grand estate in the hills above Goulburn.

Even from a distance, its grandeur was imposing—a contrast to the ruin my own life had become. A stark reminder of the heights I'd climbed, now lost to me.

My hands trembled as I reached for the intercom, pressing the button with an urgency born of desperation.

A voice crackled through, cold and impersonal. 'State your business.'

'It's Franco Conti,' I gasped, wiping the sweat from my brow. 'I'm here to see the boss. It's urgent.'

I got a pause, a moment thick with tension, sensing the scrutiny on the other side of the camera.

With an initial groan, the gates creaked open.

The gravel crunched beneath my worn shoes as I walked up the path, my shoulders hunched under the weight of my troubles.

Two menacing bodyguards waited at the entrance, their eyes hard and unyielding. One stepped forward, his hands rough as he frisked me with clinical efficiency.

Finding nothing, he nodded and let me pass.

Inside, the luxury of the Caputo estate - from gilded statues to dripping crystal chandeliers - struck me. This world was far removed from the grime and decay of the jail I'd just been released from.

I was ushered into a den, an elegant study filled with dark wood and the faint scent of expensive cigars.

A slick, ebony-haired, leathery-faced man sat behind a massive desk, his eyes glinting with the power that needed no introduction.

'Franco,' he greeted me, his voice as smooth as the silk tie at his throat. 'I hear you'd some excitement your way last night.'

I swallowed hard, stepping into the room with the nervous-ness of a man about to face a firing squad. For Leo Caputo was many walking men's nightmare, a ruthless Don and businessman who took no shit from anyone.

He'd also paid a heavy sum to bail me out of prison in return for access to my land for his enterprise.

'Don, we had a visit from the feds. My men tried to defend the farm, but we were overwhelmed in minutes. They brought in dogs, helos, and drug squads.'

His gaze narrowed. 'The lab?' He leaned back in his chair, steepling his fingers.

I braced. 'All gone. Those who survived the night, including my sons, fled into the hills. We're hunkering out in the wild for now.'

The man before me grimaced. 'What happened to '*Don, I'll keep your investment safe and triple it?*' From the sounds of it, you've lost control. Income is down; worse, the facility is lost. As well as soldiers. Some of those were my capos—good men.'

I flinched at the words, the truth of them cutting deep. 'It's all true,' I admitted, just above a whisper, hating that I had to kowtow to this fucking shit. 'But it's not because of anything I did. It's him—this fuckin' Alessio guy. He's been striking us like he's always one step ahead.'

'One man, causing all this carnage?' The Don's voice was laced with disbelief but also something more dangerous—anger. 'How did you permit this to happen, Franco?'

I had an inkling.

I'd let my obsession with *her* dictate my life.

But fotto, why had this innocent, beautiful young woman I'd pursued with jewelry and cash, sparing no time, energy, or expense, never responded to me? Why had nothing worked? I'd even fuckin' gone to jail for her.

I'd agonized in prison about her, the most alluring, perfect woman, my favorite Queen in Waiting.

Now, all that stood between her and me was some fuckin golden-haired lothario. Fuck that shit. She would be mine by nightfall tomorrow.

'I'm sorry, boss. I underestimated the situation, but I won't make that mistake again. I swear it.'

'Who is he?' the Don demanded. 'The man who hit up the feds with intel about the farm?'

'Not sure,' I lied, aware of who the Calibrese head capo was. 'But I need your blessing to obliterate him.'

Caputo's favor would give me the sanction I needed to go after a made man in the hope of restoring my fortunes and reputation and my fuckin' bride-to-be.

My voice wavered as I continued, 'I'll fix it. I'll flush him out, take care of him once and for all.'

His eyes bore into mine, searching for any sign of weakness, any reason to doubt me. After a tense silence, he gave a single nod. 'I grant you carte blanche. Do whatever it takes to get his head on a spike.'

'Last, we need refuge in your estate to avoid the feds.'

Caputo scoffed. 'You have to rectify your shit first before coming to lay more in my backyard. Go back to your farm and use it as a base. The cops are long gone. But Franco,' his voice dropped to a chilling whisper. 'If you fail or return here without finishing the job, don't bother returning. Capisce?'

I nodded, feeling the cold sweat trickle down my spine. 'I understand, boss. I won't let you down.

'Make sure that you don't,' he said, waving me away, dismissing me as if I were nothing more than a bothersome fly.

I stumbled out of the room, heart bitter, my legs weak with the weight of what lay ahead.

The bodyguards' eyes followed me as I exited the estate, but I took no notice.

All I thought about was the promise I had just made to myself. Of the woman who was meant to be mine—and the grim certainty that if I failed, I wouldn't live to regret it.

Chapter 29

ALESSIO

Midnight was cleaved by the distant roar of engines growing louder by the second.

I grabbed my gun and strode to the window.

Outside, the night was alive with chaos.

Dirt bikes and four-wheelers tore across the fence lines and the gate, their headlights cutting through the darkness.

I caught the shouts and whoops of the riders.

The Conti clan was out for blood.

'Baby.'

I turned, tagging Cleo at my back, eyes soft.

I sighed. 'Our fuckin' nightmare has come to life. Mia sola, you'll have to listen to everything I say and do it.'

My growl went over and above the revving of engines outside, hurling insults. Even from afar, I sensed the hunger for revenge that consumed them.

'What do you need me to do?'

I stepped out onto the porch, my gun at the ready.

In moments came the roar of a vehicle rushing the gate.

'We have to move,' I said, grabbing Cleo's hand and pulling her back inside. 'They'll be through that barrier in seconds.'

She nodded, her face set in grim lines as she followed me.

We paused at the entryway where we'd laid out our weapons.

We pulled on our Kevlar vests and loaded up our guns.

Then, with a long eye lock at each other and a lingering kiss, I led my woman towards the back of the house.

'Behind me, always carissima,' I growled.

We eased into the darkness and sidled along the exterior to the right of Cleo's home.

The truck's screech of metal was ear-splitting as it rammed through the gate, followed by the crunch of gravel as it roared into the yard.

The growl of engines shattered the night, accompanied by the staccato pop of gunfire.

I shoved Cleo down, where she was hidden by the stone wall that ringed the porch.

My body shielded hers as bullets peppered the ground around us.

'Stay down!' I shouted over the din, risking a glance over the edge. What I observed made my blood run cold.

Franco Conti sat behind the wheel of a massive truck, his face twisted in a rictus of rage. Beside him, his sons Bruno and Rocco leaned out the windows, assault rifles in hand, as they sprayed the house with gunfire.

Hunting spotlights mounted on the truck's roof swept across the yard, blinding in their intensity. I ducked back down, my mind racing. They were coming in hard and fast, intent to end this once and for all.

Franco's shout boomed out over a loudspeaker, thick with venom.

'Alessio! You bastard, I know you're inside! Come out and face me like a man!'

The Contis behemoth truck was circling, revving over the lawn in the front of the house, their wheels churning chunks of mud out of Cleo's front garden.

I tagged the glint of their weapons in the moonlight and the twisted smiles on their faces.

'You're gonna pay for what you did, you fucker!' Fabio yelled, raw with rage.

I raised my gun, my finger hovering over the trigger. 'Come any closer, and I'll put a bullet between your eyes,' I growled.

Franco laughed, the sound harsh and mocking. 'You think you can take us all on, tough guy?' He taunted. 'We're going to burn this place to the ground with you in it! But first, before I do, I'll need my bride.'

A surge of anger, hot and fierce, went through me.

These bastards had no idea who they were messing with. I'd faced down worse than them in my life, and I sure as hell wouldn't let them take what was mine.

I aimed my gun at Franco, my voice cold as ice. 'Last chance, assholes. Turn around and crawl back to whatever hole you came from, or I'll start shooting.'

A few of their capos on two- and four-wheelers surged forward, thinking they were likely to breach our defenses.

But my snares caught them, their dirt bikes tangling in the concealed wires I'd rigged up.

Shouts of anger and pain rose into the air as they plunged into the booby traps I'd laid out.

They fell and flailed in shallow pits lined with sharpened stakes, hidden beneath a thin brush layer.

The sound of bodies hitting the ground, followed by agonized screams, told me my snares had found their marks.

I stepped out into the open, my gun raised as I blasted at the vehicle. Explosions rang out like thunder in the stillness of the night. Franco cursed as he dove for cover.

'I've got him!' one of his sons shouted.

Moments later, the air was alive with the crack of gunfire as they returned fire.

The rigged-up truck charged toward me; its hunting spotlight was so bright that it burnt my cornea.

Franco and his sons took wild shots in my direction, shouting at how they'd had enough of my shit.

I fired back to protect Cleo, who was fighting at my side.

With no warning, a deafening roar came as the Contis truck revved even higher, its tires spinning on the gravel as it surged forward.

I stared in horror as it careened towards the giant pine tree in the front yard, Franco blinded by rage.

The impact was tremendous, the sound of shattering glass and twisting metal filling the air as the vehicle slammed into the tree and burst into flames.

But even as the thought crossed my mind, a shout of outrage tore the atmosphere.

Franco emerged from the flaming juggernaut, his face twisted with hatred as he leveled his gun at me.

The muzzle flashes lit up the dark alley as I charged forward, my pistol spitting lead.

Rocco, Bruno, and Fabio also appeared, shaken from the crash but still advancing.

I had a second to react before my rounds found their marks.

Bruno's revolver jerked out of his hand, clattering across the cobblestones.

Fabio's Beretta vanished from his grip in a shower of sparks.

The shock on their faces was priceless.

'Fuck! Impossible!' Fabio cried, flailing around to where his piece had landed in the shadows.

I kept my aim steady on them, a cold fury in my eyes. 'Not impossible. I'm just that damned good.'

Their bravado melted away, replaced by the wide-eyed look of cornered rats.

They were outmatched.

With deliberate slowness, I lowered my gun and slid it back into the leather holster under my jacket.

The brothers exchanged confused glances, but I wasn't about to play by their wishes.

I was going to beat them at my game, my rules.

I rolled my shoulders, loosening up. 'What do you say, boys? Let's settle this like men. No more guns, no more tricks. Just you and me, mano a mano.'

Fabio snarled, his face twisted with rage. 'You think you can take us both, vecchio? You're insane!'

'Crazy like a fox,' I countered with a predatory grin. 'I've been scrapping and brawling before you ever wiped your culo. You don't stand a chance.'

I shifted into a brawler's stance, fists up and ready. My muscle memory kicked in, ingrained from countless back-alley bouts.

The Contis had yet to learn what they were in for.

Bruno cracked his knuckles, trying for a badass, rugged look. 'You're going to regret this, fucker. We're younger, faster, stronger. We'll break you in half!'

'Enough talk.' I beckoned them forward with a curl of my fingers. 'Let's dance, ragazzi.'

The slow-turning gears behind their eyes were comical as they tried to decide whether to rush me together or split up to flank me. But I wasn't about to give them time to think. This ends now, one way or another.

They wanted to play the game, thinking I was just some tough guy in his mid-thirties that their youthful arrogance might push around. They were about to learn that I was no old dog and had plenty of bite left in me. And I was going to savor every instant of teaching them that lesson.

The brothers exchanged glances, then charged as one, arms open to grab me from both sides.

Amateurs.

I pivoted at the last second, letting their momentum carry them past me. Bruno stumbled off-balance, and I cracked him across the jaw with a vicious right hook. He went down hard, spitting blood and teeth.

Fabio roared in anger and came at me with a wild haymaker.

I ducked, driving my fist into his soft belly. He doubled over, gasping for air, and I brought my knee up into his face with a satisfying crunch.

Decades of pent-up rage and frustration had fueled my attacks, giving me a strength and speed I'd never experienced before.

All those years of street brawling, all those back-alley fights and barroom scuffles, had been leading up to this moment. This was what I was born for.

But I'd no time to gloat. The other Conti soldiers were already advancing in, trying to surround me.

I had to keep moving and tip them off balance. They might have outnumbered me, but I had decades of experience.

I whirled and lashed out with a spinning back fist, catching one thug in the temple. He crumpled like a puppet with its strings cut.

Two more rushed me from either flank, but I was ready. I grabbed one by the arm and used his momentum to flip him hard onto his back, then snapped a quick front kick into the other one's groin. He went down, squealing like a stuck pig.

The last two hung back, trying to circle behind me. I let them think they had me trapped, then feinted left and dove right, rolling beneath their clumsy grab. I came up in a crouch and swept my leg out in an extensive arc, taking their feet out from under them.

I pounced as they struggled to rise, hammering them with a relentless flurry of punches and elbows. I had to put them down hard and fast.

Cleo had disappeared in the rush, and I hoped she was OK.

She was badass, but this shitshow was getting out of hand.

The still-standing Contis circled me like a pack of wolves.

I settled into a fighter's stance, blood singing with the thrill of impending violence. 'Come on then, you sons of bitches,' I taunted. 'Let's finish this.'

They rushed me as one, but I was ready. I became a whirlwind of flying fists and precise strikes, my body moving on pure instinct honed by years on the unforgiving streets. One by one, they fell before my onslaught.

A piercing scream broke through the air

Cleo.

Ice flooded my entire spirit, and I jolted.

The extreme wave of shock hit hard as I twisted and spotted

her being dragged by her neck.

The man wrenching her along was Rocco as he strutted backward past the grime and wreckage of his truck.

He was flanked by Franco, who wielded a shotgun, firing in the air, a glaze of madness in his eyes.

My essence shifted to fire, and my chest scorched.

How the fuck had they overcome her?

I rushed forward when a half dozen Contis capos fell on me, answering my question.

That's how.

They'd had a dozen more men lurking, waiting until I was preoccupied.

The fuckers all tackled me to the ground.

I caught flashes, heart-wrenching glimpses of the Conti pair dragging her to a waiting second truck, where a dark figure was hunched behind the wheel.

She yelled, kicked, and screamed even as they bundled her inside.

I roared, trying to hold off my attackers, growling with frustration as they swarmed me, impeding me from getting to my woman.

Rage boiled through my veins. With a roar, I surged against the goons restraining me, desperate to get to her.

Still, they teemed at me, fists and boots raining down blows as they pinned me. I bucked and struggled but couldn't break free.

'You bastards!' I snarled. 'I'll fuckin' kill every last one of you!'

I bellowed as the SUV Franco and Rocco had pushed her into started up and pulled away.

That's when I lost my everlovin' shit.

With a rush of strength, I lifted off and threw down three attackers pummeling me.

I reached into my pants, where my hunting knives lay sheathed inside my boot.

I unleashed the sharp fuckers and began slashing.

Cutting, stabbing, gashing, splitting open sinew, vessels and muscle.

Sick, fluid resonance and screams rose around me as I moved like a god of retribution through the ranks, uncaring, unsparing, fuckin' undone with rage.

I had nothing but crimson in my vision as the lights of the errant SUV disappeared into the darkness.

Enraged even more, I lunged toward Fabio, Bruno, and their fucking clown entourage.

One by one, they fell, and those who didn't fled into the night in terror.

For my vengeance was unquenchable.

My wrath was unequivocal, and I'd only just begun.

The crunch of gravel beneath my boots joined with the distant hum of cicadas as I marched down the moonlit road.

My senses were on high alert for any sign of an ambush.

Not that anyone would try jumping me, for I appeared like a devil out of the underworld, my hair, skin, and clothes streaked with blood and gore.

I held my Sig in one hand and a deadly blade in the other as I strode along a silver-etched track, eyes hard, face harder.

I walked for an eternity, the range melting beneath my relentless pace.

Sweat trickled down my back, plastering my shirt to my flesh, but I barely took note, driven to protect what was mine.

At last, I reached a spot where the trees thinned out, and I spotted the faint glow of civilization in the distance.

Pulling out my phone, I checked it.

I was finally within network range.

Growling in relief, I tapped on a number.

Despite it being late, the call was picked up in three rings.

'Fratello, scusa,' I growled, my voice grim. 'It's Alessio. I need you to jack some shit up.'

A moment of silence fell on the other end, then the timbre, familiar rasp. 'Che cosa?'

I took a deep breath, steeling myself. 'The Contis. They've taken her. I must have Mauri and his men, as many as you can spare. It's going to be war. It'll necessitate all the help I can get to rain hell down.'

I referred to our Calibrese contingent of enforcers and capos.

The latter had moved to Australia from Italy and now worked at our import fulfillment center.

They'd be the army I needed to face the unknown.

Lorenzo's voice rumbled. 'Is she worth it?'

'Far more than all the fuckin' rubies in this world, Renzo,' I snarled with a vicious edge to my snarl. 'Shit, I can't breathe without her. Will you help me or not?'

After a long pause, Lorenzo sighed. 'You know I will, fratello. Famiglia is everything. I'll send Mauri and his best men.

They'll be your way by early morning. Fuck, I might even come along for the joy ride.'

Relief washed over me. 'Grazie, Renzo. I'll owe you.'

'You owe me nothing,' my brother added, his growl fierce. 'We're blood, Alessio. We stand together, sempre.'

I disconnected, messaged him my coordinates, and slipped the phone back into my pocket.

The die was cast.

I turned to jog through the bush back to the cabin, scowling, wrath energizing me, driving me.

I faltered halfway as a searing pain went through my side, my ailment flaring.

I fell to one knee, shaking.

With a roar, I rose once more.

Cursing the freakin' world, I fought through the shakes.

I lurched, jaw clenched in agony of body and mind that seared to the core, fuckin' wanting to burn the universe for her.

Franco had no idea what he was in for.

The Calibreses were not to be trifled with, and I would show them how deadly we could be.

MIA

My gorgeous man hung up, his hand lingering on the phone for a second before he turned to look at me.

The room was dim, and the only light came from the small bedside lamp, which cast a soft glow over the walls.

The air was thick with the quiet of the late night, the kind that wrapped like a blanket, shrouding us from the world outside.

Preceding the call, we'd been wrapped in each other's arms, lost in a session of baby-making and wild fucking with unrestrained passion.

Now, my hand rested on his chest, moving with his breath's rise and fall.

I tagged the conflict in his eyes, the pull of duty warring with the desire to stay. 'You have to go, don't you?' I asked, already knowing the answer.

He nodded, his expression pained. 'He needs me,' he rasped as if that explained everything. And in a way, it did.

I sat up, pulling the duvet around me for comfort. 'What's happened?' I asked, not sure I wanted to know.

'Alessio's been attacked,' he murmured, a shard of pain crossing his face. 'He also wants us to help him find a woman.'

I studied him and tagged the concern and care etched into Lorenzo's features.

The lines on the edges of his eyes appeared deeper, the weight of his brother's pain pressing down on him.

I wished to tell him to stay, to let someone else handle it, but that wasn't fair. This was who he was, and part of me had always admired that about him.

But it didn't make it any easier.

'Do you ever wonder -,' I started, then stopped myself.

I didn't have an idea of how to finish that sentence. *Do you ever wonder if things were different? That you didn't always have to go? That you didn't need to put your life and mine on the line so often?*

He reached out, brushing a strand of hair away from my face. 'Sometimes, bella,' he murmured as if reading my mind. 'But this is what I have to do.'

I swallowed hard, forcing back the lump in my throat. 'I know,' I whispered. 'I just wish it didn't have to be tonight. Or this week.'

We'd set aside time to work on baby-making; these seven days were the window to make it happen this month.

However, Lorenzo's family was his responsibility.

Alessio needed him, and the Calibreses never abandoned their own, always having each other's back.

Lorenzo leaned in, pressing a gentle kiss to my forehead.

'So do I,' he murmured against my skin, his breath warm and comforting. 'But I promise, I'll come back to you. I always do.'

I nodded, not trusting myself to speak.

My eyes locked on him as he dressed, his movements quick and efficient, like he'd done a myriad times before.

He strode to his safe and pulled out two weapons, tucking them into the waistband of his trousers, then threw on a leather jacket and boots.

When he was ready, he stood by the bed for a moment, gazing at me with soft regret and a love that always blew my mind.

'Ti amo, bella,' he rasped, the words heavy with meaning.

'I adore you too,' I replied, my voice trembling despite my efforts to stay strong.

He leaned down, capturing my lips in a slow, lingering kiss that felt like a goodbye and a promise.

When he pulled away, I tagged the smolder in his eyes.

307

My eyes flicked to the set clench to his jaw, radiating with a steely purpose forged with a ruthless affection.

He also showed possessiveness for his loved ones, which was the one quality that had drawn me to him in the first place.

'Be safe,' I whispered, my hand reaching out to grasp his for one last moment.

'I will,' he said, giving my hand a reassuring squeeze before he released and turned to leave.

I let him go, the door closing with a soft click behind him, and then I was alone.

The room's silence pressed in on me, the bed suddenly too big, too empty.

I curled up under the blankets, his scent still lingering on the pillow beside me and tried to hold on to the promise he had made.

He would come back. He always did. But that didn't make the waiting any easier.

Chapter 30

ALESSIO

The rumble of vehicles shattered the predawn calm.

I bolted upright on Cleo's couch, eyes so tired, gritty under my lids.

Sleep had eluded me, my thoughts in a constant battle, my mind churning with worry. I'd struggled to stay rational and not give in to the impulse to rush out into the night and save Cleo.

Not even a shower at 2 a.m. had helped settle me down. I was jacked up, missing her, on the edge of losing my shit.

I mulled the idea of storming the neighboring property alone, my paranoia ratcheting at the thought of what the Contis and Franco, in particular, were doing to her.

Mayhem, murder, and malice twisted in my heart as I waited, my only thread to sanity being the thought of Lorenzo on his way.

Now, a voice called. The sound carried from down the drive at the gate. My spirit leaped in recognition.

I pushed up to my feet and powered to the door.

Tugging on my boots, I opened the cabin door and jogged toward Cleo's front yard.

The sight that greeted me lifted my fucked up spirit.

With a jerk at the silhouettes inside the lead vehicle, I unlocked the entrance and shoved it open.

Tires crunched on the gravel as three SUVs rolled past me one by one, headlights cutting through the inky predawn darkness.

I prowled to the cars from which a dozen men were exiting.

I first tagged Lorenzo, my older brother, my mentor, my freakin' ride-or-die.

'Fratello?'

I pulled him in for a silent, extended hug.

'Calma, piccolo leone,' he murmured into my hair, using our childhood nickname for me.

Little Lion.

Not so little now.

He canted back and studied me in the weak light, patting my cheek.

'We're here now,' he added.

His words had the desired effect, and a measure of my burden lifted.

'Grazie mille.'

I gazed at the men who eased from the vehicles, stretching their arms and legs, silhouetted in the early morning mist.

Mauri and our finest capos. Mattia, Leonardo, Andrea, Francesco and Tommaso.

'We've got weapons, ammo, and soldiers. We're primed to

go when you are,' our consigliere announced.

'I'm ready now,' I growled.

'Sì, non preoccuparti, fratello. Franco Conti won't know what hit 'em.'

I curled my lip. 'We ride at dawn.'

'Indeed.'

CLEO

A weak light falling on my face jerked me awake.

I shook my head, disoriented, as I stared at the unfamiliar room, the spare cot, and the sparse furnishings.

I glanced out the window at a soulless backyard and realized it was after daybreak. And that I'd spent the night in a tiny, ugly bedroom in the Conti compound.

The experiences of the night came rushing to mind, and I groaned.

I recalled how Franco and Rocco had dragged me out of the car and thrown me in here.

As I fell to the ground, Rocco exited with a smirk, leaving me with his lecherous father.

Franco had approached me, eyes shining with lust.

'Finally mine.'

'You're out of your mind, delulu.'

His hands had pawed at me, and he'd tried to force his slobbering lips on me.

At the same time, he'd undone his trousers, releasing his

shaft, groaning as he dry rutted against my thigh.

He'd heaved against me, about to shudder into his sordid release, when I'd bitten his flopping, wet lips, raised a knee, and slammed it into his groin.

Clutching his wounded jewels, he'd slipped to his knees, where he'd lain, crying out.

I'd taken the opportunity to kick his ribs, his yells for help filling me with a macabre triumph.

Rocco had rushed in and, with a snarl, slapped me, breaking my lip.

The cut on my mouth, the mark on my face, no doubt given the trail of crimson on my hand, had been worth it.

'You won't be able to fight me tomorrow,' Franco promised, leaning on his son, attempting to cover up his embarrassment.

Both Conti scum had scowled at me before hurrying out of the room, locking me in.

It took a good hour of dry heaving and shaking on the tiny cot in the room before I shook off the disgust of the assault.

Through the night, I tossed and turned, mind racing, wondering when Alessio would come for me.

For I was certain he would. Thinking of my man's unyielding, brawling spirit was like oxygen, giving me life and filling me with hope.

Hours later, footsteps echoed in the corridor beyond, and the lock on the door to my cell jiggled as a key was rotated.

I braced as the metal entryway was pushed open.

Franco stepped with a cold sneer on his face.

He fuckin' made my blood boil, and I rushed him with a hook and sidekick, ready to hit the fucker once more.

Rocco, who'd eased in behind his father, ducked around Franco, encircling my waist.

I thrashed harder against the lean as a whip man, heedless of his blows and slaps.

'You fucking bitch,' he called out, slamming me onto the far wall.

I cried out as my head bounced off, stars exploding in my vision.

Rocco seized a fistful of my hair, wrenching my head back, eyes glittered with malice as he shoved me to my knees before him. 'Not so tough now, are you, whore?' he sneered.

Franco stepped in, lifting a hand. 'Don't call her that. Not when she's about to be my bride.'

Rocco backed off with a scowl as I sliced my eyes away from the pair of them, blinking back tears of agony.

I would not let them fall, for they'd never see my pain.

'The ceremony is at 8 a.m.'

'Fuck off.'

Franco ignored my spirited response, instead tossing a package on the bed.

'Dress, shoes, veil, wear them.'

He turned to leave.

I glared at him, then opened my mouth, needing answers. 'Why? Why are you so obsessed with me? Why go into all this trouble? All these years?'

Franco laughed, the sinister light in his eyes fading to my surprise, revealing a desperate, almost love-sick expression.

He raked his strange, dark, glittering eyes over me in a mix of affection and viciousness that was downright creepy.

'Cleo Michele, you're the one female I've never stopped thinking about. Call it a wild attachment I've never been able to let go of. I knew we were meant to be since I first noticed you as a child. I'm obsessed with you. I craved your attention. I prayed for any glimpse of you. I even forgave you the previous two times you escaped from me and for your attack last night. Because I am convinced that with you in my life, I will be a better version of me and someone you will cherish.'

Silence fell as I regarded him, feeling my anger ebb a little, replaced by scorn for his loathsomeness.

'Never, ever will I love a pedophile, a pervert, a kidnapper, and an outright sadist. One who's fuckin out of his mind thinking he's joined a pantheon of dad-bodded, middle-aged creeps and their lissome, millennial lovers. Who fantasizes and fetishizes about the glory and admiration that he imagines will be in my eyes when I look at him. To be real, I'd rather kill myself than be with you.'

Franco's eyes dilated, his mouth contorting, before he lowered his voice into a feral whisper. 'You've no choice, Cleo. The rings are set to be exchanged, and they'll bind you to me and grant us the life I've always wanted. With you.'

His eyes glittered with madness as he swept aside his vest to show me his gun.

'I also have ways to compel you to give me what I want,' he crowed on. 'So please be ready when Rocco comes for you.'

The older man's fingers reached for mine, fumbling for my hand, the roughness of his skin scraping against mine before I snatched it away.

'I can't wait to kiss you, my bride,' Franco intoned. 'And breed you. Even if it means doing it with a gun to your head.'

I stared in scorn and horror at his dry and cracked lips and closed my eyes, wishing I could disappear, that this could all be a bad dream I would soon wake from.

But when I opened them, the reality was still there.

Franco smiled, a look of triumph in his eyes as if he had won something.

Maybe he had.

He saluted, as did Rocco, before exiting the room and leaving me to ruminate on my coming nightmare.

Chapter 31

CLEO

Time passed, and without a watch, I had no idea of how long.

Rocco came for me, his sneer a cruel reminder of my vulnerability in the hideous, frothy lace dress they'd procured.

I kept my hiking boots on, part in defiance and hoping to escape this incubus somehow.

'Let's fucking get this started.' Rocco snarled and brandished a Glock, pushing me out of the cell with rough hands and herding me with rough pushes to one of their outer barns on the compound.

The air was cool, the breeze whipping my hair about, adding to my discomfort.

A storm was brewing, and heavy, gray clouds loomed ominously in the sky, sending a shiver of fear down my spine.

With a sudden, deafening crack of thunder, the rain poured down, catching us off guard.

Rocco rushed me toward the barn, my heart pounding in my chest, my breath coming in short, panicked gasps.

I hadn't expected the weather to turn like this, but somehow, the tempest was a sign of nature's righteous wrath about the unsanctioned union.

The gale raged, battering the old shed with a fury that shook its foundations. The downpour pounded against the weathered wood, and the wind howled through the cracks.

Inside, the Contis had gone all out.

Wildflowers adorned the makeshift altar at the far end of the space, and makeshift lanterns hung from the beams.

I almost puked.

The guests, a small gathering of the Conti and Caputo capos, huddled together on wooden benches.

Their faces were closed off as they stared at me take my first steps down the aisle.

I wondered if they pitied me or, perhaps, didn't care.

Rocco shifted, his boots scuffing against the floor.

I caught his eye briefly, a flicker of something passing between us. Was it hate? Pity? I couldn't tell, and it didn't matter. I was too far gone.

As I walked, the storm outside appeared to grow louder, as if trying to force its way into the space.

The wind whipped through the cracks in the walls, lifting the edges of my veil and causing the flames in the lanterns to dance.

At the altar, Franco waited, his eyes never leaving me.

He wore a simple shirt, trousers, and a wedding jacket. The outfit emphasized his yellow ex-con skin, how worn and tired the man was, and how an insane evil lurked in his eyes.

My eyes flicked around, resting on a shotgun that had been placed on the front chair, Franco's, I assumed.

I considered rushing for it and turning it on him.

Until his hand gripped my upper arm and yanked me to the altar.

I tried to free myself from Franco's grip.

The old mofo held on for life's sake, and I blinked back my rage as the officiant, a Catholic priest I did not recognize, cleared his throat.

'We are gathered here today,' he said, 'to witness the joining of two souls.'

Franco's leathery and weathered fist clutched mine with a grip that signaled more possession than affection.

His sons and the capos fixed bleary eyes on us, their faces a blur of indifference and silent judgment.

Please come soon, honey, I thought, my mind racing as the priest droned on about love and duty.

My voice was trapped in my throat, and my lips pressed together tight as I stared at the clergyman, refusing to give Franco even one iota of my attention.

I stared dead ahead, seeing nothing but my life, narrowed to a single, suffocating path.

Franco squeezed my hands, pulling me back to the present.

His smile was crooked, more of a grimace than anything else, and the yellowed teeth peeking through his mouth made me swallow hard.

He leaned closer, his breath sour and stale, as he whispered, 'You'll learn to love me, Cleo Michele. You'll see.'

I wanted to pull away, to run far from this place, but my feet stayed glued to the spot. Instead, I glared at him. 'In your freakin' dreams.'

The priest cleared his throat, signaling it was time for the vows.

My heart pounded so intensely that I was sure everyone could hear it.

Franco's voice was raspy as he spoke his lines, each word heavy with the finality of a trap closing in. When it was my turn, I faltered, the words sticking in my gullet.

'Fuckin say it,' Franco hissed, leaning into me, his claw-like hands digging sharp into me.

I glared up at him as a wave of nausea washed over me, churned by my storm-tossed soul.

Just then, a flash of lightning lit up the barn, casting everything in stark, brilliant relief.

The barn's doors flew open, and the wind rushed in with a force that sent the flames in the lanterns flickering and the flowers on the altar swaying.

A shadow stepped into view.

Tall, muscled, a golden god of wrath, menacing, breathtaking.

Two lethal weapons were brandished in his hands, and a curl of scorn played on his lips.

My entire being jolted even as my soul lifted.

ALESSIO

'One more word, or move from any of you jokers here, and I'll rip all your fucking throats out,' I growled, meaning every syllable.

The wedding party turned to face me, eyes widening and mouths gaping.

I stood at the threshold of the makeshift barn chapel, my Sig in one hand and a 12 gauge in the other.

The wind whipped my hair around, adding to my diabolical appearance, given the shocked expressions.

I didn't give a fuck, my finger resting on the trigger of my weapons, eyes trained on my woman.

That she was alive, standing, and unharmed weakened my knees.

I hissed in relief, sucking in air.

She slow-blinked as her body relaxed, gifting me with a slight, soft smile, which in itself was enough to energize the hell out of me.

I jerked my chin at her and gave her a subtle nod.

Pointing my gun in her direction and angling it to the ground in a clear message.

She obeyed, dropping to the floor.

I kicked off the festivities with a volley of gunfire.

My fellow capos materialized behind me and joined in.

Bullets pinged off the walls and surfaces, sending puffs of dust and debris.

Chaos reigned as the Contis and Caputos retaliated, weapons blazing. But we'd caught them off guard, and many succumbed before they could even draw their firearms.

Lorenzo and our capos blasted firepower in a blistering hail of ammunition.

Seeking my woman, I surged forward, squeezing rounds

from my shotgun to clear my path.

One of the Caputo soldiers fell, clutching at his chest.

Others tried to flee.

'Flank them on the left!' Mauri growled over the din of battle, directing his men to move around the side of the barn. 'Cut off their escape route!'

Projectiles whizzed overhead, shattering windows and splintering wood.

I ducked instinctively, the searing heat of a round passing close by my cheek. This was madness, an all-out war being fought for one woman.

But we had the advantage of preparation and surprise. The Contis and Caputos had underestimated us, and we'd caught them off guard.

The acrid stench of smoke and gunpowder filled my nostrils, making my eyes water.

'Hold the line, boys!' I rallied the crew, my voice booming across the vast space. 'Let's send these bastards straight to hell!'

I gritted my teeth, popping up to fire off another burst of rounds.

We were outnumbered but not outmatched. As minutes ticked on, the tide began to turn in our favor. The enemy's ranks were thinning, their attack faltering in the face of our unwavering defense.

I was about to take to the walkway and go for Cleo when a figure stepped before me.

'To get to my father and his bride, you must go through me,' Rocco growled, standing at the center of the cobbled-up aisle.

We squared off, chests heaving, eyes locked.

'Oh, I will, and I'll flay you just as I did to your brothers.'

321

He jolted. 'What the fuck?'

'Didn't you wonder where they've been all night? I don't think they're coming back home, asshole.'

'I thought -,' he faltered. 'I thought they were guarding you until Franco could get to you.'

I cocked a brow and shook my head to dissuade him of the fact.

With an inarticulate cry of rage, Rocco charged.

I sidestepped his clumsy attack and seized his arm, wrenching it behind his back.

I turned to the porch, heart pounding, and caught slices of action as Franco, the fucker, attempted to drag my woman away.

With a mighty roar, I jerked Rocco's hand upwards.

The sickening pop of a dislocated shoulder echoed across the space. I stretched his hand out and crashed my boot onto it, snarling at the satisfying crunch of breaking bones and screaming man.

Wailing, Rocco collapsed to his knees as I released him.

I stood over his writhing form, chest heaving with exertion and unleashed fury. It would be so easy to un-alive him, to snuff out his miserable life like stepping on an insect.

But I was more human than that.

Better than them.

My issue was with his father.

I turned back on Rocco's writhing, pathetic self and strode towards Cleo.

It was time to end this fucker and his perverted obsession once and for all.

I leaped over a few benches to get to her.

I needn't have.

Somehow, Cleo had wrenched away from Franco and found a shotgun.

She stood a few steps from her kidnapper, breathing so hard that I tagged the jagged inhales from where I was.

Franco, too, had a second weapon in his hand, trained at me.

I'd already whipped out my Sig, and Franco froze, eyes darting between my woman and me.

'You're dead, Alessio,' the Conti patriarch snarled, his finger tightening on the trigger. 'You and that bitch of yours.'

'Bitch? Hell, weren't you about to wife her?'

'I realize now she's sloppy seconds,' he hissed at me.

I huffed. 'You never had a chance, for she is more regal, more valuable, more impossibly more beautiful for your filthy hands even to touch. You're the scum of this earth, and I should have finished you that night long ago in Naples.'

My words enraged him, and he raised his gun.

I braced myself for the blast, my Sig rising to meet his.

But before either of us could fire, there was a loud explosion.

The shot was so forceful and delivered over a compact range that it punched a hole through Franco.

Lifting him into the air, vaulting him over the altar, where he crumpled to the ground.

Cleo rose from the ground, a shotgun smoking in her hands as she met my gaze across the makeshift chapel.

'Mia sola,' I growled, rushing to her.

'I told you I had your back,' she muttered as I pulled her up, my lips and arms all over her. 'And that his ass was mine.'

'Fuckin' right you did,' I said, pulling her tight to me. 'Fuckin' hell you did.'

She was shaking like a leaf, the rifle still clutched in her white-knuckled grip.

'Cleo, mia stella,' I murmured. 'It's over. You can put the gun down now.'

She gazed at me with wild, unfocused eyes. For a terrifying second, I thought she might turn the weapon on me. But then she blinked, and her gaze cleared.

'Is he is he dead?' she whispered.

I glanced over at Franco's prone form. 'Si, e morto. Very much so.'

Cleo let out a shuddering breath and lowered the shotgun. I prised it from her hands, then gathered her into my arms.

'You're safe now,' I murmured into her tresses. 'I've got you. I've always got you.'

'Never leave me, baby,' she breathed.

'Never.'

'Never, Alessio, never.'

She clung to me, her face buried in my chest as silent sobs wracked her body. I held her, one hand stroking her hair, the other rubbing soothing circles on her back.

'I'm sorry,' she choked out. 'I never meant for any of this to happen.'

'Shh,' I hushed her. 'You have nothing to apologize for. That bastard got what he deserved.'

Just then, a roar came from behind me.

I swiveled and caught sight of Rocco, making a desperate charge toward us, a weapon in his still-working hand, his other flopping like a string by his side.

If ever there was a fine line between wise-ass and jackass, Rocco has sprinted past it. Bounding over dumb-ass, twisting past stupid-ass, headed for the finish line of dead-ass.

His eyes were wild, his face contorted in a snarl of rage and desperation. He realized the battle was lost, but his pride wouldn't let him retreat.

I pushed my woman behind me and raised my Sig, taking careful aim.

Time slowed as my finger tightened on the trigger.

The world narrowed to me, Rocco, and the space between us.

The gun kicked against my forearm as I fired, the burst of bullets finding their mark. Rocco jerked and spun, his body dancing a macabre puppet dance as the rounds tore through him.

He crumpled to the ground, his once-fierce eyes now vacant and lifeless.

The sight sapped the remaining fight from the remainder of the Conti capos.

They broke and ran, scattering like cockroaches exposed to sudden light.

We had won, but the victory was bitter in my mouth.

Cleo's trembling hands came around me from behind as she buried her face in my spine.

I turned, dropped my weapons, and circled her waist and her nape, tucking her into me as the shock ebbed out of her.

While she calmed, I surveyed the barn, taking in the destruction and death.

So much blood spilled, so many lives lost. And for what? Hubris? Pride? Power? Control? It seemed so meaningless in the face of such carnage.

My woman shifted, and I glanced down at her, one eyebrow arched. 'You still with me, carissima?'

'Always,' she murmured.

I wanted to freeze this moment, imperfect and chaotic as it

was. Because despite the pain, the danger, and the uncertainty that lay ahead – there was nowhere else I'd ever be than by her side.

One day, she'd understand the depth of my feelings, the truth that had driven me all these years. One I'd carved into my soul, buried and only resurrected in recent days: It had always been her. It would always be her.

My north star. My reason. My home.

It was what I'd braced for. Even without full awareness of the fact, I'd always held out for her.

'Tu sei il mio destino,' I whispered, my lips turning up.

I reached out, my bloodied fingers brushing against her cheek in a promise, a vow.

'Sempre,' she murmured, her love for me and our unyielding connection softened her face.

'Famiglia!'

Lorenzo's growl had my attention.

'Che cosa?' I muttered.

Lorenzo raised a finger to his mouth, signaling he wanted silence.

In an instant, we all obeyed.

Mauri and I exchanged glances as we caught on to what Lorenzo had picked up.

We swung our eyes back to our leader.

He pressed his lips together, lifted a forefinger, and cocked it, striding forward.

We followed and stepped out in the early morning to the growing decibels of an unfamiliar yet steadily advancing whir.

Chapter 32

ALESSIO

The whup-whup-whup of helicopter blades sliced through the air, growing louder by the second.

I snapped my head up, muscles tensing.

The tension was palpable as Lorenzo stepped beside me, eyes narrowed at the gray sky that still had to reveal its prize.

His body was coiled, ready to strike at a moment's warning, his hand resting on his weapon, a mirror of my stance.

'People, fall back.' Lorenzo nodded, his eyes glinting with a predatory light.

We melted back into the shadows of the barn, blending into the gloominess, using the veil of the dark clouds above to take cover and assess the threat.

Cleo's hand found mine in the darkness, her fingers lacing tight. I squeezed once, a reassurance and a promise.

She met my gaze, her chin lifting. At that moment, I loved

her more than ever.

She fell back, her presence to my rear, crouched low on the ground.

The seconds stretched each one an eternity as a new, approaching noise ratcheted.

Through the trees, I glimpsed sleek, black metal glinting in the morning light.

At least ten SUVs raced up the Contis' driveway rapidly in a roaring convoy, the rumble of powerful engines filling the air.

Lorenzo held up a hand, a silent command to hold position.

'Who are these fuckers? Unintended collateral?' he whispered to me.

'I have a hunch,' I muttered under my breath, sliding my hand to the grip of my Sig Sauer, thumb poised over the safety. 'Uninvited company.'

Whatever this was, it didn't bode well—not with this many wheelers storming the Contis property just after we'd unalived the Head of the Conti family.

'Renzo, I'll take the lead,' I told my brother.

When he appeared to protest, I shook my head. 'This is my fight,' I growled.

He flicked his dark aqua gaze over me and then nodded.

The SUVs roared into the courtyard and formed a semicircle, a phalanx of steel and glass, each one disgorging well-armed men.

They fanned out, weapons ready, their faces stern and uncompromising.

Fuck. The Caputos must have called in reinforcements.

The chopper thundered overhead now, so close the downdraft whipped at my hair and clothes.

We observed through the leaves as the machine settled onto

the front lawn in a vortex of dust and debris in the center of the arc.

It was a great, black beast, its rotors decelerating, the airflow from its rotors flattening the grass.

I crouched low, my senses on high alert.

I tightened my grip on the Sig in my other hand, finger hovering near the trigger.

With slow deliberation, the helicopter's door opened.

A tall figure emerged from beneath the slowing blades, flanked by armed bodyguards.

Even from a distance, I sensed his power, the aura of command. He strode forward, his steps sure and purposeful.

I tensed, ready to spring into action at the slightest provocation.

The man stopped at the edge of the semicircle, his gaze sweeping over the destruction. Then, as if sensing our presence, his eyes locked on the shadows where we hid, like predators detecting prey.

'To whom do we owe the pleasure?' I drawled, nonchalant-as-fuck, stepping out of the barn's overhang.

The man smiled, a slow, dangerous curve of his lips. 'I'm Don Sebastian Caputo, head of the Caputo family. And I presume you are the man who brought the AFP down on our heads.'

I smirked back, a wolf baring its teeth. 'Guilty as charged.'

The air around us seemed to vibrate with the promise of violence.

The Don's henchmen bristled, mitts twitching for their weapons.

I raised a hand.

My crew materialized like shadows at my back, their sheer appearance and might an unspoken threat.

The Don's brows arched in surprise.

For an uptight moment, no one breathed.

The world narrowed to this - two factions on the brink of war, waiting for the other to flinch first.

The tension ratcheted up, the atmosphere crackling with it. My people, too, tautened, ready to unleash hell at my command.

I broke the impasse with a slow, deliberate movement, raising two fingers to my lips. 'Umiltà, Don Caputo,' I rasped, my voice soft, almost gentle. 'Humility, in the face of the Omertà.'

Lorenzo appeared at my side, mirroring the gesture. 'Umiltà per l'omertà,' he murmured. 'Humility for the code of silence.'

The color drained from Caputo's face as understanding dawned.

He stared at us, mouth agape, for a few more moments before he spoke. 'We caught wind of rumors that the Calibrese and the Omertà Alliance were in Australia,' he whispered, shock and something like fear in his intonation. 'But we never dreamed -'

'We are,' I said, my growl hard-edged. 'Our presence here can be soft or hard, depending on your subsequent actions.

My advice is to take your men and fuck off this area, for it's under our protection. Leave and never return, not even to the farm next door or even the entire freakin' region. Do this, and we'll be ghosts, nothing more than specters haunting your dreams. Choose the alternative and start counting your days and those of your children on Dio's green earth.'

Caputo's eyes iced over. For a split second, I wondered if he'd be foolish enough to challenge us.

The silence stretched between us, taut and razor-thin.

The Don's eyes darted from Lorenzo to me, calculation warring with self-preservation in his gaze. The gears turned in his head as he weighed his options.

The mafia leader's jaw clenched, a muscle ticking in his cheek. For a long moment, he stared at me, his expression unreadable. With a sharp jerk of his head, he raised his hand in surrender.

'Va bene,' he ground out, the words like shards of glass in his throat. 'For I'd be a scemo to cross the Sons of Honor.'

He lifted a hand, asking for permission to step forward.

Lorenzo granted it with a raise of his chin.

Don Caputo moved toward him and, in old-fashioned tradition, bowed one knee before him, head down.

It was his sign of respect, capitulation, and a request for forgiveness.

He reached for Lorenzo's hand, fumbling a kiss on his Omertà signet ring.

My brother glanced at me, narrowing his eyes.

He loathed all the godfather shit, but he had to play a role to maintain peace and order.

Lorenzo placed his hand on the older man's shoulder.

'Rise, friend, all is well.'

The Don pushed up with some effort. He gave Renzo and me a sharp, relieved glance, nodded, and turned on his heel. Moving fast, his hand whirled in a tight circle to call back his men.

They, too, had a new measure of restraint and respect in their gaze as they eyed us in cautious retreat.

They obeyed with alacrity, melting back into their vehicles as the helicopter fired up.

I glared, unmoving, as the Don and his guards disappeared into the sleek machine. It lifted into the sky, hovering for a moment as if the man inside was still trying to comprehend what the fuck had just happened.

My crew emerged from the shadows, clustering close, our hands crossed over our chests.

Behind us, silhouetting our badass figures, were the flames burning off in the still-smoking barn.

The helo banked and faded away into the heavens while the convoy revved and roared out of the property.

'Good riddance,' I growled, the tension leaching from my frame.

Cleo's hand was on my back, sliding around my waist. Her touch grounded me, bringing me back to the present.

'You OK, baby?' she murmured, her voice soft in my ear.

I turned, drawing her closer to me. 'I am,' I said, pressing my lips to her forehead. 'You?'

'Always fine when I'm next to you,' she breathed, melting into my embrace. 'But you'll need to explain what the fuck just happened there.'

'In good time, mia sola, in good time.'

We stayed that way long, watching the sun push through the storm clouds.

Morning's full brilliance began to streak across the canopy, chasing the shadows of the tempest, and the skies painted in the aftermath shades of gold and pink.

CLEO

'Fratello, won't you introduce us to your lady? The reason for all this excitement.'

Alessio's face dissolved into a soft smile as we turned arm in arm.

'This is my woman, Cleo,' Alessio growled, stepping toward his gun-toting, frankly badass entourage.

He slipped a hand around my waist, tugging me to his side, owning me, claiming me.

'I never thought I'd see the day.'

The speaker was a man in his mid-to-late thirties who carried significant gravitas. Sinewy and commanding, he towered tall and imposing, with broad upper arms and a lean, muscular frame.

But his face, a craggy-hewn sculpture of rugged masculinity and dangerous allure, caught my eye because it resembled Alessio while paying homage to the iconic figures of Italian cinema.

Dark, slicked-back hair set off piercing inky blue eyes with an alluring and threatening intensity.

He wore a stylish sweatshirt, no less, under an expensive

leather jacket that hugged his muscled, sinewed body, exuding confidence and power.

Thick thighs were encased in black jeans, and his feet were in patent upper sneakers with couturier detail.

'Never say never,' came the amused drawl from a second man.

This time, he was a bulwark of flesh and muscle.

Face hard, gaze harder, and his cold, dark, honeyed features inherited from his Moorish ancestors.

He had the stride of a wolf and the menace of a warrior, and I felt a shiver go down my spine.

'Cara, meet Lorenzo,' he growled, pointing at the designer-clad man. 'My older brother and boss of the Calibrese family.'

'Hi,' I told the man, nonplussed as his eyes raked over me, focusing on how close Alessio was holding onto me.

'The second mofo is our consigliere, Mauri,' he rasped, raising his chin to the honey-skinned man. 'The rest of the crew are our freakish capos. Mattia, Leonardo, Andrea, Francesco and Tommaso.'

I nodded to the group of men. 'Lovely to meet you. I can't thank you enough for being here.'

Lorenzo stepped forward and tugged me away from his protesting brother.

I slow-blinked at him, surprised as he enveloped me in a tight hug, my face in his leather jacket.

Emotion clogged my throat. 'I can't believe you came. All of you.'

'You're family.' Lorenzo added, kissing my cheek. 'And famiglia stays united, no matter what.'

The fear I'd tagged in Don Caputo's eyes had made me realize my man was a major badass, and so was his kin, given how the head mafioso had reacted to them.

Alessio's older sibling was a charmer, yet underneath his sophistication lay a sinister spirit that few would dare cross.

As for my man, he exuded a raw and powerful energy, like a force of nature that could not be tamed.

Hell, they'd driven off the mafia kingpin together.

I realized then that they were a formidable clan, and I was awed by their power and dominance, unwavering and unapologetic gaze.

Like a pack of wild wolves, his family was fierce regarding each other, their bond tight and unbreakable.

I never imagined I'd have this kind of support.

Not after losing so much, so young, born of a mother and father who had manipulated me and never stepped up for me.

Apart from my grandparents, I had never been shown love, and witnessing Alessio's brothers and friends rally to his side, our side, filled me with deep gratitude.

We drove back to my cabin, which was still worse for wear from the Contis' last incursion.

While I changed and fed Mauri and the crew, they cleaned up the aftermath.

Lorenzo and Alessio went into town and chatted with the local cops.

In time, my man and Lorenzo returned with tired smiles.

'The cops listened, persuaded by my Australian Federal Police connection, a badass mofo called Saint Tahana, that the showdown, while firmly in the gray from an ethics perspective, had aided the fight against crime. They were happy to let the Conti problem go away forever,' Lorenzo announced, stepping into my cabin and sinking into my couch.

'They're well pleased the Contis are gone and won't terrorize the community anymore,' Alessio rasped into my hair when he tugged me close.

I raised a brow in disbelief.

'The Contis were on the AFP wanted list for a long time. We did them a favor.'

'The Caputos?'

'We left out our business with them, affording the Don his peace.'

Alessio convinced me to leave the farm, even if just for a while.

'The place is a wreck—walls splintered, windows shattered, the cabin is not holding together,' he exhaled into my neck.

'It looks like a battlefield. We can't stay here. It's not much of a home anymore.

'Let's regroup,' he said, his voice firm yet gentle.

'Where to?' I asked, pressing my lips to his.

He took my mouth in a blistering kiss.

When he finally lifted off me, he breathed. 'Sydney, where we can rest and shake this whole thing off.'

He didn't just suggest it; he promised it, swearing he'd leave two of his men behind to guard the property and ensure the safety of my belongings.

I gave in eventually, unwilling to be surrounded by the reminder of Franco's wrath and how much he'd wanted to destroy my life, to own me.

The thought of making the journey by car didn't sit well with Lorenzo, who was itching to get back to his wife.

So he used his hideously expensive satellite phone to make a few calls and pull some strings.

A private hire helicopter was sent to us. It set down in my front yard in a whirl of leaves and dust.

I hurriedly packed a bag, not needing much from the bullet-torn cabin.

I wandered between the bedroom and living area, sighing at the stuff that I had to leave behind.

'My books, though?' I asked Alessio, running my hands over the spines on the shelves. Which had, by a miracle, survived the gunfire that had shredded most else in the house.

He pressed a kiss on my temple. 'I'll have my men pack them with care, bella, and bring them to our new home wherever that will be.'

I took an inhale and surrendered.

In less than two hours, Mauri, Alessio, and I joined Lorenzo on the flight, the roar of the blades drowning out any second thoughts I might have had.

I gave one last look at my sanctuary as the helo banked into the skies.

I was consumed by a sense of loss yet eager to move on to the next season of my life.

With the man whose arm was banded around my waist, my other hand in his, my heart and soul forever entwined with his.

Chapter 33

CLEO

S ydney was a blur at first—a whirlwind of noise and
lights that overwhelmed me, the city's din blending
into a clash of sensory overload, reminding me why
I'd left in the first place.

When we landed on Lorenzo's stunning mansion rooftop,
his wife, Mia, greeted us with warmth, her warmth melted
my trepidation.

I liked her at once and smiled as she let go of her embrace.

She then folded into her husband's arms, their passion and
love evident.

'We'll spend the night here,' Alessio advised me, his confident stride leading the way, a reassuring presence in this new
and unfamiliar place.

Stepping into this vast and luxurious home felt like crossing
into a realm of grandeur and luxury so far removed from my

reality that it left me in awe.

I peered in wonder as we meandered into the kitchen, where Mia had prepped an outstanding Italian meal.

Alessio's youngest brother, Vitto, joined us.

At first, I stared, like a country hick because *what in the actual good genes?*

Mia was out of this world stunning, and the Calibrese men were beautiful.

As was Mauri, in his silent, gruff consigliere manner.

Still, they received me, pulling me in for tight hugs that instantly made me feel one of them.

First, Mia welcomed us with an aperitivo, her smile as warm as the late afternoon sun that bathed the kitchen in a golden glow.

She had dishes of olives and nuts alongside prosecco, all ready and waiting for us on the rustic wooden table. It was a simple yet elegant start to a memorable evening.

'Salute!' Mia exclaimed, raising her glass. We echoed her toast, the bubbly sparkling wine tickling my nose as I sipped. The first savor was crisp and refreshing, promising the delights to come.

Soon, the antipasti were served.

Mia brought out platters of frito misto—crispy fried vegetables, calamari, and shrimp. Every bite was a burst of flavor, the crunch of the batter giving way to the tender sweetness of the seafood.

'Eat! Eat! There's more to come!' Mia teased, noticing my hesitation as I reached for another piece. 'This is just the beginning.'

The table became laden with dishes, each more enticing than the last. We eagerly dug in, starting with the gnocchi in a rich, savory scampi sauce. The dumplings were like little pillows of heaven, complemented by the deep, garlicky relish.

'Oh, Mia, this is divine,' I couldn't help but murmur.

Next came a tender and flavorful osso buco dish, the meat melting off the bone. It was paired with steamed spinach, and its earthy bitterness was a perfect counterpoint to the meat's richness. A simple salad of mixed greens followed, a refreshing pause between the more indulgent courses.

During the meal, the room was filled with laughter and conversation. The mix of Italian and English created a lively, warm atmosphere as everyone tried to translate for me, often speaking over each other.

'Now, this is what I call a feast!' Alessio exclaimed, leaning back in his chair with a contented sigh.

Throughout the evening, the boisterous chatter and the sharing of food and stories were a revelation to me. Having lived alone for so long, I hadn't realized how much I missed the energy and connection from a meal shared with others.

We ate surrounded by affection and conversation.

To everyone's amusement, Lorenzo, Mia's husband, re-counted anecdotes from his childhood, his eyes twinkling with mischief as he mimicked his father's stern voice.

I gained insight into Alessio's family and witnessed their devotion to each other. Their banter and soft gibes told of a deep, familial bond.

'Alessio is so in love with you,' Mia stated as we prepped the decadent dessert dish in her beautiful kitchen.

'He's everything,' I said. 'I adore him just as much, if not more.'

She hugged me spontaneously. 'I'm so happy you're in his life, in our life.'

I squeezed her back, sensing her genuine acceptance and soaking it up.

'Grazie, for the welcome. I didn't know how much I needed this.'

Mia smiled, reaching out to squeeze my hand. 'From what Lorenzo shared, you've been through the wringer. Processing it all can be difficult, so call me anytime, honey, if you need to chat.'

She winked; I beamed back, knowing I'd gained an instant sister.

We reappeared at the table with the pudding: a refreshing sorbet and a lovely tiramisu. Its layers of coffee-soaked ladyfingers and creamy mascarpone were the perfect sweet end to the feast.

ALESSIO

Just after dinner, my brothers and I, Mauri, Mia, and Cleo, lingered around the expansive table.

Our faces lit with the warm glow of the chandelier above us.

The centerpiece of the evening was the bottle of grappa that sat in the middle of the surface. Its color caught the firelight, reflecting a thousand tiny flames in the tulip-shaped glasses that stood waiting.

Lorenzo reached for the carafe, his hand steady as he poured the spirit with practiced ease.

The liquid flowed, filling each glass to the curve, where the aroma would be most intense.

Lorenzo lifted his own when the glasses were filled, and we followed suit without hesitation.

The crystal chimed as the crystal pinged together, a sound that resonated with our shared history.

'Famiglia,' Lorenzo began, his voice rich and deep, carrying the echoes of our father. 'Per tutto quello che abbiamo superato insieme. To the family. For everything we've overcome together.'

From losing our parents and our aunt in recent times to forging a new path, this was a night of remembrance.

We nodded, our eyes meeting over the rims of our glasses. Vitto, the youngest, grinned, his usual mischievousness tempered by the gravity of the night.

'To life, which gave us hell but didn't break us.'

There was a murmur of agreement, a ripple of laughter that eased some tension.

I raised my glass higher.

'E a noi,' I growled. 'And to us, who never stopped fighting. Always together.'

The glasses clinked again, firmer this time as if sealing a vow. The grappa burned as it touched our lips, warming them from the inside out.

Lorenzo set his tumbler down, his gaze sweeping over us. 'Non importa quello che viene dopo,' he said with quiet reverence. 'Sappiamo chi siamo e da dove veniamo. Nessuno può portarci via questo. No matter what comes next, we know who we are and where we come from. No one can take that from us.

Vitto grinned. 'E ora,' he said, picking up the bottle to pour another round, 'Let's drink! Because if we must fight again, we'll do it with fire in our veins and grappa in our hearts!'

The laughter this time was full and rich, echoing off the kitchen walls.

This was our time, our night, and nothing—not even the trials of life—could take it from us.

'Thank you for everything,' I murmured to Lorenzo and Mia as the night began to wind down. Cleo and I stood at the dining room door, making our much-needed exit upstairs to rest after a tumultuous few days.

Later, in bed, Cleo turned to me, stroking my hair.

'I loved all of you, honey,' she murmured. 'From your beautiful heart, ruggedness, and strength and support, which had given me an anchor in my storm-filled life. And now, your family. Every one of them is precious, baby. Thank you for letting me in.'

I buried my mouth in her nape, nuzzling her ear, searching for her skin under her cami. 'Grazie mille for loving me, cara. After years of obsessing about you, Cleo, your love and holding you in my arms is beyond a dream; it's heaven itself.'

Chapter 34

CLEO

'**M**ake me all yours til I black out.'

Alessio's demanding growl echoed in the sumptuous bedroom.

'Baby,' I breathed, 'your wish is my desire.'

I canted myself over his waist, stroking his cock, flicking my tongue over the head, and moving with teasing slowness to his pulsing base.

It was our second night in Sydney.

Alessio had outdone himself, renting us a luxurious town-house near his brother's place.

Earlier that day, we'd pulled up to an address where he'd led me inside, a slight curve on his chiseled face. 'Welcome to our temporary home, amore mio.'

I'd stepped inside the opulent surroundings.

The space was decked out with every amenity imaginable,

from gleaming marble floors and plush furnishings in rich jewel tones to a crystal chandelier casting prismatic light.

'What do you think? I spared no expense,' Alessio had growled, wrapping an arm around my waist and pulling me close.

I managed a smile. 'It's stunning.'

But I couldn't shake the uneasiness lurking beneath my skin, an itch I couldn't quite scratch. It was a palace in its own right, yet it didn't feel like me.

That said, I attempted to make it our home by loving on my man, floating on clouds in the primary bed on a king-size mattress.

I pumped the base of his pulsing member, suckling the tip, flicking a tongue over the tiny silver barbells at his apex.

He bucked, one hand thrown over his face, his other muscled hand flung into the pillows, chest heaving, thighs trembling.

Damn, having so much power over my man was causing me to get high on love and totally sex drunk.

I lifted off, staring down his pulsating distended cock, so wet, so wanting to ratchet this fever to the next level.

With a moan, I ran my hand over my skin and my nipples, pinching their throbbing ends and lower to where my clit throbbed for him.

His eyes were glazed, and he tried hard to concentrate as I squeezed the base of his member to stop him from cumming too early.

When I swiped my tongue over the tiny jewelry in fast flicks, he roared, limbs shaking.

I thrust a few times before he began to slam his hand on the pillow.

Alternating with suckling his mushroomed head, I got high

off his wild passion.

'I'm about to blow,' he groaned.

'Not without me.'

I swung a thigh over him and turned to face his legs, and with teasing slowness, I lowered myself onto him.

When his fingers grazed my hips, I whipped around to lock eyes with his dilated, impassioned leonine ones. 'No soldier, no touching, no hands. That was the deal.'

He hissed, face convulsing with desire, veins jutting from his arched neck. 'Cleo, fuck, mia stella, don't torture me.'

I swirled my pelvis over his throbbing cock, stroking his head over my clit as my other hand pumped his base, quickening. He knifed up, moaning, keening, almost undone.

'Ain't no need to cry, Calibrese,' I teased.

'Cleo!'

His growl was so feral that I lurched at the pure wildness of his roar.

With a smile, I lowered myself onto him just as his pelvis slammed up, driving his shaft into me.

'Squeeze cara, tight as you can,' he growled.

I obeyed, caressing his balls with one hand and working him harder.

I rode him with wild abandon. On and on, we flew.

'Fuck you're so hard,' I groaned. ' So thick.'

'Ride me,' he moaned. 'Harder, faster.'

All his muscles were now so taut, so braced, so taut as we rammed our sex together.

We came in a blaze of heat, wet and cum.

My hands went to the mattress as I levered myself.

My hips were a blur as my pleasure rolled in waves even as he broke the rules, grabbed my waist, and slammed more forcefully into me.

Until I fell back onto him, our bodies slicking together, shaking, panting, heaving.

His fingers ran up and down his body onto him, cupping my tits and squeezing hard.

'What a freak you are, cara.'

At first, my wild streak shocked me because I liked it hard and rough.

'You bring out the freak in me,' I sighed, my bliss still washing over me. 'You bring it out of me.'

'I think, mia bella, you were a freak long before I came along.'

We laughed as I turned to find his mouth, beauty, and essence, my entire being trembling over him as I came down from my high.

'Fuck, I adore how we've perfected how we sexin', he growled against my lips, canting his hips to enter me once more.

Damn, how he made love easy.

The following day, Alessio and I visited Nonna at her care home.

The clean, modern facility was popular with its happy, smiling residents.

We walked past pickle-ball courts, a spa, a swimming pool,

and an arts and crafts hall. Light streamed through the windows, illuminating dust motes floating in the air.

Approaching Nonna's door, I paused at the sound of voices coming from inside - Nonna's raspy chuckle mixing with a man's deep baritone.

My curiosity piqued. Pushing open the door, I was surprised to recognize Mauri.

The Calibrese consigliere was seated at Nonna's tidy living room, at her dining table, a hand of playing cards splayed in his fingers.

Nonna's eyes lit up when she spotted me. 'Cara mia! Come in, come in.'

She folded me into her powder and perfume-scented hands and blessed me with a kiss and the cross sign.

'Mauri, please explain?' I said, waving at the inscrutable consigliere and the card table.

'You know my Mauri?' Nonna nodded.

I smiled at the stoic bodyguard, not expecting to find him there. 'I didn't realize you two were friends.'

A slight smirk pulled at Mauri's lips, his eyes softening as he eyed my grandmother. 'Your Nonna is my most formidable opponent. She beats me at scopa every week.'

I raised an eyebrow, surprised that the taciturn consigliere had a soft spot for my grandmother. Who would have guessed there was more to the man than his gruff exterior?

Nonna waved a dismissive hand. 'Ah, he lets me win. Such a gentleman, this one. My favorite visitor, you know.'

Alessio leaned into me. 'He and a few of my capos were on detail, checking on her each day. Turns out he got charmed by her and ended up playing cards with her every Saturday afternoon, unveiling a side to the taciturn bodyguard I had

348

not expected.'

Nonna reached out to squeeze my hand. 'But of course, I'm always happy to set eyes on my cara nipote. Now, introduce me to this handsome diavolo d'oro.'

Alessio arched a brow. 'You know my nickname?'

Nonna laughed. 'I don't need to. I discern the fire of a lion and devil in you.'

I took Alessio's hand, my heart swelling with pride as I introduced him. 'Nonna, please meet mia amato, Alessio.'

Nonna's face lit up with joy, folding my much taller, mus-cled, golden man into her arms. 'Finally, you have a man who looks like he'd flame heaven and hell for you. Welcome to the family, my dear.'

Alessio grinned, his eyes crinkling at the corners. 'Thank you, Nonna. I'm the lucky one.'

As Nonna fussed over Alessio, straightening his collar and patting his cheek, I couldn't help but feel a twinge of amusement. She was already treating him like her own grandson despite having just met him.

But then, Nonna turned to me with a sly smile. 'You know, tesoro, I had hoped to introduce you to Mauri first. He's quite the catch.'

I felt my cheeks flush, and I glanced at Mauri, who raised an eyebrow, his expression unreadable.

'Nonna!' I admonished. 'I'm thrilled with Alessio.'

Nonna chuckled, waving her hand dismissively. 'Of course you are, dear. I'm just teasing. But you can't blame an older woman for trying to play matchmaker. I've been attempting to match him up for days,' she complained. 'Nurses, doctors, physios, all clever women, he doesn't want any.'

I peeked at Mauri, curious to witness his reaction.

The stoic consigliere was impassive. His arms crossed over his chest as he listened to Nonna's matchmaking attempts.

Alessio, on the other hand, couldn't contain his amusement.

He roared with laughter, clutching his stomach as tears formed in the corners of his eyes. 'Nonna, you're relentless!' he managed to say between gasps for air.

But Mauri remained unmoved, his dark eyes fixed on Nonna with exasperation and fondness.

'The only woman who rules my world is my cat,' he declared, his deep voice rumbling through the room.

'And me,' Nonna Guilia glared.

'And you,' Mauri growled, a soft upturn to his lips slipping through.

I smiled at the intimidating consigliere, his care for Nonna, and his feline revealing a side of him I would never have guessed existed, but it made him all the more intriguing.

Nonna, however, wasn't quite ready to give up her match-making efforts.

She fixed Mauri with a stern look, her eyes narrowing as she wagged a finger at him. 'You mark my words, young man,' she said, her voice filled with the wisdom of a woman who had seen it all. 'One day, you'll find a woman who will turn your world upside down, and not even your cat will be able to compete.'

As we pulled up chairs, I couldn't help but marvel at the unlikely friendship between these two – my spirited Nonna and the reserved mafioso bodyguard.

Nonna had a way of drawing people into her orbit, no matter who they were.

I settled in to regale her with tales as Mauri gazed on with a glimmer of amusement in his eyes.

While Alessio and I caught her up on the Contis' demise, Nonna listened with rapt attention, her eyes sparkling, with ire at first, then triumph.

'Fucking good riddance.' she snarled when I was done.

'I now understand where you get your fire from, mia stella,' Alessio rasped.

'It runs in the family,' Mauri remarked dryly, the corner of his mouth twitching.

I shot him a mock glare. 'Watch it, consigliere. You're skating on thin ice.'

He held up his hands in surrender. 'I wouldn't dream of crossing either of you formidable women.'

Nonna reached over to pat his arm. 'Ah, Mauri, you're learning. Stick with me; I'll teach you all you need to know about handling the female folk.'

The visit flew by in a blur of laughter and stories; before I knew it, it was time to go.

As I hugged Nonna goodbye, she whispered, 'You see? Even the toughest men have a soft heart if you know where to look.'

I glanced over at the love of my life, then Mauri, and nodded.

Guilia dug an elbow in my side, and we exchanged smiles.

Leave it to Nonna to find humanity in even the most hardened souls.

Chapter 35

ALESSIO

'Come, let's go for a walk on the beach. The salt air will do you good.'

I took Cleo's hand, the contact sending an electric current through my body.

She'd been restless for days now since we'd arrived in Sydney.

We spent most of it in bed; when we didn't, we explored the beaches near our temporary home.

We strolled along the shore at Manly as the sun began its lazy descent, painting the sky in dazzling streaks of orange and pink. The sand was soft beneath my bare feet, the waves lapping at the seashore.

We attempted to relax, letting the salty breeze wash over us. We dined by the water, twilight ashing us in brilliant hues as we sipped wine and nibbled on seafood.

But I sensed the crowds—the endless stream of joggers, sunbathers, and surfers—were setting Cleo's nerves on edge.

She wasn't used to the city, the constant buzz of life around us.

This showed in her silence and quiet, the white ring of anxiety on her mouth.

I tried kissing away her angst, distracting her by touching her.

It worked, and I'd never made love so much to anyone ever.

The more I got, the more I needed.

I just couldn't pull myself from her magic, her pussy, her lips, her essence.

I loved how she touched me, all her little elaborate ways that got me wild.

When we weren't fucking, I did everything in my power to distract her, spoiling her with shopping trips, day trips, anything to make me feel at ease.

The weeks blurred together in a whirlwind of activity as I endeavored to lift her spirits.

I surprised her with a trip to a luxe day spa, where we were pampered with hot stone massages and champagne facials.

As the masseuses kneaded the knots from our shoulders, I tried to release the tension, the worry for her coiled inside me, to let my fears melt away.

But her unease remained, and it ate at me, knowing nothing I was doing was working.

Not that she wasn't grateful.

She always said thank you in her soft, husky intonation.

Still, her joy had ebbed; the light in her eyes was dimming.

It was killing me.

I sensed that the city was just noise, a discomfort she wanted to escape.

I pulled her close, my arm a solid anchor on her waist. 'What's on your mind, amore? You seem a thousand miles away.'

She leaned into me so I'd breathe in her enticing scent. 'I'm sorry. I know I've been distant. It's just a lot to take in.'

I pressed a kiss to her temple. 'I understand. We've been through a freakin' shit season and need time to heal. This too shall pass.'

She gave me a wan smile.

She wanted to believe me, but she had doubts.

It showed in her troubled jade eyes as they leaked with uncertainty she couldn't escape.

I squeezed tight, wanting to reassure her that our love was enough of a balm to soothe her fractured soul.

'But it's not enough, is it, carissima?' I asked, keeping my voice soft but probing.

She glanced away, the city lights throwing radiance over her face.

'It's not,' she admitted, just above a whisper. 'I can't live here, in Sydney. It's not me.'

My brow furrowed, concern deepening. 'You want to go home?' I asked, searching her face for an answer.

Home.

The word twisted something in me.

For I, too, wanted a sanctuary, a haven with her.

'Sydney isn't it, but neither is the farm. The memories there are too dark and painful, and with the cabin gone, nothing's left for me,' she said, shaking her head.

I melted and reached out, brushing a strand of hair from her face. 'I need to find a forever haven, too, with you,' I rasped.

'Shall we search for a home together? Or will you believe in me to locate the best place for us?'

Cleo gazed into my eyes, searching. 'Out of the city?'

'Si,' I nodded.

Her smile returned, flitting on the edges of her lips. 'You pick it. I trust you.'

'Do you, mia sola?'

'You've more sophistication than I do,' she huffed. 'I'm a farm girl but one who can appreciate luxury if it's surrounded by wilderness, earth, and realness. A house isn't a dwelling with four walls. I believe it's what you build with someone who cares enough to stick around. It'll be the perfect home if we're together and in nature.'

CLEO

How could I explain that Alessio's efforts to make me feel at home in Sydney, though well-intentioned, only caused more disorientation?

The chasm between the woman I had been on my property and the one he wanted me to be seemed to grow wider with each passing day.

While I wanted to share a life with Alessio, I didn't enjoy the noise and the distractions surrounding our current reality in the city.

I spent nights in his arms, trying to hold it together. But it was no use. The cracks were already spreading, the foundations of my trust crumbling beneath my insecurities.

Surrounded by a vast, uncaring metropolis, I shrunk.

With all its glitz and glamour, Sydney was suffocating, as if I was drowning in it.

I was often sucking air, needed to escape the oppressive press of bodies and the weight of vile words.

Why couldn't I just be happy, grateful for this beautiful life Alessio was offering me?

I hated myself for my inability to embrace it, to let go of the past and step into the future he envisioned for us.

My man, credit to him, got the memo.

So it was with much relief that he had me pack a bag.

He whisked me away from the bustle of the city, driving us up winding roads that seemed to ascend into the clouds.

We were heading to Lorenzo and Mia's mountain retreat, a place they called *Blue Bliss*.

The name sounded almost too perfect, like something out of a dream, but as we climbed higher into the mountains, the weight on my chest began to lift.

The property was even more breathtaking than I imagined when we arrived. Nestled among towering peaks, the house was an elegant blend of rustic charm and modern luxury.

Expansive windows open to views of endless green forests, the sky a deep azure above. Flowers bloomed in vibrant colors, and their fragrance carried on the cool mountain breeze.

As soon as I stepped out of the car, something shifted inside me.

For the first time in weeks, I could breathe. The tension I'd been carrying in my shoulders eased, and a tear slipped down my cheek before I could stop it. The beauty of the setting, the tranquility— was overwhelming.

I loved it.

Alessio took note, of course. He always did. 'Would you like to live in a place like this?' he asked, his voice soft and filled with a tenderness that elicited a chest ache.

He was so sweet and gentle, which only made the tears faster. I tried to blink them away, but he was already brushing one away with the pad of his thumb, his touch warm against my skin.

I thought about it for a moment, letting the peace of Blue Bliss seep into my bones. 'I would,' I found myself saying, the words almost a whisper.

The stunning views of the mountains, the beautiful grounds, the overwhelming sense of serenity—everything I didn't know I needed until I stood there.

Alessio's smile was soft, his eyes shining with something I couldn't quite place.

We spent the next few days wrapped in that blissful serenity, losing ourselves in each other.

We made love in the mornings, the sunlight streaming through the windows as we tangled together in bed.

We ate simple, delicious meals, enjoying every bite as if tasting food for the first time. And we rested, letting the quiet of the mountains lull us into a calm we both needed.

There were moments when Alessio had to leave, business in Sydney pulling him away, but I didn't mind. I wandered the gardens alone, marveling at the explosion of color and life around me.

I even found myself kneeling in the dirt, getting my hands dirty as I tended to the flowers.

With each passing day, I sensed more of my true self

returning. The shadows that had clung to me since we left the farm began to fade, replaced by a sense of peace I hadn't experienced in years.

Blue Bliss was living up to its name, and for the first time in years, I wasn't just surviving—I was thriving.

Chapter 36

CLEO

One morning, Alessio woke me with a coffee on a tray covered in white rose petals.

I spotted more flower blossoms on the bed and floor scattered like a trail.

Intrigued, I got out of bed and followed the path to *Blue Bliss'* front door.

Where Alessio was waiting with an even larger bunch of ivory roses and his SUV.

Without a word, he handed the bouquet to me and led me into the car.

I protested. 'Honey, I'm in pajamas, Ugg boots, and a robe.'

'You won't need anything else fancier where we're going,' he growled.

He started the vehicle and drove out of the estate and down the valley for about five minutes until we pulled into a gate.

'What is this?' I asked in wonder as the gates opened and we swept up the stunning driveway.

We parked at the sweeping steps to a Hamptons-style house that was so breathtaking that I gasped.

Standing tall with its two stories, the homestead welcomed us with open arms.

'Welcome to *Luminescenza*, meaning luminescence. Our new home.'

Eyes blinking fast, I let Alessio lead me into the property, my heart thudding with anticipation.

The estate, nestled in the embrace of the Blue Mountains, radiated a quiet grandeur that promised a beautiful future together.

Stepping into the stillness of the house, it felt like coming home.

Expansive windows let in a golden luminosity that fell over the towering pines standing sentinel in the stunning vista beyond the glass.

There was a harmony in this space, an unspoken rhythm that the city's cacophony could never hope to match.

Six spacious bedrooms and five bathrooms, including three ensuites, awaited us.

Every detail was more charming than the previous, with joinery and exposed timber beams adding a warm, rustic touch to the elegance surrounding us.

As we walked hand in hand through the house, I imagined the life we'd build here.

The rooms, each more inviting than the last, appeared to whisper of future memories.

The formal dining was perfect for hosting dinners where laughter and conversation would flow as easily as the wine.

The heart of the home was the open-plan kitchen, a space that invited warmth and devotion.

'Baby, I can see us prepping together!' I murmured, imagining the aroma of our cherished dishes filling the air.

The piece de résistance, however, was the library.

It came complete with oversized bookshelves, a stunning mix of decor and indoor plants, comfy sofas, and a vintage rug with a modern glass coffee table.

Betters till, Alessio had transported all my books, precious, well-thumbed novels, and limited-edition hardcovers and arranged them on the shelves.

I was so stunned that my words stayed trapped inside as I ran my hands over the familiar spines, my mind spinning.

Still, there came more to explore. From the sunroom to the sitting rooms and library, I already have found a dozen favorite spots to unwind.

The wide verandas, the vaulted ceilings, and the stone fireplace in the living area promised cozy nights.

On the north terrace, I pictured us sharing meals under the wisteria's shade, warmed by the outdoor fire and pizza oven.

We discovered the 22-meter pool, the renovated cabana with a built-in beer system, and a Brazilian-style BBQ inset in lush gardens, offering peace and tranquility.

The estate also had a tennis court, horse stables, dog kennels, machinery sheds, and abundant water resources.

Lastly, we inspected the charming guest accommodations: a weatherboard timber cottage and a two-bedroom apartment.

'You like?' Alessio asked when we stood on a small knoll overlooking the property, staring back at its beauty.

'I don't like -' I declared, speaking my first words since

we'd arrived.

His eyes narrowed, and his nose flared. 'But –'

' – I adore, Calibrese. I love it a lot. Grazie, honey.'

He shut his eyes for a moment, sucked his teeth, and let out a long exhale. 'Fuck woman, I thought you hated it. Which would have killed me given how many other places I've had to tour and turn down until I found this place.'

I laughed, tugging him into my arms. 'Calibrese, you're so easy to tease. And I cherish you for it. I also adore that you took the time to search for it. It's perfect, where we can build our dreams, surrounded by love, in a home that would be ours for years to come.'

I woke to sunlight filtering through the gauzy curtains, casting a golden glow across the room.

Blinking sleepily, I stretched under the soft sheets, a contented sigh escaping my lips.

As I rolled over, I was greeted by a sight that made my heart skip a beat.

On the nightstand sat a delicate vessel filled with a vibrant bouquet of wildflowers, their petals still glistening with dew.

A steaming mug of coffee rested beside it, the rich aroma wafting through the air and enticing me from slumber's gentle embrace.

I reached for the handwritten note propped against the vase.

'Good morning, zuccherino,' it read in Alessio's scrawled script. 'I hope these little tokens of my affection bring a smile to your beautiful face. Meet me in the garden when you're ready. Ti amo, always.'

I traced my fingertips over the words, warmth blossoming in my chest.

Damn, we'd even come up with nicknames for each other: *zuccherino*, for me, as I was Alessio's sugar, and *mio leone d'oro*, my golden lion, for him.

How had I won life's lottery?

Alessio's thoughtfulness never ceased to amaze me; his tender gestures reminded me of the depth of his love.

In the past few weeks, settling into our home and finding a fresh rhythm had only revealed how much I adored him.

Given our home's proximity to Lorenzo's mountain residence and Sydney, Alessio commuted when needed.

Weekends were spent with famiglia, my new family.

Mia and I took turns hosting the Calibrese clan, and our joint barbecues, cookouts, and swim parties became legendary.

When we weren't with kin, we took advantage of the fantastic bushwalking, rock climbing, cave exploring, and hiking trails surrounding us.

There was also an abundance of wildlife, including wombats, birds, kangaroos, wallabies, and wallaroos. It was like living in a national park, a naturalist and birdwatchers' paradise, and the starry nights had to be seen to be believed.

Twenty minutes down the road was a historic stone-built pub on the edge of the mountains, and in the winter, one could stretch by an open fire.

The local village has tennis courts, quaint shops one could explore for days, and friendly, smiling locals.

As for my farm, we'd repaired the cabin and rented the spread to a grandson of the Henderson family who'd decided to take up farming.

The Conti estate was sold off to recoup the state's costs and pay back fines.

The Caputos left us well alone and, from all accounts, had shut up shop in Goulburn to refocus their efforts on their Sydney and Melbourne-based illegal vapes and drug distribution.

During the week, Alessio worked in the city with his brothers.

Which gave my introverted self a chance to regroup. I wandered in quiet euphoria through our gardens and vegetable patch, nurturing the nascent carrots, tomatoes, and chilies we'd planted.

Anticipating a bumper crop, I gathered ideas for jams and pickles from Mia and Alessio and incorporated their late Aunt Bianca's recipes into the mix.

Now, sipping the perfect brewed coffee, I breathed in the delicate fragrance of Alessio's wildflowers.

Damn, the man was a soft touch. He kept spoiling me rotten with heartfelt gestures, tender touches, and whispered words of devotion.

I returned it with joy and laughter, cooking, and long massages that ended up in melting-hot sex.

It was healing. It was heaven.

It appeared he loved life in the country, after all.

It still jolted me how much the man had transformed.

From a brooding city brawler who didn't know the difference between a tomato and grapevine to a gentleman farmer. One who nurtured chilies with a passion bordering on mania.

Thinking of him, I set the mug down and slipped from the bed.

I threw on a robe over my cami top and shorts.

Stepping out into the light-dappled garden, I spotted Alessio sunning himself on a chaise lounge on the far end of the wrap-around veranda.

He wore a pair of tight, white trunks and nothing else. Stretched out like a predatory cat, his limbs long, thick, sculpted, and freakin' gleaming in the sun like some god.

I drank in his shoulder-length mane, that fuckin' sensual beard and mustache, his muscled chest and hips that drove me wild daily.

Sensing my presence, he opened one eye, tagged me, and unfurled a hand to reach for me.

I was wet in an instant, even as I moved to his side and let his sinewed hand wrap around my thighs.

'Il mio leone d'oro,' I breathed.

His lips curled as we stared at each other, our passion and yearning ratcheting without a word shared.

His fingers reached for the edge of my cami bottoms and tugged them down.

I helped shimmy them off my feet, turning to see him lift that freakin' tight ass to slip off his shorts.

My knees weakened at the sight of his thickness, jutting, throbbing for me.

Exhaling to contain myself, I levered my leg over him and lowered my waist.

I was so soaked, to the point of leaking, and his palm curled into me, slicking all over my clit, driving me wild.

Only this man could get me so high on love, on sex, on life itself.

Hands gripping my midsection, he positioned me, then, with a curl of his lip, slid his cock in, his jeweled head driving me wild.

He buried himself to the hilt with a growl and with a smooth thrust of his groin, hitting my G-spot and plunging so deep I felt him against my belly button.

Hell, every time we slammed into each other, it seemed like I was about to fall off the edge of a cliff into a sea of ecstasy.

My hands fell onto his chest, head thrown back, pussy gripping him as he worked his hips, my pelvis sliding over his, the friction driving me wild.

While one hand stimulated my clit, a lean finger eased down my spaghetti shoulder straps, exposing my tits.

I leaned forward and offered them.

In seconds, his mouth was suckling, laving, one hand plumping so he'd have more of my nipple in his lips.

The pleasure and pressure between my thighs began to coalesce.

'Alessio, baby,' I murmured.

'Do you want my cum?' he growled.

'Si,' I breathed, 'but not until I say you can.'

He huffed in disbelief at my moxie.

I stared back at him, daring him.

He upped the ante, slamming harder into me.

I threw my head back and rode him, unable to contain all the sweetness and wild he was giving me.

When I detected the telltale flutter at the back of my spine, I jerked my eyes to meet his hot, scorching gaze.

'Now, cum for me, baby, you deserve it.'

He whipped his head back as my words gave him release.

Neck corded, veins jutting as he groaned long and loud, his

cum spurting into me in thick ropey, scorching jets.

I bucked, cumming so hard I saw stars.

We came down, panting into each other.

Alessio's head remained thrown back on the lounge chair. Eyes closed, throat working as the waves of bliss ebbed through him.

I fell onto his chest, kissing his collarbone, thoroughly fucked and spent.

Finally, he roused, tipping my chin up to meet his amber, heated eyes, soft in adoration.

His arms came around me, his lips finding mine in a gentle, lingering kiss.

'Buongiorno, mia sola, il mio zuccherino,' he murmured against my mouth. 'You slept well?'

'Like a dream,' I replied, nuzzling into his embrace. 'Grazie for the flowers, coffee, and fuck. You're too good to me, Alessio.'

He chuckled, the sound rumbling through his chest, cupping my breast, flicking my nipple. 'Hell woman, you've turned me into a love-sick diavolo.'

'Don't blame me. You're the one who came after me twice, desperate for it.'

He growled, pulling me into his arms. 'I'm much the better man for it. Fotto, carissima, you deserve all the sweetness in the world, and I intend to spend every day giving it to you.'

'You ready for more sweet?'

I arched a brow. 'What do you mean?'

He lifted a finger to stay me. 'Wait here.'

He untangled himself from me and pulled on his shorts. I reached for my cami bottoms and stepped into them as he loped off, lips curved, ass tight, sexy as fuck.

He vaulted over a fence and went into one of the barns.

Minutes later, he emerged with a hefty package in his hand.

He eased over the railing again and strode toward me, sensual as sin, golden hair ruffling in the wind.

He set down the box before me.

'What is it?'

A rustling noise came from inside, and my heart rate ratcheted.

'Open it,' he growled, affection in his gaze.

I did, easing back the flaps.

I almost died as two little faces peeked up at me.

Both were white as snow and adorable as fuck.

I gasped, reached into the crate, and held them close.

'Are you going to thank me for your baby miniature goats?'

They nibbled my ear, and I laughed, nestling myself into their taut, wriggling forms.

I set them down, and they pranced around me.

'Grazie, my love. They're so perfect,' I murmured, stroking Alessio's chin, my eyes fixed on the squirming little bodies.

'You told me a dog would be too much but that you loved goats.'

'You remembered?'

'I always remember,' he rasped. 'Everything you say and do is etched in my mind.'

I leaned in and gave him a long kiss.

'But wait, there's more.'

He reached for one of the kids who was butting his knee.

That's when I saw a small package around its neck.

Alessio extended the goat to me with a smirk. 'Cleo Michele, your whole being is so beautiful, cara. You help me to discover me. Now, I know it was less obsession and more destiny that we're together. I want to build a tribe with you, protect and provide for you. I know the past has been hard on you, but Dio, I see the divine in you. Will you do me the honor of becoming my wife?'

With shaking hands, I retrieved the velvet pouch he was extending.

He nodded as I undid the string and delved in to retrieve a stunning emerald green ring crowned by a cluster of diamonds arranged in a perfect square cut.

I gasped at it, twirling it in the air in wonder.

He set the baby goat down and reached for my hand.

'Woman, will you agree to wife me or play with your new toy?'

He growled with impatience, yet I tagged worry interlaced in his demand.

I leaned back and smiled.

'Let me think.' I teased.

'Cleo,' he snarled in warning, his face blanching with concern.

I convulsed into laughter. 'Of course honey, yes, I'll marry you.'

The look of relief on his face was priceless.

'Never thought I'd see a badass sweat as much as you did just now.'

He slid the ring on my finger, adding a scorching kiss, then, in retaliation, captured me, threw me over his shoulder, and marched to the primary bedroom.

Where he tossed me onto the bed.

Our desire re-ignited like wildfire.

Shedding our clothes, we made love again with the doors to the garden open, the wind flowing over our bodies entwined in a dance as old as time itself.

'Ah Cleo, you undo me, inflame me,' he rasped into my ear, hoarse, raw, grating. Slicking in and out of me as he growled, 'Luce dei miei occhi, the light of my life, carissima.'

'Baby, ti amo, you are my life,' I whispered, rocking under him, lips to his.

I closed my eyes, cherishing those words, committing them to memory.

Alessio's touch set my skin aflame, his reverent caresses worshiping every curve and hollow of my body. Until I thought I might shatter from the sheer intensity of it all.

Later, we lounged naked in our king-size bed, wrapped in each other's arms with a view of the blooming garden and the mini goats frolicking in the grass.

A profound sense of peace washed over me.

This was where I belonged, in the embrace of the man who had utterly captured my heart.

We basked in the afterglow of our passion as the sun descended, painting the sky in shades of gold and crimson.

In those moments, I knew that this was what true happiness was like—a joy so pure and unbridled that it threatened to overwhelm me.

As I gazed into Alessio's eyes, I tagged the same wild delight reflected and a promise of a lifetime of adoration.

At that moment, I recalled the days I'd prayed for this kind of ecstasy. Now, I didn't have to pray anymore.

He leaned in, whispering some spicy, naughty nothings in Italian into my ear.

I laughed, throwing my head back.

So elated.

So free.

So utterly in love with my *leone d'oro*, my man, my wicked and eternal obsession.

THE END OF ONE BEAUTIFUL, INCANDESCENT ROMANCE

AND THE BEGINNING OF ANOTHER

The Kings of Omertà Series will continue with Valerio and Vitto.
However ... a secret 'brother' is also about to ghost into the Calibreses' life ...
Who is he, why is he a secret, and what might his incandescent romance be?

To find out more, sign up for my email newsletter to get updates on the series.

While you wait, explore Saint & Doja's love story ...

Love to Shield You:
When her worst nightmare resurfaces to take her out,

Detective Doja Main is under fire and up the proverbial creek without a paddle. With no other options, **she does what terrifies her the most - she reaches out to Saint Tahana**, one of the scariest operators in Sydney, with the cred to match. **He is Falcon & Eagle's best shield and deterrent** ... against low-lives wishing to move in on their patch. His uncanny spider sense for danger and cool-headedness make him the guy other badasses wanted in their foxhole. Because **he's the 'get shit done' guy who always wins with the will to cut through B.S**. He's got the long-range vision to see danger before it hits and split-second reactions to diffuse the threat. Except, **he's the lover she can't resist ...** and their bond is treacherous for her defiant heart. **She might evade the war against her, only to be lost in his arms forever.**

Get it now - it's FREE on Kindle Unlimited!

Glossary of Italian terms

- *Grazie, grazie mille* – Thank you, thank you very much.
- *Grazie a Dio* – Thank God
- *Bene* – Good
- *Et tu* – And you
- *Sprezzatura* is an Italian word that refers to effortless grace, the art of making something difficult look easy or maintaining a nonchalant demeanor while performing complex tasks.
- *Come stai?* – How are you?
- *Padrone* – Boss
- *Merda* – Shit
- *Cazzo, fotto* – f$ck
- *Si* – yes
- *Scusa* – sorry, excuse me
- *Fratello / fratellini* – brother, brothers
- *Cara / Amore / Bella* – dear, beloved, beautiful, terms of endearment

- *Buongiorno* – Good morning
- *Squisito* – exquisite
- *Buona notte* – good night
- *Sempre* – Forever
- *Dimmi* – Talk to me / tell me
- *Te amo* – I love you
- *Sei pazzo* – you're crazy
- *Cosa hai detto* – what did you say?
- *Andiamo* – let's go
- *Molto romantico* – very romantic
- *Molto bene* – so good
- *Per sempre vostri* – forever yours

About the Author

Sky Gold is a best-selling author who loves to indulge in all things delicious, fun, and courageously life-affirming.

She's happily married with two bright, funny kids and lives in Sydney, Australia, a gorgeous sun-soaked beach haven.

She writes best to music and looks to the stars for inspiration. When not getting lost in her characters' worlds, she's a busy soccer, basketball, dance, and gymnastics mum who folds clothes (maybe, sometimes ...).

You can connect with me on:

- https://skyovereden.com
- https://www.facebook.com/OfficialSkyGold
- https://www.instagram.com/skyovereden

Subscribe to my newsletter:

- https://skyovereden.com/newsletter-sign-up

Also by Sky Gold

King of Omen

She's his omen of love, he's her omen of desire
...

Soon after I first locked eyes with him, Lorenzo Calibrese commanded his body-guard to kick me out of church.

The next time I saw him was when I walked right into the middle of an execution in his house. **Now I'm trapped.**

I can't escape this unholy-made man. There's no turning back now, not after what I've seen. We're forced together until the world is safe for us.

He's Italian Mafia, ruthless, heartless, cold. The King of Omertà and an omen that my world is about to change.

He's also something else—sexy as hell. Freakin' possessive too. I should run the second he puts his sinewed, sensual, scorching hands all over my body. I shouldn't let him tear my clothes off. But I do.

He's going to break me. He's going to own every inch of my flesh. He demands complete obedience, and I want to resist, I do. But my rebellious heart won't let me.

This isn't the first time I've been at the mercy of a dangerous man, but this time, I might not live long enough to tell the tale.

'King of Omen' is a Mafia romance with graphic scenes, forced proximity, a possessive MMC, a strong FMC, violence, consensual steamy sex scenes, NO cheating, and mature language. It is perfect if you love a mafia, dark + light, contemporary bad-boy romance packed with spice, steam, sass, and plenty of heat.

Get your copy today.

Love To Wreck You

☆☆☆☆☆ 'Appreciated the strong woman particularly and the strong man. Highly recommended.' - Amazon Review.

With lush looks she plays down, Doja Main is **a savvy detective, a star case closer** ... and the widow of a highly decorated undercover operative. She asks the hard questions and takes no prisoners ... **and her corrupt police bosses have taken notice**.

When her worst nightmare resurfaces to take her out, she's under fire and up the proverbial creek without a paddle. With no other options, **she does what terrifies her the most - she reaches out to Saint Tahana**, one of the scariest operators in Sydney, with the cred to match.

He is Falcon & Eagle's best shield and deterrent ... against low-lives wishing to move in on their patch. His uncanny spider sense for danger and cool-headedness make him the guy other badasses wanted in their foxhole. Because **he's the 'get shit done' guy who always wins with the will to cut through B.S**. He's got the long-range vision to see danger before it hits and split-second reactions to diffuse the threat.

Except, **he's the lover she can't resist ...** and their bond is treacherous for her defiant heart. **She might evade the war waged against her, only to be lost in his arms forever.**

Set in the stunning and glamorous eastern suburbs' beach

escapes of Sydney, 'Love to Shield You' is a steamy, heart-wrenching adult romance that's an enticing, irresistible, happy-ever-after. It is recommended for mature readers only.

Get 'Love To Shield You' Today.

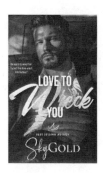

Love To Wreck You

He wants to wreck her for her family's sins.
Her love might just wreck him instead.

☆☆☆☆☆ 'An amazing enemies-to-lovers read.' - Amazon review.

☆☆☆☆☆ 'With plenty of heat and tension, this (is) a captivating journey of love amid conflict.'

———

Ash Falconer is a ruthless, cool-headed leader on and off the battlefield. He fights the urge to wreck the one woman whose family has wrought so much destruction in their wake. But he's torn by his unbidden attraction to her. Falling for her could wreck his plans to seek justice.

Cece Mirren wants to build a fresh life for her and her son. She has no idea Ash thinks of her as the enemy. While he drives her up the wall with his cold and confounding attitude, Cece feels a wild pull to him. But craving him is dangerous because Ash is the one man who may just wreck her.

Get Your Copy Today.